Thinblade

Sovereign of the Seven Isles: Book One

by

David A. Wells

THINBLADE

Copyright © 2011 by David A. Wells

Map by Carol L. Wells

Edited by Carol L. Wells

www.SovereignOfTheSevenIsles.com

To Mom and Dad.

NORTHPORT

BLACKSTONE
KEEP

HEADWATER

BUCKWOLD

NEW RUATHA

GLEN
MORILLIAN

THE
GREAT
FOREST

WARRENTON

SOUTHPORT

HIGHLANDS REACH

ISLE
OF
RUATHA

KAI'GORN

Thinblade

Chapter 1

Alexander let the arrow fly. It was a clean shot, easily two hundred feet across the pasture. The wolf yelped and squealed in pain before stumbling to the ground and mewling for a few moments until it fell still and silent. The other wolves scattered a bit, looking for the threat.

"Nice shot," Darius said as he drew, sighted, and loosed his arrow. It glided silently in a gentle arc and hit another wolf in the haunch. The wolf barked in pain and hobbled into the wood line. Darius frowned.

Abigail loosed her arrow and missed again. She muttered something under her breath.

Their father had sent them to hunt a pack of wolves that had been killing calves in the north pasture. They'd been at it for a few days and were finally having some luck.

"Be still. They haven't seen us," Darius said as he nocked another arrow.

Alexander shot again. He wanted to be done with this and go home. Another wolf fell. His arrow had caught it broadside, pinning it to the ground.

Darius and Abigail both hit the same wolf.

"Hey!" Abigail shot her brother a dirty look. She hadn't gotten anything all morning and now her first kill was compromised by her older brother's arrow.

He smiled, nocking another arrow.

Abigail scowled, then abruptly drew another arrow and took careful aim of an empty wood line. She relaxed the tension on her finely crafted composite bow and rested it in her lap as she sat astride her horse, huffing at the lack of a target.

"Let's go get our pelts." Darius clicked to his horse, urging her forward. Alexander and Abigail followed.

Alexander relaxed the focus on his vision and looked for the telltale colors of a living aura. When he was about thirteen, he discovered that he possessed magic. Magic wasn't common, but it wasn't exactly unheard of either. His parents both had it. When he realized what the colors were, he started training himself to see them whenever he wanted. After eleven years of practice it had become second nature.

He saw the colors of three wolves just inside the wood line; one aura was fading. That was one of the things the colors told him: dead things didn't have an aura. The wolf that Darius had shot was dying and its colors were going dark.

"Two left," Alexander said as he rested his bow on his saddle horn. He scanned the range for any potential threats.

That was when he saw the man on the horse. Only, he saw him a second too late. A long black arrow drove straight through Darius's leather breastplate and into his chest with such force that it didn't stop until six inches of the shaft were sticking out of his back. Darius grunted, slumping forward in his saddle.

Alexander loosed a quick shot at the man, then dropped his bow into its sheath.

Abigail cried out, "Darius!"

Both moved up alongside their wounded brother.

Alexander grabbed him by the back to steady him in his saddle, carefully sitting him up straight so he could get at the arrow. He grabbed the shaft close to the breastplate and snapped off the feathered end.

Darius cried out in pain.

Abigail sobbed her brother's name through freely flowing tears.

Alexander fixed Abigail with a hard look. "Grab his reins."

He took hold of the arrow, pulled it through and slipped it into his quiver.

Darius let out a strangled wail of pain and slumped forward, unconscious.

Alexander swung his leg over the side of his horse and expertly switched horses, sliding behind his brother. He pulled Darius up and held him against his chest with one hand while taking the reins from Abigail with the other. He turned for the northern ranch house and kicked the horse into a fast but steady walk.

Abigail took the reins of Alexander's horse and turned to look for the man who'd attacked her brother, but he was nowhere to be seen.

They made it to the ranch house within an hour. About thirty-five people lived there, including house staff and the hired hands that worked the northern property. More importantly, they had a healer, a wagon, and fresh horses.

As they came into the yard, Alexander called out, "I need the healer!"

The head cook turned and rushed off to find the resident healer.

Alexander turned to a group of three ranch hands and barked his orders, "I need a fresh horse saddled and ready to ride right now."

They looked at him in surprise, but didn't react.

"Now!" Alexander bellowed, causing them to spring toward the stables.

Abigail quickly dismounted to help Darius down off the horse. The healer came rushing up at the same time and helped her slip him gently to the ground.

As the house staff descended and the healer went to work, Alexander pulled Abigail aside. "Ride to the manor house and tell Lucky what happened. I'll be right behind you with Darius."

The stableman ran up, leading the fresh horse Alexander had demanded.

"Just in time," Alexander said as he took the reins and handed them to his sister. "Ride fast." He helped her into the saddle and slapped the horse on the rump. Abigail goaded the horse on as he sprang into a gallop.

Alexander knew it was bad.

Darius was dying.

"Stableman, prepare your fastest wagon with your best team of horses to carry my brother to Valentine Manor," Alexander commanded. He didn't like ordering people around, but today was different.

The stableman nodded, "Right away, sir." He turned and ran toward the stables, shouting orders along the way.

Alexander returned to Darius to get a report from the house healer. He could see from the look in the man's eyes that his fears were justified. The healer had no magic and could do little more than stop the bleeding, put healing salve on the wounds, and bandage him up.

The stableman pulled up a few moments later with a two-horse carriage that looked fast enough. Alexander and the healer supervised the loading of his brother. They placed him on a pallet covered with straw mats and layered wool blankets, gently lifted the whole pallet into the back of the wagon, and covered him with more blankets to keep him warm. The healer climbed aboard to attend to Darius during the trip while Alexander took his place at the reins.

Four of Valentine Manor's security men trotted up on horseback and took positions around the wagon to provide protection along the way. The ride seemed tortuously long to Alexander. He checked frequently with the healer but the answer was always the same: No change.

When Alexander turned the wagon off the main ferry road and up toward Valentine Manor, he saw Anatoly and twenty of his men riding toward him fast.

"Is he alive?" Anatoly called out as soon as he was close enough to shout.

Alexander gave a curt nod and could see the relief on Anatoly's face. Anatoly motioned for his men to continue ahead as he stopped to talk with Alexander.

"What happened?" His voice was level but his face had a look of pent-up thunder. He'd all but raised the three of them. Anatoly Grace had been the family man-at-arms for over twenty years. He was their mentor and their father's best friend. But more than that, he was the family protector, and one of his charges had just been badly hurt.

Alexander quickly told him what he knew: "A man on a horse caught us by surprise from the wood line and hit Darius. I sent an arrow at him and then took Darius to the north ranch house."

Anatoly nodded, "Good man." He kicked his horse into a gallop and over his shoulder called out, "I'll find him."

Alexander smiled grimly. The man on the horse wouldn't get away, Alexander was sure of that much.

He continued up the road and moments later saw a second party on horseback moving at full gallop toward him. It was his parents and Lucky with his assistant in tow and Abigail, racing ahead with her silvery blond hair glowing in the sunlight.

They came up in a rush as Alexander stopped the wagon.

Duncan Valentine was off his horse before it could stop. He hit the ground running, took one step on the side of the carriage, vaulted onto the buckboard, climbed over, and knelt down next to his son.

Lucky stayed mounted so he could see into the carriage for his initial assessment. He didn't like what he saw.

Bella Valentine looked into the back of the carriage and gave a low tortured moan when she saw her eldest child. Her face went white.

As his family arrived and swarmed the carriage, Alexander could feel the burden of responsibility slip away. He stepped off to the side of the road and sat down. The shakes soon followed.

"Are you all right?" Abigail asked softly as she sat down next to him. He nodded to her and smiled tightly even though he couldn't stop shaking. She sat quietly for several minutes, simply offering him the comfort of her presence.

"Lucky says his chances are good." She sounded a bit too worried to be reassuring. "Come on." Abigail stood up and offered Alexander her hand. "Let's go home."

The wagon started moving again with Lucky and the healer in back and Duncan and Bella in front, driving the wagon toward Valentine Manor.

Chapter 2

Darius was unconscious and could breathe only when he was rolled onto his side. Lucky had done everything he could do. He'd worked through the afternoon trying to save the young man who was heir to Valentine Manor.

Lucky, Aluicious Alabrand, was a master alchemist. He stood just under six feet tall, wore a crown of silver-white hair around a bald head and carried his ample belly as if it were a testament to his skills in the kitchen. He was an able healer, but he feared that Darius was beyond his ability. The young man had developed a fever that wouldn't respond to any of Lucky's potions, and he couldn't figure out why. Darius should be healing, but he was getting worse. Lucky looked at the door to the waiting room.

He dreaded going out to face his patrons, the Lord and Lady Valentine. It was all the worse that he was an old and dear friend of the family and had been Darius's principal teacher for his entire education. He loved the boy and could hardly swallow the lump in his throat as he rose from his dying patient's side.

When Lucky came out of the house infirmary, Bella sobbed at the look of anguish on his face. Duncan, Lord of the House, stood straight-backed at his wife's side, his face ashen and set.

Lucky took a deep breath and composed himself before speaking, "I've done all I know how to do and he's still getting worse."

Alexander suddenly had a thought. He shot to his feet and abruptly left the room.

"Alexander," called his mother through her crying.

"Let him go," his father said quietly.

Alexander ran to the stables and found his saddle. He still had the arrow that had impaled his brother. He ran back to the infirmary, burst through the door, and walked straight up to Lucky, arrow in hand.

"What if it was poisoned?" Alexander held up the arrowhead to Lucky, who looked Alexander in the eye for a moment, nodded once, then snatched the arrow and headed for his workshop in haste.

Alexander felt suddenly deflated once again. For a moment he could take action to help his brother, but now he could only wait. He went to his brother's side and took his hand. "Hold on, Darius. Lucky will figure this out and make it right."

From somewhere behind him, Abigail whispered, "He has to."

Late in the evening, it became clear that Darius was dying. In his last hours, the small room filled to overflowing with family and friends. He was loved by everyone who knew him. Even the toughest ranch hands cried without shame.

Lucky determined from the arrowhead that it had indeed been coated with baked-on poison. The effect had been slowed because the arrowhead hadn't lodged inside Darius but instead went straight through him. Unfortunately, even a small dose of the poison was deadly and there was no antidote.

Darius was dying.

Amidst the mourning, Anatoly strode in, caked in road grime. "Found him," he growled with angry satisfaction. He stopped short when he took in the scene of the people in the room.

"Is he gone?" the big man-at-arms asked softly.

Duncan shook his head and motioned toward his dying son. Anatoly went to Darius's side to say his goodbyes. As Anatoly took his hand, Darius gasped his last breath. Bella and Abigail wailed in anguish almost in chorus. Duncan sat heavily and stared blankly while tears streamed down his face.

Abigail buried her face in Alexander's shirt and wept. He held his sister and felt a kind of anguish wash over him that seemed boundless and all-encompassing. Before this moment he didn't even know this kind of pain existed.

His big brother was dead. His best friend. His protector. His hero. Gone.

The whole of the world would never be the same again. The finality of it was terrible. The sudden void was utterly without mercy.

Alexander succumbed to the pain of it. He gave himself over to it. Let it fill him. He held nothing back, allowing the hurt to find its way into every crevasse of his psyche. He stood there for a long time, holding his sister and feeling immeasurable sorrow while tears streamed down his face.

Her presence brought him back from the hopelessness. She was still alive. His family still needed him, now more than ever. He had to put his emotions in perspective, mourn his brother's death, and live his life.

Then it hit him and his eyes snapped open. The pain of his sorrow shifted into cold anger. "Anatoly … who did you find?"

Anatoly stood, anger on his face in spite of the tear streaks running through crusted dirt from his eyes to his chin.

"We found the man who shot Darius. He's shackled and locked in the holding cell. Four of my best men are guarding him." Anatoly grinned tightly with absolutely no humor. "You got his horse, by the way. Nice shot."

Everyone stood and faced Anatoly.

Duncan asked, "What has he said?"

"Quite a bit, actually. After some persuading, mind you." Anatoly gestured for everyone to step out of the room where the lifeless body of Darius lay.

"He's a member of the Reishi Protectorate. About a month ago he was sent to locate and kill Darius. He doesn't know why, only that he has orders from the General Commander of the Protectorate. He made his way from Tyr, found Darius, and shot him with a poisoned arrow." Anatoly gave his report in the detached manner of a soldier but it was clear to everyone in the room that he was hurting as much as anyone.

"Why would someone from the Reishi Protectorate want to kill my brother?" Abigail asked. "The Reishi are dead. They've been dead for two thousand years."

Anatoly looked down, shaking his head. "The prisoner doesn't know why," he said softly. "He claims he was just following orders."

"If he was following orders, then a better question is why was he ordered to kill Darius?" Duncan said. "Anatoly, did he speak my son's name?"

"Yes. His orders were to kill Darius Valentine."

Bella touched her husband's arm, "It can't be … can it?"

Duncan took his wife's hand and squeezed reassuringly as he shook his head, as much for his own comfort as hers. "The Reishi Protectorate is more rumor and legend than anything these days." Duncan frowned in thought. "Lucky, what do you know of the history of the Reishi Protectorate?" He doubted the old alchemist knew any more than he did, but Duncan Valentine was thorough and knew events often turned on the smallest details.

Lucky leaned forward. "Little that will shed light on the motives behind your son's murder, I fear." Lucky closed his eyes and dredged his memory. "The Reishi Protectorate served as the royal guard for the Reishi family during the two thousand years that the Reishi Sovereigns ruled the Seven Isles. For much of those many years the people lived in peace until the last Reishi Sovereign took up necromancy. He quickly descended into madness and tyranny. It was a very dark time. The First Reishi Sovereign discovered the secret of making Wizard's Dust, so they had many true wizards and more than a few mages and arch mages. Their power was unrivaled for millennia.

"Their cruelty was their downfall. One of their own house stole the secret of Wizard's Dust, their most jealously guarded secret, and distributed seven copies of the process, one to each of the Seven Isles. The Sixth Reishi Sovereign responded by declaring open war on any non-Reishi magic. That was the beginning of the Reishi War. It raged across the Seven Isles for nearly two centuries. After untold destruction, the war ended with the death of the Sixth Reishi Sovereign and the loss of the secret of Wizard's Dust.

"To this day, the Reishi Protectorate believes that the Reishi line will rise again to claim its rightful place as rulers of the Seven Isles. Over the centuries they have become more of a secret society or a cult than anything else." Lucky sighed, "Most people don't even believe they still exist."

Alexander stood abruptly. "I want to talk to the prisoner," he said and started for the door.

Anatoly looked to Duncan, who nodded slightly. The big man-at-arms fell in behind the new heir to the House of Valentine.

Alexander looked at his brother's killer through the cell bars. The man was helpless and yet Alexander wanted to hurt him just the same. He wondered what that revealed about his own character.

He relaxed the focus of his vision, and the colors of the man's aura began to shine. He was evil, cowardly, and absolutely terrified. Alexander was coming to rely on his ability to see a person's colors. It was so revealing.

"Do you know why you were sent to kill my brother?" Alexander's voice was flat and detached. He couldn't afford to let emotions get in the way of discovering the truth.

"No! I told your big ox back there the same thing," he said, pointing at Anatoly with his chin.

Alexander watched his colors. The man was telling the truth.

"What is the purpose of the Reishi Protectorate?"

"We protect the Reishi line," he blurted out, happy to answer a question that was common knowledge.

"The Reishi are dead," Alexander replied.

The killer shook his head vigorously. "No, they're not," he said firmly. "There's one left."

Chapter 3

"What do you mean there's another Reishi?" Alexander asked.

Alexander stood a few inches taller than six feet. He was well built and strong from working on the range. He had handsome features and light brown hair cut to medium length. His most striking feature was his eyes. He had his father's eyes, only more so. They were soft brown with flecks of gold in the irises that glittered when he got angry.

They were glittering now.

The prisoner looked furtively at Anatoly standing behind Alexander before answering. "There's an obelisk on one of the islands of Tyr. Prince Phane Reishi is inside ... for now, anyway," he said with a nervous titter.

"For now?" Alexander asked.

"The obelisk came alive a month ago, all swirls and lights floating around on its surface. The old scrolls say that means Prince Phane will come out of his long sleep very soon." The prisoner believed what he was saying. Alexander was sure of it.

He frowned while he thought about his next question. Abigail and his parents were standing behind him, beside Anatoly.

The air grew strangely still. Alexander felt every hair on his body stand on end just before a magical shock wave passed through the room. Awareness of Phane flooded into everyone's mind. They all stood mute, looking at each other for confirmation of what they had just experienced.

A moment later, Alexander felt a sudden burning on the right side of his neck. For all the world, it felt like he was being branded with a hot iron. He cried out and stumbled backward trying to escape the shocking pain. It lasted for only a moment, but it was blinding in its intensity.

Alexander found himself sitting on the floor gasping, his hand pressed tightly over the side of his neck, and his family standing over him looking worried.

"Let me see." Bella's voice was strong but forlorn. He looked up at his mother blankly, still shaken by the sudden pain and stunned with confusion about its source. She looked back as if to say "Well?"

Alexander removed his bloody hand. There, on the right side of his neck, was the ancient glyph of the House of Reishi branded by fire into his flesh. The wound was still fresh. Bright red blood was smeared around the burn where he'd pressed his hand. It hurt.

Alexander was marked.

The ancient story of the curse was true. Bella Valentine's face went shock white. She stood straight and looked at her husband. Each was a mirror of the other's feelings. Anguish, fear for their son, and iron resolve. The time was here. The curse had been invoked.

"Alexander, we need to talk about this. Let's go upstairs," Duncan said as he helped his son to his feet.

When Alexander came close to the bars of the cell, the prisoner lunged with a sharp piece of wood he'd splintered off the leg of the bed. Duncan and Alexander were unaware, but Anatoly was watching closely. He was prepared. He had a short sword in hand.

"Death to the Marked One!" the prisoner cried out as he lunged.

Anatoly shouldered Alexander aside and thrust with his sword. He caught the prisoner straight in the middle of the chest and stopped him cold. They stood looking each other in the eye.

"I've failed ... oh, no."

Anatoly saw a look of panic as the light faded from the assassin's eyes. He fell off the end of Anatoly's sword and was dead when he hit the ground.

"Anatoly, increase security and tell the stableman to have horses ready for everyone at dawn." Duncan Valentine always knew this day was possible but he never actually believed it would come. It had been two thousand years since the end of the Reishi War. His father had told him the story of the curse as he lay on his deathbed. Now the curse had been invoked and his son knew nothing of his destiny. He looked hard at Alexander with love and hope.

Duncan put his hand on Alexander's shoulder. "My son, I have much to tell you."

Anatoly returned from issuing his orders, cleaning his blade off as he entered the room. "Duncan, let's have this conversation in your hall. It's more easily defended and I suspect Alexander will want a glass of wine or two by the time you're done."

They made their way to the great hall of Valentine Manor. It was a huge central gathering room capable of accommodating a hundred people or more. The ceilings were vaulted and soared thirty feet into the air. The windows were high on the walls and too narrow for a man to fit through easily. The long room was lighted by three enchanted chandeliers that magically glowed on command, prized possessions of the Valentine household.

In the center of the room was a polished oak table stretching the length of the hall, with cushioned chairs all around. Everyone who mattered most to Alexander was at the table ... everyone except Darius. His head was swimming and the pain of the burn on his neck was still distracting. He sat with one hand on his neck and the other on his forehead. His eyes were closed and he was still a bit stunned by all that had happened.

His mother handed him a cool damp cloth for his burn. He took it with a forced smile.

Darius was dead.

It didn't seem real. Every time he tried to face it, he felt an abyss of pain rise up from the pit of his stomach and threaten to claim his sanity. He simply could not make his mind comprehend a world without his big brother in it. How could such a thing be possible?

He'd felt the warning spell wash over him. He knew without question that Phane Reishi was walking the world again. He couldn't explain how he knew, but that didn't change his certainty. He also knew that Prince Phane would not stop until he ruled the entire Seven Isles. All of the dark stories of the last Reishi Sovereign and his sadistic son now seemed real. Until now, they'd been nothing but bedtime stories used to frighten unruly children into sleeping quietly at night.

And then there was the issue of the burn on his neck. Everything about it was unsettling, but especially the timing. He had been burned, marked with the glyph of the Reishi, only a moment after the warning spell had washed over him. The spell that had just warned the whole world about the coming of Prince Phane had marked him.

Alexander didn't know the significance of that but it worried him greatly.

Duncan sat at the head of the table, Alexander to his right with Abigail next to him. His mother, sat across from him at his father's left. Lucky sat next to her.

Alexander looked up as Anatoly came to the table and took the chair next to Lucky. "The room is secured. I barred every door myself and posted a man outside each entrance. Horses and a fast wagon are being prepared. Your traveling gear is being made ready as well." Anatoly was a soldier before all other things. He was in his element in a way that Alexander had never actually seen before. He had a certainty of purpose about him that projected an almost infectious confidence.

"Thank you, Anatoly." Duncan took a deep breath.

"Listen well, Alexander, there may not be much time." Duncan was all business in spite of his red and swollen eyes.

Bella sat still and straight, her face etched with pain and purpose. Abigail hadn't stopped crying since Darius died. She took Alexander's hand under the table. He returned a reassuring squeeze and gave her a quick look.

"This is the story your grandfather told me in the last hours of his life." Duncan paused for a moment to let the words sink in before continuing. "Two thousand years ago, at the end of the Reishi War, Prince Phane Reishi cast a spell of desperation. His family had been defeated, the Reishi Isle was overrun and he knew the castle would not hold. So he fled. He hid himself inside a magic obelisk located somewhere on one of the islands of Tyr. Within the obelisk, no time would pass, allowing Phane to escape justice and flee into the future."

Duncan stopped as Alexander began shaking his head. "What does any of this have to do with me?" He was exhausted. Nothing made any sense.

"Be patient, Son," Duncan said quietly. "The Rebel Mage discovered Phane's obelisk and tried to destroy it but failed. He realized that when Phane woke, the world would be totally unprepared for his power and ambition, so the Rebel Mage placed a magic circle around the obelisk to warn the future, to warn us. That magic circle was what we just felt. The Rebel Mage's magic circle warned everyone alive that Phane Reishi walks the Seven Isles again."

Alexander interrupted again, "That still doesn't explain the burn on my neck."

"No. The burn on your neck is the result of a curse." Duncan stared at Alexander for a moment to emphasize his words but spoke again before Alexander could object.

"The story my father told me says that an ancient bloodline was cursed. Our bloodline. We have remained hidden for centuries to protect our line for this day. The Rebel Mage feared that the Reishi Protectorate would discover his curse and eliminate our entire line, so our family went into hiding many centuries ago. The story says that the eldest son of our line would be marked when the Arch Mage Prince awakes. You've been marked, Alexander. It's no longer just a story."

Alexander sat slack-jawed and looked at his father. Abigail's hand tightened around his.

"You are the one marked by the Rebel Mage. The old story says that you must defeat Prince Phane or the world will fall into darkness and tyranny for a thousand years." The calm, quiet pronouncement fell like a sentence on his life.

He was cursed.

Who was he to even think about picking a fight with an arch mage? He didn't want to fight. He didn't even want to be heir to Valentine Manor. He just wanted to live his life.

He started laughing without any humor at all, then stood up abruptly, knocking his chair over. "This is crazy." He walked several steps from the table, running his hands through his hair and then stopped in front of a mirror hanging on one wall of the great hall. He hadn't actually seen the mark on his neck yet. When he looked at it for the first time, his blood ran cold as ice. It was the ancient glyph of the House of Reishi. He'd seen it in history books from his father's library, but to see it burned into his flesh was a shock.

"None of this can be happening," he said while running his hand through his soft brown hair.

Anatoly stood and said, "My Lord."

Alexander whirled on him. "What did you just call me?" The world of sanity was spinning dangerously out of control. Anatoly had helped raise Alexander. He'd been his friend, mentor and protector for Alexander's whole life. And now he was calling him, "My Lord."

"My Lord," Anatoly said deliberately and looked firmly at Alexander in the way he always did when he wanted to drive home an important point in a lesson.

"Anatoly, I am not 'Your Lord' so stop calling me that. I'm Alexander, nothing more." He was getting angry. Nothing about this day made any sense. He shook his head, turned and left the room.

Bella looked to Abigail and motioned for her to follow after her brother. "Give him some time, Anatoly," she said. "He'll come to understand his responsibility."

Anatoly sat back down. "We may not have time," he said flatly. "The assassin that killed Darius was sent to kill the Marked One. The Reishi Protectorate knew Darius would be marked by the curse. He represented a threat to their charge. What do you think they're going to do when they find out Alexander bears the mark?"

"We should leave in the morning at the latest." Lucky sounded resolute and forlorn at the same time. He relished the comforts of home and the cooking of his own kitchen, but he was loyal without fault and he knew the peril they now faced.

"Agreed," Duncan said as he took his wife's hand. She nodded. "We'll make for Glen Morillian. The Rangers will swear loyalty to Alexander on the strength of the brand on his neck alone. They've been waiting for him for millennia. He'll be safer there than anywhere."

The second part of the legend was the Rangers. They had been created by the Rebel Mage as well. Their purpose was to serve as protectors of the bloodline until this day arrived, then to serve the Marked One in his quest to preserve the Seven Isles from the ambition of Prince Phane. Anatoly was a Ranger.

He nodded, "I'll send word to the Forest Warden and the Wizards Guild in New Ruatha." He started for the door. "My birds will make better time than any horse and have far less chance of being intercepted."

"I'll prepare what potions I can for travel and store the rest," Lucky said as he stood to leave.

Bella caught his hand briefly. "Lucky, would you look in on the children before you attend to your lab?"

"Of course," he said.

"It's been a long time since I wore my armor. I hope it still fits." Duncan tried to smile at his wife but it faded too quickly.

"We'd best get ready," Bella said with a mixture of sadness and resolve.

Duncan took her hand. "He's strong. The Old Rebel Wizard chose well." He squeezed her hand to get her to look up at him. He hated the pain he saw in her eyes; it made his chest hurt. What he had to say didn't help matters.

"Phane is loose on the world. Our son is marked. All we can do now is support him and guide him with all we have." He held her eyes with his commanding gaze until she nodded acceptance of the world as it was.

They had the kind of relationship that often involved complicated and esoteric discussions. One topic of interest was people's propensity to see the world as they wished it to be, rather than as it actually was. Bella and Duncan both emphatically agreed that reason depended on accurate facts. And accurate facts only came from an honest and unbiased assessment of the situation. Deal in what is, not what if.

She was tough. He knew that better than anyone. They were holding hands as they left the great hall.

Chapter 4

Jataan P'Tal stood facing the obelisk not ten feet from the edge of the magic circle that surrounded it. He stood straight with his feet shoulder width apart and his hands clasped loosely behind his back. About a month ago, the surface of the obelisk had begun to swirl and flow as though it were alive.

Since then, Jataan P'Tal, General Commander of the Reishi Protectorate, had posted a senior officer to greet Prince Phane when he emerged. It was his turn to stand watch. He believed that a good commander should be willing to do any duty he asked of his men.

He was a soldier. He didn't complain.

The sun had set an hour ago and the clear sky was fading from a deep luminescent blue to sparkling black.

Abruptly, the obelisk shot through with cracks and fissures running all across its surface. Jataan stiffened. The cracks glowed white, then the obelisk began to crumble. Starting slowly from the top, chunks of black stone broke away and crashed to the ground. They shattered into powder on impact, leaving little more than a dark stain where they fell. In a matter of seconds the entire obelisk was gone. Prince Phane Reishi stood in the center of a black stain on the ground surrounded by an ancient magic circle. For a moment, he was completely motionless.

With a sudden gasping breath he became conscious, staggering slightly to keep his feet. At the very moment that he sucked in his first breath in two thousand years, the magic circle glowed brightly, increasing in intensity for a few seconds before it detonated with a wave of magical energy.

Jataan was struck full in the face and thrown flat on his back from the impact. The magic circle was gone. The wave of magical energy spread out across the entire Seven Isles. Every living soul would feel it.

The last Reishi Arch Mage was awake.

Jataan shook off the shock and bounded to his feet. He took three purposeful strides toward Prince Phane, stopped abruptly, stood at attention and gave the traditional Reishi salute—fist to heart.

Jataan P'Tal was a little man. He stood only five and a half feet tall and looked a little soft, even slightly portly. His hair was black and close-cropped. His complexion was swarthy. His eyes were black and he wore clothes to match. No weapon could be seen on his belt but he always had a knife somewhere.

"I am Jataan P'Tal, General Commander of the Reishi Protectorate. I am at your service, Prince Phane." Jataan spoke with complete calm assurance and punctuated his oath of service by going to a knee and bowing his head deeply. He waited.

A moment passed. Prince Phane assessed the situation and grinned. "Rise, General Commander P'Tal." Phane's grin turned into a broad smile.

Prince Phane stood just over six feet tall and had a perfectly proportioned build. His wavy brown hair reached to his shoulders. His face was strong and handsome and his smile was almost ridiculously charming. But his eyes did not smile. They were soft brown with glittering flecks of gold in the irises and they looked like eyes that had witnessed unspeakable atrocities … and liked it.

***

"It is very gratifying that you've kept this little piece of the Great Reishi Empire intact for so many centuries," Prince Phane said with ever-so-slight mockery while he gestured around at the tent.

Jataan P'Tal stood passively. They had retired to a set of command tents set up on a small hill near the site of the obelisk. Phane was eating with enjoyment and gusto. He praised the food between mouthfuls. After he'd eaten his fill he took up a bottle of dark red wine and emptied it into a large flagon, patiently shaking out the last drop. He inhaled the bouquet of the wine deeply, lifted the huge cup with a shameless smile, and took a long pull.

He set the cup down and sighed with delight. "I haven't eaten in ages, you know," he said with a conspiratorial wink. When Jataan didn't react, Phane sighed. "Very well, General Commander, report." Phane sat back with a smirk and waited.

Jataan cocked his head, "My Prince, I command a force of intelligence assets spanning all of the Seven Isles and numbering approximately twenty thousand. I also have about fifty thousand total combat forces at my command but it will require some notice to assemble them."

Phane looked at him and waited silently.

"The Reishi Protectorate controls this island within the Isle of Tyr. Our purpose for the past two thousand years has been to wait for this day. Our sworn duty is to protect the Reishi Sovereign and his line. We are currently aware of one threat to your life and we have taken measures to eliminate it." Jataan was a general officer giving his report. He spoke matter-of-factly and without emotion.

Phane smiled, "A threat, you say? Tell me more." His smile took on a slight menace that even Jataan P'Tal found somewhat unsettling. Prince Phane had boyish good looks and big brown eyes that glittered with the telltale gold flecks of the Reishi line. Jataan reminded himself to be on guard.

"The Old Rebel Mage cursed an ancient bloodline to rise on this day to oppose your claim as Sovereign of the Seven Isles. The legend says the curse will be triggered by the warning spell released when you awoke."

Phane held up his hand, "You refer to the magic circle that surrounded my obelisk, yes?"

Jataan nodded.

"What exactly did the circle do when I was released?" Phane leaned forward with intense interest.

Jataan P'Tal frowned. "A great wave of magical force expanded outward from the circle. It knocked me from my feet and stunned many of my men. All felt it. I believe it may have been felt on all of the Seven Isles. Your arrival has been announced, My Prince."

Phane picked up his flagon of wine and looked intently into it for a moment. Jataan was silent. Phane very deliberately took another long pull from the oversized cup.

"The Old Mage is a nuisance even two millennia after his death," Phane shook his head. He stared into the cup again as if the wine might provide a solution to his troubles.

"Tell me of the threat sent by the Old Mage." Phane spoke deliberately.

For the first time in a very long time, Jataan P'Tal actually felt a little flutter of nervousness. A drunken arch mage was dangerous.

Jataan straightened and began his report anew. "The spell takes the form of a curse on the eldest son of the chosen line. He will be marked. This mark will allow him to access hidden storehouses of magic. The legend says he will defeat you with the ancient magic he will find. The story has been corroborated by two master-level prophet wizards over the past two thousand years."

"Does this story say what magic this brave champion will find?" Phane asked almost disinterestedly.

"The only item mentioned is the Thinblade of the House of Ruatha," Jataan answered.

Phane looked up sharply and smiled, "Go on, General Commander."

"The Protectorate has discovered the last remnants of this ancient bloodline. They are concealed as a secondary noble house on the Isle of Ruatha under the name of Valentine. When your obelisk came to life a month ago, I dispatched an assassin to kill the eldest son of the family. My assassin is reliable," Jataan P'Tal concluded, and having finished his report, stood silently.

Phane sat quietly for a moment, nodded and said, "General Commander, let's find out how reliable your man really is." Phane stood and held out his hand toward the tent wall. His eyes lost focus and he relaxed as he touched the firmament with his mind. He released the magic through his will and commanded the door of his Wizard's Den to open.

After a moment, the air in front of the ancient arch mage began to shimmer. Then, quite suddenly, an area of space coalesced into an open doorway leading to a place beyond and apart from the real world.

Jataan had heard stories about the Wizard's Den spell before, but he'd never actually seen one. It took an arch mage to cast such a powerful constructed spell and it had been two thousand years since an arch mage had walked the Seven Isles.

The door to the Wizard's Den was a simple open archway. Jataan leaned slightly to see behind the magical portal. It vanished from sight when he did.

"Huh." Jataan P'Tal was a man of few words.

Phane smiled slightly at his General Commander and walked casually through the door, whistling a tune as he went. Jataan followed. He found himself in a stone room with a vaulted ceiling. A hearth occupied the wall opposite the door; a fire was burning brightly. Lamps spaced out along the walls provided ample illumination. A comfortable-looking bed was pushed into one corner of the room with a trunk at the foot. Along the same wall in the opposite corner stood a finely crafted armoire. A large table occupied most of the wall opposite the bed with a bookshelf taking up the rest. A simple, cushioned wooden chair was pushed in under the table and a more comfortable-looking chair faced the fireplace. The place looked almost homey.

On the table was strewn all manner of books, maps, scrolls, and other odd scraps of parchment with arcane writing in ancient and long-dead languages. There was also a finely crafted mirror in an ornate gold and silver frame resting in the middle of the table. It was oval, about two and a half feet tall and a foot and a half wide.

Phane stopped in the middle of the room and looked around as if he expected something to be out of place. He nodded his satisfaction and took a seat at the table in front of the mirror.

Jataan stood just inside the doorway looking around casually.

When Phane touched the mirror, it began to shimmer. "Show me the Seven Isles," he commanded.

The surface of the mirror seemed to ripple. As the ripples calmed, an image began to appear. It looked like a map of the Seven Isles, except there were clouds. Jataan realized with a shock that he was seeing the entire known world from impossibly high in the sky.

"This threat you speak of is on Ruatha?" he asked Jataan.

"Yes, My Prince, House Valentine, just south of the Great Forest, between Highlands Reach and Southport." Jataan's eyes didn't leave the mirror as he spoke.

Phane nodded and touched the glass where Ruatha was and the island grew to fill the whole mirror. He touched it again just south of the Great Forest and the image grew impossibly fast. Jataan felt a flutter in his stomach like he was falling. Phane searched about until he found the house he wanted. He placed his finger on the mirror frame and the image began to move toward the house, only more slowly.

Jataan P'Tal was not easily impressed, but the power of this mirror set his mind racing.

Phane guided the image through doors and into the manor. He searched methodically until he found what he was looking for. He watched as Alexander sat at a large table and listened to his father explain the curse on their bloodline. He could hear every word of the conversation through some magical effect of the mirror as if it were taking place right in front of him.

Phane smiled, "It would seem that your assassin has succeeded and failed all at once. He killed the elder brother but he killed him before the mark was made."

"So it would seem, My Prince. I will send a squad at once." Jataan looked to Phane for confirmation of the offer but the Reishi Prince was deep in thought.

Phane looked up abruptly. "Ah … no, that won't be necessary. I have another idea." Phane stood and gestured toward the door.

They exited the Wizard's Den and Phane waved his hand toward the door. It snapped shut with a high-pitched popping sound and vanished in an instant.

"Go get me your worst soldier," Phane commanded offhandedly as he found a tray of food on a side table and placed it carefully on the table in front of his chair.

Jataan frowned inwardly but said, "Yes, My Prince," and left the tent. As he walked down the small hill toward the encampment, he wondered what the Reishi Prince had in mind. No matter, he thought, he had his orders. He was the General Commander of the Reishi Protectorate. He had been raised from birth for this moment. He would do his duty, come what may.

When he came into the small sea of tents that housed his forces, a sentry saluted. Jataan returned the salute with practiced precision. He called out into the open night, "Lieutenant," then stopped and waited with his hands clasped behind his back.

Moments later, the officer on duty appeared out of the shadows, came to an abrupt halt and saluted. "Yes, General Commander?"

"Lieutenant, go get your worst soldier and have him report to me immediately." Jataan was becoming uneasy but he wasn't sure why. He stood silently, hands clasped behind his back, and surveyed the encampment. The sentry on duty fidgeted nervously in the presence of his General Commander. Not five minutes passed before the lieutenant returned with a soldier in tow.

It was clear that the soldier had been sleeping. He was still buckling his poorly kept breastplate and he'd forgotten his shield. He ambled up to the General Commander and came to attention. Almost as an afterthought he added a sloppy salute.

Clearly this man was not cut out for the life of a soldier. Jataan P'Tal looked him up and down. He nodded to the lieutenant, said, "Come with me" to the soldier, turned on his heel and started for the command tent on the top of the small hill. He could hear the soldier shuffling along behind him.

He wondered again what Prince Phane had in mind for this young, poor excuse for a soldier, before he entered the dimly lit tent.

"I have the soldi…" Jataan P'Tal stopped mid-word at the threshold of the tent. The unkempt soldier stumbled into him from behind, then recovered quickly and backed off a step while trying to peer around the short, portly General Commander.

Prince Phane stood with his back to the entrance facing a circle drawn on the ground in blood. His left hand was slick with it from a cut on his wrist that looked self-inflicted. Drops of the thick red liquid were still dribbling from the wound but Phane didn't seem to notice.

Inside the circle was a creature of shadow and malice. Jataan couldn't quite discern where the creature ended and the darkness around it began. It was as if the beast was not quite solid, more a shadow, yet deadly real nonetheless.

When it saw the General Commander, it lunged for him and abruptly crashed into the invisible barrier of the magic circle surrounding it. The noise it made was like nothing Jataan P'Tal had ever heard. The combination of a dying pig's squeal and metal scraping against metal. Phane looked over his shoulder and laughed with a mixture of glee and menace. Every hair on Jataan P'Tal's body stood on end.

Jataan P'Tal was a battle mage. He understood magic in a limited way. His connection to the firmament was strong but could only be established when he was in a fight. This magic was something else altogether.

This was necromancy. The magic of the dead. The magic of the netherworlds. The magic of evil. He didn't know Phane was a necromancer. None of the old writings in the archive of the Reishi Protectorate spoke of this. Jataan P'Tal's inward frown deepened but he showed nothing.

"My Prince, I have the soldier you requested," he said as he entered the tent and drew the now terrified soldier into the dimly lit, cloth-walled chamber of horrors.

Phane turned and spoke jovially, "Ah, there you are, my boy. Come in, come in." Phane's boyish good looks and friendly demeanor stood in jarring contrast to the monster in the magical cage behind him. Jataan P'Tal thought idly that he would never turn his back on such a beast.

Phane didn't even acknowledge Jataan. He walked to the soldier and smiled warmly. "Would you like some wine? Perhaps you're hungry?"

The soldier stood at rigid attention, his face pale and his knees trembling, as he tried to fix his attention on his newly awakened Prince. Try as he might, his eyes kept slipping back to the horror in the circle of blood. The horror looked back with insatiable hunger.

"No, thank you, My Prince," the soldier said as he went to a knee and bowed his head.

"Stand," Phane commanded. The soldier complied but couldn't help looking at the thing in the circle again. It was still staring at him with a mixture of anticipation and madness.

Jataan P'Tal stood to the side and took it all in. He took a mental inventory of everything in the room he might use as a weapon. As was his custom, Jataan P'Tal was armed with only a pair of concealed knives. He rarely required more and when he did, there were usually plenty of weapons lying around for him to choose from.

"Nonsense," Phane said as he patted the soldier on the cheek with his bloody left hand, leaving a lurid red handprint smeared across the terrified young man's face. "I insist." The edge in his voice only served to punctuate the command and heighten the young soldier's fear.

Phane guided him to the table, sat him down in a chair that faced away from the beast, and poured him a flagon of dark red wine. He took a seat to the soldier's left and pushed his platter of meat, cheese, and vegetables over. "Surely you wouldn't refuse the hospitality of your Prince," he said with a genuine smile and a graciousness that only served to elevate the tension in the air. Phane seemed to revel in it.

The soldier took a piece of meat from the platter with trembling hands, all the while looking to Phane for permission. Phane smiled. "Eat ... have some wine." He pushed the flagon closer to the soldier, causing some of the wine to slosh out onto the table.

"Thank you, My Prince." The soldier lifted the flagon with shaking hands and took a long drink. Wine dribbled out the sides of the cup, down his face, and onto his breastplate.

Phane sat back and smiled warmly. "Good. I have a very important mission for you." The soldier set the flagon down with about two fingers of wine left in it. He was clearly eager to have his orders and be on with his duties.

Jataan P'Tal stood passively beside the entrance and watched. The beast in the circle of blood stared intently at the soldier.

"It seems that there is an assassin intent on killing me," Phane said with exaggerated sadness while he wrapped a cloth around his bloody wrist. "I've been trapped in a rock for thousands of years and I'm released from my prison after all this time only to find that people still want to kill me." Phane shook his head sadly.

"We won't let that happen, Prince Phane." The soldier actually looked a bit worried for Phane's safety. "How can I serve you?"

Quality soldier or not, this young man's loyalty was clear. Jataan made a mental note of it.

Phane nodded somberly as if making up his mind. He looked the soldier right in the eye and said, "I'm sending you to kill my would-be assassin."

Confusion stole across the soldier's face; he swallowed hard, held his head up bravely in spite of the fear that gripped him, and said, "I live to serve the Reishi."

Jataan was almost impressed, but he was even more concerned. The man he'd sent to kill Darius Valentine was a well-trained assassin and he'd failed. This young man was a poor excuse for a soldier. Clearly he would not succeed, and there was still the matter of the beast in the circle eyeing the young man intently.

Phane stood. "I know that you do." He looked almost touched by the show of loyalty.

When the young soldier stood and stepped aside from the chair, Phane stepped into him, planted his bloody left hand on the soldier's chest, and shoved him backward into the circle of horrors. Jataan stiffened imperceptibly.

The young soldier fell into the waiting arms of the shadow beast trapped in the circle of blood. A look of shock and disbelief sprang to the young man's face. Phane smiled warmly; Jataan's blood ran cold as the insubstantial beast swirled into a dark and inky shadow that engulfed the soldier.

Jataan P'Tal could see the dying man try to scream but no sound came out of the black vortex that surrounded him. Then the darkness began to flow into the soldier while his body stood limp as if it were being held up by puppeteer strings. When the darkness had completely invaded the soldier, his body fell in a heap on the ground.

For a long moment he didn't move. Then he slowly stood. What Jataan P'Tal saw behind those dark eyes was no longer human, no longer a thing of the world of life.

"I have given you a soul, now you will do my bidding. Do you agree?" Phane asked the possessed corpse before him. The husk of the soldier replied with a sound that was not human, could not be human. Jataan didn't understand but Phane seem satisfied with the response. "Very good. You will hunt and kill young Alexander Valentine. You may have any soul that gets in your way." The man that was no longer a man began to tremble with anticipation.

"Kludge!" Phane bellowed into the darkness around him; not a moment later the shadows coalesced into another creature of the netherworld. This one Jataan P'Tal recognized.

It was an imp.

His level of discomfort was rising with each new revelation about the character of his Prince. Jataan P'Tal was not a particularly good man but he wasn't evil either. He was a man sworn to serve, trained from birth to be loyal to the Reishi line. He had never considered the true cost of that loyalty, until now.

An imp was a creature of the netherworld, a being of malice and evil. Jataan P'Tal had never actually seen one before but he had seen renderings in old magical texts. He knew they only manifested in the world of the living when summoned as a familiar by a very powerful, and very evil, wizard.

The little demon stood about a foot and a half tall with three clawed fingers on each hand. It had leathery batlike wings and a tail ending in a sharp black spike. Its hide was ashen grey leather that hung loosely on its humanoid form. Its head was bald and smooth and the skin of its face was pulled tight. Its nose was narrow and sharp but not as sharp as the row of dirty-looking, spike-like teeth behind its thin black lips. It wore only a loincloth with a small knife hanging from its belt.

As distasteful as this little monster was, the thing that bothered Jataan the most was its hateful yellow eyes. When it looked at him, he could see the calculating malevolence behind those close-set nightmare eyes. All in all, the little beast made his skin crawl.

"Ah ... there you are, Kludge." Phane smiled warmly at his familiar. "I have a task for you. Take this zombie demon through the netherworld and deliver it to Valentine Manor on the Isle of Ruatha. Do you understand?"

"Yes, Master." Its voice was gravelly and dripped with fawning subservience. Kludge nodded and wrung its hands while its little wings beat feverishly to keep it hovering at eye level with Prince Phane.

Jataan P'Tal had seen plenty of magic in the course of his life but nothing like the power he'd witnessed this night. He was coming to understand the true nature of an arch mage's power. Now he knew that the stories of old were not exaggerated myths and legends. They were true and literal. For the first time since he was a child, Jataan P'Tal felt a chill run up his spine.

Kludge flew to the zombie demon inhabiting the corpse of the unfortunate soldier and seized him. An inky darkness grew to engulf them both followed by a thump that expanded outward like a shock wave. When it passed through Jataan, he felt an unearthly chill course through him, then the inky darkness faded like smoke and both Kludge and the demon were gone.

"That ought to do it," Phane said and started whistling to himself while he worked the cork loose from another bottle of wine.

Chapter 5

Alexander's mind kept skipping from one catastrophe to the next as he burst out of the room and past the guard at the door. He didn't think about where he was going, he just went.

Darius was dead. His big brother. His best friend. His protector. His confidant. His captain. It just didn't make sense. How could he be dead? They were shooting at wolves just this morning.

Phane was loose. Until an hour ago Phane was just a story about a long-dead and unspeakable evil, but the warning spell had changed all that. Now Alexander had a firm picture in his mind's eye of the Reishi Prince and understood the dark nature of his character with a clarity that he frankly didn't want. Alexander could only imagine the suffering Phane might cause. He was an arch mage from the time of the Reishi War. There was no one in all the Seven Isles as powerful as Prince Phane Reishi.

Alexander could still feel the dull ache of the brand on his neck. He was marked by a curse. He'd been chosen by another long-dead arch mage to lead the Seven Isles against Phane ... and Prince Phane, the only living arch mage in the whole world, knew it.

Alexander couldn't make his mind settle on any one of the three. The enormity of each was just too much to bear. He pushed it all away and focused on quieting his mind. He cleared it the way Lucky had taught him, this time not to explore or develop his limited understanding of magic but to keep his mind from considering the matters pressing in on him.

He found himself standing on the turret of the watchtower. Alexander had always liked high places and often came here to think. This time he'd made his way here without even knowing where he was going. He stood resting his hands flat on the low stone wall of the turret.

He stared up at the stars and let the cold air wash over him as he took slow deep breaths. Winter was half over. It would be time to start early planting in a few months. Alexander wondered if his world would ever be the same again.

"I knew I should have come here first," Abigail said softly as she silently glided up beside him. His sister was his best friend. She was a couple of years younger than him but she had enough self-assurance to hold her own with anyone. Abigail was also strikingly beautiful, a fact that worried Alexander when he saw how the ranch hands looked at her. She was tall, only a few inches shorter than him, had long silvery blond hair and pale blue eyes that seemed to see right through people. She wore a cloak to ward against the cold and looked sidelong at his shivering. "Come inside, you've got to be freezing."

He didn't move.

"Fine, I'll just go get you a cloak then." Abigail punctuated her statement with a look that said "I'll show you," then turned and strode off without so much as a rustle.

Alexander stood there for a while just breathing and staring at the stars.

When he felt a hand on his shoulder, he assumed it was Abigail. No one else was likely to sneak up on him and he hadn't heard anything.

"I guess I am a little cold," Alexander said as he turned to face his sister. What he saw was something else altogether.

It was the silhouette of a man traced against the night in a faint silvery light. He could see right through him. Alexander was so startled that he stumbled back against the turret wall, lost his balance, and started to topple over. The silhouette lunged forward and the silver lines that defined him became brighter. He grabbed Alexander by the shirt and pulled him back from the brink of a four-story fall, then abruptly disappeared. Alexander felt the air around him go colder still. He could suddenly see his breath as he sat on the floor with his back to the turret wall trying to make sense of the experience.

Abigail came up the stairs a few moments later. Seeing Alexander sitting on the ground, she quickly looked for a threat. When she didn't see one, she walked to Alexander and offered him her empty hand. She held a heavy, fur-lined, leather cloak in the other.

He took her hand and stood. He wasn't sure what to make of the ghostlike man. He didn't want to add more stress to the family, so he decided to keep the encounter to himself for the moment. He took the cloak from his sister and threw it over his shoulders.

"Mom and Dad are taking us to Glen Morillian in the morning. You need to pack your things," Abigail said in a small voice.

Alexander was suddenly struck by the pain and fear in her voice. He put his arm around her. They stood silently for a moment, taking comfort in each other.

They heard Lucky huffing and puffing as he came up the stairs behind them. "Ah ... there you are ... I've been looking everywhere for you." He stopped to catch his breath when he reached the top of the stairs. Lucky was slightly rotund, not terribly overweight but certainly not fit and trim. He loved his food far too much and he spent his days in his workshop whenever possible.

He looked at the two of them as if carefully searching for the right words. With a resolute nod, he found his voice. "Alexander, your life will be more difficult now. You have an obligation that cannot be ignored."

He looked to Alexander's sister. "Abigail, you must stand by your brother, now more than ever."

He stopped as a tear slipped from his eye. "I miss him, too," he said, hugging them both. He stepped back. "Both of you go pack and then get some sleep. You'll need it. We'll be off at dawn." He turned and made his way down the stairs.

Alexander decided to ignore everything until after he'd gotten some sleep. Maybe it would all be less insane in the morning. He followed his sister down the tower stairs and said goodnight as they each went to their rooms.

He fell into his bed and managed to get his boots off before rolling over and falling asleep still fully dressed. His dreams were fitful. Everything that had happened collided into an improbable collage of events, distorted and filled with dread. At one point he woke with a start at the clear and vivid image of an arrow driving through his brother's chest.

He sat up gasping. The lamp had burned out and the room was dark.

Alexander sat on the edge of his bed, breathing deeply in an effort to slow his racing heart. He'd just calmed himself when the silvery outline of a man abruptly materialized not three steps in front of him.

He sat bolt upright, staring at the apparition. It wavered slightly and the temperature of the room suddenly fell by ten degrees as the ghost came into clear and sharp focus.

Alexander was nearly paralyzed with fear. Surely Phane couldn't have sent another assassin so quickly. Panicked thoughts flooded through his mind. Of course, Phane would know where he was; Phane was an arch mage and Alexander was the one marked to kill him.

Then the apparition spoke. "I am the ghost of Nicolai Atherton. I will not harm you, Alexander." He faded almost totally out of sight, then came back just as suddenly. The temperature in the room fell noticeably again.

"You are in great danger." His image sputtered and crackled, flaring brightly before dimming to the point of invisibility.

Alexander stood. "What danger?" He could see his breath. He felt his heart racing. Goose bumps erupted all over his body and a chill raced up his spine. The temperature fell yet again. Ice began to crystallize on the mirror. Alexander's fingers hurt from the sudden cold.

This time there wasn't even a ghost, just a disembodied voice yelling from far away. "Find the Thinblade," he said and then he was gone.

Alexander slapped his hands together and rubbed them back and forth. The cold was soaking into him so he threw his top blanket over his shoulders before pulling on his boots.

He pushed open the shutters to the cool night air, which felt almost balmy next to the freezing air in his chambers. It was still the dead of night. There was no hint of light on the horizon.

Alexander could see from the light in Lucky's workshop that the old alchemist was up and about, no doubt packing his laboratory away for safekeeping. Lucky was never happier than when he was conducting some experiment or other, except maybe when he was cooking a meal for someone. He loved to tinker and always said: "Trial and error is the path to discovery."

Alexander decided he'd had enough sleep. His pack was mostly ready since he hadn't taken the time to unpack from the wolf-hunting trip. He opened it and replaced a few items with their clean counterparts, cinched it down tight and set it next to the door. Next, he went to his weapons cabinet and selected his favorite set.

Alexander was the son of a minor noble. House Valentine had considerable land holdings, so Alexander had access to money. He didn't take it for granted but he wasn't afraid to spend it to get what he wanted. In this case, Alexander had always been a student of military history. He loved weapons and stories of war.

When he was five he started practicing next to his brother, with Anatoly as their master-at-arms. Alexander was skilled with a sword, a spear, and a bow. He wasn't a seasoned warrior by any means but he was well trained in the use of his weapons.

He chose his favorite long sword. The blade was thin but strong, light, and well balanced. It was a fine piece of craftsmanship and Alexander was more familiar with it than any of his other swords. He slipped a small knife inside each boot and clipped them in place, then slid his throwing knife into its sheath on the back of his belt.

He picked up his heavy long knife and looked at it. Its oak handle was well worn and smooth, the brass pommel was polished to a shine, and the blade was old steel but sharp and well cared for. His father had given him this knife on his seventh birthday. He'd carried it every time he'd left the manor house since then. He took a set of three extra throwing knives and then he checked his short bow, found a few extra bowstrings, and filled his quiver with broad-point hunting arrows.

Alexander was suited up a few minutes later in his leather breastplate, greaves, and bracers. His finely crafted long sword hung on his left hip; his long knife on his right. He hoisted his pack on one shoulder and a set of saddlebags on the other, gathered his bow and quiver, and left his room. He stood for a moment looking at the door to his bedroom, took a deep breath, turned abruptly and headed for Lucky's workshop.

Chapter 6

He decided to face his problems head on. He would follow his teachings. He would deal with what is, and he would do so with reason, courage, and morality. All of his childhood lessons took on new meaning. They weren't just theories anymore.

The Reishi Arch Mage, Prince Phane, was awake. Darius was dead because of it. Alexander was marked. And Phane knew.

Oh, and he was seeing a ghost.

Alexander suddenly chuckled mirthlessly at the insanity of it all. "Darius, may you find peace. I will mourn you properly, but not today." He spoke under his breath, putting his grief away for later. His brother was dead. He couldn't change it, so he set it aside. He couldn't afford to let himself indulge the pain that swirled in his soul lest it overwhelm him.

Phane was probably going to try to kill him, and soon. Now that Alexander was awake and his head was clear, he could feel alarm starting to build. They had killed Darius. Then Alexander had received the mark. They would come for him as soon as they realized they'd missed the Marked One.

He picked up his pace slightly. The ghost had told him he was in "great danger" and to "find the Thinblade." And why exactly was he seeing a ghost? Alexander wanted to talk to Lucky about it. Maybe he would know more.

The house was already awake with staff bustling about preparing for the family's departure. Word of Darius's murder had spread like wildfire and everyone was both sad and angry.

Alexander nodded good morning to the few stable hands in the courtyard. They seemed slightly more deferential today than ever before. He knew it was because of the mark, and the fact that he was now heir to Valentine Manor.

"Lucky?" Alexander poked his head into the door of the shop. The room was cluttered as usual. Books, scrolls, vials, and jars were stacked here and there. All of the shelves were crammed full of ingredient containers. There wasn't a flat space in the place without something on it.

Lucky and his assistant were busy boxing up jars of odd-looking things used in the preparation of potions. Next to the door was a set of traveling robes, a stout oak staff, a pack, and a set of saddlebags. Lucky hated to travel but looked to be ready to go at a moment's notice. Alexander became even more concerned; Lucky was taking the situation very seriously.

Alexander stepped inside and said, "Hi, Lucky."

The rotund alchemist turned, "Ah, my boy." He turned distractedly back to his assistant. "No, no, no ... put that one over there," he said, pointing to a stack of boxes.

He turned back to Alexander, "I'm afraid there's just no use for it. I'll never be able to pack up everything before dawn." He looked somewhat distraught. This little workshop was where his heart was most at home.

He stopped short and looked hard at Alexander. "What's happened?"

Lucky had helped raise and teach Alexander. He knew him as well as anyone. He could see that there was something bothering Alexander.

"I've seen a ghost," he said.

Lucky's brow furrowed. He nodded thoughtfully. "Come and sit, have some hot tea and breakfast while you tell me about it."

Lucky was a good cook and always had some form of food to offer. Today he had a sheet pan of warm biscuits with fresh butter and strawberry jam. Alexander was suddenly hungry. He ate his first biscuit quickly.

"I saw him the first time last night on the tower after Abigail went to get me a cloak." Alexander had just swallowed the last bite of his first biscuit and was breaking another open while he spoke.

"The first time?" Lucky asked around a big bite of biscuit slathered with jam and butter.

Alexander nodded, "I saw him the second time about half an hour ago in my room." He looked at Lucky to see if he believed him. Lucky was frowning in thought but gave no hint of doubting Alexander, which was a relief, because he wasn't sure he believed it himself.

"The first time, on the tower, he put a hand on my shoulder. When I turned and saw him, I was so startled that I leapt backward and started to fall over the tower wall." Alexander looked a bit sheepish. "He grabbed me by the shirt and pulled me back from the edge, then everything got really cold and he disappeared. I think he saved my life."

Lucky frowned in thought and motioned for him to continue while he chewed. Lucky always claimed he did his best thinking while he was chewing.

Alexander took another bite and continued. "The second time, just now in my room, started with a bad dream. I woke with a start and sat up on the side of the bed. When I looked up, he was standing right there."

"Back up a moment. The ghost actually touched you, twice?" Lucky was still chewing.

Alexander nodded.

"Only the most powerful ghosts can actually manifest physically," Lucky said as he motioned for Alexander to continue, while taking another big bite of biscuit smothered in jam.

"When I looked up and saw him beside my bed, he told me his name was Nicolai Atherton. He called me by name and said he wouldn't hurt me. Then he faded out of sight, came back suddenly, and said, 'You are in great danger,' then he flickered out again. The room started to get much colder and I heard him yell from very far away, 'Find the Thinblade' and then he was gone."

Lucky's frown deepened.

They both ate in silence for a moment while Lucky digested what he'd just heard. "I believe I've heard of Nicolai Atherton but I don't remember where. Perhaps we can find some reference in the library at Glen Morillian." He stood and took two more biscuits along with a big dollop of butter and a couple of heaping spoonfuls of jam.

"As far as the Thinblade goes ..." Lucky's voice trailed off in thought as he slathered butter on a biscuit.

Alexander waited a moment before he couldn't help himself any longer. "What about the Thinblade?"

Lucky looked up and smiled. "Ah yes … well … the seven Thinblades were created by the First Reishi Sovereign and given as gifts to the seven Island Kings. Each is a longsword said to be the length of a man's arm, the width of a man's thumb and black as onyx. It gets its name from the thickness … or rather thinness … of the blade. When you turn it sideways it's so thin you can't even see it. Each Thinblade is bound by Reishi magic and cannot be broken. It's said that a Thinblade can cut through anything with almost no resistance. Most have been lost since the end of the Reishi War."

"Maybe the ghost knows where it is?" Alexander mused.

Lucky grunted his agreement as he cleaned off the breakfast table. He was making a plate for his assistant when Abigail came in carrying all of her gear and wearing her armor, a sight that always made Alexander a bit nervous.

"Ah … my dear, you're just in time for breakfast," he said, holding up the plate of biscuits with butter and jam that he'd just prepared for his assistant. Abigail smiled.

"I can always count on you, Lucky." She dropped her gear by the door and strode to the table, touching Alexander on the shoulder in greeting as she sat down next to him. She started in on the plate of biscuits. Abigail was thin but she didn't eat like it.

Alexander watched her for a moment until she'd taken a few bites, then casually said, "So … I saw a ghost last night."

She stopped chewing. "What do you mean you saw a ghost?" She covered her mouth as she spoke.

Alexander recounted his two encounters with the ghost while Abigail ate her breakfast. She listened carefully as always. When he finished, she considered what he'd said for a moment before launching into a litany of questions. "Who's Nicolai Atherton? Why is he a ghost? Why is he bothering you? How does he know your name? What does the legend of the Thinblade have to do with any of this?"

Alexander held up his hands to slow her down. He wasn't even fazed by her string of questions; inquisitiveness was in her nature. "All good questions and I can't answer a single one. We're hoping we can find more information in Glen Morillian. If we can't find what we need there, I think we'll have to go to the Wizards Guild in New Ruatha."

Lucky nodded his agreement.

Alexander looked out the window. There was just the faintest hint of light on the horizon. Dawn wasn't too far off. He could hear people going about their chores in the yard. The day was about to begin. Abigail resumed eating while Lucky made up another plate for his assistant who was busily packing the little workshop into storage boxes.

Outside in the courtyard, an inhuman shriek cut through the still predawn air. It was a sound like nothing Alexander had ever heard, a sound born of madness and hate. His blood ran cold. For the briefest moment he froze in utter terror. Whatever had just made that noise was here to kill him. He was certain of that.

The alarm bell rang. Lucky was up and to his travel packs in a blink. He quickly dropped his plain woolen robes and donned his travel robes. They were much warmer, had an oiled leather topcoat, and were lined with dozens of pockets, all filled with potions, powders, and salves. He took up his travel bag and ordered his assistant to find shelter in the cellar. The young man scurried off.

Alexander and Abigail followed his lead, picking up their weapons and gear. They heard shouting and then the ring of steel. The three of them emerged into the courtyard from Lucky's workshop to a pitched battle between three of the Valentine house guard and a single man armed with only a sword.

Then the man shrieked again and Alexander knew he wasn't a man, at least not anymore. A man couldn't make a noise like that.

Everyone froze for a moment, and the man that was not a man lunged at the closest guard. It was a reckless attack; he left himself completely open. The guard thrust with his short spear, driving hard straight through the midsection of the intruder. It was a kill strike and the guard knew it. What he didn't yet know was that his enemy was already dead.

Alexander let his eyes go out of focus. The colors he saw made him catch his breath. The man that was not a man was indeed already dead. He was a corpse, animated by a creature from the netherworlds. The colors of his aura made Alexander's eyes hurt and his soul squirm. They were not the vibrant colors of life but the inky darkness of death.

The man that was not a man smiled as the spear drove through his belly. He grabbed the haft and pulled it through his gut to get closer to the shocked guard. A moment later the man that was not a man drove his sword cleanly through the guard's breastplate and into his heart, then cackled with a whining, scraping, rasping voice that was altogether unhuman. He watched with rapt attention while the guard died on the end of his blade.

Alexander stood staring at the creature's aura. He saw a palpable hatred for life, visceral evil, and a coiled, tortured rage, drunk with the chance to lash out at the living. He also saw a pulsating power that was much greater than anything he had ever seen before.

But the thing that frightened him the most happened when the guard died. The guard's colors flowed into the man that was not a man and the demon's darkness swelled. Alexander focused his vision and steadied his resolve.

Once the life was gone from the guard, the man that was not a man stood and pulled the spear through himself slowly as he looked casually over his shoulder at one of the two remaining guards. Then the man that was not a man moved.

He spun with inhuman speed and hurled the spear at the guard he'd been leering at. The short spear struck him in the stomach with such force that it drove clean through his body and clattered to the ground, trailing blood several dozen feet behind him. The guard slumped to his knees and keeled over.

The last guard backed off slowly, looking around wildly, clearly hoping for reinforcements. Defending against bandits or assassins was one thing. This was something else.

Then the man that was not a man locked eyes with Alexander. He tipped his head back and shrieked with a piercing intensity that nearly brought Alexander to his knees.

The last guard stood his ground between the man that was not a man and Alexander but it wasn't clear if it was courage or paralyzing fear that held him fast.

The intruder lunged so quickly that the guard only had time to raise his shield. The thing backhanded the shield, and Alexander could hear bones in the corpse's left hand break from the impact. The guard turned with a grunt from the force of the blow, leaving his left side exposed. The man that was not a man drove his sword into the guard's ribs but this time he didn't pay any attention to his kill. This time the man that was not a man was looking straight at Alexander.

The thing sprang into a headlong sprint. Alexander and Abigail drew their swords almost as one. Lucky pulled a small clay pot out of his bag. The man that was not a man drew closer and Lucky prepared to throw his clay pot, when a blindingly bright ray of argent light stabbed down from the second-story balcony of Valentine Manor.

Bella Valentine stood on the balcony, wreathed in golden light and flanked by a half dozen archers. She was an accomplished witch. Her mother had been a sorceress and had taught Bella about magic from an early age. From her outstretched hand she directed her magic down on the man that was not a man. Her light revealed the creature's true nature for all to see. The ugliness of its form was only exceeded by the ugliness of its nature.

The man that was not a man screamed in pain and flipped over backwards, retreating from the light. He regained his feet and shot Bella a murderous look as he snarled and keened in pain. Half a dozen arrows peppered him without any visible effect.

Duncan and Anatoly burst into the courtyard flanked by a dozen of the house guard.

Lucky didn't hesitate. He threw his clay pot with perfect accuracy. It hit the man that was not a man straight in the chest. The clay pot shattered on impact, splattering magical liquid fire the color of free-flowing lava that ignited everything it touched.

Flame quickly engulfed the possessed corpse. He shrieked again and fell as the fire consumed him. Alexander thought he saw a shadow rise up out of the flames, but dismissed it as his father and Anatoly came up around them.

"It's time to go. Get your horses."

Duncan Valentine was all business. It had been many years since his house had been attacked and he was fighting mad. Alexander and Abigail knew better than to argue. They made straight for the stables while Lucky went to get his wagon. He never traveled light.

Before Alexander could reach the stable gate, he heard the shriek again. He whirled to see the house guard who had been speared in the belly standing with his guts hanging out of the fresh wound. He was looking straight at Alexander.

From the balcony, Bella called out, "Zombie demon!"

She cast another ray of blinding argent light at the newly animated corpse. It screamed and gibbered as it leapt back out of the light, looking for a way to get to Alexander.

Alexander didn't know what a zombie demon was but he could see that his father and Anatoly did. They began barking orders at the growing number of house guard in the courtyard. Duncan grabbed Anatoly by the shirt and said something to him before turning to face the demon in his yard.

Anatoly turned and ran straight for Alexander and Abigail. "Get your horses! Right now!" he bellowed as he ran toward the stables. Lucky came out from behind his workshop driving his wagon fast. Anatoly barked to Lucky, "Head for the gate!"

Alexander and Abigail emerged from the stables mounted on their horses and saw the fire in the yard. Duncan Valentine was ordering his men to use fire against the attacker. Bella's light was effective at corralling the creature but couldn't kill it. Fire had felled the first possessed corpse. Duncan clearly figured it should work again.

Anatoly mounted his big warhorse quickly and motioned for them to follow Lucky, while he positioned his horse to block the zombie demon's view of Alexander. Already three of Anatoly's men had fallen. He looked back and heard Duncan shout, "Get them out!" Anatoly nodded once, turned away from his best friend, and urged his horse into a gallop.

He found Alexander and Abigail waiting with Lucky just outside the main gate. "Let's go," he said tersely as he rode past. They fell in behind him, looking back to see the flames growing from the courtyard of their home.

"Wait!" Alexander cried and reined in his horse. "Where are Mom and Dad?"

Anatoly wheeled around and pulled up close to Alexander. He spoke quietly but with deadly firmness. "Your mother and father are fighting the zombie demon to buy you the time you need to escape with your life. Do not waste their sacrifice."

He heard Abigail let out a small whimper. Anatoly slapped Alexander's horse on the rump. The horse leapt into a gallop and Abigail's horse was startled into a run as well. Soon they were running away from their home as fast as they could ride.

When they crested the last hill, Alexander looked back to see his home fully ablaze in the early dawn light. "Please let them survive this," he said under his breath before turning back to the road.

Chapter 7

Alexander was standing watch in the dead of night. They'd ridden since dawn as fast as Lucky's wagon would go. It had been a miserable day. The drizzle had started early and was still falling. The wind had blown steadily in their faces all day, and it was cold. Not cold enough for snow, but close.

His heart ached at the loss of his brother. The hard riding had occupied his mind for most of the day but now he was alone in the dark with nothing but his grief. He stood facing the wind, embracing the punishing cold while tears quietly rolled down his cheeks and mingled with the raindrops falling on his face.

He felt adrift in a sea of despair. When he wrenched his mind from thoughts of his brother, he was blindsided with stabbing and sudden worry for his parents. He didn't even know if they were still alive. Lucky told him that a zombie demon couldn't stand the light of day. That it would have retreated into the netherworld with the first rays of the sun. That was some consolation but not much. He could still see Valentine Manor ablaze when he closed his eyes. His home was gone. His family scattered or murdered.

Thoughts of his parents led to guilt. He left them to fend for themselves against an unhuman enemy. Despite repeated assurances from Anatoly and Lucky, he felt like he'd betrayed them. He should have stayed and fought. He should have protected his family.

It was all too much to take in at once. He couldn't get his mind around the terrible day that had forever altered the course of his life. Too much had happened. Too many terrifying questions remained unanswered.

Yesterday morning he was the second son of a minor noble. He had a plan for his life. He'd chosen the plot of land where he was going to build his home. He was going to raise cattle like his father had. All he wanted was a simple life. A family. A home. A connection to the land he drew his sustenance from. Alexander wasn't ambitious. He didn't need to be. Darius was heir to Valentine Manor. Alexander would have followed his brother anywhere. And now ... Darius was gone. Valentine Manor was gone. His future was cloaked in darkness.

His anger began to build again. All this pain for what? Because of some curse cast thousands of years ago. No ... not a curse. All of this pain could be pinned squarely on a man who should have had the good sense to die two millennia ago.

Prince Phane Reishi.

A gust of wind blew the icy rain into his face. He heard someone stir from under the oilskin tent. Anatoly emerged quietly to take his turn at watch.

"You are relieved, My Lord," Anatoly said quietly as he came up beside him.

Alexander spun and grabbed the big man-at-arms by the coat. "Don't call me that." His rage had come quickly and he knew it was misplaced. Anatoly didn't flinch or resist. Instead he stepped close to Alexander and drew him into a hug.

He held him tightly for a long moment, then released him and held him at arm's length by the shoulders. "The days to come will be hard, Alexander. But you must face your duty. Many depend on you now."

"I didn't ask for this and I don't want it." His face was a mask of misery.

Anatoly looked back with the maddening resolve that Alexander knew all too well. "Be that as it may, this is your duty now. You have only one decision to make. Will you accept the responsibility you have been given or will you run from it?"

Alexander stood silently, tears flowing down his face, and stared back at his old teacher as if refusing to answer the question would negate the reality of the situation.

"For what it's worth, Alexander, I already know the answer to that question because I know you, maybe even better than you know yourself." Anatoly clapped him on the shoulder. "Now go get some sleep. It'll be dawn soon."

They rode hard from dawn to dusk for the next two days and made the outskirts of Southport late in the afternoon on the third day.

Southport was a sprawling port town on the west coast of Ruatha a couple of days' ride from the south edge of the Great Forest. It was a major trading hub that shipped the cattle, grain, and corn produced on the fertile plains and grasslands of southern Ruatha to other ports all around the Seven Isles. Goods of all varieties were in turn shipped into Southport to make their way inland along the three well-traveled roads that went north, east, and south.

Alexander had been here several times with his father and brother to sell herds of cattle and bushels of wheat and to buy wagonloads of all manner of goods needed to run Valentine Manor's vast estate. He knew it wasn't a place to let your guard down. It was home to all kinds of people, from reputable merchants, tradesmen and sailors to thieves, con artists and cutthroat murderers. It was the kind of place a person could get lost in.

The houses on the outskirts of town were mostly run-down and poorly kept. The people who inhabited them were about the same. Alexander checked his sword to make sure it was loose in its scabbard.

"We should find an inn with a stable where we can have a hot meal and a warm, dry bed for the night," Anatoly said as he reined in his horse a few paces from the gate.

Southport had a wall surrounding the city in a half circle that radiated away from the seaport. It wasn't much of a wall anymore. There were many places where one could find a way in without passing through a gate, but not with horses, let alone a wagon.

The disinterested guard came out of the small shack looking annoyed to be out in the rain again. "State your business." He seemed impatient. The drizzle left tiny dark spots on his damp oilskin cloak.

"We're travelers in need of shelter for the night," Anatoly said from atop his big horse as he flipped a silver coin to the man. The guard caught it, gave the coin a hard look and nodded. "Very well then, be on your way."

He leered at Abigail and her long blond hair when they rode by. Alexander relaxed his focus to look at the guard's colors. He saw a mix of lust, greed, and petty selfishness, but no threat. He returned a hard look and the guard pretended to take a sudden interest in his reports.

They passed through the gate and into the city to the sucking sound of horses' hooves in muck. The place stank of manure and human waste. Alexander kept his guard up and his pain at bay. Anatoly's words from a few nights ago nagged at him again and he pretended that he hadn't yet made up his mind, but somewhere deeper he knew that he had.

As they made their way through the sea of buildings toward the center of town, Alexander caught a glimpse of something on one of the rooftops but it was gone behind a brick chimney before he could make out what it was. He shook his head as he recalled his father's words: "There are strange things in the big city, best to leave them be and attend to your business." Good advice, but something about the thing bothered him. It looked almost like a tiny man with wings.

Alexander allowed himself to relax his guard once they were in their room at the inn with the door firmly locked and barred. He reminded himself to be grateful for the small things as he took a seat at the long table occupying the center of the main room. It was a simple table with simple chairs. Abigail was ladling thick stew from the heavy iron pot that had been sent up from the kitchen.

"Thanks, Sis," Alexander smiled up at her as she placed a heavy wooden bowl in front of him. Lucky sat across from him and rubbed his hands together at the prospect of a hot meal. He looked tired but despite his fatigue, Alexander could see the light of genuine joy in his eyes as he took a chunk of warm bread and slathered it with rich yellow butter. Alexander had always envied Lucky's ability to put his troubles aside when presented with a good meal.

"The room is secure and easy enough to defend if need be." Anatoly took a chair next to Lucky and put his short sword on the table, nodding his thanks to Abigail when she placed a steaming bowl in front of him.

The aroma of the stew triggered Alexander's hunger. He poured himself a flagon of cider while Abigail dished a bowl of stew for herself. She took her seat next to him and he raised his glass. Lucky stopped short of his first bite, looking almost sheepish.

"May the Lord and Lady of Valentine Manor fare as well as we do this night." Alexander's toast was simple but heartfelt. All raised their flagons.

They ate in silence. Everyone was hungry and glad to have a hot meal in a warm and dry room. The past few days had been cold, wet, and filled with fear. They didn't know if they were being pursued but could only assume that they were.

After they had eaten their fill and the kitchen staff had cleared the table, Anatoly secured the room again. He bolted the door and checked the windows in the main room and the two bedrooms to be sure they were secure. Lucky followed after him and sprinkled a silvery dust on the windowsills and at the base of the door.

Alexander gave him a quizzical look. Lucky responded with a wink and said, "Just in case." He always had some potion, powder, or salve for nearly any situation.

"I'll stand first watch," Anatoly said in spite of his obvious exhaustion.

Lucky shook his head, "Nonsense. We have more need of sleep than we do of a guard. The room is secure and the entrances are spelled. No one will get in without me knowing about it."

Anatoly frowned and looked to Alexander.

Alexander suddenly felt very tired. He'd always looked to his father and brother to make the decisions. He never realized what a burden it must have been for them. After a moment he nodded, "I agree with Lucky. We all need a good night's sleep."

Anatoly frowned again and said, "Very well, I'll sleep on the couch; it'll certainly be more comfortable than the floor and I can keep an ear on the door. Besides, I don't fancy sharing a bed with Lucky," he added with a brief grin as he unrolled his bedroll on the oversized couch.

Alexander was asleep as soon as his head hit the pillow. Abigail was breathing deeply in the big bed before he'd even stripped down to his nightshirt. Despite his worry, he slept soundly without any dreams.

He woke with a start. It felt like only a few minutes had passed since he'd lain down. He rolled over and looked at the window to see that the sky was just starting to glow with the coming dawn.

Then the layer of dust Lucky had sprinkled on the windowsill pulsed brightly. Alexander sprang out of bed and drew his sword. He heard a scuffle coming from the main room before he made it to the door.

He burst into the large room to see Anatoly holding a smaller man down on the table with the point of his long dagger at the man's throat. Without a glance toward Alexander he barked, "Bar the door!"

Alexander slammed the door shut and threw the bolt as Lucky emerged from his room holding a brightly glowing glass vial high in his left hand and a long knife in his right. Abigail stood in the doorway to their room dressed only in her nightgown but with her short bow in hand and an arrow nocked and ready.

Anatoly growled into the sudden silence, "How many men do you have with you?"

The man pinned to the table sputtered, "No one else … just me … don't kill me … I've come to help you." His words tumbled out quickly.

Anatoly grunted, obviously not convinced.

Alexander relaxed his vision. What he saw surprised him. The intruder's colors were those of a good man, perhaps even a fiercely good man. He saw loyalty, reverence for life, and courage. He also saw that the man was telling the truth.

"Anatoly, let him up," Alexander said quietly. Anatoly looked to him for confirmation. He nodded slowly. "It's okay … I don't believe he's a threat."

Anatoly grunted again. "That remains to be seen," he said as he released the intruder while still pointing his long dagger at the man's chest. Anatoly stepped back and allowed the man to stand while deftly removing the intruder's knife from his belt.

The intruder looked straight at Alexander, "You would be Darius Valentine, yes?"

Anatoly tossed the intruder's knife away and grabbed him again by the throat. His long dagger pierced the intruder's tunic right over his heart and he pressed the point against him firmly enough to draw just a drop of blood.

"Choose your next words very carefully." Anatoly was in a foul mood.

Before the intruder could speak, Alexander asked, "How do you know my brother's name?" Abigail came up alongside him, tension still on the string of her short bow.

"Your brother … but you bear the mark." He looked genuinely confused, but only for a moment before a look of sadness came over him. "Your brother is dead then." It wasn't a question but a statement of realization.

Abigail repeated the question with a hard edge to her voice. "How do you know my brother's name?"

He looked back to Anatoly who still held him by the throat with a long knife to his heart, then back to Alexander and Abigail. "It's somewhat of a long story and we haven't the time at the moment. There is a small contingent of Reishi Protectorate in Southport and they are aware of your presence. They're searching for you and will likely find you soon. We must flee if you are to have any hope of living through the day."

Alexander shook his head slowly. "You still haven't answered my question and we aren't going anywhere until you do."

The intruder looked at the resolve in Alexander's face and nodded stiffly. "I could explain more easily if you would kindly let go of my throat." He forced a smile as he looked at Anatoly.

Anatoly looked to Alexander, who nodded. Anatoly released him again, still pointing his long dagger at the intruder's heart.

The man stood, made a brief show of brushing himself off, turned to Alexander and Abigail bowing deeply and said, "My Lord and Lady Valentine, I am Master Bard Jack Colton and I am at your service."

He stood six feet tall and looked to weigh about 160 pounds. He had dirty-blond hair, a fair complexion, and piercing blue eyes the color of the top of the sky a moment after the sun sets. He was altogether too good-looking and possessed a kind of charisma that was a mixture of youthful charm tempered by the confidence of more real-world experience than someone his age ought to have. His clothes were simple and ordinary. His way of speaking and his bearing were not.

"Since the time of the Reishi War," Jack began, "the Bards Guild has passed the story of the Marked One from one generation to the next. When my father told me the story, I set out on a quest to find the true bloodline, your bloodline, which led me to House of Valentine. When I discovered the truth of your line a few years ago, I moved to Southport so I would be ready when the Reishi Arch Mage awoke."

"Stop … you're rambling. How do you know of my brother?" Alexander was getting mad. "I won't ask again."

Jack glanced at Anatoly who was standing dangerously close with his very sharp long dagger still poised to strike. He took a deep breath. "Darius Valentine was the eldest son of the House of Valentine. Your house has hidden the cursed bloodline for centuries. Your brother was supposed to defeat the Reishi Arch Mage, Prince Phane, and deliver the Seven Isles from a thousand years of darkness."

"Darius is dead," Alexander said flatly. "He was murdered less than a week ago by an assassin."

Jack closed his eyes and took another deep breath. "I am very sorry for your loss, My Lord. That sad fact explains the mark you bear on your neck. The eldest son of the cursed bloodline will be marked when the Arch Mage Prince awakes. With your brother dead, the task falls to you." Jack Colton closed his eyes as if he were dredging his memory. "That would make you Alexander and you Abigail, yes?"

"You have our names, and much more it would seem. What is your interest in us? Why have you broken into our room and how did you find us in the first place?" Alexander noticed that Lucky had already packed his things and was nearly ready to go. Apparently, he was taking Jack Colton's story seriously.

"I found you because I have been waiting for you to arrive since the warning spell alerted the Seven Isles to the coming threat. I broke into your room to warn you of the danger you are in and my interest in you is obvious. I want to be the one to write the songs of your story."

Lucky started laughing, "Sounds like a bard to me. What does your sight tell you, Alexander?"

Alexander frowned, "It tells me we should trust him."

Anatoly frowned too, as he stepped back and shrugged. "Sorry about the nick, Mister Bard …"

"Actually, it's master bard, but you may call me Jack." His smile was warm, comical, and disarming all at once.

Anatoly grinned in spite of himself, "Very well, Jack, but know this," his grin turned menacing, "if you're lying, I *will* kill you."

Jack's expression turned deadly serious. He appraised Anatoly for a moment before nodding solemnly. "Given the nature of the coming storm, I for one, am glad to see that the Marked One has such a devoted protector." He strolled over to his knife on the floor, retrieved it and returned it to the sheath on his belt. "I've also read the stories of Prince Phane … and they still give me nightmares. He must be stopped or I fear the whole world will fall into darkness."

Jack took a seat at the table. "The Reishi Protectorate is looking for you as we speak. If we stay here, they will find you. The only question is when."

"Very well then, you can finish your story on the road," Alexander said as he turned back to his room.

Chapter 8

They began gathering their things and preparing to leave.

Lucky took a chair opposite Jack and introduced himself, "Aluicious Alabrand, Master Alchemist and Valentine family tutor." He gestured toward the room where Alexander and Abigail were packing. "My friends call me Lucky."

Jack inclined his head in formal greeting. "It is an honor and privilege to meet you, Master Alabrand."

"So, Master Colton, where did you train?" Lucky spoke while he laid out a breakfast of cold biscuits, berry jam, and butter.

"Please, call me Jack," he said.

Anatoly grunted in the background as he packed up his bedroll.

"My father was the master bard of New Ruatha. He trained me from the time I was old enough to speak." Jack looked pleadingly at a biscuit.

Lucky nodded eagerly; he was always happy to share a meal. "Ah ... so you know of Kelvin, the Guild Master of the Ruathan Wizards Guild ... Oh what's his last name? I'm terrible with names."

Jack nodded and smiled gently at the test, "Gamaliel ... Kelvin Gamaliel, Guild Mage of Ruatha and the finest magical craftsman in all of the Seven Isles ... or so he likes to claim," he added with a wink.

Lucky chuckled at the friendly gibe. Kelvin didn't so much boast of his talent as state the truth of it without discomfort.

"He once crafted a necklace of warding for my father," Jack said around a bite of biscuit. "It was the damnedest thing I ever saw. Once, an arrow would have killed my dad for sure, but the necklace glowed and the arrow stopped dead in the air not three feet from burying itself in my dad's chest, hung there for a full count, then fell to the ground." Jack shook his head slowly as if marveling at the wonder of it. "Boasting or not, the Guild Mage is okay by me."

Anatoly finished packing his bedroll and joined the two at the table just as Alexander and Abigail came out of their room packed and ready to go. "So ... Jack, tell me about the Reishi who are looking for young Alexander here," Anatoly commanded.

"I know only what my people tell me. In the few years I've been here I've developed a network of sources, some more reliable than others, who bring me information concerning the happenings about town. They all know I'm especially interested in any activity of the Reishi Protectorate."

Alexander and Abigail set their packs next to the door and took seats at the table. Alexander motioned to Jack to continue as he helped himself to a biscuit.

"About a month ago, I caught wind that agents of the Reishi Protectorate were meeting. They don't usually do that so I started poking around. When I learned that Phane's obelisk on Tyr had started acting funny, I made sure to pay every gate guard, bartender, and innkeeper in the city to send word the moment they spotted you. Then I got a few of the Reishi Protectorate drunk and talked them out of what they knew." Jack smiled conspiratorially and winked at Abigail.

"It's amazing what a man will tell you when he's had a bit too much to drink."

Anatoly grunted, nodding his agreement. "Do you know how many men the Reishi have in the city?"

"I'd say about thirty, and only a handful of those have any real experience in a fight. The one I'm most worried about is a wizard named Rangle." Everyone sat up a bit straighter at the mention of a wizard. "Rangle is pretty good with fire. He works for the Southport Smithy and Iron Works. I wouldn't want to tangle with Mercado, the master smith, either; he's an ox of a man with arms as big as my thighs. Those two are likely to be leading the hunt for you." Jack glanced out the window at the growing dawn and said, "And I suspect they are looking even as we speak. I'm sure they know you're in town."

"How can you be sure?" Lucky asked. "We only arrived just last night."

"Same way I knew you were here; they paid the gate guards to tell them when you arrived. Although, I doubt they were as thorough as me so they're probably going from inn to inn looking for you right now, hence my humble suggestion that we be on our way quickly."

This time it was Alexander who spoke. "But how would they know we would come to Southport?"

"They know you'll likely be heading for the Rangers in Glen Morillian so you'd just about have to come through here." Jack was growing visibly impatient. "My Lord, we really should be on our way."

"Master Bard ..." This time it was Abigail who spoke only to be quickly interrupted by Jack.

"My Lady, you simply must call me Jack," he said with his most charming smile.

Abigail actually blushed. Alexander thought to himself that there was a first time for everything.

"Very well," Abigail said, struggling to regain her composure. "Jack, if they knew Valentine Manor was home to the cursed bloodline, why didn't they come for us sooner? Why not attack when they discovered our secret?"

Jack smiled again, this time with a hint of puzzlement. "That I do not know. I suspect the General Commander of the Reishi Protectorate saw no point in killing you until it became clear that Phane would wake. From what I know of the man, he appears to value life and only kills when necessary. Of course, that is only speculation on my part. He may have only recently become aware of your lineage."

Abigail nodded in thought but before she could speak again, Anatoly motioned for silence. Everyone stood as one at the sound of several sets of heavy boots coming up the stairs. Anatoly motioned for them to grab their gear. It sounded like half a dozen men were gathering outside their door.

Everyone in the room jumped when a heavy hammer smashed into the door. The frame cracked and the wood around the bolt gave way, sending splinters flying into the room, but the bar across the door held.

Anatoly took up his war axe, Abigail nocked an arrow, and Lucky went to the window to see if they could get out that way.

Alexander acted without hesitation. He stood, swept his chair aside with one hand and drew his long sword with the other. Before the heavy hammer could crash into the door again, Alexander took a long step and drove his sword through a newly formed crack in the door. A man screamed. Alexander hoped it was the man with the hammer but it wasn't. When he drew his sword back, the hammer fell again. This time it struck higher, at the level of the bar.

The door held, but only just. Alexander knew it wouldn't withstand another blow like that. They were about to be in a pitched battle with a superior force and he felt surprisingly calm, almost like he was watching the scene unfold on a stage.

Anatoly tipped the long table up to provide some cover. Alexander found himself between it and the quickly failing door, so he vaulted over it just before the door burst from the force of another hammer blow. The bar shattered and the broken door swung wide and slammed into the wall, revealing a cluster of armed and armored men in the hall poised to rush the room.

The first man through the door fell back with an arrow sticking out of his breastplate. Abigail stood, feet planted, face set in stone as she drew a second arrow from her quiver.

"Grab the table and push!" Anatoly commanded.

Alexander and Jack took hold of the table and helped Anatoly use it like a cross between a battering ram and a shield wall to drive the next man back and block the door at the same time. Another arrow whizzed past them and buried itself in the shoulder of another enemy.

Lucky came up behind them just as they heard a whoosh followed by the shattering of glass. A wave of heat and the bright orange glow of fire rose up behind them. The wall facing out onto the street was ablaze.

"Rangle is hurling fire at the windows to make sure we can't get out that way," Lucky reported.

They were trapped.

Abigail loosed another arrow but it glanced off a shield.

Jack Colton was surprisingly calm in the midst of the sudden violence. He was squatted down low, lending his weight to the table to keep it in place blocking the door. "I don't suppose there's another way out of here?" he asked no one in particular in the most nonchalant sort of way, almost like he was asking if someone could please pass the butter.

Lucky actually chuckled, "I believe I might be able to help with that. Anatoly, where's your rope?"

The big man-at-arms motioned toward his pack on the couch, then took a swipe with his axe at an arm that had the poor judgment to come over the table.

The heavy hammer slammed into the table and drove it back about a foot, just enough for a man to slip between the table and the wall only to be pinned there as the three pushed back. Another hit with the hammer and he'd be in the room. The enemy had a couple of heavy shields held high to protect against Abigail and her bow. She stood, arrow nocked, waiting for a clear shot.

Alexander called out, "Lucky, whatever you're doing, do it faster."

Lucky came out of his room with a clay fire pot in hand.

Anatoly looked twice at his old friend. "You sure about this?"

Lucky shrugged, "Desperate times and all. Quickly, all of you get into my room." Abigail scooped up her pack and went without a word. The three holding the table released their pressure just as the hammer struck again driving the table back several feet.

Anatoly spun. He knew the man pinned between the table and the wall would be free the moment the pressure was off. When the enemy slipped into the room, Anatoly used the momentum of his spin to bury his axe blade in the man's chest, cutting him nearly in half at the torso. Blood flowed freely.

Alexander and Jack were moving toward Lucky's room, followed by Anatoly as Lucky tossed his clay fire pot through the doorway. It broke against the shields and splashed liquid fire into the hallway. Smoke began to flow along the ceiling, both from the now burning curtains covering the windows and from the new conflagration in the hall caused by Lucky and his well-placed fire pot. The screams of burning men could be heard over the growing roar of the fire.

Inside Lucky's room, they were met with a three-foot hole in the floor, burned around the edges as if by some type of potent acid. Anatoly's rope was secured to the bed and trailed down the hole. Abigail was already in the room below, which was thankfully unoccupied.

She called out quietly, "Come on," and motioned for them to follow.

Lucky went next, followed by Jack, then Alexander, and finally Anatoly. They could hear shrieks of pain coming from the hallway above as they slid down the rope. The fire was growing and the other guests were in a panic to get out of the building. As guests fled, more soldiers raced up the stairs to reinforce the Reishi Protectorate in the hall above, leaving a clear route to the kitchen where they could flee out the back door.

Anatoly cracked the door just enough to see down the hall. "It's clear this way."

Alexander took a look out the window. Wizard Rangle stood across the street, looking up. He was flanked by a dozen men with crossbows. Fortunately, they were all looking at the second floor. "We have to move fast. Anatoly, lead the way to the kitchen and out to the stables. We have to get out of here before they realize we're not still in our room."

Anatoly considered for a moment. "Agreed, but they'll have men waiting for us at the stables, probably with crossbows. Jack, do you know of another way out?"

"I'm afraid not," Jack answered. "There's a way into the Southport underground a few buildings down but that can't help us unless we can get there." Just then they heard the bells of the fire brigade. "Perhaps the authorities will provide us with the distraction we need."

Alexander had his bow out with an arrow nocked. "I'd rather face whatever's out back than that wizard and his crossbowmen. I say we go out the back way and hope we can make it to the stables in one piece."

Anatoly nodded, slung his war axe, and drew a throwing knife in each hand. "Hit them before they hit you and move fast." He checked the hall again, stuck his head out, then back in quickly. "There's one at the end of the hall guarding the door to the kitchen."

Alexander took a deep breath. He'd never killed a man before, unless you count the guy he just stuck with his sword through the door, but he didn't even know if that guy was dead. "Open the door for me," he said as he put tension on his bowstring.

Anatoly nodded, positioned himself and looked to Alexander for the go. It happened very quickly. Anatoly swung the door wide, Alexander glided into the hallway, drawing his bow as he moved. The enemy saw him and pulled his crossbow up to take aim. Alexander was faster. The soldier took the arrow straight in the chest and staggered back with a look of confusion and disbelief. He looked Alexander straight in the eye for just a moment before slumping to the floor.

"Move!" Anatoly commanded as he turned the young Lord of Valentine Manor away from the first man he had ever killed and toward their escape route.

Alexander obeyed, even drew another arrow, but all he could see in his mind's eye was the shock and surprise of the man he'd just killed. He felt like he might throw up.

Then he heard the shout of a guard from the staircase above. "They're downstairs!"

Alexander's heart skipped a beat when he heard the sound of heavy boots running in the hall above. The shock of killing a man slipped into the background of his mind, and the need to survive shouldered its way into his consciousness, demanding his full attention.

They made it to the kitchen, which was now deserted because of the fire. The door leading outside behind the inn was standing open. There was only an alley between the inn and the stables, and the side door to the stables stood open.

Anatoly stopped and crouched at the door to poke his head out. He yanked it back quickly. Crossbow bolts whizzed past and glanced off the side of the building from both directions. There were men at either end of the alley and probably in the stables. They were trapped again and more men were coming from behind. They only had moments before they'd be in a pitched battle in tight quarters.

"Over here ... it leads down to the cellar." Jack had found a trap door in the floor of the kitchen. The stairway leading down was steep but sturdy. The air in the cellar was rank and musty.

"What if it's a dead end?" Anatoly said as he unslung his war axe. "I'd rather face 'em where I have room to work."

"We might be able to get into the underground from down there. I know for sure there are passages that run down the street out front. Besides, we won't do well against all those crossbows." Jack made his case while he took a kitchen rag, wrapped it around a long wooden spoon, and lit it on fire from the stove.

Anatoly still looked skeptical.

Alexander made up his mind for him. "I'd rather not be caught in a crossfire. At least they have to come down the stairs before they can get a clear shot off, and we can shoot at them from the dark."

The cellar was dank and musty but well stocked. The shelves were lined with tightly sealed jars filled with all manner of vegetables and preserves. A few jars contained chickens. Boxes and crates were stacked all around the low-ceilinged room. But there was no door out.

Anatoly was the last one down. "You picked a fine spot for a last stand, *Master* Colton," he growled as he pulled the trapdoor closed, then worked a leather strap free from his pack to tie the hatch closed.

Alexander enlisted the assistance of Lucky and Abigail in stacking a few of the heavier crates for cover.

Jack was busy examining the walls, for what, Alexander didn't know, but didn't take the time to ask. The room above filled with the sound of heavy boots and the shouts of at least a dozen men as the enemy burst in from both entrances. They sounded confused and angry, each group accusing the other of letting their quarry escape.

There was a moment of quiet before the men of the Protectorate began to search for another way out of the kitchen. Alexander knew it wouldn't be long before they found it.

"Here! Anatoly, bring your axe." It seemed that Jack had found what he was looking for. "This wall is all that separates us from the Southport sewers. Can you knock this wall down right here?" Jack pointed at a spot in the wall.

Anatoly gave the bard a grim look, spun his war axe around to bring the long spike on the back of the gruesome-looking weapon to bear. With a mighty swing, he shattered a single brick, leaving a small hole in the wall. Cool, foul-smelling air flowed in from the sewers beyond. He gave Jack a quick smile and picked a brick several rows down for his second strike. As the brick shattered, the men above found the trapdoor and tried to open it. Anatoly's leather strap held.

He swung at the wall again and another brick shattered into dust. He was picking his targets carefully to weaken the wall enough so that he could push a large section through all at once.

Alexander and Abigail stood behind the hasty barricade of crates, looking from Anatoly to the trapdoor, wondering who would break through first. Alexander had an iron grip on his fear. He knew without doubt that there were powerful forces hunting him, trying to kill him for an accident of birth. He also knew they would kill his sister as well. He thought of Darius and deliberately changed the pang of grief he felt into anger. There would be time for mourning later, but he had to live through the day first.

Anatoly shattered another brick. Then the big man with the hammer struck at the hatch in the floor. Alexander could see a sudden sliver of light through the now cracked floorboard. He knew the trapdoor wouldn't last long under the punishing force of the blacksmith's hammer. But that wasn't what worried him the most. He could hear the fire engulfing the front of the inn above. Once the trapdoor was open, he had no doubt that Wizard Rangle would fill this small cellar with flame. They probably wouldn't even get a shot at any of the soldiers before Rangle sent a gout of fire down the hole to burn them out.

Another brick shattered and Anatoly followed by smashing into the wall with his shoulder backed up by his considerable weight. A small section of the brick wall fell into the sewer with a muted splash. Fetid air flowed into the cellar. The hole was almost big enough for Abigail but no one else. Anatoly stood back and took another swing, again carefully picking the brick he wanted to attack.

The broken floorboard in the trapdoor shattered into splinters under the weight of a second hammer blow. "Be ready, men," said the blacksmith. Then an arm snaked into the hole and fished around for the strap that was holding the door closed. The arm found it and unlatched it just as Abigail's arrow found him. The man shrieked with the sudden pain of having an arrow driven clean through his forearm. He tried to snatch his hand out of the hole but the arrow caught on the boards as he yanked up and he screamed even louder as his flesh tore.

Alexander drew back on his bow and took aim. Anatoly broke through another brick. The trapdoor was thrown open with the man's arm still through it; the heavy door crashing over on top of him with a thud. He wailed in agony again while he tried to work his arm free.

Anatoly smashed another section of the wall and motioned Lucky to get through into the sewers.

Alexander took careful aim and loosed his arrow. It just slipped through the open trapdoor and drove into the ankle of one of the men standing on the floor above. He would have given Abigail a cocky little grin if the situation wasn't so desperate and if his heart wasn't hammering in his chest.

Jack was through the hole in the wall and into the sewers. Alexander had another arrow ready. Abigail sent an arrow at the hole. It made it through but didn't find a target. Then Alexander heard what he'd been expecting to hear.

"Stand back, let me set them on fire."

It was Wizard Rangle and he was getting ready to send fire down on them. In the confined space of the cellar it wouldn't take much to fill the room with flames and kill them all.

Alexander gave Abigail a gentle shove toward Anatoly, shouting, "Go, both of you!"

He didn't look back as he raced around the crates to the base of the steep stairs with an arrow half drawn. He looked up to the kitchen above and saw Rangle drawing power for his spell. Alexander could see the glittering of magic in the wizard's eyes as his power coalesced. An almost insubstantial ball of fire began to form between Rangle's outstretched hands. Alexander snapped his bow up and let the arrow fly. The wizard cried out when the arrow drove right through his left shoulder and stuck out the top of his back. The fire that hadn't yet formed fizzled out and Rangle threw himself out of harm's way.

Alexander dashed to the hole in the wall and scrambled halfway through. Anatoly grabbed him and drew him through the rest of the way. The look on the big man-at-arms' face as he roughly set Alexander on his feet was one of boiling anger.

"We'll talk of this later, *young* Lord Valentine."

The passageway was a good eight feet across with an arched ceiling at least that tall. There were two-foot ledges on either side and a fetid, stinking, slow-moving canal of raw sewage four feet across running down the middle of the dark corridor.

"This way."

Jack was at the end of a corridor, motioning frantically for them to follow, when Alexander heard men starting down the stairs into the cellar. He drew another arrow, but before he could take aim, Anatoly gave him an angry look.

"Not this time. Get moving."

Lucky was fishing around in his bag. "I believe I have something that will slow them down a bit." He drew out a glass vile that was stoppered at each end and separated in the middle by a thick glass divider. In each half of the vile was a liquid of a different color, dark red on one side and a milky white on the other. With a mischievous little grin he unceremoniously tossed it through the hole into the cellar. "Come along now," he said as he shooed the rest of them away from the sound of shattering glass.

Jack led the way with the dim light of his makeshift torch. When they made it to the end of the corridor and rounded the corner, a strange hissing noise rose up from behind them, followed by screaming.

Alexander's heart raced as they moved away from the horrible screaming. "What was that?" he asked his old tutor.

"Oh, just a set of compounds that are completely harmless by themselves, but when put together release a thick gaseous vapor that burns like acid. It's especially nasty if you inhale the stuff. I'm afraid those men in the cellar won't make it." Lucky gave him a look and a shrug that was at once proud and guilty.

Alexander had known the old alchemist for his entire life. He didn't have a mean bone in his body but clearly his rotund, jovial tutor did have mettle.

Chapter 9

They moved as quickly as they could along the narrow, slippery ledge without risking a fall into the sewage canal. The stench was so overpowering, Alexander almost gagged.

Jack seemed to know where he was leading them. He took each turn or passed it by like he was in familiar territory. Alexander couldn't understand why anyone would willingly set foot in such a place. It was as filthy and unpleasant a place as he'd ever been ... except maybe back in the little cellar where he thought they were going to be roasted alive by Rangle.

The light from Jack's makeshift torch began to sputter.

Anatoly stopped and asked, "Where are you leading us?" There was a hint of wariness in the question.

"There's a hidden door just up ahead that leads into the basement of one of the local merchants. He's a friend and, um, well, business associate. We can go through his shop to get back on the street." He handed the spoon-made-into-a-torch to Abigail and used his knife to cut a strip of cloth from the bottom hem of his tunic, which he then carefully wrapped around the burning end of the torch to keep it from going out. He took it back and started moving again.

Jack stopped so abruptly that Anatoly bumped into Alexander in the dark as the four of them halted behind the bard. He raised his torch, looking carefully at the wall. After a minute of searching, he found a loose stone and pushed on one side. The brick swiveled, allowing access to a lever. Jack pulled the stiff metal rod and pushed on a two-foot-wide by four-foot-tall section of the wall.

They found themselves inside a cool, dry storage room lined with wooden shelves crammed with boxes, jars, cartons, and other containers. Jack carefully closed the secret door and started for the stairs leading up.

Anatoly caught his arm. "What should we expect at the top of those stairs?" Anatoly was charged with protecting Alexander and Abigail. He took his duties seriously. Jack had been helpful and was probably telling the truth about his motives but that wasn't good enough. Anatoly needed to be sure.

Jack stopped and nodded. "My associate is usually in the showroom of his shop during the day or in the workroom just off the showroom floor. The room at the top of the stairs is a storeroom in the back of the shop. It will probably be empty and it has a door leading out the back. If we're quiet, we should be able to slip out into the alley without anyone even noticing." Jack was clearly offering as much information as he could. He seemed to be going out of his way to earn the trust of the big man-at-arms.

"Does your friend have any employees or others who might be in the storeroom?" Alexander asked. He allowed his vision to go out of focus so he could see Jack's colors. He wanted to trust the bard, but the events of the past week had reinforced his father's lessons about trust. Deception was the most powerful weapon in the arsenal of evil. A simple lie was all it took to undo whole nations. Believing a lie could cost you your life.

"His wife works with him. I don't think he has any other help." Jack didn't shy away from the questions and the colors of his aura were clear and honest.

Alexander nodded.

"Okay, once we're in the alley, what's our plan? The Reishi Protectorate isn't going to give up that easily. They probably have spies all around town. We left our horses back at the stables, not to mention Lucky's wagon. Suggestions?" Alexander had decided that he was going to accept the mantle of leadership. He didn't like it, but it was the only sensible thing he could do given the circumstances.

Lucky cleared his throat. "I'd like to get the contents of my wagon, if we can do so without notice. Many of the items I brought along are of great value and may prove very useful in the future."

"We're going to need horses to get to Glen Morillian," Anatoly mused. "I suppose we could make our way back to the stables at the inn and take a look. We might get lucky. Then again, they'll probably have someone watching our horses in case we come back. The alternative is finding horses on our way out of town and leaving ours at the stables. I don't much like that option but it might be the safest route."

Alexander turned to Abigail for her input. She looked almost startled to be consulted but recovered quickly and frowned in thought. "Our horses are healthier and better cared for than any we'll find for sale and Lucky is probably understating the value of his wagon," she gave him a smile before she went on. "Jack, does the Reishi Protectorate know you? Would they have any reason to suspect you're with us?"

The bard frowned for a moment. "I can't see how they could. I've only just met you and I've been careful to keep my true purpose here a secret."

"Is there any way you could get our horses for us while we waited nearby?" Abigail asked.

Jack nodded slowly, "I think I could. I have a friend that operates a large stable just outside of town. I could pose as one of his men and tell the fire brigade I'm moving the horses to his stable. I doubt anyone would get in the way; they'll be too busy with the fire."

"There's still a good chance that the Reishi Protectorate will be suspicious of anyone trying to take our horses. They're likely to follow you." Alexander frowned as he thought out loud. "Do you have anyone in town that you trust, anyone who would be willing to help us?"

"Of course, my apprentice Owen. In fact, I have him waiting with fresh horses in a little farmhouse just north of town. But that doesn't help us with Lucky's wagon. If the tricks I've seen him pull out of his bag are any indication, I believe he's quite right about the contents of his wagon being very useful."

Anatoly, ever suspicious, asked, "Why is your apprentice waiting with fresh horses?"

Jack smiled and shrugged. "I believe in being prepared. I knew you were going to pass through here and I wanted to be ready to help. I've used every resource at my disposal for just that purpose." He almost looked self-conscious as he went on. "Whether you like it or not, My Lord, your story will be sung for a thousand years. I intend to be the one to write those songs." Jack smiled briefly at the thought, then looked Alexander straight in the eye. All humor and good cheer left his face. When he was sure he had Alexander's attention, he continued.

"I also know a little bit about Prince Phane. If he wins, then everyone who loves life and freedom will lose. I've read some of the histories of the Reishi War. Phane took delight in torturing his rivals. He sacrificed innocent children to the netherworld in his efforts to master the dark magic of necromancy and brought about the fall of whole countries with simple, yet apparently very convincing, lies. He is powerful, cunning, utterly ruthless, and absolutely driven by a sense of personal entitlement. In his view, the Seven Isles and every last soul alive belong to him by right."

Silence settled into the dim room as Jack Colton's pronouncement sank in. "You have been marked. If the Seven Isles have a chance, it rests with you. If you fail, hope will die for a thousand years."

Some of the color drained from Alexander's face as the magnitude of his burden settled in on him. He took a deep breath and nodded. "Very well then, we make for the farmhouse and your apprentice. We'll send him to retrieve our horses and Lucky's wagon while we head for the forest. I'd rather have our own horses but the risk is too great at the moment. There's no telling what Phane can conjure so we can't risk holding still for too long and I'd rather not make it easy for the Reishi Protectorate to pick up our trail."

Everyone nodded in agreement.

"Jack, you go up the stairs first. Anatoly, bring up the rear," Alexander commanded.

The narrow alley was empty when they slipped out of the little storeroom. Wagons, carts, and people filed by on the streets to either end of the space between the two buildings. The brick walls were black and wet with the morning dew; some sort of fungus grew in splotches here and there. From the angle of the buildings it looked like very little direct sunlight ever fell on these walls. Jack closed the door gently behind them.

"We should head this way. I think I can keep us off the main streets for most of the way and I know of a few breaches in the walls we can use to avoid the checkpoints at the city gates."

They moved through the city like shadows, keeping to the dark and untraveled passages between the buildings. It was like moving through tunnels. The only people they encountered were the underclass who lived in the recesses of society and foraged on the scraps of others. A few tried to demand a coin here or there but Anatoly had only to brandish his war axe to convince them to recoil back into the shadows.

By noon they made it to the outer wall without drawing any attention. Jack had proven to be a careful and knowledgeable guide. He knew the city well and made each turn with confidence. He peeked around a corner to peer down the alley that led to a breach in the outer wall and just as quickly snapped back behind the corner.

"We have a problem," he whispered to Alexander.

"What is it?" Anatoly growled before Alexander could ask.

"There are city guards at the breach. It's just a crack in the wall. They shouldn't be guarding it." He shook his head. "Why would city guards be there?"

"They've probably been paid," Abigail said. When everyone looked at her, she shrugged. "You don't really believe it's a coincidence do you?"

Alexander shook his head, "Of course not. How many did you see, Jack?"

"I saw three, but there are probably more; they travel in squads of seven, a commander and six guards."

"Is there another way out of the city?" Lucky asked.

"There are several other breaches in the walls but none close by and I'd bet they're all being watched as well," Jack answered.

"Are there any buildings that butt up against the wall?" Anatoly asked. "We might be able to go over the wall from a rooftop."

"I'm afraid not. The wall runs along a perimeter road. If we want to go over we'll need a rope or a ladder and we'll have to risk being seen by guards along the road," Jack said, shaking his head.

"What about under? Do you know a way through the Southport sewers that passes under the outer walls?" Alexander spoke calmly, but he could feel a sense of fear rising within him. He felt growing certainty that these men had been paid to kill him.

"The sewers are all barred where they flow under the walls. I doubt we could get through and we'd have to backtrack quite a bit to find a way into the underground. We could make our way to the docks and try our luck on the water but I suspect we'd run into the city guard there too," Jack said.

Alexander nodded. Anatoly stood silent, arms folded on his chest, waiting for Alexander to make a decision. Alexander could feel the big man-at-arms appraising him while he deliberated. He felt the burden that had been placed on him by an ancient curse. The mark on his neck still hurt when his collar chafed against it. He knew from his own studies of the Reishi War what would happen if Phane was allowed to reestablish the House of Reishi under his command. He'd seen it back at Valentine Manor when the zombie demon attacked. Creatures of the netherworld would haunt the innocent people of the Seven Isles at the whim of a tyrant and murderer.

But more than any of that, Alexander wanted to live. He wanted his sister to live. He desperately hoped his parents were still alive. He hadn't asked for any of this. He didn't want it, yet here he was.

Trapped.

He knew they couldn't wait around until dark. Phane had abilities far beyond Alexander's understanding. He could summon agents from the netherworld to hunt them. He could probably divine their location and send word to the men searching the city for them. In truth, there was no telling what Arch Mage Prince Phane Reishi could do.

The two things that Alexander knew for certain were that Phane would offer him no mercy and that he couldn't afford to underestimate the Reishi Prince. The night he watched his home burn had convinced him of that.

In the back of his mind he knew what had to be done. He just desperately didn't want to do it. Until just a few hours ago, Alexander Valentine had never killed a man. As they'd fled through the alleyways, he'd tried to keep the thought of it away from his awareness, tried to push the cold truth away into the dark recesses of his mind where he wouldn't have to face it.

Now, standing in the narrow alley, weighing his choices, he called the ugliness of the deed out of the shadows and stared it full in the face. He,

Alexander Valentine, had killed a man. He considered the truth of it and felt a sick feeling well up in the pit of his stomach. A wave of nausea swept over him and then he heard the words of his father: "Motives matter." It was one of his father's favorite sayings and one that Alexander could always count on hearing every time his dad had occasion to reprimand him. The sickness in his belly subsided with that thought.

He hadn't sought out that man to kill him. That man had brought death to his door. Alexander was fighting to survive against those who were trying to kill him. He had committed no crime. Yet men, armed with steel and magic, were trying to murder him. Alexander had never done anything that justified the forfeiture of his life. He was entitled to live until he had. The man he'd killed had died in the commission of a crime. He'd come to kill and had died instead. Justice done. An emotional hardness began to take shape within him.

The men guarding the gap in the wall were little better. If they'd been paid to kill him, then they were the enemy, but Alexander had to be sure. They might just be city guard following orders. He couldn't justify killing innocent men just because they were in his way.

When he looked up from his thoughts, all eyes were on him. "Jack, I need you to do a little scouting for us. We need to know if those guards are being paid to find us or if they're guarding the gap for another reason. Can you do that?"

Jack nodded, "No problem. I'll go around these buildings and come down the street, have a little chat with them and be on my way. Once I'm out of sight I'll make my way back here."

"Sounds good. We'll be here," Alexander said.

Jack headed off down the alley.

Alexander made his way to the corner of the building so he could watch from the shadows when the bard approached the city guard. He didn't have to wait long before he heard what sounded like drunken singing. Sure enough, Jack Colton, master bard, came into view, weaving and singing loudly, with a flagon of ale in hand. Where he'd gotten it was a mystery to Alexander; he'd only left just a few minutes before.

Jack approached the guards and raised his glass. "A toast to the city guard of Southport, the finest city guard in all the Seven Isles." He was talking loudly and slurring his words ever so slightly. The guards looked at Jack and then at each other.

"Move along, there's nothing to see here." The squad commander was all business.

"But I was going through the wall. You guys don't usually guard the cracks in the walls." He looked both ways conspiratorially and leaned in, speaking in an exaggerated whisper. "What's going on?"

Alexander relaxed his focus so he could look at the guard's colors.

"Fugitives are loose in the city. No one gets through the wall. Now move along." The guard rested his hand on the hilt of his short sword.

Jack stepped back in a show of innocence holding both arms wide. "What'd these fugitives do? Maybe I've seen 'em." He swirled the ale around in the flagon before taking a drink, all the while looking a little unsteady on his feet.

"They killed their family and burned down their parents' house."

Alexander's blood ran cold. The guard's colors revealed a corrupt character and his words were lies.

Jack blurted out, "Hey, is there a reward for their capture?"

The second guard chuckled. "Who said anything about capturing them? The Reishi are offering a hundred gold sovereigns for their heads."

"Hold your tongue, you fool," the guard commander snapped as he shot his subordinate a murderous glare. "There's no reward, now move along!" he said, taking a few steps toward Jack.

"Okay, okay, I was just askin'," Jack said, stumbling backwards. He started down the road and turned to shout, "I just wanted to help." Then he quickly disappeared around the corner when the guard took two purposeful strides toward him.

Alexander withdrew around the corner again. He had his answer. A deadly calm filled him. The flutter in his belly vanished. The sweat on his hands dried.

He looked straight at Anatoly, still standing quietly with his arms folded across his chest, and said, "We have to kill them quickly and get through the wall before they can call for reinforcements."

Anatoly grinned ever so slightly, Lucky nodded slowly, but Abigail nearly gasped. "Alex, we can't just kill them. They've done nothing to harm us. They're just city guard doing their job."

Just then Jack came up the alley.

Alexander looked his sister in the eye and shook his head to disagree with her but addressed his command to Jack, "Report."

"They've been paid by the Reishi Protectorate to kill you. The price is for your head, not your capture. There are two guards on this side of the wall, one standing in the breach, another two on the other side of the wall and a crossbowman on the rooftop of this building here. I didn't see the seventh, but I'd wager he's armed with a crossbow and perched on a building on the other side of the wall with a good view of the breach."

Before Alexander could speak, Anatoly nodded and said quietly, "Well done, Master Bard."

Alexander couldn't help smiling. "You certainly do have a flair for the dramatic." He clapped Jack on the shoulder, "Well done, indeed."

He turned back to his sister. "Abigail, these men are hired killers. They've accepted money for the job of ending your life. In doing so they've forfeited their right to draw breath." He looked at her without flinching. "We have to kill them to escape with our lives."

She didn't look away from her brother's scrutiny and only considered the new information for a moment before nodding. "I agree. What's your plan?"

"I'd like to take the crossbowman out first. Do you think you can make it up that drainpipe and onto the roof without him hearing you?"

She nodded. "Then what?"

Alexander considered for a moment. "Jack and Anatoly, you go around these buildings so you can come down the street toward the guards. Jack, tell them you brought help. All you want is the description of the fugitives so you can have a chance at the reward. Abigail, you'll be waiting on the back of the roof, out of sight, until you hear Jack and Anatoly coming. Once they're close enough, you stick an arrow in that crossbowman's back and then head for the front of the building." He looked at her to make sure he had her attention. "Have another arrow ready, use it if you have a good shot, otherwise climb down onto the awning over the shops in the front, and get back on the ground so we can move. When I hear the guy on the roof fall, I'll put an arrow into one of the guards at the breach. Then Lucky and I will head for the wall. At that point we fight our way through."

"A sound plan," Anatoly said grimly as he unslung his war axe. "Keep an eye out for the other crossbowman. Once we're through the wall, we'll have to move quickly into the back allies before more guards arrive." He looked from Alexander to Abigail. "Remember your lessons. Let your training guide your hand."

Chapter 10

Abigail was quiet as she made her way up the drainpipe and onto the roof. The peak of the roof ran parallel to the front of the building and was gently sloped so she had cover but wasn't in danger of falling off. She quietly crawled into position and nocked an arrow. She stole a glance over the peak of the roof and saw that the crossbowman looked bored. Her heart was pounding so loudly she was afraid he might hear it. She schooled her breathing and waited, just out of sight.

Alexander stood in the shadows at the back of the alley, which ran forty or fifty feet to the perimeter road between two buildings. It was another twenty feet across the road to the guards. He waited, still as a statue, arrow at the ready with just the slightest tension on the string.

Lucky stood just around the corner, leaning against the building.

Moments ticked by.

Then Alexander heard Jack. "Hey, I brought help." The slight slur was back in his voice. Alexander couldn't see him from where he stood but he could picture the wobble in his stride.

The guards were not amused. The sergeant on this side of the wall drew his short sword and called for the guards on the other side of the wall to come through.

Alexander heard Jack protest, "Hey, come on, we just want a chance at the reward is all."

The sergeant pointed with his blade, "Not a step closer or you're both going to rot in the guardhouse dungeon." The rest of his men drew their blades and fanned out across the street. Five men against two.

"Alright already, we didn't mean nothin' by it. We just wanted a chance at the reward." Jack and Anatoly slowed their approach but didn't stop. "My friend here is real good with his axe. We could work together and split the gold."

Abigail took a slow, deep breath and held it as she drew her bowstring back to her cheek. She sighted down the shaft just like Anatoly had taught her, just like she'd done countless times in the past. The whole world faded away. It was just Abigail and her target.

She let her arrow fly.

It was a perfect shot. The arrow drove into the guard's back, straight through his heart and twelve inches out the front of his hardened leather breastplate. He toppled wordlessly off the roof and crashed onto the corner of the awning that covered the raised wooden walkway running along the front of the building. She was up and moving, drawing another arrow along the way.

There was a moment of stillness, an instant before the reality of the attack sank into the five guards. Alexander loosed his arrow into that moment. His target was the squad sergeant. The man stood facing Anatoly and Jack, pointing his sword at them. Alexander sent his arrow into the unarmored place just under the man's right armpit that was exposed by his raised arm. The sergeant stiffened and his eyes went wide before he slumped to his knees and fell over on his side.

Anatoly had his war axe resting nonchalantly on his shoulder. He took one step toward the guard standing to the left of the dying sergeant, pulled down sharply on the handle of his axe, leveraging it off his shoulder, and flipped the blade over in a high arc with surprising speed. The first three inches of the razor-sharp crescent blade cut into the guard's forehead down to the bridge of his nose, cleaving the front half of his head in two. Anatoly unceremoniously kicked the man in the chest to free his axe from the bone of his skull before the man could fall.

Only moments had passed. Alexander raced to the front of the alley where it spilled out onto the street. He stopped, standing over the corpse of the crossbowman who only seconds before had stood on the building above, and nocked his second arrow. The three remaining guards had regained their wits. The closest one spotted him and raised his round shield. Alexander calmly adjusted his aim and sent his arrow into the man's thigh. The guard screamed and collapsed with a thud, writhing around on the ground in agony.

Just as Abigail made it to the front of the roof, she caught motion coming from a rooftop on the other side of the wall. It was the second crossbowman. She threw herself flat on her back as the short but fast crossbow bolt sailed toward her. It sliced across the top of her left shoulder. Had she been standing, the bolt would have caught her square in the left side of her chest.

She slid toward the front of the roof. Her arrow came free and skittered over the edge. She struggled to gain purchase but the shakes came loose under her and she continued to slide.

Anatoly faced the last two guards. Jack circled to the left, and they let him because they were clearly more worried about Anatoly. Anatoly stepped to the right and smashed that guard's shield with the blade of his axe, rolling around the left side of the man and propelling himself into a tight spin. He finished behind the guard with his crescent-bladed war axe whistling around from the spin, catching him in the back of the neck. The guard's head came free and spun end over end, trailing lurid streamers of blood, hovering in midair for a moment before it followed the body crashing to the ground in a crimson pool.

The final guard turned to face Anatoly. Jack slipped in and unceremoniously knifed him in the back. He fell forward with a look of surprised shock.

Abigail slipped over the edge of the roof and crashed into the awning. It broke her fall only partially as it gave way under the sudden load. She hit the ground hard amidst a shower of roofing shakes and splintered awning.

Alexander, seeing that the immediate threat had been eliminated, went to his sister. "Abby, are you okay?" he asked urgently, kneeling beside her.

She tested her limbs to make sure nothing was broken and nodded tightly. Blood soaked through her tunic at her shoulder.

Lucky rushed up, knelt alongside Alexander and began fishing around in his bag. "Lie still and let me tend to your shoulder. Can you move your legs? Does anything feel broken?" He was all business.

She shook her head slightly and gritted her teeth through the pain. "Crossbow on the roof," she gasped in pain when Lucky went to work on her wound, "other side of the wall," she managed through clenched teeth.

Lucky looked up at Alexander. "Go, I'll take care of her."

Alexander gave her hand a squeeze, then turned and shouted to Anatoly, "Crossbow on the roof." Anatoly stopped short before going through the wall. Alexander and Jack came up alongside him.

"Alexander, follow me through with your bow ready."

Anatoly was a soldier at heart. He was in his element. He picked up the corpse of the sergeant and slung a shield across the dead man's chest. Holding the man in front of himself, he went through the crack in the wall. The crossbow bolt drove clean through the shield, through the sergeant's leather breastplate, through his body and three inches out his back. Anatoly tossed the body to the ground and spun out of the breach to give Alexander a clear shot.

He didn't waste it. The crossbowman was reloading. Alexander's arrow caught him in the chest and drove through him clear to the feathers. The guard staggered back a step before toppling over backwards.

The battle had taken only seconds. A handful of people stood looking at the spectacle in shock and amazement. Moments later Lucky and Jack helped Abigail through the breach in the wall and they started moving into the poorer neighborhoods surrounding the Southport city wall. They made their way quickly but quietly through the shantytown that sprawled out onto the plains north of the city, avoiding contact with others as much as possible. The few people who did cross their path took one look at Anatoly and his bloody war axe and looked the other way.

Abigail recovered quickly and was moving on her own in no time. The bandage on her shoulder soaked through but it looked like the bleeding had stopped.

Jack led them in a winding path through the maze of haphazard houses until they reached the edge of town.

"The farmhouse is just over that rise," Jack pointed at a small hill that rose up out of the fertile farmlands that gave Southport its purpose. "If we skirt the hill on that side we should be able to make it there unnoticed."

Alexander looked around. They hadn't drawn any attention and it didn't look like they'd been followed. He nodded and they moved out away from the protection of the city's concealment.

Alexander felt naked out in the open, vulnerable. If they were spotted by the wrong people before they made it to the farmhouse, they were in trouble. They rushed across the seemingly vast expanse of farmland, looking behind them for signs of pursuit but saw none. It looked like the city guard had lost their trail.

Minutes later they reached the safety of the little farmhouse. It was a simple house made from rough-cut timber with a shake roof and a broad, covered porch. Not far from the house, set close to the hillock that sheltered the cozy little estate, was a sturdy-looking barn with a stable and fenced paddock. There were half a dozen healthy-looking horses grazing lazily in the afternoon sun.

Under different circumstances it would have been almost idyllic. Before the events of the past week, Alexander had always pictured himself living in a simple farmhouse like this one. He had no desire to be Master of Valentine Manor. That had always been Darius's destiny. His brother was the rightful heir, and he'd relished the role. Now he was gone. So many things changed that day.

Alexander pulled his thoughts back to the present when a short, stocky fellow came out of the house and onto the porch. He wore the simple clothes of a farmer. His broad shoulders looked to be a match for any job you might find out on the open range. He scanned the group approaching and, seeing Jack, raised a hand in greeting. He looked about ready to call out a greeting but a quick gesture from the master bard silenced him. He waited patiently as they came onto the porch.

Jack led the way. "Owen, it's good to see you. We have guests. May I present Lord Alexander Valentine." Owen bowed formally. "His sister, Lady Abigail Valentine; Master-at-Arms, Anatoly Grace; and Master Alchemist, Aluicious Alabrand." Jack indicated each in turn. "This is my trusted apprentice Owen. He's been minding the house for me."

Owen smiled broadly. He had a simple, forthright nature about him and looked entirely comfortable in his own skin. Alexander let his focus slip so he could see Owen's colors. His aura was about as honest and innocent as Alexander had ever seen.

"It's an honor to meet you. Please come in. I have stew on the stove and a kettle of hot cider waiting." Owen opened the stout door and took up the familiar role of host.

The beef stew was simple but hearty. Owen had a sheet pan of biscuits and a lump of rich yellow butter to go with it. Alexander couldn't remember the last time a meal had been so satisfying. He was warm, his belly was full, and he felt safe for the first time in a week.

He sat in a comfortable chair near the warm stove with a mug of hot cider. He took time to simply savor the moment. The events of the past week danced at the edges of his awareness and the danger they represented only served to heighten the value he placed on the simple pleasures of warmth and safety.

Owen and Jack were busy clearing away the dishes from the meal and cleaning the little kitchen. Abigail had taken refuge in a large overstuffed chair that threatened to swallow her slight frame while she nursed a large mug of hot cider. Lucky was comfortably sprawled out on one of the two couches that framed the low table in the middle of the sitting room and was already snoring gently. Anatoly was the only one not taking the opportunity to relax. He stood at the window, scrutinizing the empty fields that lay beyond.

Alexander smiled. He thought of his parents. His father was fond of afternoon naps. Most days after lunch, Duncan Valentine could be found in his reading room, dozing in his favorite chair. His mother played at being his guardian, keeping the noisy children from disturbing her husband while he slept.

He realized just how much he had taken the simple treasures of his childhood and family life for granted. The love, guidance, and protection of his parents had just always been there like they were a natural part of the world, as dependable as gravity and as predictable as the sunrise. He swallowed the lump growing in his throat, sat up a bit straighter and took a deep breath to clear his head.

Owen and Jack finished up in the kitchen and came to sit on the couch opposite Lucky. The sun hadn't set but the light of day was beginning to fade. It would be dark soon and they had a long way to travel in the coming days. Alexander decided that he had some questions.

Chapter 11

On the road from Valentine Manor to Southport he hadn't been able to focus on anything but his grief for his brother and his worry for his parents. He still didn't know if they had survived the zombie demon but he decided to believe that they had. His parents were resourceful, tough, and determined. They had both undergone the mana fast and survived it, and although neither had chosen to pursue mastery of magic, they were both capable of wielding power far beyond Alexander's understanding. Not that he understood much about magic.

He cleared his throat. "Anatoly, would you join us, please? Abby, give Lucky a nudge, would you?" He motioned to the snoring alchemist with his chin.

She smiled as she reached out to poke him on the shoulder. He grumbled, snorted and came awake abruptly, sitting up in a rush as he did. Abigail chuckled softly. Alexander smiled. Anatoly even grinned at his old friend's bleary eyes and disheveled hair as he took a seat next to him on the couch.

"Owen, thank you for your hospitality. This is the first time I've felt warm, safe, and full in several days," Alexander said.

Owen smiled with unabashed pleasure at the sincere compliment. "You are most welcome, Lord Valentine. It is a privilege and an honor to be of assistance in your quest."

Alexander smiled a little at the formality. "Owen, please call me Alexander." He raised a hand to stifle the protest he could see building on Owen's face. "As for our quest, well, that's what I wanted to talk about."

"Anatoly, you're a Ranger. We're headed to the Rangers of Glen Morillian." Alexander looked at the big man-at-arms. "Why? What do the Rangers have to do with this?" He gestured to the mark on his neck.

Anatoly nodded the way he always did before launching into a lesson, marshaling his thoughts like they were legions on a battlefield.

"Your parents never had a reason to explain it all to you." He took a deep breath. Lucky sat forward, silently offering to assist in the explanation. "Your bloodline was cursed two thousand years ago by the Old Rebel Mage, Barnabas Cedric. I don't know much about him because he was so secretive and careful. I suspect they will be able to tell you more about him in Glen Morillian. I do know that he was the leader of those who fought against the Reishi Sovereign. When Malachi Reishi vanished, Prince Phane attempted to rally the remaining forces of the Reishi Army but they were destroyed in a terrible battle. Unfortunately, Prince Phane escaped and fled with his life. The Rebel Mage hunted him but was always one step behind the Prince. He knew that Phane could not be allowed to fade into hiding or he would regroup and the war would start all over again. When Phane realized that he would never be able to hide from the Rebel Mage, he did something entirely unexpected. He cast a spell originally created to imprison the most powerful of wizards, but he cast it on himself."

Alexander interrupted, "Why would he do that?"

Anatoly looked around the room. Everyone waited in rapt attention.

Alexander could almost see Jack taking notes in his head.

"Phane knew he couldn't escape," Anatoly continued with a shrug. "At least not anywhere on the Seven Isles. The Rebel Mage was a crafty old wizard and he'd managed to find Phane wherever he hid. For several years they played this game of cat and mouse until Phane simply had enough. So rather than constantly running and hiding, he fled to a place where he knew the Rebel Mage couldn't follow. He fled into the future. The spell he cast stopped time for him and him alone. Within the obelisk of dark magic that has encased him for the past two thousand years, no time passed for Prince Phane." Anatoly shook his head both marveling at the feat and disgusted by the result.

"But why wouldn't the Rebel Mage just destroy the obelisk?" Alexander was starting to wish he'd spent more time reading the ancient histories in his father's library.

"He tried. The story says he tried for a year to destroy the obelisk. He simply couldn't. Nothing he did had any effect. He even tried to dig it up and move it, thinking he would take it out to sea and cast it in." Anatoly grinned at that. "Imagine Phane's surprise when he woke up on the bottom of the ocean?" Anatoly shook his head. "The thing wouldn't budge.

"The Rebel Mage was distraught," Anatoly said. "He knew he'd cursed the world of the future to a terrible fate. When Phane woke, there would be no one with enough power to stop him. He'd be able to dominate the whole of the Seven Isles without challenge."

"Why was he so sure there would be no one able to stop him? And what does this have to do with the mark on my neck?" Alexander could feel a rising sense of frustration. He'd kept these questions at bay for the past several days and now that he was facing them, he felt like he understood less with each answer.

Lucky took up the story. "Prince Phane is the last arch mage. He is the only arch mage alive anywhere on the Seven Isles. There are none who can hope to defeat him with magic."

Alexander took a deep breath to suppress the feeling of hopelessness in the pit of his belly. "If there aren't any wizards who can hope to kill him, then how am I expected to do it?" Before Lucky could answer, Alexander asked the more important question. "Why me? Why was I marked? Why was our bloodline cursed?"

Lucky took a deep breath, pursed his lips and began again. "We don't really know why the Rebel Mage chose your bloodline, only that he did. You see, when he realized that Phane would be loosed on an unsuspecting future, he conceived of a plan to protect the future as best he could. The major parts of his plan that we know of are the curse, the magic circle, and the Rangers." Lucky held up his hand to forestall Alexander's next barrage of questions.

"We don't know why he chose your bloodline, but the purpose of the curse is to identify the champion who will lead us in the coming struggle for freedom. The magic circle he placed around the obelisk served to warn the world that Phane was awake and to activate the curse by branding you with the glyph of the House of Reishi. The Rangers exist to serve you in the coming war."

Alexander was aghast. He sat, mouth agape, and stared at Lucky as if he'd just grown an arm out of his forehead. The questions were tumbling through his mind so quickly that he couldn't grab hold of one and blurt it out. It was surreal. To think that he, a glorified ranch hand, was going to lead the Rangers against the tyrannical ambitions of a two-thousand-year-old arch mage. Alexander started laughing. Abigail looked worried. Jack and Owen shared a furtive glance but Anatoly and Lucky didn't waver.

He chuckled as he looked into his mug of cider, then nodded and took a long pull, draining it completely. He swallowed, wiped his mouth on his sleeve and resumed staring into his empty mug.

"Why aren't there any arch mage wizards?" Alexander finally found a question he could put words to.

"Ultimately, that was what the whole war was fought over. The Reishi had originally discovered the secret to making Wizard's Dust..." Lucky's voice trailed off as Alexander put his head into his hands.

"Every time I ask a question you go off about something else and set a dozen more questions rattling around in my head," he complained.

"Patience, my boy," Lucky said. "It's a complicated explanation that requires some groundwork. These are things you should have been taught years ago but your parents insisted that you be allowed to just be a boy. They believed as we all did, that Darius would be the one marked if the curse was activated in this generation.

"Now, where was I... ah yes, the short answer is, there are no more arch mage wizards because the secrets to achieving that level of mastery were lost in the war. You've heard of the mana fast?"

Alexander nodded.

Lucky continued, "The mana fast is how wizards and witches are made. After much preparation and training and once their master wizard consents, an apprentice will undergo a weeklong fast, consuming nothing but water and Wizard's Dust. It's a trial of character that can be fatal to those who are unprepared and even to some who are. During this week of fasting, the apprentice undergoes great changes." Lucky paused for emphasis. "They become open to the firmament that underlies all of creation.

"Once an apprentice has survived the mana fast, he becomes a novice wizard and the real work begins. Linking one's mind to the firmament is always dangerous. Without sufficient discipline and control, a person's mind can become lost in the stuff of creation."

Alexander held up his hands to stop Lucky from continuing. "Okay, so wizards are made with the mana fast. Why can't anyone become an arch mage?"

Lucky nodded. "An arch mage is made with a second mana fast, except the mage's fast is longer and the quantity of Wizard's Dust required is much greater. The truth is, if one could procure a sufficient quantity of Wizard's Dust and survive the mage's fast, one could become an arch mage. However, the process is supposed to be much more dangerous. The old histories state that over half who attempt it are lost and that the odds of surviving such an ordeal improve significantly with the assistance of another arch mage. Since the time of the Reishi War, those few wizards who were able to acquire enough Wizard's Dust to make the attempt all perished. Over the centuries, Wizard's Dust has become more and more scarce. Those who do come by it usually find far more productive uses for it."

Alexander nodded as he considered his next question. "You told me my vision, the way I can see colors, comes from Mom and Dad. Isn't that a form of magic?"

"It is, but it's much more limited than the kind of magic a wizard or witch can wield. Wizard's Dust is all around us. It's a natural part of nature. It's in the water we drink, the food we eat, and even the air we breathe. In its natural form, it's a dust so fine that one grain can't even be seen. It is the very stuff of life. Without it we wouldn't even exist. The first wizards, even before the Reishi, found that this magical substance existed in high concentrations in certain natural springs. Those who drank this rare water found that they were able to wield small magic. Much later, they discovered that they could use the waters of these sacred springs to perform the mana fast. This discovery marks the dawn of wizardry.

"Your ability to see colors exists because you have an unusually high concentration of Wizard's Dust in your blood because of your parents. They both survived the mana fast, so they both possess a greater amount of Wizard's Dust and they passed some of it on to you."

Abigail frowned, "Why didn't Darius or I get any magic?"

Lucky nodded as he continued. "Not all who have naturally high levels of Wizard's Dust in their blood manifest abilities. In fact, it's very rare for one who hasn't survived the mana fast to be able to use magic to any significant degree at all."

"Okay, next question. What's the firmament, why is it dangerous and how does a wizard use it to make magic?" Alexander was determined to learn as much as possible about magic while he could. He'd questioned Lucky about it in the past but the old alchemist would never reveal much. Alexander always suspected his parents had told Lucky to avoid the subject but he was never sure why.

He remembered the day he told his mom about the colors he could see. She'd looked very worried, even frightened. He spent the rest of the afternoon being peppered with questions by his father, mother, and Lucky. After that, Lucky had worked with him to control and guide his vision but revealed very little about magic in general to his young student.

"The firmament is the substance of creation. It underlies all of reality and provides solidity to all that you see and feel." Lucky smiled at the frowns of confusion all around him. "The firmament is unformed reality. As we move through time, the firmament is the stuff of the moment. There is no existence in the past or the future, only in the now. That is the firmament in action. The moment of reality that just passed is gone because the firmament manifests only in the present moment. The moment of reality it will create two breaths' time from now is only a possibility." He looked hard at Alexander for a spark of understanding.

Alexander's brow drew down for just a moment before his eyes went wide. "If the moments yet to come are only possibilities and a wizard can control the firmament, then he can make it do his bidding. He can shape the way the firmament manifests reality according to his will." Alexander's voice trailed off in wonder.

Lucky smiled broadly the way he always did when one of the children answered correctly. "Exactly right," he said with a firm nod. Then he waited for the inevitable questions that would follow.

He didn't have long to wait. "But then, why is it so dangerous? Why do wizards get lost in it?"

It was the question Lucky had expected, the next logical question. "When your mind is in the firmament, the possibilities are infinite. The only boundaries are those you bring with you. A wizard without a clear vision of what he wants to happen can easily get lost in the boundless possibilities. Time does not exist within the firmament, so while a wizard is sorting through infinity for the outcome he desires, his body can wither and die. The second danger is a lack of discipline. Linking one's mind with the firmament can be a rapturous experience. Without a firm connection to one's real existence, a wizard can simply forget that he even exists and be swept away in the ecstasy of limitless creation."

Lucky was about to go on but Anatoly touched his arm to silence him. "Alexander, I know you have many questions but now is not the time. We still have a good distance to travel and we're hunted by more than just men. We'll move faster tomorrow if we're all well rested. Besides, you've learned enough tonight to think on for the time being."

As if on cue, Alexander yawned. He felt weariness settle on him like a heavy blanket. He nodded, "It has been a long day."

Chapter 12

There was a firm but measured knock at the door. Phane smiled suggestively at the serving maid standing off to the side of his table. He'd decided to take dinner in the study of the rather modest keep that was his new home.

"My dear, please take my plate and bring me a bottle of wine. Tell the cook I'd like some of that dark red, very dry wine he served at dinner two nights ago."

Dora was seventeen years old, stood five feet eight inches tall with a slender build and pretty, long auburn hair tied back in a ponytail. She wore a simple serving girl's dress that was off-grey in color and low cut. She was uncomfortable serving her new Prince but her family needed their place in the keep and her service was part of the price of their room and board.

She answered Phane in a little voice, "Yes, My Prince, right away."

Phane sat back in his chair to give her the space to remove his half-finished dinner while he leered at her shamelessly. She blushed and cleared his table quickly.

Dora opened the door, balancing her tray in one hand, and bowed her head to the General Commander who stood, hands clasped behind his back, waiting patiently just outside the door. When Jataan P'Tal saw the young maid, he stood aside to permit her to leave on her errand.

"Good evening, My Prince." Jataan said nothing else while he waited for Phane to acknowledge him.

"Ah yes, Commander P'Tal, come in."

Jataan P'Tal stepped up to the table but said nothing.

Phane regarded him for a long moment. "I have it on good authority that the men of the Reishi Protectorate on the Isle of Ruatha have failed to apprehend the fugitive in Southport. It would seem that he is proving to be more trouble than either of us thought."

The serving maid came to an abrupt stop at the threshold of the door with a bottle of dark red wine and a large silver goblet. She waited for the Prince to call her in.

He smiled past Jataan P'Tal and said, "Come in, my dear." He kept smiling as he watched her bring the wine to his table. He took a hard look at the bottle and nodded. "Very good, my dear, please close the door on your way out." He watched her start to leave.

Just when she reached the door he said, "Oh, one more thing."

She stopped and turned. "Yes, My Prince?"

He looked at her as if he were seeing right through her. Then, with a smile that could only be described as lewd, he asked, "Have you ever been with a man?"

Dora blushed furiously while struggling to compose herself. She opened her mouth as if to speak but nothing came out. Phane smiled like he was watching a bug squirm on the end of his knife. "Well?" he asked with a slight edge to his voice.

"No," she finally stuttered. She looked like she would rather be anywhere else.

Phane smiled even more broadly, a boyish, innocent smile that looked like joy itself. "Excellent, bring another bottle of wine just like this one to my quarters in an hour."

Jataan P'Tal didn't think her face could turn any more red than it was but he was wrong. He could clearly see the wild terror dancing in her eyes as he watched Phane toy with her.

She managed to murmur, "Yes, My Prince," before she turned and fled without closing the door.

Phane chuckled to himself while he worked the cork loose from the bottle of wine and poured half of it into the oversized silver goblet. He held the goblet almost reverently as he swirled the wine for a moment while breathing deeply of its bouquet. He chuckled to himself again before taking a long drink. Jataan stood quietly and watched him savor his wine.

Phane looked up abruptly as if Jataan's presence had interrupted his reverie. "I will be sending a little surprise for the Rebel Mage's puppet. I expect that he will not escape this time. However, I must be sure, so I'm sending you as well." Phane looked intently at Jataan P'Tal's impassive face for a reaction.

Jataan P'Tal was the General Commander of the Reishi Protectorate. He had risen to the post by setting his feelings and opinions aside in favor of a single-minded devotion to the protection of the Reishi line. He didn't hesitate.

"I will make arrangements to leave in the morning."

Phane nodded slowly before taking another drink from his goblet. "I don't expect he will live through tomorrow night but I need to be sure, and I have another reason for sending you." He looked up at Jataan as he poured the rest of the bottle into the goblet. "I need you to bring me his head, especially the part of his neck that was marked by the Rebel Mage's spell. I may be able to glean some information of value from it.

"If he is able to elude death before he reaches Glen Morillian, you will have to go in and kill him there. Take what men you need. I'll send Kludge with any new orders, and, Commander P'Tal, I will be watching." Phane smiled ever so slightly at Jataan P'Tal's almost imperceptible reaction.

The General Commander saluted, fist to heart. "It will be done, My Prince."

An hour later Phane lounged comfortably in the overstuffed chair in his personal chambers. He whistled to himself while he waited for the serving girl. Kludge sat on top of a bookshelf eating a rat. Phane smiled when he heard the timid knock at his door.

He reached out with his magic to feel for her fear. It was palpable. He could sense it even through the door. She would do well.

He took a deep breath, got up and strolled to the door. She was trembling. How delicious, he thought. Phane looked her up and down, very deliberately, and smiled his most lascivious smile. "Please, do come in." The words dripped off his tongue.

Dora hesitated as she held out the bottle and goblet, still trembling and clearly terrified. She looked like a trapped animal who wanted to run for her life.

Phane cocked his head and let his smile slip away. She shrank away from his look and meekly entered the room, heading straight for the table. He closed the door and bolted it while looking over his shoulder at the young woman. She jumped at the sound of the bolt being thrown but didn't falter. She went to the table, opened the wine and filled the goblet. When she was finished, she carefully positioned herself so the table was between her and Phane.

"If there's nothing else, My Prince, I'll leave you to your wine." She stood, eyes on the table, waiting for his dismissal. Phane simply stared at her until she looked up timidly.

"Oh, but there is…" He smiled at her trembling. "I have something very special in mind for you tonight."

"Please, My Prince, may I go to my quarters now?" She sobbed slightly.

Phane soaked up her fear. He drew it in and savored it. "No." He pronounced it like a sentence.

She started to protest but he cut her off. "Come with me. Leave the wine." Then he turned and went to a door leading from his well-appointed main room.

She followed hesitantly. He could still feel her fear. How exquisite this would be.

He led her into a perfectly circular room of bare stone about forty feet across. In the center of the floor was a double-ringed circle of inlaid gold with complicated symbols inlaid in silver packed into the six inches between each gold ring.

Dora stood at the threshold of the door, clearly confused.

"What? You thought I was going to take you to my bed?" Phane shook his head in mock disappointment, then suddenly snatched the front of her dress and ripped it clear down to her waist, exposing her breasts and causing her fear to spike into panic. She tried to back out of the room and away from Phane but he grabbed her by the wrist, jerked her past him and tossed her to the floor. He threw the bolt on the door and cast a simple binding spell to prevent it from being opened.

"Oh no, my dear, you won't enjoy the comforts of my bed this night." When he strolled past her, she skittered away from him toward the door. He regarded her calmly while she struggled but failed to unbolt the door. "I'm afraid there is no escape, my dear."

Phane began his spell. He chanted a dark and guttural incantation over and over again.

Dora sat with her back to the door and sobbed with her arms wrapped around her knees to cover her exposed breasts.

The air within the circle began to darken until it took on the consistency of black smoke. Then it got darker, more opaque, and substantial. It whirled slowly in a column that stretched nearly to the vaulted ceiling. The light of the lamps that ringed the room seemed to be soaked up by the swirling vortex of darkness, dimming the entire room. Phane continued to chant. The darkness grew to fill the circle.

When Dora saw a pair of hateful yellow eyes looking out of the inky blackness at her, she screamed. She could just make out the shape of a giant wolf's head in the dark. And it was staring right at her. She wanted to scream again but she was frozen with terror.

Phane abruptly stopped chanting. Two more pairs of eyes appeared, all staring at Dora. Her fear had transformed into a visceral, breathless panic. She was frozen by the deadly glare of the now three sets of hateful yellow eyes looking right at her from out of the inky blackness.

"I bind you to my will!" Phane spoke the words of command with such force that Dora could feel the power of his pronouncement echo in her chest. All three sets of eyes turned at once to Phane. He smiled tightly.

"Take form on the Isle of Ruatha. Hunt Alexander Valentine and kill him. He was last known to be in the vicinity of Southport. These are my commands." Prince Phane's voice reverberated around the circular room.

As one, the three nether wolves howled. It was a sound that no living thing could make. Dora screamed again and shut her eyes tightly.

Phane smiled at her as he reached out for her with his magic. She felt a viselike grip around her ankle but could see nothing there. She screamed again with renewed panic when the invisible grip started dragging her slowly toward the circle and the darkness and the hateful eyes. She struggled for her life, kicking and begging, but Phane's spell pulled her toward her doom.

When her leg entered the circle, the jaws of the nearest nether wolf snatched her by the ankle and jerked her into the swirling darkness. She screamed and wailed as the three beasts tore her apart and devoured her. When her screaming died out, the slowly whirling column of blackness began to fade. In just moments the air cleared and the room brightened. There was nothing left of Dora except a few scraps of her dress and the stain of her blood on the floor.

Prince Phane nodded in satisfaction and started whistling as he turned toward the door.

Chapter 13

Alexander woke to the smell of breakfast cooking. For a moment he almost forgot where he was. In that in-between state, not quite asleep, not quite awake, he almost thought he was back at Valentine Manor in his very comfortable bed, but only for a moment.

Reality hit him suddenly and just as suddenly he was wide awake. Abigail was just rousing in the farm hand's bunk on the other side of the small room. Alexander's bed was lumpy and uncomfortable but the blankets were warm and it beat sleeping on the ground. He sat up and stretched. Abigail came fully awake with a start. She sat up, quickly looking for trouble. Seeing that there was none, she flopped back onto her pillow with a groan.

Alexander smiled gently. "Good morning. Smells like breakfast is about ready."

She groaned again and waved him off. Abigail was not a morning person and Alexander knew it. He'd teased her about it often enough when they were children. That time seemed so long ago. He suddenly felt a stab of guilt for every unkind thing he'd ever done to her. She was his sister and quite possibly the only family he had left.

"I'll keep a plate warm for you," he said quietly before he left the little room.

Everyone else was already up and about. Lucky sat at the table slathering a fresh biscuit with thick blackberry jam. Anatoly stood at the window looking out over the fields, while nursing a mug of steaming hot black tea. Jack and Owen were bustling around in the kitchen preparing breakfast.

Alexander got himself a cup of tea and took a seat at the table next to Lucky.

"Good morning, my boy," Lucky said around a mouthful of biscuit. The old alchemist was as cheerful as ever. Alexander marveled at how easily Lucky could find delight in the smallest things. He supposed it was a talent that his tutor had cultivated for many years.

Breakfast was hearty and filling. They had skillet-fried potatoes, spicy sausage, scrambled eggs, and fresh biscuits with jam and butter. There was more than enough for everyone to eat their fill and then some. Jack seemed to be in his element, playing host and ensuring that his guests were well fed. Owen followed his lead with practiced ease.

When everyone had stopped eating, except Lucky, Anatoly stood. Before he could say a word, Lucky sighed in resignation and nodded up at his old friend.

"I suppose it's about time we were on our way." He took one more biscuit before he too stood.

"Jack, I'd like to take a look at the horses, if I may." Anatoly was clearly anxious to get moving. He seemed to be on edge, as if he could feel their hunters closing in. His tension was contagious and soon Alexander started to feel an urgent need to be on the road as well.

"Of course, we might as well take the saddlebags out to the stables on our way," he said motioning to the five sets of saddlebags piled next to the door that were already loaded with food and traveling supplies. Anatoly nodded to the bard and scooped up two sets of the fully loaded leather bags and threw one over each shoulder.

Not half an hour later the five of them were mounted on their horses. It was a clear morning and the wind was still. It would be a good day for traveling. Owen stood at the stable gate as they said their farewells to the bard's jovial apprentice.

"I expect I'll be two or three days behind you with Master Lucky's wagon and your horses. By the end of the week, we'll all be safe in Glen Morillian and enjoying the hospitality of the Forest Warden's table." He gave a wink and a nod to Lucky.

"Thank you, Owen. Be safe in your journey. If you meet trouble on the road and need to travel more quickly than my wagon can carry you, there's a leather bag under the buckboard. The contents of that bag are the most important to me. Everything else can be replaced." Lucky shook hands with Owen and the party was off.

The forest was a good two days' travel to the north if they stuck to the road, but Anatoly and Alexander both reasoned that the Reishi would have men along the road searching for them. While slower, it would be far safer to travel parallel to the road through the farm fields that stretched from Southport to the forest.

They made reasonably good time over the uneven ground. More importantly, they didn't come across anyone but a few farm hands here and there and they were more interested in preparing the fields for planting than in anything else.

After a full day of uneventful travel, Alexander was starting to feel the sense of urgency fade. Maybe they would make it to Glen Morillian without drawing the attention of the Reishi Protectorate. He didn't really believe that but he took comfort in the possibility.

They found a depression in the rolling landscape and made camp for the night. It was an ideal spot that offered protection from the wind and shielded their small fire from view. The night was clear and cold and the little cook fire offered welcome warmth.

After a meal of camp stew and hard biscuits, they began to lay out their bedrolls. Alexander was tired from the long day of travel but he was feeling optimistic. A little voice in the back of his mind was beginning to wonder what they would do once they reached the forest city, but he shoved it away. He had enough to worry about in the present. Tomorrow's problems could wait until then.

Once they had their bedrolls set out, everyone sat quietly staring into the little fire, taking comfort in the flames.

Alexander was deep in thought about the forces of magic. He was going over everything Lucky had told him the night before, trying to put each new piece of the puzzle into its correct place in his expanding understanding of reality.

The fire suddenly drew down and went out. The air around them became frigid. Alexander could see his breath in the light of the half moon rising above. Anatoly stood, drawing his battle axe in one fluid, but silent, movement.

Alexander knew what was coming next. He'd felt this kind of sudden cold before.

When the ghost flickered into existence, everyone gasped and stood in alarm. Everyone except Alexander. He sat where he was, albeit a little straighter.

The glowing silhouette grew brighter, then dimmed and shimmered as though he was struggling to maintain his connection to the realm of substance. The coals of the fire went from red to black and the ghost brightened.

Everyone was frozen with fright or disbelief. Anatoly started to take a step to place himself between Alexander and the apparition, but Alexander stopped him.

"Hold, Anatoly. He means no harm. Let him speak."

The big man-at-arms looked at Alexander skeptically but did as he was told.

The ghost of Nicolai Atherton flickered and wavered in the moonlight. He fixed Alexander with a gaze that made him wonder if the ghost could even see any of the others at all. The ghost looked around as if searching for a threat in his unseen world before speaking. "Danger comes. Phane has summoned nether wolves to hunt you."

No sooner had he given his warning than he turned abruptly as if to face an enemy and then flickered out of existence. A moment later, an inhuman howl shattered the night, followed by another ghost that flickered into view and darted through the campground toward Nicolai Atherton. Alexander didn't get a very good view of the second ghost except for the ornate crest of the House of Reishi emblazoned on his breastplate. As everyone stood frozen in fear and disbelief, they heard the ghost of Nicolai Atherton call out from a place beyond the world of life, "Flee!"

Lucky and Anatoly looked at each other. Abigail and Jack looked at Alexander.

Alexander stood and took command. "Anatoly, prepare the horses. Everyone else, strike camp quickly. We ride in three minutes."

Without looking to see if anyone even heard him, Alexander turned and began rolling up his bedding. A moment later everyone else sprang into action. The camp was struck in minutes and they were riding carefully through the night by the light of a half moon.

"We're going to have to risk the road. I don't know what nether wolves are, but I think I'd rather face the Reishi Protectorate, and we can move faster on the road, especially at night," Alexander said. He could just barely see Anatoly nod his agreement as he rode beside him through the darkness.

They reached the road after only about an hour of careful riding across the uneven cropland. Anatoly stopped them for just a moment. "If we come on a camp, don't stop to fight, just ride. It'll take them a few minutes to get on their horses, so we'll get a head start. Our best hope is speed."

They rode through the night with as much speed as they dared. It was dark but the light of the moon was just enough to keep them on the well-traveled road. Alexander could feel the tension and almost smell the fear of the others. Fighting men was one thing, but ghosts and nether wolves, whatever they were, was something else altogether.

As the night wore on they all began to suffer from exhaustion. The horses were getting tired and slowing down until finally, Alexander ordered a halt. They needed to stop for a few minutes to rest. They dismounted and Lucky fished around in his saddlebag for some dried fruit that he passed around. Their rest break was brief. Alexander felt a growing sense of uneasiness. He knew they wouldn't survive an encounter with creatures from the netherworld at night out in the open. He didn't know how far away the creatures were, but he didn't want to take any chances.

"We need to get moving. We'll walk our horses for a few hours. They need some rest or one of them is liable to collapse."

The night was cold and calm. The stars glittered in the sky as the half moon began to slide toward the horizon. They'd been traveling for several hours when Alexander came to an abrupt halt.

He saw the campfires a long way out. He guessed that the Reishi were a mile ahead and camped right on the side of the road. Dawn was still a couple of hours away, so they at least had darkness and surprise on their side.

Alexander heaved a sigh. "We can go around or we can go through. Neither option sounds very good at the moment. Going around will put us out in the open with exhausted horses when the light comes up and going through gets us into a fight that we probably can't win." Alexander stared off toward the enemy trying to find a better option.

Abigail shook her head, "It's too bad we can't steal their horses."

Alexander spun around and smiled at his little sister. "Who says we can't?"

Anatoly was incredulous. "Are you kidding? You want to walk into a hornets' nest when we could just go around?"

Alexander smiled fiercely. "Exactly," he said with a firm nod. "Lucky, Abigail, and Jack will take our horses around the camp to the west. Give them a wide berth. They may have lookout posts a fair distance from their camp. Move quickly but stay as quiet as possible. Anatoly and I will meet you on the road north of the Reishi camp. Be ready to ride because I suspect we'll have a swarm of hornets after us."

Anatoly stood staring at Alexander with his arms folded across his chest. "How do you propose to sneak into their camp without notice?"

Alexander grinned. "I'll explain along the way. Let's go. We'll need the darkness to make this work."

Anatoly harrumphed and shook his head but didn't object.

They moved down the road quickly but quietly. Alexander let his vision go out of focus every ten steps or so. He was looking for the telltale glow of a human aura. He had always had an advantage in the dark. He could see people's colors, even at a distance, even in complete darkness, and even if he couldn't see them with his normal vision.

When Alexander saw the first sentry posted along the road, he stopped and motioned to Anatoly in the dim light. They moved to the east of the road and quietly crept up on the guard. He was sitting with his back against a large stone jutting out of the ground alongside the road. When he coughed quietly, Anatoly marked his position. The big man-at-arms moved with surprising stealth as he circled the mercenary in the blackness of night. Once he reached striking range, he lunged over the top of the rock with his long knife and brought the blade down over the surprised guard's head and into his heart with one stroke. The sentry didn't even have time to scream. Anatoly took the dead guard's heavy crossbow but left the quiver of bolts with the fresh corpse.

They made it to a slight rise on the road. Alexander could see the entire camp from their position and could clearly see the larger, less complicated colors of the horses. They were picketed together as he hoped they would be. He pulled Anatoly down and whispered to him in the darkness. "The horses are off to the side of the main camp and it looks like there are only two guards near them." He pointed into the night to give Anatoly a general direction of their destination.

"How many men in the camp?" Anatoly asked.

"Looks like about thirty. I only see four standing watch, but there are probably a few lookout positions farther out."

Anatoly nodded and they started moving. The two men guarding the picketed horses sat on either side of a small fire. They were clearly not concerned that they would be attacked. Anatoly and Alexander could see they were passing a jug back and forth. Two more men were sleeping not far from the fire.

Anatoly had taught Alexander and Darius how to move through the night, how to test each step for footing and noise before they committed weight to it. It was a game they played when they were children. Alexander was good at it. They moved without a sound.

They made it to a boulder resting on the open plain and crouched behind it. Anatoly handed Alexander the loaded and cocked crossbow and drew a heavy throwing knife from his belt. Not thirty feet away, the light of the fire silhouetted the two guards. Anatoly threw his knife first, followed closely by Alexander's crossbow bolt. The heavy knife buried itself up to the hilt in the side of the first guard's neck. He stiffened and slumped forward into the fire. The second guard's eyes went wide a moment before the crossbow bolt plunged into the side of his chest. He tried to gasp but couldn't. He pitched forward into the fire and dropped the jug, which shattered on the rocks ringing the fire.

The two guards sleeping nearby stirred at the sound. One sat up and looked toward the two men slumped into the fire. Their hair was starting to burn, mixing foul-smelling smoke with the cloud of steam from the cider that had splashed into the hot coals.

Alexander and Anatoly were up and running. Anatoly drew his short sword and headed for the remaining two guards. Alexander sprinted through the night the short distance to the horses.

The two guards who'd been sleeping came fully awake when they saw Anatoly coming for them. The first struggled to free himself from the blankets of his bedroll before the charging man-at-arms could reach him. He just managed to get to his feet but was still wrapped in his blanket when Anatoly ran him through. The second man came up out of his bedroll, sword in hand, with a loud battle cry. He slashed at Anatoly, who deflected the blow with the heavy bracer he wore on his left arm, running him through as well.

Alexander worked quickly. He was pretty sure the alarm would be raised, so he didn't let the battle cry of the now dead guard distract him. He had a set of five horses strung together, one to the next, with ample lead lines between them so they could all run freely. He left the first horse tied to the picket and went to work on the second string of horses when Anatoly rushed up.

The rest of the camp was coming alive. Men sleeping not fifty feet away were struggling to get free from their bedding and take up their weapons. The camp leaders were shouting orders. Alexander knew they didn't have much time.

"Anatoly, cut those horses free." He pointed to the second picket line.

Anatoly didn't hesitate. He used his razor-sharp short sword to quickly free the horses. He could hear men running toward them. As he cut the last horse loose, Alexander rode up next to him and handed him the reins of a horse with another four horses tied to it in a long string. Anatoly swung up onto the bare back of the horse just as a crossbow bolt whizzed past his head. Alexander had already spurred his string of horses into an almost reckless dead run through the predawn blackness. Anatoly kicked his horse into a gallop.

They raced toward the road at an angle that took them clear of most of the onrushing soldiers. Both leaned into their horses and held on for dear life as they barreled through the night. Fortunately, the road was close enough that they reached it before the camp could come fully awake. The few soldiers that tried to stop them found themselves in a cloud of dust as Alexander and Anatoly raced away with a string of fresh horses each.

As they put distance between themselves and the now furious Reishi Protectorate soldiers, Alexander relaxed his guard. He felt a thrill of triumph. His plan had worked. They'd secured fresh horses and scattered their pursuers' mounts into the night. It would be dawn before the soldiers could gather enough horses to give chase, and with a string of horses each, Alexander knew they would be able to outpace any pursuit.

Anatoly rode up beside him, and Alexander flashed his old teacher a cocky grin. Then the sky behind them burst into an orange glow. Alexander's smile quickly faded when he looked back to see a jet of bright red-orange fire rising from the camp they'd just raided. The flame rose high into the air and fanned out into a disc of brightly glowing fire to form a halo over the entire camp, providing the enemy with ample light to round up their remaining horses.

The feeling of triumph quickly faded. He just caught the reproving glance from Anatoly when a sentry stepped out of the darkness and shot him with a crossbow.

Chapter 14

Alexander was caught by surprise. The heavy, steel-tipped bolt tore into his left shoulder. He lurched back and nearly lost his hold on the horse. For a moment that seemed to drag on for hours, Alexander struggled to keep from falling. Sharp, hot pain coursed through his shoulder and radiated into his arm, neck, and chest.

So many things tumbled through his mind in that moment. He'd let his guard down. He could have seen the sentry a mile away if only he'd remembered to look. He felt foolish and ashamed. He could lose everything in one moment of cockiness. He imagined the look his father would give him if he could see him right now.

He thought about how close the bolt had come to his heart and lungs. Just a few inches to the right and a couple of inches lower and he'd be dead. Who would look after Abigail if he died? She'd already lost so much. What of the war that was coming? He'd been chosen, for better or worse, as the one to lead the battle against Phane. What would become of the world if he fell? How would his parents feel to learn their only remaining son was dead? All for a stupid mistake. All because he had indulged a childish emotion rather than relying on the cold hard reality of reason.

He caught his balance and pitched forward, resting his chest on his horse's neck, the feathers of the bolt running down the left side of the animal's body.

Anatoly didn't even bother with the soldier. Instead, he took the reins of Alexander's horse, checked to make sure he was conscious and still holding on, and rode on into the night.

Alexander held on and just focused on breathing. He could feel blood oozing from around the shaft of the heavy bolt. Rhythmic jolts of pain shot through him with each stride of his horse as the steel tip of the bolt scraped against the inside of his shoulder blade. He tried to focus on his breathing and not the pain. They rode for what seemed like days. When the sky began to brighten, they saw the others riding toward them from the side of the road. Alexander tried to console himself with the knowledge that his plan had worked … more or less.

In a blink, Anatoly was off his horse and helping Alexander to the ground. "Lucky, tell me you have some healing salve in your bag. Alexander's been shot."

Alexander gasped in pain as the bolt was jostled while he dismounted his horse. Abigail leapt off her horse and was at her brother's side in a heartbeat. Jack took the two strings of horses and led them into the grass off to the side of the road. The horses were winded and excited. It wouldn't do to have them stomp on Alexander while Lucky did his work.

Alexander lay flat on his back in the middle of the hard-packed road. He could smell the dirt and his own blood. He felt cold and he hurt. Pain radiated from his shoulder and pulsed with every heartbeat.

Tears streamed down Abigail's face, leaving streaks in the travel dust, but otherwise she was calm and steady as she cradled her brother's head in her lap.

Lucky quickly assessed the situation. "How long do we have before the Reishi are on us?" Anatoly always admired the way Lucky went calm in the face of danger.

"Not more than half an hour." He actually thought it would take them longer to catch up but wanted to err on the side of caution.

Lucky nodded. "You'd best help Jack with the horses. We'll be ready to go in a few minutes."

Anatoly gave Alexander's hand a squeeze before he stood and went to help Jack saddle fresh horses.

Lucky gently probed and prodded the area around the bolt, all the while explaining to Alexander what he was doing and why. It sounded like any other lesson the old tutor might give. Except this one had a practical exam that went along with it. Alexander wasn't exactly numb to the pain; he was just getting used to it. He could see the colors of both Lucky and Abigail. He supposed that was because he didn't seem to have the energy to keep his eyes focused.

Lucky wrapped a leather thong around the base of the bolt where it jutted from Alexander's shoulder and cinched it down tight. Then he took his belt knife and scored the bolt shaft a few inches from the knotted leather thong. Once he'd cut deeply enough that he could break the shaft, he fished around in his bag and came out with a wooden dowel about five inches long. He leaned over Alexander and looked him in the eye. "This is going to hurt. Bite down on this." Then he popped the dowel into Alexander's mouth.

What happened next threatened to render Alexander unconscious. Lucky took the shaft and pulled the tip of the bolt back toward the entry wound, then slid the knotted thong down to the point of entry to keep it from going any deeper. He cinched the thong down tight and wrapped it around Alexander's shoulder, tying it tightly to keep the bolt in place. Then he snapped the bolt off where he'd scored it. Alexander screamed and clenched down on the dowel. Lucky spread a salve on the wound and tied a bandage around Alexander's shoulder. Then he took a couple of leaves from a pouch, removed the dowel from Alexander's mouth and replaced it with the leaves.

"These will dull the pain. Chew on them until I tell you to spit them out, but don't swallow them."

Lucky finished the job by tying a makeshift sling for Alexander's left arm. Alexander's head was swimming but the pain was becoming less important. It was still there. It still hurt. It just seemed to be less urgent. The numbweed was doing its work.

Anatoly returned with a big strong horse saddled and ready to ride. "Abigail, you'll have to ride with Alexander. He won't have the balance or strength to ride on his own."

She nodded tightly and helped her brother to his feet. She and Anatoly helped Alexander into the saddle and Abigail climbed up behind him. Within minutes they were riding as quickly as they dared toward the forest.

Alexander felt the pain in his shoulder in a steady, pounding rhythm. His head was clearing with the cold air in his face. He knew they were in trouble. The sun was just rising and the enemy would be coming fast. It was nearly a day's ride to the forest and even then they wouldn't find safety. It was several days from the edge of the forest to Glen Morillian. With his injury, they would be much slower than their pursuers and they dare not stop and fight.

After a morning of agonizing riding, they stopped on a rise to saddle fresh horses. They could see their enemy in the distance, a dozen men on horseback maybe an hour behind. Alexander thought to himself that at least they would have fewer men to face since he'd managed to steal some of their horses and scatter the rest. When they remounted, Alexander insisted on riding on his own. He wasn't in great shape but he knew they would make better time if he wasn't doubled up with Abigail.

Lucky protested but Alexander simply mounted up. "We need speed. I'm slowing us down. Besides, the pain has subsided some," he lied, "and I'm starting to feel stronger."

Anatoly and Lucky exchanged a look before mounting up themselves.

They rode hard all afternoon and into the evening, changing horses every few hours. Each time they stopped, they could see the enemy in the distance and it looked like they were gaining ground. The speed Alexander had bought them with fresh horses, he had cost them with his wound.

His failure nagged at him. He knew he could have prevented his injury if he had just been mindful, if he'd just been focused instead of letting his emotions distract him. He tried to push it from his thoughts. He told himself it was in the past and he should learn his lesson and let it go, but he couldn't. It just kept slipping back into his mind. He would catch himself dwelling on it and realize that he'd been turning it over and over in his mind for several minutes without even realizing it.

They crested a small rise just as the sun sank past the edge of the world. Alexander reined in his horse. The rest of them followed suit. They could see the forest in the distance but that wasn't what caught Alexander's eye. The old forest gate tower was still glowing orange with the last rays of daylight. It stood atop a flat, rocky plateau just west of the road at the edge of the forest. Shadow slowly crept up its walls, chasing the orange rays of sunlight into the night. In ages past, this place had been a guard post belonging to the Ruathan King, but now it was a dilapidated ruin, crumbling under the weight of inattention. It was also the most defensible place for miles around.

"Lucky, can you get this out of my shoulder if we have the time and safety for you to work?" Alexander asked.

"Yes, I believe so," Lucky said. "Once it's removed, I have a salve that can heal your wound very quickly, but I can't use it until I can cut the bolt out first and we have some time for you to rest."

Alexander wasn't looking forward to that. His shoulder had settled into a dull, palpable ache. He set aside his pain and fear and raced through all of their options. They could continue into the forest, at night, in the dark. Not a good plan. They could leave the road and try to elude the Reishi Protectorate, but their horses would be easy to track, and striking out on foot wasn't an option. If the ruse didn't work, they'd be run down without any chance of escape. They could stand and fight. That would be stupid. The remaining choice wasn't perfect but it was better than any of the others.

"We'll hole up in the old forest gate tower. Hopefully, we can hide, but if we can't, it's the best place we have to make a stand." Alexander looked at Anatoly, expecting an objection.

Instead, the big man-at-arms took a deep breath and nodded slowly. "The Reishi are about an hour behind us. That should give us some time to improve our fortifications before they arrive. Besides, I'm tired of running."

They rode hard for the tower plateau. The more time they had to make preparations, the better their chances for survival. Alexander was exhausted, sweating and in growing pain when they reached the base of the abrupt granite plateau. It looked like an oblong section of the plain had been thrust up fifty or sixty feet into the air. The rocky walls drove straight up from the ground. There was only one way to the top. A path had been cut into the face of the rock wall starting at the base on the northeastern side and running completely around the west side of the plateau and finally reaching the top at the southeast corner. The path was about six feet wide and offered only a foot-high curb of stone for a railing along its outer edge.

They led the horses up the path in single file through the quickly fading light. Despite the stones cluttering the path, it was solid and sturdy. They reached the top and found the entire plateau ringed on its outer edge with a low stone wall broken only by the stout gatehouse at the top of the path.

The gatehouse was a simple stone building with a passage that formed a tunnel about a dozen feet long and only about seven feet high. They walked their horses through the ancient fortification. Alexander could see where stout oak doors used to be hinged but they had long since rotted away. As he passed through the gatehouse, he caught glimpses of the moon through the arrow slits cut along the walls. The rusted and broken remains of a portcullis were now little more than a reddish stain on the ground.

The tunnel opened onto the top of the plateau that stood a hundred feet long and seventy-five feet wide. It looked much bigger from below. The outer wall that ringed the entire edge was only about three feet tall but it was still intact. The guard tower in the center of the plateau hadn't fared nearly as well over the centuries.

The building had two parts. The first was a single-story, square, stone room about forty feet on a side. The walls were thick stone but the east wall facing the road had partially collapsed and the stout wooden beams that used to support the flat-topped roof had long ago rotted to dust, leaving what was left of the room open to the sky. The tower was attached to the large square room at the western side and rose a good forty feet into the quickly darkening sky. The ground all around the tower ruin was thick with rich green grass.

Anatoly unslung his war axe, handed Jack the reins to his horse, and entered the square room through the open door. He disappeared into the old structure for a moment and returned, nodding to himself. "Lucky, the tower's the most enclosed place in the building. All of the floors are gone so it's open to the sky but it'll shield light better than anywhere else. Abigail, Jack, we need to do a quick assessment of our tactical situation and make preparations for battle."

Lucky took his bag and led Alexander into the tower. Alexander sat down on his pack heavily and gently probed his wounded shoulder. Now that they'd stopped, the pain seemed to slam back into him and he could feel his exhaustion quickly catching up with him. He sat quietly, just trying to conserve his energy, while Lucky tacked a blanket from his bedroll over the entrance to the door and took two little candle lamps from his bag. Despite their small size, they created ample light for Lucky to work by and with the blanket over the door, Alexander guessed they would be all but invisible from the road.

"All right, Alexander, let's get your bedroll laid out and have you lie down."

Alexander felt dizzy when he stood but steadied himself and motioned to his bedroll on his pack. Lucky unrolled it, and Alexander, gratefully, lay down. He felt like all of his strength drained out of him as he let his body go limp. He tried to focus on his breathing and not the pain, but it was a losing battle.

Lucky used Alexander's pack for a seat and set out a series of items on a flat rock nearby. He had ample bandages, a couple of jars of salve, a vial of clear liquid, a pouch of numbweed leaves, a pair of sharp-looking knives, and a bottle of spirits. He fished two of the numbweed leaves out of the little leather pouch, rolled them into a ball, and held them in front of Alexander's mouth.

"Open up," he said as he popped them in. "Now chew those into a pulp but don't swallow them. That's important; they're poison if swallowed."

Alexander nodded. He'd had numbweed before. In fact, Lucky had given him some earlier this very day. He knew what to expect. He would start to feel numb, hence the name. First his face, then his hands and feet, and finally his whole body would feel somehow distant and fuzzy. At this point, he welcomed it. He was tired of the gnawing pain in his shoulder.

Lucky began removing the sling and bloodied bandages from around the wound. He cut the shirt from around Alexander's shoulder, exposing the angry-looking injury with the business end of an immobilized crossbow bolt still sticking out of his flesh. He gently and carefully cleaned around the wound with a damp cloth. Alexander could feel the shadow of pain but it was distant, somehow less urgent than he knew it should be. Lucky looked closely into his eyes.

"All right, Alexander, it's time to begin. Spit out the numbweed and take this bite piece."

Alexander knew he wasn't going to like what was coming next, but he did as he was told. Just as he settled the little wooden dowel between his teeth, Abigail came into the stone tower. She made sure to refasten the blanket over the doorway to keep the light of Lucky's two little work lamps from shining down to the road. She knelt at Alexander's side and took his hand.

"I'm here, Alex. Anatoly is setting up defenses. He seems almost happy to be preparing for a battle." She smiled as she shook her head. A long lock of her silvery blond hair fell free and she hooked it behind her ear before she continued. "Jack is following him around and taking orders like a trained soldier. The Reishi are about half an hour away and riding by torchlight."

He felt like he was listening to his sister from underwater. He could hear what she said and knew it was important but just couldn't make his mind translate the words into meaning. He smiled and nodded as he gave her hand a squeeze.

Lucky took a good look at Alexander, then turned to Abigail and said, "It's time." She nodded and switched from kneeling to sitting cross-legged with her brother's hand held firmly in both of hers, then nodded at Lucky. He gave her a little smile. Lucky had helped raise both of them. He loved them like they were his own children.

First, he removed the leather thong that was holding the tip of the crossbow bolt in place. Alexander closed his eyes in anticipation of pain but it didn't come. Next, Lucky splashed some spirits on the area of the wound. Alexander winced and bit down on the dowel in his mouth. The pain was hot and sharp even through the numbness.

Lucky took the smaller of his two little knives and carefully washed it with the spirits. He examined the wound to see where the blades of the bolt were. It was a three-bladed bolt. He would have to make three cuts, one for each blade, so he could draw the bolt out without ripping a chunk of flesh from Alexander's shoulder.

"This is going to hurt. Are you ready?"

Alexander nodded tightly.

Lucky took a deep breath and began.

The shock of the first cut was stunning. Alexander bit down hard on the dowel and gasped. In that moment, the effects of the numbweed seemed to evaporate in the face of a pain they couldn't contend with. The second cut sent shooting, white-hot agony into every recess of his body. He felt like he was drowning in an ocean of torment. There was nothing but pain. No enemy. No fear. No grief for his dead brother. Everything in his world, every part of his awareness was filled to overflowing with agony. The third cut threatened to claim his consciousness. He held his eyes clenched shut. His teeth clamped onto the wooden dowel in his mouth and his breath came in quick little gasps. He felt like he was sliding into an unforgivable darkness, and then he heard his sister whimper ever so slightly and he realized he was crushing her hand.

He focused on her, on his need to not hurt her, and forced himself to relax his death grip on her hand. In that moment of distraction, Lucky drew the head of the crossbow bolt out of his shoulder. He nearly screamed. His eyes snapped open and he started panting around the dowel.

Lucky was talking him through the operation gently while he worked. "The bolt is out, now I just have to clean the wound, pack it with healing salve, and bandage it." He sounded very reassuring somewhere off in the distance past a battlefield of pain.

It wasn't long before Alexander was lying quietly with a fresh bandage around his now much-improved shoulder and Lucky was packing his things back into his travel bag.

Alexander felt as if he were floating gently on an ocean of agony that only moments before he'd been drowning in. The pain was still there. It still occupied the very center of his awareness but it was not nearly as insistent, not nearly as urgent as it had been. He focused on his breathing in an effort to wrest his consciousness away from the pain and exert some form of control over his experience of the moment. Second by second he began to have little bits of success. He wasn't sure if it was from his efforts or the result of the healing salve that Lucky had liberally packed into his wound before dressing it with a clean bandage.

Anatoly came to the doorway but didn't disturb the blanket. "The Reishi have turned off the road and are approaching. Douse the light if you can." Alexander heard the big man-at-arms move off into the night just before the world went dark.

Lucky spoke in hushed tones. "Abigail, you should go help Anatoly. I'll sit with Alexander while the salve does its work. It shouldn't be too long before his shoulder is mended."

Alexander felt his sister pat the back of his hand before she stood and left the pitch-black tower. His shoulder felt warm and it was itching but he didn't seem to have the energy to reach up and scratch it. He drifted somewhere on the edge of sleep for what seemed like a long time. When he woke, the pain was nearly gone and his shoulder felt almost whole again.

Chapter 15

He lay still in the dark, listening. He could hear the shadow of voices drifting up from the plain below. "Lucky?"

"I'm here," he said in a whisper.

"How long have I been out?"

"Several minutes. The healing salve renders you unconscious briefly while it finishes its work. How does your shoulder feel?"

"Much better," Alexander said as he sat up. He could still feel a slight pain where he'd been injured but it was nothing he couldn't handle. "What's happening?"

"The Reishi are at the base of the plateau. I suspect they'll send some men up to search the ruin within minutes. Normally, I would insist that you rest for at least a full day before doing anything physical but under the circumstances, perhaps we should go see if Anatoly could use our help."

Alexander rubbed his shoulder. Magic always amazed him. The wound was completely closed over. Only the roughness of a scar remained where less than an hour before a crossbow bolt had been buried in his flesh. He stretched his arm gently this way and that, then rolled his shoulder to get an idea of his limitations. The shoulder was stiff and still hurt when he put a strain on it, but otherwise it felt better than he could have hoped for.

He dug into his pack and found his spare shirt and his cloak. The air was cold and he started to shiver almost as soon as he sat up from under the blanket Lucky had draped over him.

Alexander crept up behind Anatoly, who was kneeling behind the eastern edge of the low wall that ringed the top of the plateau.

Anatoly glanced back and whispered, "Good to see you up and about. How's the shoulder?"

"Not quite mended but well enough. What's the situation?"

Anatoly motioned over the wall, "There's about a dozen of 'em and that fire wizard is with them. They just started picketing their horses."

Alexander peered carefully over the low wall. He let his vision go out of focus but didn't see any more than he expected. There were twelve men and twelve horses. He could hear someone barking orders and then half a dozen men with torches started out toward the plateau.

"What are our defenses?" Alexander asked quietly.

"We piled a bunch of stones in the gatehouse tunnel to slow them down and create a choke point. There are arrow slits all along the entrance tunnel so we can probably hold them there. We also put stacks of stones the size of a man's head all around the perimeter wall and on top of the gatehouse. If we do it right, they won't be able to get enough men up to the top of the ramp to be a problem. My only real concern is that wizard."

Alexander took another look at the group of men approaching. He let his vision go out of focus so he could see their colors. He'd used his little bit of magic so often that he just took it for granted. He couldn't imagine how limiting it must be to only see with normal vision. He could tell by the colors of the six men headed their way that the wizard wasn't among them. People who'd been through the mana fast had a deeper mix of colors with more intensity and their aura usually extended farther around them, giving off a brighter glow. Just one more little piece of vital information that he could see and others could not.

"We may get lucky. The wizard isn't with the group that's on the way up."

Lucky came up alongside them and carefully peered over the wall. "Abigail is on the gatehouse with her bow, and Jack is at the western perimeter wall with a large stack of rocks. I've quieted the horses and given them something to soothe their nerves so they won't get spooked and start running if we have to fight. You say the wizard isn't with that group headed our way?"

"No, it looks like he's still back at their camp." Alexander tested his shoulder again. He was feeling stronger despite his fatigue.

"Odds are they don't know we're here, probably just sending scouts to make sure," Lucky mused.

Anatoly spoke softly, "Agreed. We can make short work of these six from Jack's position. I recommend we hit them by surprise and thin their numbers. The rest of their soldiers will be here in the morning, no doubt. The fewer men we have to face in the light, the better our chances."

Alexander nodded, "Lucky, stay here and warn us if the other six head our way. We'll throw a few rocks at them and see if we can't knock them off the path before they know what hit 'em."

Anatoly and Alexander stayed low and close to the tower. The element of surprise was their best weapon and they didn't want to squander it with carelessness. They gave the picketed horses a wide berth and made their way through the darkness to Jack's position.

"Alexander, it's good to see you up and about. You gave us quite a scare back there," Jack whispered. He was sitting with his back to the low stone wall between two stacks of rocks. He had also lined the top of the wall with a rock every foot or so for a dozen feet in each direction.

Alexander peeked over the wall. It was twenty feet to the narrow path below and another thirty feet from the path to the ground. There was no cover. It was the perfect place for an ambush.

He thought back to his childhood lessons. He could hear the words of his father's lecture in his mind: "Surprise and deception are two of the most formidable weapons you will ever have. More battles have been won by clever use of surprise or deception than by larger numbers, superior weapons, greater skill, or even magic. Each depends on the essential element of belief. If you can create a false belief in the mind of your enemy and exploit that belief, they will fall and you will prevail."

Alexander knew that they would win this battle and they would win because they had the element of surprise. It suddenly occurred to him that he had lost the last battle, in large part, because he had allowed himself to be surprised and it had very nearly cost him his life.

When he heard the six men coming up the path, his mind snapped back to the present. He relaxed his vision and scanned all around for any sign of life that he wasn't aware of, but saw none. Six men came around the corner of the plateau and into view. They were walking single file, each carrying a torch, and they were complaining about being assigned to scout the plateau. Each wore the crest of the Southport city guard. Alexander supposed they had been bought by the Reishi just like the other guards. He wondered if the Regent of Southport was actually the one who was in league with Phane. It made sense. The Reishi Prince would bribe the most powerful and influential people he could in order to secure power over the Seven Isles.

Alexander, Jack, and Anatoly each stood quietly in the darkness and each took a heavy rock from those placed along the top of the wall. They waited until the first three soldiers passed and the remaining three were directly below them. As one, they carefully tossed their rocks into the night. There was no need to heave them. They didn't need to add any force or power to their impromptu weapons. Each rock weighed a good twenty pounds or more. All they needed to do was toss them accurately and let gravity do the rest. Each small boulder sailed through the darkness, gathering frightening speed. Smoke swirled violently when the rocks passed out of the darkness and into the sphere of light cast by the enemy's flickering torches.

The first rock was a direct hit. The soldier crumpled to the ground in a heap as the rock caved in his skull despite the protection of his helm. The second rock struck the next in line on the back of his left shoulder. He pitched forward in surprise and stumbled right off the edge of the path, plummeting thirty feet to the ground without so much as a whimper. The third rock smashed squarely into the base of the last man's neck. He fell forward flat on his face and didn't move again.

The next salvo of boulders was away before the first three had a chance to understand or react to the attack. One took a direct hit to the face when he spun and looked up. He fell in a broken and bloody mess. The next dodged quickly enough to avoid the boulder hurtling toward his head but lost his balance in the bargain and went over the edge, screaming briefly before the ground silenced him. The third managed to leap backward and get his shield up just in time to take a solid hit. He fell backward but the heavy rock glanced off his round shield. He was back on his feet more quickly than Alexander would have thought possible. The last man standing ran for his life.

Anatoly was ready. He cast his next stone off the edge in an arc that brought it down in front of the fleeing guard. The moment the rock was away, Anatoly raced along the wall to the next position where he'd placed stones. The rock he tossed missed but he hadn't been trying to hit him. He wanted it to come down in front of the fleeing soldier to slow him down and it worked like a charm. The soldier stopped short when the rock shattered on the path in front of him, and then he looked up, raising his shield, for the next attack. Anatoly cast a stone aimed for the glint of moonlight off polished steel. The rock scored a direct hit against the shield. The force of it propelled the soldier off the path as if he'd been tossed by a giant. He hit the ground with a terrible thud and the night went silent.

All three waited for a moment in the dark before they collectively breathed a sigh of relief. They started for the east side of the plateau to see if the rest of the Reishi hunting party had been alerted. They came up alongside Lucky from his left, moving low and quiet. Abigail approached from the right. The remaining six men were busy making camp. They appeared to be unaware of the death of their scouting party, but Alexander knew they'd be missed soon enough.

"Alex, how's your shoulder?" Abigail sounded concerned and relieved at the same time. She knew firsthand how well Lucky could heal if given the time and his bag of tricks, but she wanted to hear it from her brother.

"Still a little stiff, but better than I have any right to expect," Alexander said. "We killed the six that were headed up to scout the plateau. I expect the rest will become suspicious sooner rather than later."

"We left a couple of them back on the trail," Jack said. "If we tossed them over before any more came up the path we might be able to use the same tactic on the rest. I'll run down and tidy up if one of you will keep an eye out for me."

"I agree," Anatoly said. "You head down the path and I'll keep watch from the north side. Lucky, let us know if any of 'em head our way." He waited until everyone nodded agreement before moving off into the night. Jack disappeared into the dark, leaving Alexander and Abigail with Lucky to watch the enemy camp.

The soldiers were cooking dinner over an oversized fire. The night air was getting cold and the moon had risen, casting its eerie glow over the world. It was more than enough light to see by.

One of the men got up from his seat around the fire and walked out of its circle of illumination to peer up toward the plateau. Alexander was sure the man couldn't see them but he felt uneasy just the same. The man returned to the fire and spoke to the only man dressed in robes. The man in robes nodded and took one last bite of his dinner before walking a few paces from the fire. He stood facing the plateau and started chanting.

A chill raced up Alexander's spine. He relaxed his vision and saw the man's aura flare as he called his magic. "He's casting a spell," Alexander whispered tensely.

In unison, the three of them turned and sat with their backs to the wall. A moment later a white-hot streak of flame rose high into the sky above them, casting a harsh light that threw hard shadows as it moved overhead. Moments later it faded into nothingness and the world plunged abruptly into darkness again.

"A signal, I suspect," Lucky said. "He'll be expecting the scouting party to answer soon."

They heard Jack before they could see him. The flare had ruined their night vision.

"It's me," he whispered, moving up next to them in the darkness. "What was that?"

"Lucky says it was a signal," Abigail whispered to Jack, who crept up alongside her, making sure to stay low.

"They'll be coming soon then. The path is clear of bodies. I'll go find Anatoly." Jack disappeared into the darkness again.

Sure enough the six men at the camp were all standing and watching the plateau, waiting for a signal of some sort. Alexander knew that they would come soon. He was worried about the wizard.

After a few minutes, the enemy began to gather their gear. Each of the five men in armor lit a torch and all six started for the plateau. They hadn't made it ten steps when the night was shattered by an otherworldly howl that stopped the men in their tracks and made Alexander's blood run cold. Before the first terrible howl went silent it was joined by another and then another. Alexander broke out in a cold sweat. He knew in an instant what they were.

Nether wolves.

Creatures summoned from the depths of the netherworld, the plane of death. Beasts brought forth into this world by Phane Reishi for the singular purpose of hunting Alexander down and killing him. Before the shrieking yowl from the beasts in the distance ended, both Jack and Anatoly were at his side.

Alexander's night vision had once again adjusted to the light of the moon. He looked Anatoly in the eye and for the first time in his life he saw fear there. The big man-at-arms could stand before any human foe with a good chance of living through the fight, but this was something else. The quality of the noise the nether wolves made spoke to Alexander's life essence. He knew at a visceral level that they were not of this world. They were not bound by the rules of life and death because they were already dead.

Lucky sighed, "This may be a problem." He sat down and started rummaging through his bag.

Jack was almost calm except for a slight tremor that ran through his voice. "Well, at least the Reishi have decided against an attack."

The Reishi had indeed stopped heading toward the plateau and were instead busy setting out firewood at points in a circle surrounding the main fire of their camp. The wizard was urgently directing where each stack of wood was to be placed.

"Whatever made that noise sounds like it's still a long way off. We have some time to prepare." Anatoly had quickly regained his composure. "Lucky, tell me you have something in that bag of yours."

Almost as if on cue, Lucky produced a small metal canister about two inches in diameter and four or five inches long with a metal cap screwed and wired tightly in place. "I'm afraid this is all I have capable of defeating such a beast." He looked at it almost fondly.

Abigail frowned, "What's it do?"

"Ah, my dear, this is a very rare creature of great and terrible power. It looks like nothing more than a puddle of thick black water but when it comes in contact with nearly any other thing, save glass, stone, or dirt, it will transform that which it touches into more of itself. It's really quite dangerous. If I were to cast it into the forest it would transform everything for several miles into nothing but more of itself. All of the trees, bushes, and animals would be lost to it. When the rays of sunlight touch the creature, it turns to ash almost instantly."

"That sounds awful. Why would you have such a thing?" Abigail asked, wrinkling her nose.

Lucky smiled good-naturedly, "Sometimes your enemy is best defeated by introducing him to another enemy."

Anatoly chuckled softly.

Jack looked like he was taking notes in his head again.

"Sounds like we'll have to be very careful about how we use that stuff. I don't want to destroy the forest and I don't want to get any of us killed by it either," Alexander said while he watched the Reishi make preparations for the coming threat. It seemed odd to him that they were clearly just as afraid of the nether wolves as Alexander was. He wondered if they might kill each other but thought it was too much to hope for.

"I agree," Lucky said. "It would be best used in a place where it can be contained, like the gatehouse tunnel. There isn't any grass there, just stone and dirt. If we catch one of the creatures in the tunnel, it would be consumed in just a few moments. The puddle of slime that remained would have nothing to feed on so it wouldn't spread and it would offer the added benefit of effectively sealing off the gatehouse entrance. Anything that tried to pass would be consumed as well. Of course, our horses would be trapped up here and we'd have to climb over the wall and drop down to the path to get out ourselves."

"Let's call that a last resort," Alexander suggested. "The more you talk about that stuff, the scarier it sounds."

Abigail nodded her agreement.

"Let's try to get some rest while we wait. It sounded like it'll be a while and those Reishi certainly don't look like they're going anywhere tonight. I'll take first watch," Alexander said, pulling a blanket from his bedroll to ward off the chill night air.

For all the impending threats, the rest of the night was quiet. Those who could sleep did so fretfully. Mostly they waited with a sense of dread weighing down on them. The watch kept a close eye on the Reishi camp down on the plain below but none of the Reishi strayed from the protection of their firelight. About an hour before dawn, the still night air was shattered again by the keening, shrieking howl of the nether wolves. This time they were much closer.

Chapter 16

Alexander sat bolt upright from his half sleep. He was on his feet, moving to the low perimeter wall in a blink. His heart pounded in his chest, so he schooled his breathing to calm his near panic at being abruptly awakened by such a terrifying noise.

Anatoly had just relieved Lucky on watch and was looking intently into the darkness in the direction of the otherworldly howls. Alexander came up alongside him quietly, still keeping low to avoid the notice of the Reishi. He didn't really care much who or what planned to kill him, dead was dead, and he'd learned a hard lesson the day before. He was determined to be mindful of every possible threat. He scanned the plain below and relaxed his vision. He reminded himself not to take his ability for granted. It had saved him more than once. He saw the nether wolves almost immediately.

Out in the darkness, he saw the opposite of life. The three beasts coming for him were holes in the world to his second sight. Their auras were not the rich colors of life, but instead splotches of impossible blackness moving through the night and they were coming fast. They bounded toward the fire of the Reishi camp faster than any horse could run.

All of the soldiers in the camp were up with weapons at the ready and the wizard was chanting. Alexander saw his aura swell when he sent his intention into the firmament and commanded reality to bend to his will. It happened suddenly. His aura abruptly collapsed back in on him and a stream of white hot flame arched from his outstretched hands and leapt to the first of the piles of firewood that had been laid out in a circle around their camp. The flame flared, grew into a blaze, then arched from the first pile of firewood to both of the piles on the left and right. Fire flowed from the wizard's hands, jumping from each pre-positioned pile of wood to the next until the flames formed an unbroken circular wall surrounding and protecting the Reishi camp.

By now, everyone was up and looking over the wall with Alexander. A week ago he'd been hunting wolves on the north range of his father's estate. So much had changed in such a short time. His brother was dead, murdered. His family home had been set ablaze. He didn't know if his parents still lived. He'd been chased from his home and hunted. He'd been nearly mortally wounded. He'd killed. And now wolves were hunting him.

"They're coming," he whispered as he watched the darkness bound through the night. "Three of them."

They held their breath.

And then the creatures arrived.

Three inky black beasts. They looked almost like wolves except they stood five feet at the shoulder and their impossibly black, leatherlike skin was pulled taught around their skeletons. They were completely hairless and ran on oversized feet with claws like the talons of a giant raptor. Their heads were large and their snouts were long and wide. It looked like they could easily fit a man's head between their huge jaws lined with razor-sharp teeth and fangs.

They stopped at the edge of the firelight thrown off by the circle of protection cast in flame by Wizard Rangle. They walked around the camp, staying just at the edge of the light, gnashing their teeth and snarling toward those behind the fire. The soldiers were terrified. They stood huddled around the central fire with their crossbows loaded and cocked.

The nether wolves made a complete loop around the fire ring before they stopped suddenly. All at once, their heads snapped toward Alexander. He felt an icy tingling of dread flash through every fiber of his being when the glowing yellow eyes of the nether wolves locked on his position. They tossed their heads back and howled in unison.

And then they were coming.

Anatoly was up and running for the north edge of the perimeter wall, barking orders as he went, "Lucky, Abigail, get on top of the gatehouse. Jack, Alexander, to the west wall."

Alexander and Jack raced past the frightened horses to their post at the west edge of the wall. Alexander heard the crash of rocks as Anatoly ran along the north wall pushing pre-positioned stones over the edge.

"They're coming!" he bellowed while he ran to join Jack and Alexander at the west end of the plateau. He arrived just before the first pair of eyes came around the bend on the path below. In the darkness, all that Alexander could see were glowing yellow eyes the color of hate looking up at him. The beast seemed to laugh as it slowed to peer at its prey.

Alexander and Jack tossed stones in unison, followed a fraction of a second later by Anatoly. The beast dodged the first two stones with ease by sidestepping a few feet closer to the edge of the path. Anatoly cast his stone exactly where the beast would have to go to avoid the first two. He caught it squarely in the hindquarter and knocked it over the edge. It caught the stone curb with one of its claws and managed to stop its fall until the stone itself gave way. The beast shrieked in rage, plummeting to the ground thirty feet below. Unlike the soldiers they'd killed earlier, this beast bounded to its feet only a moment after it hit the ground, gave one angry look up toward its prey, and started running around the plateau toward the base of the path.

The sky was just beginning to lighten with the coming dawn. The dusky light made the creature that came around the corner next look like a living shadow cast against the stone of the path. It actually stopped and looked up toward them in defiance when they cast their volley of stones. All three found their mark. The beast took the brunt of the attack as it hunkered against the wall. The force of the impact would have killed a prized bull, but it only stunned the nether wolf, knocking it to the ground but not off the path. The third nether wolf bounded over its stunned companion and loped up the path toward the gatehouse.

Anatoly hurled another stone with all his might at the monster lying on the path below and scored another direct hit. It sounded like bones broke but still the beast stirred and came to its feet, looking up and snarling. Alexander and Jack cast yet another set of small boulders at it. This time they drove it from the path, spiraling to the ground below. It hit hard and didn't get up right away. Alexander thought maybe there was some hope that the creatures could be killed, and then the beast staggered to its feet and looked up at him again.

"To the gatehouse," Alexander commanded as he turned and sprinted to the only high ground they had left.

By now the horses were in near panic. They could smell the unnatural enemy coming toward them and were straining to break free of their tethers. Alexander ignored them and made his way to his sister as fast as he could.

The first nether wolf to fall off the ledge rounded the corner more warily this time and hesitated as Jack and Anatoly cast one last stone each at the beast. Both fell short but succeeded in slowing the thing down by a few steps.

The gatehouse stood nine feet tall, eight feet wide and a dozen feet long. The top was ringed on three sides with a low wall and was open on the end where the gate passage led onto the plateau. As Alexander raced toward the gatehouse, he saw Abigail loose an arrow down toward the path.

He leapt up the side of the wall and caught the rope Lucky and Abigail had used to climb up. Even with the stiffness in his shoulder, he had more than enough adrenaline-fueled strength to climb the wall. Lucky caught his hand and helped him the last few feet. Jack was right behind him and Alexander cleared the way so Lucky could help him to the top as well. Abigail let another arrow fly.

Alexander unslung his bow, stepped up next to his sister and took aim. The beast charging up the trail toward them already had two arrows sticking out of its bony shoulders. He could see the hate in its eyes and the malice of death itself powering the beast as it bounded toward them. He and Abigail released as one. Their twin arrows drove side by side into the heavy bone of its forehead. The creature flinched and stopped for a moment to shake its head wildly. It tipped its head back, arrows still sticking out of it like the horn of a unicorn, and howled with unearthly fury.

Alexander found himself in a strange place. Time seemed to be moving more slowly. Everything was clearer, more focused. He could see the bony skeleton of the creature beneath the taut black leather that covered it. He remembered all of the lessons he'd ever learned about battle and war and strategy all at once. They all flowed together into a background symphony of skill and instinct and the singular purpose to survive. In that moment, he understood at a basic level all of those things he'd learned about war in an academic way but had never actually experienced outside the safety of his imagination.

He'd never felt a more serene calm in all of his life.

There was no fear, only stillness. A quietness that filled his soul and gave him a kind of comfort he'd never known before. The comfort one can only feel when he discovers his purpose in the world. He knew in that moment that the Old Rebel Mage had chosen well.

He released his next arrow with confidence. He knew before he drew it from his quiver where it would land. It drove into the place where the creature's heart would have been if the nether wolf actually had a heart. Abigail nearly matched his shot for speed and accuracy, driving her arrow into the beast's chest not an inch from Alexander's mark. The creature gibbered and mewled as it shook wildly to dislodge the arrows. When it came close to the edge of the path, Anatoly heaved a stone with all his strength from the top of the gatehouse and caught the creature on the side of the head. It pitched off the top of the path and fell the full fifty feet to the ground below, shrieking with a ghastly howl that was silenced by the ground.

The next came loping up the trail but rather than charge, it stopped thirty or forty feet from the gatehouse, then crouched and sprang straight up to the perimeter wall. It caught the top of the wall with talons that cut into the stone itself, then scrambled up and over onto the plateau. The second nether wolf to be driven from the path came around the corner. Abigail and Alexander fired in unison. Both hit the beast in the shoulders but it kept coming as if nothing had happened.

The one on the plateau was moving toward the gatehouse in a crouch, as though it was preparing to spring. Anatoly pushed Lucky and Jack into the far corner to give himself room to work, took his war axe in both hands and planted himself in a firm stance. He eyed the beast with his best battle grin and watched it gather speed for its attack.

Alexander and Abigail sent arrows with speed and accuracy into the nether wolf coming up the path, but it had taken half a dozen hits already and it still kept coming. It sprang at them, and Alexander sent one final arrow into the creature's chest. The nether wolf sailed up toward the top of the gatehouse. Abigail pulled Alexander down just as the beast passed over them and stumbled off the other side of the gatehouse onto the plateau.

The other nether wolf sprang at Anatoly, who knew that once a creature or a man left the ground their course was set. Unless they were a bird, they couldn't change direction in midflight. He used that simple piece of knowledge to his advantage. The moment the huge black wolf left the ground, Anatoly sidestepped to his left toward the front of the gatehouse and spun, swinging his axe in a tight arc. When the creature landed on top of the gatehouse, Anatoly caught the front of its right leg, cleanly chopping it off just below the shoulder joint.

There was no blood, no gore, just the snap of bone and the tear of its black leather skin. The beast crashed into the little eighteen-inch wall that ringed three sides of the gatehouse roof. It tried to regain its footing, but Jack and Lucky rushed in as one and shoved the creature off onto the plateau. Anatoly picked up its leg and peered over the edge, waggling it at the beast before he tossed it over the edge to the plain below.

The nether wolf watched its leg sail over the edge of the cliff while the other beast regained its footing, turned and sprang from a standstill onto the top of the gatehouse. This one didn't go over the edge but instead stopped and spun to face Alexander and Abigail, leaving its hindquarters exposed to Anatoly, Jack, and Lucky.

Abigail struck first. She still had her bow in hand and an arrow nocked. She sent it straight into the creature's mouth and out the back side of its head. The beast flinched but then snapped its jaws shut on the arrow and shattered it.

Alexander dropped his bow and drew his sword. He had plenty of training with a long blade but it had all involved fighting another man with a sword. This was different.

Anatoly struck next, a great downward stroke with all his might onto the rump of the nether wolf. His axe sliced cleanly through the beast's left hindquarter in a blow that should have crippled it. Instead, it turned, quick as a cat, and backhanded Anatoly in the chest hard enough to send him sailing off the top of the gatehouse and onto the plateau below. He hit the wall of the square barracks building, fell forward to the ground, and lay still, face down in the lush grass.

Alexander took full advantage of the moment of distraction that Anatoly's attack had bought him. When the nether wolf turned to swat at Anatoly, it exposed the back of its neck. Alexander brought his sword down with all his might and fury. His strike was true. The nether wolf's head came free and the beast crumpled into a heap of broken bones in a bag of black leather. The head rolled up against the low wall and Alexander watched the glow fade from its eyes.

As he brought his sword down, his mind registered all of the other things happening around him: Anatoly flying off the gatehouse; Jack and Lucky casting stones down at the three-legged beast on the plateau in a desperate effort to distract it from the man who had, just moments before, tossed its leg off the cliff; Abigail shouting behind him, "Here comes another one," followed by the telltale twang of her bowstring. He even registered the rising light in the sky and the Reishi camp still huddled inside the protection of their ring of fire on the plain below.

He came to the edge of the gatehouse roof next to Lucky and Jack and saw the three-legged nether wolf moving to pounce on Anatoly who was still lying face down, either unconscious or dead.

Alexander called out, "Your master sent you for me!"

The beast turned and made eye contact with Alexander. The depth of hatred he saw in those glowing yellow eyes made his hair stand on end. The beast very deliberately looked at Anatoly and then back at Alexander again before moving toward the stunned man-at-arms. The message was clear. Alexander would watch his friend die. The beast almost laughed as it opened its huge jaws wide enough to take Anatoly's whole head.

Then Abigail screamed.

Alexander whirled to see the third nether wolf, the one they had shot in the head and sent off the top of the plateau, hurtling through the air toward his sister. She had sunk an arrow into it and was defenseless. He was torn. In an instant, two of the last people he had left in this world could be taken from him. Their lives would be lost protecting him. All of the calm certainty he'd felt moments before melted away into the kind of fear that can only be felt at the idea of losing a loved one.

He was paralyzed with it, sick with helplessness. In that eternal moment, he was torn between throwing himself toward his mentor or his sister. And yet, he knew he had no power to stop either attack. Both were going to die and he couldn't do anything to prevent it. Once they fell, the nether wolves would kill him as well. He saw the magnitude of his failure stretch out into the coming centuries: countless innocent people suffering and dying for nothing except the depraved malice of a single man who craved power over the lives of others and was willing to kill for it. He watched the nightmare unfold in slow motion, powerless to affect the outcome. Despair flooded into him and filled him with a kind of hopelessness he didn't even know existed.

Chapter 17

Then the first rays of sunlight stabbed out from behind the horizon. In that instant everything changed. The beast that sailed through the air toward his sister abruptly transformed into nothing more than a cloud of heavy black smoke. The inky cloud stopped in midair and sank quickly to the ground where it was drawn into the cracks between the stones of the path as if it had been inhaled by the earth itself. Alexander spun to see that Anatoly lay unconscious but alive. There was no trace of the three-legged nether wolf.

Everyone stood stock-still in the sudden silence. The immediate threat was gone, banished by sunlight. Alexander glanced to the Reishi camp and saw that they hadn't yet moved. He slammed his sword into its scabbard, slipped over the edge of the gatehouse, and dropped to the ground. He was kneeling beside Anatoly in three steps. The big man-at-arms was just starting to come to. Alexander looked up and nodded at Lucky, who started down off the gatehouse using the rope.

"Jack, keep an eye on the Reishi camp. Abby, watch the path; we can't afford to be surprised right now."

Jack nodded, slipped off the gatehouse and headed to the perimeter wall. Abigail nocked another arrow.

Lucky knelt next to Anatoly just as he came awake with a start. He got to his knees with a wince and looked around wildly for the threat.

"Anatoly, the wolves are gone. We're safe for the moment," Alexander tried to reassure him so he wouldn't hurt himself with any sudden movements.

Anatoly looked to Lucky for confirmation and got a nod and a gentle hand on his shoulder.

"Why don't you lie down and let me have a look at you?" Lucky said reassuringly.

Anatoly nodded through obvious pain as he gingerly eased himself back to the ground.

"What happened?" he asked with his eyes closed.

Lucky nodded to Alexander while he rummaged through his bag.

Alexander took a deep breath before he began. "The truth is I'm not really sure. One moment we were losing the fight badly, then the sun broke over the horizon and the nether wolves turned to smoke and just disappeared."

Anatoly opened one eye and frowned up at Alexander.

He shrugged and continued, "Couldn't have happened at a better time, that three-legged wolf was just about to crush your skull and the one we pincushioned and sent off the top of the plateau came back and was about five feet from landing on top of Abby." He shuddered. "For a second there I was sure we were all done for. It was a pretty helpless feeling."

Anatoly nodded, "It's one thing to place yourself in harm's way and quite another to watch those you care about risk their lives."

Lucky rolled a couple of numbweed leaves into a ball and held them in front of Anatoly's mouth with a gesture and a look.

Anatoly scowled up at his old friend, "You know how much I hate that stuff."

Lucky nodded. "It'll do you good. Open up," he said with a little too much good cheer.

Anatoly obeyed and started chewing the foul-tasting painkiller. "That's only two of 'em, where'd the third one go?" he asked while he chewed.

Alexander smiled grimly, "I took its head off when you distracted it. It's nothing but a leather bag of bones up on top of the gatehouse."

Anatoly nodded his approval. "Good man. What about the Reishi?"

"Jack's keeping an eye on them," Alexander said. "I think they were pretty terrified by the nether wolves. Can't say I blame 'em."

Lucky produced a glass vial of clear liquid from his bag. "How are you feeling, Anatoly? Is the numbweed working yet?"

Anatoly nodded.

"Good. Alexander, let's help him sit up."

Anatoly winced in pain as he struggled to sit.

"Go ahead and spit out the numbweed." Lucky handed him a water skin to rinse his mouth out. "Now drink this." Lucky handed over the vial. "It'll help you heal. It's like the healing salve except it works from the inside."

Anatoly took the vial, inhaled deeply, held his breath, and downed it quickly. He made a face as he tipped up the water skin and took a long drink. "That tasted awful. It'd better work," Anatoly said before he closed his eyes and eased himself back to the ground.

"I'm going to go check on the Reishi and the horses," Alexander said. "How long before he'll be back on his feet?"

"He should be up and about after a short nap, say half an hour. I'll stay with him," Lucky said as he sat down on his bedroll and started rummaging around in his bag. He produced a hard biscuit and handed it to Alexander.

Alexander nodded his thanks with a chuckle and headed off to have a look at the Reishi camp.

He crept up next to Jack, keeping low to avoid being seen from the plain below. He wasn't sure if it mattered at this point but it was better to be safe. "How's it look?" he asked, peeking over the low perimeter wall.

"They haven't left that charred circle surrounding their camp but they're keeping an eye on the plateau. See that one standing at the edge of the circle looking our way?"

Alexander nodded.

"They've rotated a few men through that watch post so everyone can eat. It's a good bet they know we're here. But I'm more worried about that." Jack pointed out over the plain at a cloud of dust rising from the road off in the distance. "I suspect the rest of the soldiers we stole the horses from are headed this way. Once they get here, we're stuck."

Alexander nodded, "It looks like they're a few hours away. We might have to make a run for it before they get here. I don't really want to spend another night up here."

Jack nodded thoughtfully. "I've been thinking about that too. Did you see how those nether wolves turned to smoke and went to ground? I've read about things like that from accounts of the Reishi War. I don't think they're dead." He looked over at Alexander. "I think they're just waiting for the sun to go down."

"You mean they're still here?" Alexander asked as he started to look around with alarm.

"I believe they are," Jack answered. "By the time the sun goes down, I think we should be a long way from here."

"Agreed, we'll make a run for it as soon as Anatoly is well enough to ride. I'm going to check on the horses." Alexander patted Jack on the shoulder and moved away in a crouch.

When he passed the gatehouse, Abigail pointed off toward the road. Alexander nodded at his sister's warning. He stopped at Anatoly's feet and gave Lucky a questioning look. Lucky shrugged and motioned for him to be quiet so as not to wake the man-at-arms. Alexander started to go but stopped for a moment to take a hard look at the ground where the nether wolf had been standing just before the sun came up. The spot looked perfectly normal until he relaxed his vision and looked with his second sight. He caught his breath and a chill crept up his spine. The patch of ground radiated the same darkness he'd seen when he looked at the nether wolves.

He looked to Lucky and whispered, "We leave as soon as we can ride." Then turned and went to check on the horses.

The grass had been cropped in the area around their picket line and the horses were stretching to reach the lush green shoots just beyond their tethers. Alexander reached into one of the saddlebags and found a bag of carrots Owen had packed for them. He walked among them, petting them, soothing them, and feeding them their treats. They were restless and hungry but, all things considered, they were in pretty good shape. Once he'd made his rounds through the horses, he got into another saddlebag and found some biscuits and dried fruit. He went back to Lucky and saw that Anatoly was awake.

"How are you feeling?" he asked, offering them both some breakfast.

Anatoly nodded, "Much better. I should be ready to ride soon. Turns out Lucky's foul-tasting potion was good for something after all."

Alexander chuckled and moved on to the gatehouse. He took enough fruit and biscuits from the little bag for himself and Jack and tossed the rest up to Abigail. She caught it without a word and smiled her thanks to him.

He handed Jack breakfast and knelt down next to him to take another look at the Reishi camp. They were still in the confines of their circle of fire and the riders in the distance weren't making very good time. It looked like they were still more than an hour away.

"You were right about the wolves. I think they took refuge from the sun in the ground. We need to be very far away from here by sunset." Alexander took a bite of dried apple and chewed slowly while he thought it over and tried to formulate a strategy. They still had half a dozen enemy to get past with more on the way. If he was right, the ones coming this way were moving slowly because they were riding double. Since he'd stolen ten of their horses they had more men than mounts.

"Anatoly should be ready to ride soon," Alexander said absently around a mouthful of biscuit while he turned their situation over in his mind.

Jack nudged him and motioned to the Reishi Camp. The men were arming up and the wizard was standing at the edge of his circle chanting a spell while he looked up at the plateau.

Alexander watched in helpless fascination as the wizard's magic began to take shape. Between his outstretched hands floated a large undulating sphere that looked like a soap bubble two feet across except it was filled with swirling orange-red liquid fire. He looked straight up at Alexander and released the bubble of liquid fire at them. It rose toward the edge of the plateau, quickly gaining speed as it went.

Alexander called out, "Take cover!"

He and Jack ducked behind the low perimeter wall. The wobbling ball of liquid fire streaked over their heads, past the little wall that was sheltering them, and crashed into the old guard tower about halfway up its side. It burst with a splash and sent droplets of red-hot flaming liquid cascading down into the ruined square building that used to serve as a barracks. Had the east wall of the low square building not been collapsed in, the liquid fire would have splashed against it instead and covered Alexander and Jack in white-hot death. As it was, little droplets of the caustic, flaming, magical liquid had splattered all over the side of the tower and inside the square building. A few drops had splattered over the wall and landed just feet from Anatoly and Lucky, who were crouching against the outside of the square building's south wall.

Alexander stared in shock. The liquid fire burned into the stone of the tower wall, eating away at what was left of the tower's structural integrity. He knew it would be only minutes before the tower would fall. He saw the splattered fire all around and gave thanks that no one had been hit.

Then he saw a hawk circling overhead, which seemed to be watching the whole thing with intense interest.

He spun and looked back down at the plain below. The wizard was casting another spell.

"Time to go," he said to Jack. "Start clearing the gatehouse tunnel of that pile of rubble."

He headed toward Anatoly and Lucky and stopped at the gatehouse just long enough to help Abigail to the ground. She gave him a quick look, then stepped into the tunnel and started heaving head-sized boulders off the edge of the cliff. Jack stepped up beside her while Alexander went to get the horses. Lucky and Anatoly were already there when he arrived. They were busy tying the skittish horses into strings of three, one string for each rider. Alexander heard the flaming whoosh of another bubble of liquid fire as he raced to help prepare the horses. This one hit the perimeter wall right where Alexander and Jack had been only moments before. Droplets of liquid fire splashed over the edge and covered the grass leading up to the collapsed wall of the barracks building.

All of the horses were strung together and ready when Abigail and Jack ran up, breathless from the hard work of clearing the tunnel.

"All clear," Jack managed as Anatoly handed him a set of reins and Alexander handed Abigail hers.

They walked the horses quickly through the gatehouse and onto the narrow path before mounting up and riding single file down to the plain below. When they came to the place where they'd staged their ambush on the west side of the plateau, the tower came crashing down with a terrible noise. The horses bolted in fear. It was all Alexander could do to keep his horse on the path. He careened around the corner and came onto the long straight stretch of the gently sloping ramp that ran along the north face of the plateau and saw yet another opportunity to die.

Chapter 18

Rangle was conjuring more liquid fire. Alexander had nowhere to go. If the bubble filled with hot death hit the ramp before he made it to the plain below, he would be engulfed in fire. The alternative was to ride his horse off the edge of the path and fall a dozen or more feet to the ground with two more horses following right after him.

Then he saw the other riders. There were five of them coming from the forest to the north, and they were coming fast. At full gallop they each loosed an arrow at the wizard and his little group of hired killers. One of the wizard's men called out in pain when an arrow struck home. Wizard Rangle turned just as the arrow meant for him drove cleanly through his right forearm. The bubble of fire floating between his outstretched hands was nearly fully formed. If he lost control of the spell, it would burst and consume him. In a panic, he cast it away to splash harmlessly onto the field only twenty feet in front of him.

Alexander charged down the ramp. He reached the ground and guided his horse to the left toward the riders who had saved him, while at the same time relaxing his focus and allowing their colors to shine through. What he saw filled him with hope. He headed right for them as they sent another volley of arrows toward the Reishi camp.

This time the wounded wizard was ready. He erected a plane of red hot air in the path of the arrows. It wasn't hot enough to actually burn the arrows or even catch them on fire but it was hot enough to ignite the feathers that guided the shafts. All five arrows spun wildly out of control and fell short. The enemy mounted quickly and headed for the road, preferring retreat now that Wizard Rangle was wounded. Alexander had no doubt that they would regroup with their reinforcements and attack again.

Alexander's group slowed when they approached the five riders who had come to their rescue. Alexander showed his open hand in greeting.

The lead rider responded in kind and then called out, "Master Grace?"

Anatoly chuckled as he rode up alongside the lead rider and clasped his hand in greeting. "Erik Alaric. You were but a boy when last I saw you. How are your parents?"

"They're well. Father received your message a few days ago and sent us to find you and offer our assistance," Erik said, surveying the rest of the faces riding with Anatoly.

"Erik, may I present Lord Alexander Valentine. He was marked on the night Phane woke," Anatoly said, motioning to Alexander.

Erik stiffened in his saddle. "So the old stories are true." He extended his hand to Alexander. "Lord Valentine, we are at your service."

Alexander coaxed his horse forward and took Erik's hand. "I don't know much about the old stories, and frankly my father is Lord Valentine. Call me Alexander. I'd like to thank you for driving off the Reishi. Your timing is excellent ... that wizard was about to light us on fire. These are my companions.

You already know Master Grace." Alexander glanced Anatoly's way to see his slight scowl at the formal title. "Master Aluicious Alabrand, our family alchemist; Master Jack Colton, the Bard of New Ruatha; and Lady Abigail Valentine, my sister." She also scowled at him for the formality, only more openly than Anatoly.

Erik bowed in his saddle to each in greeting as Alexander introduced them. "I am Erik Alaric, eldest son of the Forest Warden. This is my Second, Chase Covington, my brothers Duane and Kevin, and my sister Isabel."

Each nodded to Alexander as they were introduced, except Isabel. She tossed back the hood of her cloak and gave him an appraising look. Her eyes were piercing green and sparkled with both intelligence and intensity. She seemed to measure him in a glance. He didn't waver or flinch but instead held her gaze. For just that fraction of a moment, Alexander was lost in her eyes. She was as beautiful as any woman he'd ever seen. Her hair was chestnut brown, her skin was clear and healthy, and her features were perfectly proportioned. She wore her armor and sat atop her horse with practiced ease. She was a woman whose substance overshadowed her considerable beauty.

He pulled his eyes away from her with an effort he hoped nobody had seen and turned back to Erik. "How many days to Glen Morillian?"

"Three if we make haste. It looked like you had only six men hunting you. With our numbers they shouldn't pose that great a threat even with a wizard. You needn't worry for your safety, Alexander." Erik was a few years older than Alexander and wore a mantle of confidence. He'd been born the son of an important noble and raised as a Ranger. He was sure of himself and his skills, and it showed.

Alexander paused for a moment to gather his thoughts. He needed their help and knew it would be best offered if they were more fully aware of the threat, but he didn't want to waste any more time with idle conversation out in the open. And he wanted as much distance as he could get from the plateau and the nether wolves when night fell.

"If it were just those men I would agree, but there is much more hunting us than a squad of men with a wizard. They retreated to regroup with their main force of twenty more about an hour up the road. But that's not the worst of it. Just before dawn we were attacked by three nether wolves."

Chase interrupted, "That's not possible. Nether wolves are fairy-tale creatures. They only exist in myth. It must have been some large forest wolves. We can handle those."

Alexander shook his head slowly. "No. These were creatures summoned from the netherworld by Prince Phane and sent to kill me. They attacked just before dawn and they would have killed us all if they hadn't been driven off by the light of the sun. We were able to destroy one of the three but the other two are still up there." Alexander pointed to the plateau.

This time it was Lucky who interrupted. "Alexander, are you sure? How can you know they're still up there? I saw the one hovering over Anatoly turn to smoke and fade away when the sunlight hit it. Isn't it more likely that they were killed or driven back to the netherworld?"

Again Alexander shook his head. "They're still up there, Lucky. They just turned to smoke and took refuge from the sunlight in the ground. When the sun sets they'll rise again, and I for one would like to be a long way from here when they do."

Jack agreed, "Lucky, I've read about creatures such as these. They can't stand the light of day, but they will not abandon the task they were summoned for until they succeed or are destroyed."

Chase spoke again, clearly incredulous, "You say you killed one of these nether wolves. How can you kill a creature that's already dead?" He looked to Erik. "I say they were just forest wolves."

Alexander was becoming annoyed. They didn't have time for this but he needed their help. "You're wrong. I killed the nether wolf by cutting off its head. Arrows didn't work. Knocking them off the top of the plateau didn't work. Crushing them with boulders didn't work. But taking the beast's head off killed it."

Jack, Lucky, and Abigail all nodded in agreement.

Erik looked to Anatoly for confirmation. Alexander didn't know how they knew each other but he could clearly see that Erik respected and trusted Anatoly.

"Lord Valentine speaks true." Anatoly gave a reproving glance to Chase before continuing, "These were creatures of the netherworld, not forest wolves. I know this because I cleaved the leg off one of them and it didn't bleed. When I picked up the leg and tossed it off the plateau, it felt deathly cold to the touch. As for Alexander killing the beast, I didn't see it happen because the creature had already bested me and I was unconscious, but Master Alabrand here tells me that Lord Valentine cleaved the head off the beast with one clean stroke. What's more, if Lord Valentine says they are still alive, then they are still alive and will be a threat just as soon as the sun sets."

Erik took Anatoly's words seriously but Chase was clearly not willing to believe their story. Alexander didn't have time to argue. He knew the truth and he knew they would as well once the sun set.

"Enough of this." Alexander pulled down his collar to reveal the mark burned into the side of his neck. When he was certain each of them had a clear look, he continued. "Take me to the Forest Warden by the fastest route possible or stand aside."

He held Erik with his eyes and waited for an answer.

Erik appraised him for a moment, then nodded slowly. "By your command, Lord Valentine," he said with a little grin as he nudged his horse into motion.

Alexander caught the slight smile Isabel gave him just out of the corner of his eye.

They rode hard for the forest road. When they reached the place where the road entered the forest, Isabel called out, "The enemy has regrouped. I count twenty and they're coming fast."

Erik nodded back to his sister.

Alexander was riding right next to Erik. He couldn't imagine how Isabel could know the enemy was coming. They were too far away to see and the cloud of dust they lifted off the road in the distance revealed little about their numbers.

"How can she know that?" he asked Erik.

Erik smiled over at Alexander. "Her hawk told her." His smile broadened at the look of confusion on Alexander's face. "Maybe she'll introduce you when we stop for the night."

Alexander puzzled over that as they rode. They stopped only long enough to switch to fresh horses at noon and grab some jerky to eat while they traveled. Alexander had been into the southern edge of the Great Forest where it met his father's lands, but never this deep. The sheer size of the trees awed him. He felt a sense of humility under the ancient giants that stood like silent sentinels alongside the meandering roadway. It looked like the road had been cut to avoid the largest of the trees as it wound through the forest. While they rode, he caught glimpses of wild deer, rabbits, squirrels, and all manner of birds.

The forest was teeming with life. When he relaxed his vision and let the colors shine through, he was nearly overwhelmed by the sheer magnitude of the life energy surrounding him.

Erik took his command seriously and rode at a relentless pace, pushing the horses right to their limits but never any farther. All five of the Rangers were excellent riders. They'd probably spent as much time in a saddle as Alexander. The only ones suffering from the grueling pace were Lucky and Jack. They weren't accustomed to such hard riding but they didn't let their discomfort slow them down. Alexander could see they were both hurting, but neither of them complained. Both knew what was at stake as well as anyone.

They made good time but Alexander knew it wouldn't be enough to outpace the nether wolves. He worried that the cover of the trees would protect the beasts from the light of the sun. He started to feel certain that tomorrow morning just before dawn they would be attacked again. About an hour before dusk, Alexander signaled for a stop. The horses were exhausted and everyone was in need of a break, but more than that, Alexander felt a growing need to find a safe place to take refuge for the night.

"Erik, we need someplace secure where we can rest for the night," Alexander said. "I expect the nether wolves will catch up with us about an hour before dawn and I'd like to be in a defensible position when they do."

Erik frowned, "Do you really think they'll be able to catch up with us? We made good time today."

Alexander nodded, "We did, but they run faster than a horse and it's midwinter so the nights are longer than the days. They'll attack just before dawn. We need to be ready or we won't survive to see daylight." Chase harrumphed under his breath. Alexander ignored him.

Alexander was too tired to be angry and he was coming to like and respect Erik. The man could ride. And he knew his horses well enough to get all he could out of them without hurting them. He'd do well on a ranch.

"We also have a platoon of soldiers with a wizard to consider," Alexander added. "If they push on after dark, we could end up in a fight with them in the next few hours. This is your forest, Erik, where do we stand the best chance?"

Erik nodded in thought. "We're close to the south fire tower but we'd have to leave our horses on the ground. About two hours up the road is a Ranger's sleep shack. It's got a stables and supplies and there are probably a few more men there, but it isn't well defended." Alexander could see that Erik was becoming more worried as he thought through their situation.

"Erik, Lord Valentine is right about one thing," Isabel said. "There are twenty men no more than an hour behind us and riding hard."

Alexander frowned. "How can you know that?"

Isabel smiled at his question and her face lit up like the sunrise. "My hawk told me."

Alexander looked around and Isabel's smile widened. "He's not here; he's floating over the enemy about an hour behind us."

"I don't understand." Alexander knew magic came in many varieties but he was baffled. "If the hawk isn't here, then how can it tell you the enemy is following us?"

"Slyder is my familiar. I can see through his eyes if I want to," she said, as if such a thing were commonplace.

Alexander's jaw dropped open. He'd never even heard of such a thing. He knew magic could manifest in almost impossible ways and infinite variety but he had a hard time wrapping his mind around such a thing. Then he thought about his own second sight. Most people looked at him with that "prove it" look before they took him seriously, so he decided to give her the benefit of the doubt.

He blinked a couple of times before his surprise transformed into a smile of wonder. "I'm impressed. I'd like to meet Slyder sometime."

Isabel nodded with genuine joy and excitement. She was proud of Slyder and happy for an opportunity to show him off.

Anatoly cleared his throat to gently bring everyone back to the issue at hand. "Is Falls Cave near enough to reach by dark?" he asked.

Erik nodded, "I believe it is. It's certainly big enough and the path in is narrow enough to defend. I like it. If we push, we can be there in an hour."

The path to Falls Cave was much narrower than the forest road. They had to ride single file alongside a stream running through a narrow canyon. The path was old and overgrown but it had been cut well so it was still passable.

The light faded quickly under cover of the thick, evergreen canopy. Soon they were moving through the shadows of the forest by torchlight. It was treacherous and slow but that actually gave Alexander some hope for greater safety through the night. It was entirely possible that the soldiers tracking them would miss their trail in the dark and continue along the road.

The evening gloom of the forest abruptly opened to the darkening sky at the edge of a large forest lake. Stars were just starting to peek through as the sky faded from blue to black.

Erik pointed across the lake to the waterfall on the far side. "This trail leads to the cave behind the falls. We'll camp inside. With any luck we'll have a quiet night."

Almost as if on cue, the gentle sounds of the forest were interrupted by the shrieking howls of the nether wolves off in the distance. It was an otherworldly sound that made every hair Alexander had stand on end. If death could scream, it would sound like that. The forest fell silent.

Chapter 19

The five Rangers looked to Alexander as one.

"I wouldn't count on a quiet night. They'll be here before morning," he said.

Chase muttered, "I've never heard anything like that."

Alexander shook his head, "Neither had I until last night. Erik, lets get into that cave."

The narrow path ran along the edge of the lake, with the water only a few feet below to the left and a stone cliff face reaching more than fifty feet into the sky on the right. The path had been cut into the stone, but the work looked very old. Everyone was silent, their thoughts, no doubt, on the coming threat. The path wound around behind the waterfall and into a cave that extended deep into the face of the cliff.

They dismounted and walked their horses for the last few hundred feet because the path was slick from the spray of the falls and the footing was treacherous. The entrance was a good ten feet high by fifteen feet wide and the trail stopped at the far edge of the cave mouth.

Once inside, the cave opened up considerably. It formed one large round room about fifty feet across and twenty feet high at the top of the natural stone ceiling. Despite the waterfall flowing overhead, the floor was mostly dry. Given the circumstances, it was an ideal place to make camp.

Everyone was tired after such a long day of hard riding. Camp was made quietly and quickly so everyone could get to sleep as soon as possible. Light was kept to a few torches and dinner was cold jerky and some hard biscuits with jam. Alexander was checking on his horse when Isabel approached him in the dark.

"Lord Valentine?"

He turned and saw her with a medium-sized bird on her arm. "Please, call me Alexander. Every time someone says 'Lord Valentine' I look over my shoulder for my father." He could see her smile in the flickering light of the torches.

"Alexander it is. I'd like to introduce Slyder, my hawk." She held her arm up so Alexander could see the grey speckled hawk perched on it. "He likes it when you rub under his chin."

Alexander obliged and the bird leaned into his affections without hesitation. He chuckled. "Slyder looks smaller than most of the hawks I've seen before."

Isabel nodded, "He's a forest hawk. They hunt birds in the trees, so they have to be a bit smaller and more agile. You've probably seen the ones out on the plains. They get much bigger."

"That makes sense," Alexander said while scratching Slyder's chin. "Was Slyder the hawk I saw floating over the watchtower when that wizard started trying to light me on fire?"

"That was him," she answered. "I couldn't tell for sure if you were the one we were looking for, but I could see that the wizard and his men were Reishi so we decided to run them off. I'm glad we did."

"Me, too. I thought he had us for sure," Alexander said as he patted his horse on the neck and headed toward the small campfire. Isabel walked with him, fidgeting nervously with a lock of her long chestnut hair.

"Alexander, do you really think those nether wolves will be able to find us in here?" she asked, motioning to the cave.

He took a deep breath and nodded. "They'll be here before morning and we'll need to be ready or we won't see the sunrise." When he stopped to face her, he expected to see fear in her eyes, but what he saw was resolve and determination with only a hint of nervousness.

"You fought them and survived. What can we do to prepare?" she asked.

He told the Rangers everything he knew about the beasts. He left nothing out. There was no argument or disbelief this time. Everyone had heard the howl at dusk and knew at a visceral level that the creatures that uttered that terrible sound were not of this world. He remembered that they didn't like flame so he asked the Rangers to stack every torch they had next to the small fire. He knew they would have a deadly fight on their hands and it would arrive before dawn, but he took heart in the knowledge that the nether wolves could be destroyed.

Alexander actually slept soundly despite the coming threat. When he lay down, he did so with the knowledge that everything that could be done had been done. He expected his racing mind to keep him awake but he found that place of calm certainty he had discovered during the battle with the nether wolves. He easily set aside all of his worries and did what he knew he must. He slept. Tomorrow would bring new challenges and he needed to be well rested to meet them.

He woke with a start to the sound of howling. The nether wolves had arrived. It was still dark outside, so he couldn't be sure what the hour was. They sounded like they were at the head of the forest lake.

Everyone in the cave sat bolt upright at the sound and immediately began scrambling to prepare for the attack. When Alexander relaxed his vision and let the colors of his companions shine through, he saw a lot of fear but he also saw resolve.

He raced to the mouth of the cave to meet the attack. Wood was thrown on the fire and the torches were lit. In moments the cave was brightly illuminated and cast golden light out onto the back of the waterfall. Under other circumstances, the flickering dance of firelight against the falling water would have been beautiful, but right now Alexander didn't have time to enjoy it.

Using his second sight, he looked out along the trail that skirted the edge of the lake for the telltale aura of darkness that gave away the nether wolves' position.

"They're coming," he said.

Isabel came up alongside him and tossed Slyder into the air. She closed her eyes and tipped her head back slightly. A moment later she inhaled sharply and her eyes snapped open. She gave him a sidelong glance with a fierce little smile as she drew her sword.

"Well, you were right about one thing, Alexander, those are definitely not ordinary wolves."

Anatoly came up beside them a moment before the first nether wolf came into view. It was bounding toward them quickly along the water-slicked path. Its footing didn't falter because its razor-sharp talons gouged into the stone with each step. The three-legged beast behind it moved with less grace but no less speed.

The first nether wolf charged Anatoly low and fast. Alexander and Isabel backed off to give the big man-at-arms room to work with his war axe. He spun out of the way of the attack and brought the spiked pommel of his axe into the shoulder of the beast with tremendous force. The beast staggered sideways toward the ledge and one leg slipped over. It scrambled to keep from falling into the water.

Alexander seized the opening despite the second beast bearing down on him. He stepped forward quickly and kicked the beast in the side of the head, propelling it over the edge and into the water. He heard a snarl followed by a splash.

Anatoly set himself to meet the charge of the second beast. He judged the speed of the monster and swung with all his might in a powerful horizontal stroke but the nether wolf leapt at the last moment and cleared the scything blade of his war axe. The creature sailed through the air toward Alexander. He tried to turn to meet the attack but the beast crashed into him before he could get his sword around. He toppled into Isabel and they both fell to the ground with the three-legged nether wolf on top of them. Its giant head crushed into Alexander's chest. It struggled to get its one good front leg under it so it could rise up and attack. It grunted as it got its footing, sending a burst of deathly cold breath that smelled like the inside of a crypt into Alexander's face. When it reared back to strike, Alexander smashed it in the side of the head with the pommel of his sword just as it lunged forward, sending its gaping jaws snapping into the dirt beside him, narrowly missing his face.

Isabel scrambled backward from under Alexander and drove the point of her sword over his shoulder and into the beast's glowing yellow eye socket before it was able to regain its feet. It flinched back, giving Alexander just enough room to roll away and get to his knees. He came up facing the one-eyed, one-legged beast. It was in a perfect position to lunge at him until Anatoly brought his great axe around in another mighty swing. This time his target was the creature's right hind leg. His stroke was true. The beast toppled to the side, snapping at Alexander as he scrambled backwards to get out of range of its powerful jaws.

He and Isabel both gained their feet in unison. The four other Rangers charged the downed beast with swords drawn. Anatoly struck again, cleaving through the beast where its spine met its hindquarters. The four Rangers brought their swords down across the back of the nether wolf, cleaving it into sections. It came apart under the onslaught and Alexander saw the glow of its one evil yellow eye fade away even as it inched toward him, snarling and snapping.

Everyone stood still in the sudden silence, looking at the fallen beast. It was nothing but dry, black leather and white brittle bones. There was no blood or gore, nothing to prove that the thing had ever been alive.

A moment later, the last of the three beasts reached out of the water and dug its razor-sharp talons into the stone path of the cave entrance. With one mighty heave, it vaulted out of the lake and stood dripping wet and glistening black in the mouth of the cave. Its glowing yellow eyes were the color of hate as it locked onto Alexander and bolted toward him.

Isabel was closest. She brought the point of her sword up and stepped in to engage the giant creature. It slapped her blade aside, lowered its shoulder, and lunged forward into her midsection, sending her sprawling while at the same time putting it into position to strike at Alexander.

He didn't hesitate. He spun when the creature bounced off Isabel and brought his sword around in a whistling backhanded arc. He powered his attack with fury and total commitment, fueled his strike with rage and loss. He caught the beast cleanly across the neck and cleaved its head off in a stroke. The giant wolf head tumbled to the ground. Its eyes went dark and its body collapsed in a heap of bones and leather.

Alexander paused in the sudden, stunned silence for only a moment before rushing to Isabel's side. She was trying to get up and groaning with the effort.

"Lie still. Lucky, bring your bag!" Alexander called out without looking. "You'll be all right, just don't try to move. That thing hit you pretty hard."

"Nonsense," she said through gritted teeth, "I'll be fine."

Alexander smiled. "The fight's over," he said, gently pushing her back down. "Let Lucky take care of you."

She relaxed slightly and winced at the pain. Then Lucky was there, calmly asking her questions about her injuries. Alexander stood and backed off to give the alchemist room to work. Her brothers stood around her, exchanging worried looks.

"Lucky's good at this. She'll be fine," Alexander offered. They didn't look convinced but didn't interfere.

The whole fight had lasted only a few seconds. Alexander looked out the cave entrance and saw that dawn was coming. He knew the Reishi were still out there and had probably heard the baying of the nether wolves. They needed to move soon.

Abigail came up alongside him as he stood looking at Isabel lying on the ground. "You all right?" she asked softly.

He smiled over at her and nodded. "We should move soon. Would you and Jack get the horses ready? I imagine they're pretty spooked right about now."

She gave his hand a squeeze and nodded. "She'll be okay, Alex."

He smiled his thanks for her reassurance.

"Anyone else hurt?" he asked.

The others shook their heads.

"Good. We need to move soon. Let's get camp struck and prepare to ride."

Erik frowned, "I don't think Isabel will be able to ride anytime soon. I'd feel better if we gave her some time to heal." Her other brothers nodded their agreement.

Alexander smiled, "She'll be up and ready to ride sooner than you think, but I understand your concern. We won't move until she says she's ready."

Erik, Kevin, and Duane all snorted in unison. "She'd say she was ready right now, broken ribs and all," Kevin said shaking his head.

Alexander put his hand on the Ranger's shoulder. He was just about Alexander's age but stood a couple of inches taller and weighed probably thirty pounds more. "We won't move until she's ready, Kevin. She just saved my life. I don't want her hurt any more than you do."

Kevin looked Alexander in the eye for a moment before nodding. He leaned in and whispered so Isabel couldn't hear him, "She's our little sister. We're all pretty protective of her."

Alexander smiled and deliberately looked over at Abigail. "I know exactly what you mean."

Half an hour later the camp was struck, breakfast had been made, and the horses were ready. Lucky had given Isabel a draught of his healing potion and she had lapsed into the deep sleep that it brings on while it does its work. After Alexander packed his things and had a bite of breakfast, he went to Isabel's side where Lucky sat waiting for her to wake.

"I'll sit with her, Lucky. Go ahead and gather your things and have some breakfast," he said quietly.

"Don't let her get up too quickly. The potion makes you dizzy for a few minutes after you wake," Lucky said before he got to his feet and ambled off to get a bowl of porridge with nuts and honey. Alexander had been grateful for a warm breakfast after days with nothing but cold biscuits, dried fruit, and jerky.

He sat on his pack next to Isabel and watched her sleep. He studied every line of her strong yet feminine features, the way her hair framed her face, and the gentle curve of her neck. She was beautiful in a way that made his heart race. He found he was smiling gently when she opened her intense green eyes. She looked up at him and smiled back a little sheepishly.

"I guess I let that thing get the best of me," she said as she started to sit up. Alexander gently stopped her with a hand on her shoulder.

"Just lie still for a few minutes. That stuff Lucky gave you can leave you feeling a little unsteady. As for letting that thing get the best of you, nonsense. You bought me the moment I needed. If you hadn't slowed it down, I'd probably be dead right now."

She smiled more broadly, "I think you overstate the part I played, but I'm happy to take any praise I can get."

Alexander felt like he could simply look into her eyes all day long and be perfectly happy.

Erik came up alongside him and knelt down next to his sister. "How you feeling?" he asked.

She took a deep breath, "I'm starving, what's for breakfast?" She sat up with only a slight wince. "Wow, I really expected to be in a lot more pain. You were right about Lucky. He fixed me up good. I'm ready to ride whenever you are. After some breakfast, that is," she added. Erik and Alexander helped her to her feet.

They took a few minutes to help Lucky gather some parts from the nether wolf carcasses. He said the talons, teeth, and even bits of bone might be very valuable ingredients for his potions. Once they'd collected everything he wanted, they threw the rest into the lake.

It was full light when they walked their horses out along the narrow, waterfall-sprayed path that led to the head of the lake and the seldom-used trail that would eventually connect with the road to Glen Morillian.

It was a quiet morning of travel. Alexander rode just behind Erik, who led the way. He'd insisted on the order so he could scan the path ahead with his second sight just to make sure they weren't walking into an ambush. He'd learned the value of an abundance of caution in the last few days and wasn't about to let his guard down now. Phane was serious. Alexander had to be just as serious.

Even with the wariness he felt, he couldn't help marveling at the beauty of the forest. It was ancient and magnificent. The evergreen trees soared into the sky and radiated such rich and beautiful colors that Alexander began to feel a deep sense of connection to the web of life all around him. He tried to soak it in and open himself to the simple goodness of it while at the same time keeping his guard up. He found it was a difficult balancing act but well worth the effort. Through it all he found his mind returning to Isabel.

He was the son of a minor noble and he'd been of age to marry for several years, so he'd had women express interest in him. But he'd never had any real interest in them. He found a few of them attractive enough but none so much that he was willing to give up working his father's ranch and marry.

None of them had any real substance.

They were daughters of other minor nobles who grew up indoors and didn't want to get their fancy clothes dirty. He knew he wanted a wife and family eventually but always figured he would wait a few years. He was still young and he wanted to do more before he settled down and started a family. He recalled his father's advice on the matter: "You'll know it's time when you meet the right woman and she tells you it's time."

As the morning wore on, Alexander was able to put the terror of the past few days behind him and focus on the beauty around him and the possibilities that lay before him. He didn't know what Glen Morillian would bring but he did know it would give him the opportunity to spend some more time with Isabel and for some reason that seemed more important than anything else, even the fact that the most powerful wizard in all of the Seven Isles was trying to kill him. He almost laughed at the absurdity of it.

They stopped for lunch in a little clearing with a freshwater spring bubbling into a shallow pool and running off in a rivulet that flowed into the trees. The grass was green and lush and there were plenty of bright green shoots sprouting up all around. It looked like the little meadow was optimistically trying to get a jump on spring. The place made Alexander smile.

They sat around a campfire enjoying the peaceful setting while Lucky prepared a camp stew. There was something about cooking that always made Lucky light up like a little kid. He was in his element when he had a chance to make a meal for someone. Of course, he enjoyed sharing the meal even more than he enjoyed preparing it.

The horses lazily cropped at the grass while the ten of them talked amongst themselves. Isabel's brothers and Chase sat in a little group and recounted the battle with the nether wolves. They commented on the fact that no one had reported even seeing a creature from the netherworld in nearly two millennia and wondered aloud at the implications. They were young soldiers mentally preparing for the war to come. Anatoly sat quietly sharpening his axe while Lucky worked on the stew. Abigail sat with Jack, listening raptly to one of his stories about an incident at the court of New Ruatha that had her laughing.

Alexander walked with Isabel on the edge of the meadow, talking quietly about their childhoods. By an unspoken agreement, neither of them brought up the coming war or the danger that surrounded them. Instead they spoke of simple things. They compared their experiences growing up. Each had been raised in a different setting, Alexander on a ranch and Isabel in the forest, but they found that they both had similar experiences. Both had very strong ties to family. Both had grown up more outdoors than indoors and both loved life and the world around them. Alexander felt a kind of simple joy in her presence that he never really knew he could feel.

They moved on all too soon and reached the road leading to Glen Morillian by midafternoon. The road was wider and well maintained so they could make better time, but they were still a day and a half away from the safety of the mountain city. And they still had the Reishi to worry about. Alexander renewed his vigilance by frequently scanning the path ahead with his second sight. Even with his caution, it was Isabel who saved them.

Chapter 20

"Erik, stop," she called out. "There's an ambush a mile ahead. Looks like about twenty men and that wizard." She closed her eyes and tilted her head back as she looked through Slyder's eyes. Alexander still marveled at the simple power of such a thing.

"They're lined up on Flat Top Rock with crossbows. Their horses are picketed in the meadow just the other side of the cliff."

To Alexander the description meant nothing but he could see that Erik and the other Rangers knew exactly where she was talking about.

Erik shook his head. "They're in a perfect position. If we try to get through on the road, it'll be a blood bath."

"Is there another way?" Alexander asked.

"Not on horseback," Erik replied. "We could go on foot but it'll take three days from here. Still, that might be our best option."

"What about at night? We could slip by in the dark. They wouldn't be able to see us well enough to hit anything," Chase offered.

Now it was Alexander's turn to shake his head. "That fire wizard can light up the sky like it was daylight. I've seen him do it."

"Is there a vantage point we can attack them from?" Anatoly asked with a look of coiled menace.

Erik shook his head again. "They've definitely picked a good spot for their ambush. Flat Top Rock is the highest ground in the area and the road wraps around it with a drop-off on the other side. If they catch us there, we're as good as dead. Plus, the only way to get up on top of it is from the far side."

"What about through the forest?" Alexander asked. "Is there a way to go around Flat Top Rock through the forest on the side opposite the road?"

Erik nodded. "We could make it on foot but there's no way we could get our horses through there. Once we're on the other side, then what?"

Alexander smiled and looked at Anatoly. "Isabel, can they see their horses from where they are?"

"No," she said shaking her head, "too many trees in the way."

"How many men are guarding their horses?" Alexander asked innocently.

"I only saw two," Isabel answered. "What are you thinking?"

Anatoly regarded Alexander with a hard look. "You wound up with a crossbow bolt in your shoulder the last time you tried this. Are you sure this is a good idea?"

Alexander shrugged. "The sooner we get to Glen Morillian, the better. Who knows what Phane is busy conjuring for us tonight? It's either this or we go the long way."

"What exactly are you talking about?" Isabel asked in a tone that said she meant to have an answer.

Alexander smiled, "We're going to sneak through the woods and steal their horses. We'll be on our way before they know what happened."

Isabel's mouth opened for a moment before she started laughing. "I like it," she said at the same time Chase said, "Are you crazy?"

Erik started laughing as well. "All right, but there's no sense in losing our horses and I don't want the Reishi to find them wandering along the road. Chase, Kevin, and Duane will take our horses back to the meadow we had lunch at and wait for reinforcements. The rest of us will steal the enemy's horses and ride for Glen Morillian."

Jack added, "We have a friend, probably with a wagon, traveling alone and following a few days behind us. If you see him, please give him safe passage. His name is Owen."

Kevin nodded, "We'll keep an eye out for him."

Chase frowned, "Are you sure this is a good idea, Erik? If you get into a fight, you'll need all the help you can get."

Erik nodded to his Second. "Chase, we'll be fine. The whole point is to avoid a fight in the first place. When we reach the fortress gate, we'll send a strike force to clear the woods of the enemy and escort you home. Just keep your guard up and don't engage the Reishi unless you have to."

They dismounted and repacked the things they needed from their saddlebags into their packs, strung the horses together for the three Rangers to lead back to the meadow, and headed off into the woods with Erik in the lead. He moved through the forest with silence and ease. Alexander watched how he placed his feet when he walked and tried to imitate him. He didn't understand why Erik stepped the way he did until he tried it, then he discovered that his footing was quieter and left less evidence of passage. They moved slowly to stay as quiet as possible. The distance that would have taken them less than an hour to cover on horseback took the better part of the afternoon, but they made it to the edge of the meadow on the far side of Flat Top Rock without being noticed.

Isabel reported that the Reishi were still on Flat Top Rock, waiting to spring their ambush, and there were still only two men with the picketed horses. Alexander and Erik unslung their bows. Erik pointed to a place where they could get a good angle on the two bored-looking guards who were sitting at a small cook fire.

They moved quietly into place and took aim side by side. On the count of three, each released an arrow. Both had flawless aim from countless hours of practice reinforced with real world experience. Both of the guards slumped over dead with an arrow through the heart. Alexander relaxed his vision and scanned the meadow. They were alone with the horses. For a moment he thought that it had been too easy, but then he reconsidered. Forewarned is forearmed. Isabel had told them about the enemy. Without her warning, they would have walked into a hail of crossbow bolts and liquid fire. He remembered another of his father's lessons: "Knowing more than your enemy knows usually leads to victory."

Erik whistled like a bird and Alexander heard the birdcall answered from the place in the wood line where the rest of the party was waiting. They emerged and made for the horses.

Quietly and carefully they traveled up the road in the growing darkness. After a mile or so they lit a few torches so they could keep moving in the early night, hoping to put as much distance between themselves and the Reishi as possible. They pressed on until they were confident that they couldn't possibly be followed before stopping for the night.

They had a cold dinner and made camp. Isabel picked a spot near Alexander to lay out her bedroll. She laughed quietly in the darkness as she worked.

"You should have seen the look on that wizard's face when he discovered his horses were gone."

Alexander stopped. "You were watching?" It still amazed him that a person could see through a bird's eyes.

"Of course, I wouldn't miss that for the world. I kept checking back to see when they'd notice. That wizard with the bandage on his arm was furious. He actually lit a tree on fire." She giggled again, delight and mischief all wrapped up together.

Alexander chuckled, "Without your warning, today would have turned out much differently. I still have a hard time imagining how it must feel to see through the eyes of another creature. What's it like?" Alexander asked as he lowered himself down onto his bedroll and lay back to look up at the stars.

"Well, I can see a lot better through Slyder's eyes than I can through my own. He can see farther and clearer than I can even explain. And sometimes it makes me a little dizzy when he's flying and I'm standing still." She lay down on her bedroll and got comfortable.

"Your forest is so beautiful and so filled with life," Alexander said. "Glen Morillian must be a truly magical place."

Isabel paused. When she spoke she lowered her voice to be sure only Alexander would hear her. "It has dangers all its own, Alexander. There is often intrigue, deception and betrayal at court. I fear your arrival will only magnify the webs of lies the courtiers spin. Be careful who you choose to trust."

He rolled on his side but couldn't see her in the dark, so he relaxed his vision and let her colors become visible. He hadn't looked at her with his second sight for more than a moment. Now that he did, he saw her true beauty. Her colors were clear and strong and revealed a quality of character, strength of spirit, and basic goodness that he'd seen in precious few others. And there was absolutely no fear.

He smiled gently into the dark and said, "I choose to trust you." He couldn't see her face but he could see that her aura swelled.

"Good night, Isabel."

"Good night, Alexander."

Morning came quickly. Alexander felt like he'd just gone to sleep when he woke to the first light of day. Isabel was curled up in her bedroll a few feet from him. He opened his eyes and lay quietly watching her sleep. He realized in that moment that he was falling in love with her. Maybe he already had.

Her eyes fluttered open. She saw him looking at her and gave him a smile that was as clear and beautiful as the dawn.

They rode hard all day. The horses they'd stolen were in worse shape than their horses but they still made good time. They had two horses each plus a few extra, so they were able to switch mounts throughout the day. They ate while they rode up mountain switchbacks that wound ever higher toward the fortress gate of Glen Morillian. The air grew thin and cold and they began to see snow packed heavily on the sides of the well-cleared roads. There were no trees growing out of the steep mountainsides. Still the road took them higher, until late in the day, just after dusk, they came to a stone fortress built right into the side of the mountain.

The road opened onto a wide flat platform that was part natural and part cut into the face of the mountain itself. About a hundred feet from the face of the imposing stone fortress was a half ring of stone laid into the ground. It was about seven feet across and encircled the entire fortress from the cliff wall on one side around to the other and there were ancient-looking symbols carved into it. Other than the stone ring, the entire platform looked like an assembly area. It had been cleared of snow and there was evidence of large numbers of horses moving about, mostly along the road.

The fortress was really just a stone wall fifty feet wide and fifty feet tall that protruded four or five feet from the face of the mountain. There were no openings until about twenty feet up where there were three rows of arrow slits placed close together one on top of another. It looked as if they could be manned from three corridors running the width of the fortress wall, one above the next.

Seventy-five archers could fire on the field at once from nearly complete protection. In the center of the fortress wall was a single door that stood fifteen feet tall by twenty feet wide. It was made of stone and was solid and seamless. Otherwise, the fortress wall was simple stone without adornments, banners, or ornaments of any kind.

Erik called out as they approached, "Open the gate." He halted the horses twenty feet from the large stone wall.

Alexander could more feel the vibration of it than hear the huge stone block begin to lower. It was set two feet farther into the mountain than the outer fortress wall and slowly started to sink into the ground. Once it stopped, he saw that the top of the huge stone block now served as the floor of the entryway into the fortress. The gate stone was a good twenty feet thick. No battering ram ever built could have cracked this gate. He began to wonder what had prompted the construction of such an impregnable fortress.

They traveled down a hundred-foot hallway lined with arrow slits on each side and riddled with murder holes in the ceiling. It was a death trap for the uninvited. Alexander had read about fortresses and siege warfare but he'd never seen such a clearly military construction in his whole life. The walls surrounding Southport were a joke compared to this. Even the fortifications of Highlands Reach paled next to the overt military nature of this structure.

The long hallway spilled out into a well-lit courtyard that was built into an enormous cavern inside the mountain. The ceiling reached more than a hundred feet overhead and barracks and stable buildings lined the walls. Suspended from the ceiling by a network of chains were giant oil reservoirs that fed dozens of wicks surrounded by hundreds of carefully placed mirrors each angled to direct the light into the cavern.

He stopped and simply looked around in wonder. Isabel smiled at him and he felt suddenly foolish. His life had been so simple compared to hers. She had grown up surrounded by a kind of splendor that he could only imagine. This place was the stuff of stories. At that thought, he glanced over at Jack who was looking all around in wonder himself, no doubt cataloging everything he saw for later use in a song.

"The fortress gates were constructed during the Reishi War," Isabel offered.

"Gates? You mean there's more than one?" Alexander asked.

"There are five," Isabel answered. "Each one guards an entrance to Glen Morillian. All five were built during the war to protect the valley within from attack by the Reishi. This is probably the most well-defended place in the entire Seven Isles. When we get to the palace, I'll show you my father's map. It's a little model of the whole valley, complete with mountains, rivers, lakes, roads, and buildings. It's really something. I used to sit and stare at it for hours when I was a girl. Come on, the stables are this way."

Alexander followed while trying to take in the austere magnificence of the place. Everything was in order and good repair. There was no ornamentation whatsoever, but that only served to magnify the dimensions of the accomplishment. All along the walls were stairs and walkways and smaller tunnel openings. The place didn't just encompass the cavern and the face of the fortress but stretched out into the mountain itself in a number of different directions.

They were met at the stable by a middle-aged man in a Ranger's uniform.

Erik dismounted and saluted. "Master Gatekeeper, it's good to see you." Erik took his hand. It was clear that they were friends. "May I present Lord Alexander Valentine, the bearer of the Mark of Cedric."

The gatekeeper looked sharply at Erik for confirmation, which he seemed to get from the Ranger's eyes, before he turned to Alexander and bowed formally. "My Lord, we are at your service. You have only to command it and your wish will be done."

Alexander nodded to the man even as a chill raced up his spine.

Erik waited a moment to see if Alexander had any requests before speaking. "My Second and my brothers are at the spring meadow on the old trail to Falls Cave. Between here and there are twenty enemy soldiers accompanied by a wizard."

The gatekeeper nodded. "I will send an adequate force to rout the enemy and collect your brothers and your Second. May I ask how you got past them?"

"Lord Valentine devised a plan to make our way around the enemy unseen and unnoticed and steal their horses. In one stroke we avoided their ambush and left them on foot."

The gatekeeper chuckled, "Well played, My Lord. Now if you'll excuse me I have enemy to attend to. My administrator, Hodge, will see to your needs."

"Thank you, Master Gatekeeper," Alexander said. "One other thing. We have a friend, probably traveling by wagon, headed our way. Please inform your men that he should be given safe passage. His name is Owen."

"It will be done, My Lord." The gatekeeper nodded and left to attend to his duties.

They turned their horses over to the stable hands and followed Hodge to a nearby building that looked more like an inn than anything else. Alexander soon discovered it was temporary lodging for those traveling to and from Glen Morillian. They were each given a room while a small army of servants leapt into action. Hot water was brought to each of their chambers. The servants offered to clean their traveling clothes and provided comfortable robes for the evening if they wished. Once everyone had a chance to clean up and rest for a bit, they were informed that dinner was ready.

They gathered at the large table in the main room of the lodging house. Alexander was glad to see everyone had chosen to take advantage of the comfortable robes that were offered.

When he saw Isabel, his heart skipped a beat. She wore a forest-green robe that clung to her well-toned figure just enough to be alluring without being too revealing. She had loosely tied back her chestnut-brown hair with a golden ribbon that seemed to bring out the sparkle in her eyes. All traces of the tomboy were gone. She was all woman now. Alexander couldn't help but smile.

The food was simple but hot and plentiful. They served a well-seasoned beef roast with potatoes, carrots, and onions along with a heaping tray of freshly baked biscuits. For dessert they served a fruit salad glazed in honey sauce. After days of travel rations, Alexander took the time to savor the meal.

With every course, Lucky stopped the serving girls and asked a whole series of questions about the preparation of the meal until they finally told him they didn't know and went and got the chef. Lucky insisted that he sit down and they talked about food and cooking for an hour while everyone ate.

Conversation stayed light and frivolous. No one wanted to spoil the simple pleasure of a good meal with talk of the dangers ahead. There would be time for that all too soon. Jack regaled them with stories of scandal at the court of New Ruatha that he'd witnessed as a child. Alexander couldn't quite tell where the facts ended and the embellishments began, but he marveled at Jack's seemingly effortless ability to hold everyone in thrall. He clearly reveled in the telling of a good story and was masterful in his delivery. Alexander started to understand the young bard a little better. More importantly, he noticed how Abigail was looking at him. He'd never seen her look at a man like that before. It made him happy to see the unabashed joy that Jack brought her.

Before he wanted it to end, dinner was over and the servants were clearing away the dishes. On cue, both Alexander and Erik yawned, followed only a moment later by everyone else at the table. It had been a long couple of days, so they all retired early to get a good night's sleep.

Chapter 21

Breakfast was served early the next morning. It was a hearty meal of scrambled eggs with chunks of ham and skillet potatoes along with biscuits and jam. The frivolity of the night before was replaced with a somber mood. They would reach the palace of Glen Morillian by evening. Alexander knew that the duties he'd inherited would weigh heavily on him in the days to come. He also knew that there was a very real chance he would not survive the coming war with Prince Phane and the world he'd grown up in would fall into darkness. When he forced himself to look the situation squarely in the eye, he couldn't help but sense madness scratching at the edge of his consciousness.

After a quiet breakfast they walked to the stables. Alexander was surprised to find different horses saddled and ready for them. Their new mounts were healthier and better cared for. The stable master said he wanted to give the horses they'd ridden in on time to recuperate from the long journey. His saddle, weapons, and gear were strapped onto a white saddle horse with a brown splotch on his forehead. Alexander patted the side of his neck as he spoke softly to his new steed and the horse leaned into his affections. He was a magnificent animal, full of spirit and intelligence. Alexander fished around in his saddlebags and produced a carrot. His new mount eagerly took the treat and nuzzled Alexander for more.

They traveled down a long straight tunnel cut through the heart of the mountain. All along the ceiling grew greenish-yellow lichen that emitted an eerie light that illuminated the corridor well enough to ride by. Once his eyes adjusted to it he thought he might even be able to read under the strange glow. They rode at a steady pace for almost an hour before the light of day could be seen at the end of the arrow-straight shaft through the mountain. When they emerged it was midmorning and Alexander got his first glimpse of the Glen Morillian valley.

It was as idyllic a place as he could ever have imagined. The long tunnel through the mountain spilled out onto a high mountain ledge big enough to assemble a battalion. The space had been cut from the granite of the mountain itself. From this altitude, Alexander could see that the entire valley was ringed with an impassable mountain range that acted as a natural defense. The mountains rose sharply from the valley floor below, reaching high into the sky. He could see rolling grasslands, patches of evergreen forest, and crystal blue lakes with mountain streams running between them.

The roadway down from the imposing altitude wound through the foothills after a series of switchbacks cut into the face of the stone mountains. By noon they arrived at the valley floor. It wasn't exactly warm but it was a great deal warmer than it had been at the altitude of the tunnel opening.

Alexander spent the afternoon riding through a dream. The entire valley was dotted with small family farms. The fields were well kept and the herds he saw were healthy and fat. The forests they meandered through boasted giant trees that looked like they were trying to challenge the mountain's claim to the sky. People were friendly and greeted them or waved as they passed.

There was little conversation during the afternoon ride. Erik led the way at a good pace. Not a hard ride but fast enough that it made little sense to try to talk. Occasionally, Abigail would get Alexander's attention and point out some new piece of scenery around a bend or over a hill. She was clearly just as awed by the perfect-looking little valley community as he was.

Then they came out of a little wood and saw the city itself. The outskirts of town consisted of simple cottages and houses all neatly lined up along well-ordered streets. Each house had a yard and a garden plot of its own; most were surrounded by well-kept, sturdy little fences meant more to mark a person's property than to keep people out or animals in. The place looked well maintained, as though everyone took pride in their property. The cobblestone streets were well made and clean.

The squalor Alexander remembered from the streets of Southport was nowhere to be seen. There were no beggars and the people on the streets moved with a purpose as if they had someplace to be or something of value to do. People were friendly enough and a few took an interest in them as they rode through, but Alexander suspected their glances had more to do with Abigail and Isabel than with him.

He rode beside Erik as the Ranger guided them through the streets. He could hear Abigail and Isabel talking to one another while they moved toward the center of town and the palace. Alexander hoped they would become friends. His sister's opinion was important to him and he took her counsel seriously. She was younger, but she often had a way of seeing things in a different light. He rode silently, content to be alone with his thoughts as he took in the industrious little city tucked away in the shelter of the secluded mountain valley.

The true splendor of it all lay in the center of town. There was no wall around the palace, but instead a simple stone walk a good seven feet across that formed an unbroken circle surrounding the entire garden grounds. On one side of the circular walkway, the city was built up with buildings of all sorts lined up against the outer edge. On the other side were carefully manicured gardens stretching to the walls of the single building in the center of the palace grounds: a magnificent white marble castle that looked like it belonged in the stories Alexander's mother had told him when he was a child.

Each corner of the seven-sided fortress formed a circular tower that reached up above the thirty-foot walls into the sky. Four of the towers were capped with conical spires done in gold leaf that caught the sunlight. Each stood a different height and each was topped with a flagstaff flying a colorful pinion. The remaining three outer towers culminated in platforms surrounded by crenellated battlements. From the central building rose another two towers, both with greater girth and height. The taller tower was topped with a broader conical spire also done in gold leaf and flying the flag of Glen Morillian; the second culminated in a sheltered watchtower with an open-air bell. Stone-railed walkways connected several of the taller outer towers with the central towers as well as the main building itself, which stood a good three stories above the outer walls.

The structure looked like a fortress that had never faced a siege. Its white walls were polished and unmarred by violence. Its grounds were sculpted and scrupulously well maintained. Alexander suspected that any attack against Glen Morillian had probably started and ended at the fortress gates high in the mountains.

When they crossed the circular walkway surrounding the palace grounds, Alexander noticed that the smooth, unbroken granite walk was inlaid with ancient-looking symbols in pure burnished silver. Along each edge ran an inlaid band of gold an inch wide. The sheer weight of the precious metals set into the circle surrounding the palace grounds would have been enough to buy a small kingdom. Alexander began to wonder if it served some other purpose than simple decoration. In most cities, the entire guard force would have to be continuously deployed just to keep people from prying out little chunks of gold and silver in the dark of night.

Only moments after they passed over the inlaid circle and entered the palace grounds, the castle bell tolled once, bright and clear. Alexander could hear the echo return from the surrounding mountains in the distance.

The gates to the palace stood open and looked like they hadn't been closed in a very long time. Erik rode through like he lived there but even he was somewhat surprised by what greeted them within.

An entire regiment of Rangers filled either side of the courtyard. Each dressed in identical brown leather armor and woodland green cloaks. Each stood at attention with a long spear, butt end down, at his right side and a sword on his left hip. Down the middle of the courtyard lay a clear path leading to a reception party surrounding an older man and woman, each also dressed in the uniform of the Rangers. The only thing that differentiated the man at the center of it all was the red sash he wore across his chest. Otherwise, his uniform was the same functional leather armor and warm, fur-lined, forest-green cloak that the rest of the Rangers wore.

Alexander again felt that tingle run up his spine. He glanced over his shoulder at Abigail and saw she was worried as well. Erik halted the procession twenty feet short of the reception party and dismounted. Alexander and his companions followed his lead. Once they were on the ground, a number of stable hands seemed to materialize out of the formation and take the reins of their horses. Erik gave Alexander a look that said, "Follow me," then turned and walked to the man in the red sash.

"Father, it is my honor to announce Lord Alexander Valentine, bearer of the Mark of Cedric." His clearly spoken words reverberated into the silence that followed.

Alexander stood stock-still before the big man. He was taller than Alexander and easily forty pounds heavier without any trace of fat. His face was weathered and his sandy blond hair was starting to show a hint of grey. He appraised Alexander for a long moment before stepping forward.

In a low and rumbling but gentle voice that Alexander suspected could fill the entire courtyard, he said, "Lord Alexander, you are welcome in Glen Morillian. May I see the mark?" Alexander puzzled a moment at the title. People had been calling him Lord Valentine, as was the custom for addressing a minor noble. The title Lord Alexander meant something else altogether. The tingle of dread returned.

Alexander got the distinct impression that his host was a man who didn't have time for superfluous nonsense and decided that the big man in the red sash reminded him of Anatoly. Without a word he pulled the collar of his hooded cloak down and revealed the mark burned into the side of his neck. Murmurs rippled through the assembled Rangers.

The man in the red sash stepped forward to look more closely at the intricate pattern burned into the side of Alexander's neck. After a moment of close examination he took a few steps back and held Alexander with his steely blue eyes for just a moment before speaking in a booming voice that did indeed fill the entire courtyard.

"I am Hanlon Alaric, Warden of the Great Forest, Commander of the Rangers and the Keeper of the Royal Bloodline. I am at your service, Your Majesty."

As if the words that tumbled out of the man's mouth weren't enough to freeze Alexander to the spot, what he did next threatened to overwhelm his sanity. Hanlon Alaric, a man with three important titles, went to his knee and bowed to Alexander. In unison, every Ranger in the courtyard followed his lead. A moment later Alexander was looking around almost wildly to find that everyone in the whole place was on bended knee offering their fealty to him. His heart caught in his throat when he saw that Erik, Isabel, and even Anatoly were bowing as well. Jack had even gone to his knee. The only people who remained standing were Lucky, who was looking around with a big stupid grin on his face and Abigail, who gave Alexander a look that meant she thought he was in big trouble.

The look on her face mirrored his feelings. He was just a glorified ranch hand. If these people knew who he really was they would probably toss him in a dungeon for his presumption alone. A moment later he realized with a growing sense of alarm that everyone was still on bended knee. He tried to speak but nothing came out.

He deliberately cleared his throat before speaking. "Rise," was all he could get out.

The situation was teetering on the edge of madness. Warden Alaric stood, followed a moment later by all of the Rangers with a precision that only comes from long-practiced discipline. He glanced over at Anatoly for an explanation and got only a shrug that said, "I'll tell you later." He also saw that Isabel was looking at him a bit differently.

He extended his hand to Hanlon as he found his voice, "Your sons and your daughter saved my life. I am in your debt."

Hanlon smiled with pride as he took Alexander's hand. His grip was firm and honest.

Alexander let his vision slip out of focus and saw that Hanlon Alaric was a man of courage, strength, and fierce loyalty. Alexander decided that he liked him. In the back of his mind he noted that Hanlon Alaric was also Isabel's father.

Hanlon turned to Erik and Isabel with a smile. "You've done well." He held each of them in turn for a moment with a look of fatherly approval.

It reminded Alexander of the way a look from his father could make his heart swell with pride. Then Hanlon stepped past his children and regarded Anatoly for a moment with a stern look that broke into a boyish grin. He and the big man-at-arms clasped arms in greeting.

"It has been far too long, my old friend. It seems like only yesterday when you and Duncan and I were riding together in the border wars."

Anatoly embraced the Forest Warden. "Only yesterday indeed, the mountain air has been kind to you," he said as he stepped back to look at Hanlon. "You don't look a day over fifty," he said with a mischievous grin that Alexander had seldom seen.

Hanlon scowled at the good-natured jibe. "So where is Duncan, anyway?"

The question brought the seriousness back to Anatoly's face in an instant. "We have much to discuss," was all he offered in answer.

Hanlon seemed to pull the mantle of authority back around him like a cloak against the cold of loss and nodded solemnly.

He turned to Alexander. "Please, Your Majesty, come inside. As Anatoly has said, we have much to discuss."

Alexander nodded stiffly. His head was reeling. His grief for his brother and worry over his parents was now fresh in his mind from Hanlon's question. Alexander wanted some answers and he meant to have them tonight.

"We certainly do," he said, motioning for Hanlon to lead the way.

The inside of the palace was warm and well appointed with simple yet elegant furnishings. The broad marble hall they entered through was lined with a long, dark-green carpet that covered only the middle of the hall and left the polished stone floor bare for a few feet on either side. Lighting was provided by mirrored oil lamps hanging from brass sconces at even intervals along the walls. Fine tapestries and paintings of natural settings occupied the spaces between the lamps. It almost gave the feeling that one was walking outside through a collage of the most beautiful scenery Glen Morillian had to offer.

Hanlon led Alexander and his companions through the maze of the palace. The rest of the reception party followed behind whispering amongst themselves. Alexander started to wonder about those people. He assumed that the middle-aged woman in the Ranger's uniform was Hanlon's wife. A few of the others were also dressed as Rangers but others were in robes or more fancy and expensive attire. Some looked like nobles or courtiers while others were perhaps advisors.

Alexander hadn't taken the time to examine them with his second sight, but in the light of Isabel's warning, he intended to do so. He felt decidedly out of his element. This was a place where things may not be as they seemed and danger could present itself in ways not easily defended against. He resolved to keep his guard up and to offer his trust only to those who had earned it. What he needed more than anything was answers. He had so many questions but was afraid that in asking his questions he would reveal weakness or vulnerability to those who might wish him harm. He needed to get Hanlon and Anatoly alone where they could have some privacy but he suspected that might not be an easy task given the intense interest his arrival had stirred up. There was so much he didn't know, so much he didn't understand, and so many expectations behind the many eyes that watched him now.

Alexander had always been more comfortable out on the range herding cattle or directing one of his father's harvest crews. He was simple at heart. He valued candid and blunt speech but feared he would not find it here, at least not in open court.

Hanlon led the procession into a big room with a long rectangular table set in the center. Comfortable-looking, ornately carved oak chairs ringed the table and lined the two long walls. High overhead, the arched ceiling was made almost entirely of fine crystal glass that allowed ample light into the room during daylight. Finely crafted oil lamps hung in a row several feet over the center of the long table and lined the walls in evenly spaced sconces. The floor was carpeted in a rich red that gave the room an air of authority. It was clear that this was where important matters were discussed and disputes resolved. This was the heart of the court.

Everyone filed in and several of the reception party wearing finery and jewels casually took seats at the table as if they belonged there. Alexander was at a loss. He didn't know where to sit or what was really happening until Hanlon went to the head of the table and motioned to Alexander.

"Please, Your Majesty, I would have you sit at the head of my table."

Alexander nodded his thanks as he took the richly adorned chair carved with images of every sort of woodland creature imaginable. Hanlon took the seat to his immediate right and the woman who stood with him in the reception party took the chair to Alexander's left. A Ranger or a person dressed in finery occupied every other seat at the table. Isabel directed Alexander's companions to seats along the wall on his right and both she and Erik took seats with them.

His sense of alarm was beginning to rise. He couldn't imagine what these people expected of him. This was entirely out of the realm of his experience. He felt like a fish out of water and was terrified that he would wind up flopping around helplessly in the eyes of these people that he'd traveled so far to seek shelter from.

What's more, Hanlon had called him "Your Majesty" at least twice. The first time Alexander's mind had been in a daze and he'd scarcely heard him but the second time there was no mistaking it. On top of that, he'd also addressed him as Lord Alexander. By custom, only kings were addressed by first name. And now, the Forest Warden and Commander of the Rangers had seated him at the head of his council table with a room full of nobles and courtiers who were all looking at him like they expected something.

As everyone got settled into their seats, Alexander let his vision slip out of focus and took in the colors of those around the table. The colors surrounding the Rangers were clear and bright for the most part and he judged them to be honorable servants of the Forest Warden.

The nobles and courtiers were something else altogether. Their colors were muddy and base with the quality of color that Alexander had come to understand indicated guile and dishonesty. He was beginning to feel a growing sense of alarm when his gaze fell on the man sitting to Hanlon's right. He was dressed in simple charcoal-grey robes with a thin hem of dark green embroidered with intricate black filigree. Alexander saw in an instant that he was a wizard. He was looking back at Alexander with intense interest, almost as if he could sense what Alexander was doing. Alexander refocused his vision when the room fell silent as Hanlon stood to speak.

Chapter 22

"Two thousand years ago, after the Reishi were defeated, Prince Phane fled from those loyal to the Old Law and, with the aid of his dark magic, retreated into the future. The Old Rebel Mage, Barnabas Cedric, saw the danger and made preparations so that we would have a chance of withstanding the darkness Phane would bring to our world. You are all aware of the message delivered into your minds by the magic circle placed around Phane's obelisk. Mage Cedric's first preparation for our survival succeeded. He warned us of the danger. His second preparation is more complex." Hanlon stopped for a moment to be sure he had everyone's undivided attention.

When he was satisfied, he continued, "He secreted away the last surviving heir to the throne of Ruatha and created an order of soldiers to protect that Royal Bloodline until the time came for that line to reclaim its rightful place as the rulers of Ruatha. You are all aware of the title I bear, the Keeper of the Royal Bloodline, but few of you truly understand the significance of that duty. For two thousand years, the Keepers of the Royal Bloodline have preserved and protected the line of the Ruathan Kings in anticipation of this day. Only a handful of Rangers are aware of the true purpose of our order and all who know have been forbidden from speaking of it until I fulfill my duty and name the heir to the throne."

Alexander felt that now all-too-familiar icy chill race up his spine when Hanlon looked his way.

The Forest Warden held out his open hand toward Alexander. "I give you Lord Alexander, your rightful King and Master of Ruatha."

Alexander could hear nothing but the pounding of his heart in the silence that followed. He tried unsuccessfully to school his growing panic. He glanced to Abigail and saw in her wide blue eyes a reflection of his dismay. When he looked to Anatoly, the look he got back was the one that said, "Pay attention." The old man-at-arms had known all along.

Alexander was floundering. He knew he needed to keep his composure or risk undoing the authority that had just been heaped upon him. At an instinctive level he understood that a ruler did not survive long after he abdicated his power. He knew without doubt that his survival and that of his sister depended very much on his actions in this moment. If he showed weakness, the vultures would begin circling. Phane would no doubt make offers of power and wealth in exchange for Alexander's death, and many of the nobles at the table would likely be more than happy to strike such bargains.

With a sheer act of will, Alexander wrested control of his emotions and shoved them aside before he stood to address the court. The assembled nobles each watched with keen interest. Alexander felt like a bug in a jar.

"Lords and ladies, thank you for your warm welcome. The threat we face is grave. In the coming months and years all will be called upon to sacrifice for the cause of defending the Old Law. If we fail, our children will know only darkness under the tyranny of Prince Phane." Alexander scanned the room to see how his words were being received. He saw that the Rangers were taking him seriously but the nobles and courtiers clearly didn't like the notion that they would be required to make sacrifices.

"Over the coming days and weeks I will call on many of you for your counsel. We face an enemy the likes of which has not walked the Seven Isles in two thousand years. I hope I can count on all of you in this fight." He made a point of deliberately scanning the room with his second sight before sitting down. The moment he sat, three nobles tried to stand at once.

The first to his feet looked toward the other two to yield the floor, which they did. Alexander could see the unspoken words pass between them with the furtive looks they gave each other. Now he began to feel more like a lost child who'd wandered into a den of lions than a bug in a jar.

The noble who retained the floor was a short man with a pinched face, a slight build, and wavy shoulder-length hair the color of a carrot. He had delicate hands with painted fingernails and wore several jeweled gold rings. His clothing was spun of fine silks and embroidered with gold and silver thread. He looked ridiculous to Alexander but clearly fit right in with the other nobles and courtiers.

"Your Majesty," he began with just the slightest hint of sarcasm, "I wonder if I may see the Thinblade?" His request was made with the utmost innocence as if he were a child in awe of some new discovery.

Alexander was at a loss. He didn't have the Thinblade. He'd never even heard of the Thinblade before the ghost of Nicolai Atherton told him to find it. And worse, Lucky had told him that most of the seven Thinblades were lost at the end of the Reishi War. Before Alexander could attempt an answer, Hanlon interjected.

"Truss, you know full well that the Thinblade was lost when the House of Ruatha fell." Hanlon was clearly agitated by the man. Alexander decided he liked the Forest Warden even more.

The overdressed noble reacted with feigned innocence. "Warden Alaric, I only hoped that our young new king would have the Thinblade, which as we all know is the only true badge of an Island King, so that he might easily bring the other Ruathan territories in line. Without it, I fear that many of the noble houses of Ruatha will not swear fealty to him and his vital cause."

He bowed with mock humility before continuing. "If he could produce the Thinblade, this council would, of course, bow to his authority without hesitation. However, since the Thinblade is, as you said, lost, we must deliberate before accepting the rule of this young man simply on the strength of a mark on his neck."

He looked almost embarrassed, as if he was saying something he didn't want to have to say. "I hope you understand, Your Majesty, Glen Morillian is ruled by a council of nobles and we cannot, under our law, simply bow in fealty to you without a deliberation and a vote." He smiled sheepishly, then added hastily. "Of course, you can count on my support in this matter ... Your Majesty." The last was spoken just as he sat down.

Alexander could see out of the corner of his eye the anger growing on Hanlon's face and he could also see the look of satisfaction on the faces of many of the nobles seated around the table. It was apparent that these men were accustomed to backroom dealing, subterfuge, and treachery. He could also see that they each had significant egos. As much as he wanted to speak his mind to the little man, he didn't yet know enough about the circumstances to allow his emotions to rule him. He remembered in a flash the crossbow bolt in his shoulder. He'd gotten that wound because he allowed emotion to cloud his reason and obstruct his view of the battlefield. He heard one of his father's admonitions in the back of his mind: "Be driven by emotion but ruled by reason."

Without allowing even a hint of anger into his voice, Alexander spoke without standing. "And your name is?" he asked with just a hint of disdain.

He held the little man with his gold-flecked eyes until he stood, seeming somewhat less certain of himself. He replied, "I am Rexius Truss, at your service." The little man bowed slightly.

"Very good, Master Truss, I will count on your pledge of support in this matter."

Again Alexander locked eyes with the little man. The gold flecks in his eyes glittered with anger. The little noble looked a bit unsettled but he still attempted to smile while taking his seat. It was exactly the effect Alexander had been hoping for. He knew how unsettling his eyes could be when he got angry. The gold flecks in his copper-brown irises tended to glitter just like his father's. He'd seen his father look at him in that way a time or two and it always made him want to be somewhere else. After Truss took his seat, Alexander scanned the room and caught just out of the corner of his eye the twin looks of mischievous satisfaction worn by both Abigail and Isabel.

The looks worn by the other nobles were more cautious and less bold than just a moment before. Alexander decided that in putting them back on their heels, he'd scored a small victory. It was enough for now.

"Warden Alaric, we've had a long and arduous journey. Perhaps we should adjourn this council for today and reconvene at a later time," Alexander suggested.

Hanlon gave him a satisfied little grin before standing. "This council is adjourned," he pronounced offhandedly. He clearly had little patience for the nobles seated around the table.

The meeting broke up with groups of two and three nobles going off in different directions while talking quietly amongst themselves. All except Rexius Truss. Alexander expected the overdressed little man to accost him but he didn't seem interested in Alexander at all. Instead he headed straight for Isabel. Alexander made sure he was within earshot when Truss took hold of Isabel's arm and turned her toward him as if she were a possession.

"I trust you've had ample time to consider my proposal." He smiled his fake little smile.

Isabel gently but firmly pulled her arm away from him. "Duke Truss, I have considered and reconsidered and the answer is still no. Now if you will excuse me..."

Truss interrupted her, "You simply must reconsider. As you well know, my house is the wealthiest in the entire valley. Our union would strengthen both of our families and unite Glen Morillian for the coming struggle. If not for me, please accept my offer for the sake of our land and our people." He reached out and took her by the elbow again.

Alexander walked up behind him and interrupted as if he hadn't heard a word of their conversation. "I believe you promised me a tour of the palace, Lady Alaric," he said with as much innocence as he could manage.

Just a flicker of confusion flashed across her face before she seized the lifeline he'd thrown her. "Of course, Your Majesty. Please excuse us, Duke Truss." She pulled her arm away and took Alexander's arm instead as they quickly left the room.

Once out the door and into the hall, Alexander leaned in and whispered, "Please get me away from all these people."

She chuckled softly and led him down the hall. When they turned into a side corridor, Alexander noticed Truss watching them with a look of smoldering anger that he tried without success to hide. Alexander decided he didn't like Rexius Truss.

Isabel led him through a confusing maze of corridors, hallways, and rooms until they came to a landing on a spiral stairway leading both up and down. Alexander guessed they must have been in one of the main towers rising up out of the center of the castle, but he didn't have time to ask because Isabel hadn't slowed down since they had turned the corner from the main hall.

The stairs wound up ever higher. Alexander felt his lungs burning. He raced to keep up with Isabel's long strides as she bounded up the stairs. There were landings every so often and a few doors leading out of the sides of the tower that Alexander presumed led to the open-air bridges he'd seen spanning the distance between several of the towers. Finally, the stairs ended at the top of the bell tower. It was an open-air platform with six pillars in a ring around the outside edge holding up a stout-looking roof with a heavy crossbeam that supported a giant brass bell. The rocker arm that was attached to the crossbeam had a heavy rope trailing down through a small hole in the floor.

Isabel walked in a circle, hands on her hips, around the bell while she caught her breath. Alexander just stopped and put his hands on his knees and breathed deeply. When he stood up, she was looking at him and smiling broadly.

"Thanks for the rescue," he said. "I think I was more at ease fighting those nether wolves than I was in that room full of nobles."

Isabel laughed, "I thought you handled yourself nicely. I especially liked the way you put Truss in his place. And besides, I should be thanking you for saving me. He would have hounded me until I went and hid in my room."

Alexander looked down for a moment trying to find a delicate way of asking the question that was burning through his mind. In the end, he decided to just be himself, blunt and to the point. "You aren't really going to marry that guy, are you?"

She smiled again and sat down on one of the benches lining the outside of the tower. "No, at least not if I have anything to say about it," she said.

Alexander sat next to her. "Why wouldn't you have a say in the matter? It's your life."

She looked up with a shrug. "The politics of court are complicated. Truss asked my father for permission to court me. My father is the head of the council but he only has one vote so he needs the support of the nobles to govern Glen Morillian. He gave Truss permission but told me it was entirely my decision. That was a year ago. I think my parents are becoming impatient. I'm expected to marry.

It's my duty." She heaved a sigh before continuing.

"There are a number of men from various noble families who have asked for my hand but I've put them all off. I don't want to marry any of them. They're all spoiled and soft. Besides, I want to ride patrol with my brothers. I want to see the world." She stopped when she saw Alexander looking at her. "Probably sounds stupid after all you've been through."

He shook his head, "Not at all. My father always told me to follow my heart. He's a wise man and I think that may be the best advice he's ever given me."

Isabel smiled at that. "What about you? Do you have someone special back home?"

Alexander shook his head slowly. "No, not back home." She didn't catch his meaning.

The sky was getting dark. The sun had long since fallen past the ring of mountains and the stars were just starting to shine through. It was a beautiful night. He decided to change the subject.

"I see what you mean about not trusting anyone. That council meeting felt more like a nest of vipers." Alexander took a deep breath, "Isabel, I didn't know until your father announced it that I was the heir to the Ruathan Crown. This is all happening so fast I feel like I'm struggling to keep my head above water."

"But how could that be?" she said. "My father said you've been trained your whole life for this."

Alexander shook his head, "Maybe Darius was trained for this, but I wasn't. I didn't know about any of this until two weeks ago." The memory of his brother's murder ghosted across his face.

"I don't understand? Who's Darius?" Isabel seemed slightly alarmed at the revelation.

"He was my big brother. He was murdered by the Reishi two weeks ago." Alexander couldn't help the tears that filled his eyes. He hadn't allowed himself to mourn his brother properly and it was starting to eat away at him.

Isabel covered her mouth with her hand as she stared at him with wide eyes, shaking her head quickly from side to side in denial while reaching out to take his hand. Her eyes filled with tears that spilled out and tumbled down her cheeks when she blinked.

"Oh, Alexander, I'm so sorry. I can't imagine the pain you must have bottled up inside you. If one of my brothers were killed I'd curl up into a ball and cry for a month."

Her simple human understanding and sympathy was all it took to undo Alexander's carefully constructed bulwark of emotional control. He sobbed once into the growing darkness. He tried to draw it back in, to regain control. When Isabel took his head, drew it to her shoulder, and gently put her arms around him, that was all it took. He broke down and cried for the loss of his big brother. The pain welled up in him like a torrent, and he let it. He didn't try to stop the flow of anguish. He cried unabashedly on her shoulder for several minutes until he felt like a great weight had been lifted. His sense of inner calm felt like it was restored as he released his grief.

When he looked up into Isabel's eyes in the growing moonlight, he could see the streamers of tears glistening down her cheeks. He sniffed, trying to regain his composure and smiled at her almost sheepishly. "Some king I turned out to be, huh?"

At that she forcefully took him by the shoulders and held him out at arm's length so she could look him directly in the eye. "Any man who would not cry for the loss of his brother is not worthy of being called a king." Her piercing green eyes glistened with tears and intensity.

He smiled gently, "That sounds like something my mother would say. She would like you." He sniffed again and took a deep breath to clear his head. "Thank you, Isabel. I didn't realize how much I needed that. Since the day he died I've been running for my life. I've kept everything all bottled up inside. I feel much better now."

She wiped the tears from her face and stood, turning to face the city below. "We should get back. My parents will be expecting us at dinner soon."

Almost on cue, Erik called out from below, "Isabel, are you up there?"

She smiled at Alexander as if to say, "I told you so" and called down to her brother, "We're on our way down."

She led him through another maze of corridors, passageways, and rooms until they reached the Alaric family dining hall. Just before they entered, Isabel stopped and took a good look at Alexander. She gently wiped a single tear from his chin and nodded her approval before opening the door.

Chapter 23

Everyone was there and already seated around the table. Erik had just arrived a few moments before them. Hanlon and Emily Alaric sat to either side of the empty chair at the head of the table. Lucky, Abigail, Jack, and Anatoly all sat around the table looking at Alexander when he entered. The only person he wasn't sure of was the wizard in the charcoal-grey robes.

"I was just giving Lord Alexander a tour of the palace," Isabel said with perfect innocence. Abigail gave him a look. He knew she would have questions later.

Not a moment after he took his seat, the servants started bringing platters of food to the table. It was a simple and wholesome meal of roasted venison with potatoes, carrots and onions served with thick, flavorful gravy, a green salad, and fresh bread still hot from the oven with plenty of rich yellow butter. Alexander realized the moment he smelled the roasted venison that he was starving.

Apparently, everyone else was hungry as well because the meal was enjoyed in near silence except for the occasional request for more gravy or another slice of bread. When the meal was done, Alexander sat back and took a deep breath.

"Thank you, Lady Alaric, for this meal and for your hospitality. For the first time in two weeks I almost feel safe."

Emily Alaric frowned slightly, "Almost?" she questioned. "You have nothing to fear in my home."

Alexander smiled a small smile, "Those nobles have to be around here somewhere."

Hanlon and Anatoly looked at each other and laughed out loud. "Your Majesty," Hanlon started to say when Alexander raised his hand and cut him off.

"Hanlon, please call me Alexander."

The Forest Warden shared a brief look across the table with Anatoly and nodded his agreement. "If you wish, but only in private. In public, your authority must not be questioned. The nobles don't like your presence. They're happy with the way things are and feel threatened by the change that you represent. It's vital that you be recognized as the King of Ruatha if we're to have any chance against Phane."

"Agreed," Alexander said, then turned to the wizard. "I know everyone at this table except you, Wizard. Please introduce yourself." Alexander decided that this was the time to get his questions answered.

"I am Master Wizard Mason Kallentera, Chief Counsel to Warden Alaric and I am at your service, Lord Alexander."

"Very good, I have a number of questions. First, Anatoly, how long have you known that my bloodline is the true Ruathan line?" There was a slight edge to Alexander's voice that brought everyone into focus. What had, a moment before, been a fine meal was now a King's council.

"I've known your entire life and longer," he answered the question without hesitation and held Alexander's gaze as he did.

"Why was I not told of this sooner?" Alexander tried to keep his building anger out of his voice.

"I took an oath to keep that knowledge secret until such time as the Keeper of the Royal Bloodline named the heir, plus your father forbade it," Anatoly answered openly. "He said he wanted you to grow up without the weight of the world and the burden of such terrible responsibility resting on your shoulders. He felt that there would be plenty of time once you'd grown into a man to reveal the truth to you." Anatoly hesitated a moment before continuing. "Also, this responsibility was never supposed to be yours." He looked down for a moment to wrestle with his own grief at the loss of Darius.

Alexander glanced at his sister and saw she was struggling to maintain her composure so he decided to change the subject. He knew she hadn't yet taken the time to grieve and he knew from recent experience how much weight that placed on her heart.

"Who is Nicolai Atherton?" he asked no one in particular.

This time it was Hanlon and Wizard Kallentera who shared a look.

It was the wizard who spoke. "If I may, Nicolai Atherton was Barnabas Cedric's first apprentice. He was an arch mage of great power in his own right and the person who succeeded in killing Sovereign Malachi Reishi, although at great cost to himself. May I enquire about the source of your interest in Mage Atherton?"

Alexander nodded and answered offhandedly, "His ghost is haunting me."

The table fell silent. All eyes were on Alexander but it was Wizard Kallentera who spoke first. "Are you certain?"

"Quite certain," Alexander said, nodding. "The first time he came to me was the night Darius died, the night this mark was burned into my neck. He appeared right in front of me while I was standing on the tower of Valentine Manor. I was so startled that I stumbled backward and nearly fell over the wall. He grabbed me and pulled me back. The next time was early the next morning. He appeared in my room just after I woke. He told me that I was in danger and that I must find the Thinblade. The third time he appeared in our camp the night after we left Southport and warned us that Phane had summoned nether wolves to kill me."

Abigail spoke into the deadly silence that followed. "I saw the ghost at camp outside Southport. If he hadn't warned us about the nether wolves, we would have been caught out in the open by the beasts. His warning saved us."

Lucky, Anatoly, and Jack nodded their agreement.

Wizard Kallentera started to ask another question, but Alexander cut him off. "How did Mage Atherton die?"

Wizard Kallentera took a deep breath and began. "Mage Atherton captured a book of necromancy spells during an attack on one of the Reishi strongholds. Within, he found a spell to summon a creature from the netherworld called a shade. A shade is a creature of surpassing power. It has no physical form in this world but instead appears as a shadow in the air. It can possess a person and use his body for as long as he remains alive, then move on to possess another. It can also move into the aether, and that is the power that Nicolai Atherton summoned the shade for."

Alexander interrupted, "What's the aether?"

"It's the plane of spirit. It's the place your soul goes when you die, before you move on to the light or the darkness. It exists in the same space as our world but it has no substance. The aether is the place where ghosts live." He let this last statement settle in before he continued.

"It was said that some few, very rare wizards, could send their minds into the aether. If such a thing is possible, none alive today can do so. What the shade could do was much more dangerous. It could take a person's physical body into the aether and that is why Mage Atherton cast the spell he found. He knew that if Malachi Reishi died, the Sovereign Stone would remain. Prince Phane would claim it and the war would rage on."

Alexander raised his hand and interrupted him again. "What's the Sovereign Stone?"

"The Sovereign Stone is the source of Reishi power. It's a blood-red corundum of unusual size suspended from a gold chain. It was created by the first Reishi Sovereign and served as the badge of the Sovereign of the Seven Isles for nearly two thousand years. The full extent of its power is unclear but the one thing that is known is that it contains the life memories and personalities of the previous Reishi Sovereigns. Using the Stone, the current Reishi Sovereign can confer with his ancestors.

"The power of such a thing is enormous. All of the magical knowledge coupled with all of the political secrets known by all of the previous Reishi Sovereigns was available to the current holder of the Sovereign Stone. As long as the Stone was in this world and a Reishi still lived, the world was in jeopardy. That's why Mage Atherton took such a dangerous and desperate chance. He summoned a shade to push Malachi Reishi physically into the aether, Sovereign Stone and all.

"What he didn't count on was the malice of the shade, and not being trained in necromancy, he failed to understand the nuances of the spell. He paid with his life for that failure. The shade possessed him and used his body to mount the attack against Malachi Reishi. Nicolai Atherton, possessed by the shade, seized Malachi Reishi and shifted them both into the aether. A physical body cannot survive for more than a few seconds in the cold and airless aether. Once the shade had done as it was summoned to do, it went back to the netherworld and left the souls of Malachi Reishi and Nicolai Atherton trapped forever between the world of life and the afterlife. His desperate actions ultimately won the war but at great personal cost. As long as his body remains in the aether his soul cannot pass into the light."

Alexander sat quietly and stared at the table for a moment, deep in thought. Such desperate choices had been made to end the Reishi War. Such terrible powers had been brought to bear. He had no magic to compete with the things that Phane could do. He started to wonder again what he could really do to live up to this impossible inheritance. He'd barely survived the trip to Glen Morillian and he hadn't even considered his next step. Ultimately, he would have to assemble an army under the banner of the House of Ruatha, but he wasn't even sure he could convince the minor nobles of Glen Morillian to follow him, let alone bring the ruling houses of the various Ruathan territories under his command.

"Where's the Thinblade?" he asked without looking up.

Wizard Kallentera started to answer, "It was lost…" when Hanlon interrupted him.

"I believe that it may be in the catacombs of this fortress."

All eyes were now on Hanlon Alaric. He cleared his throat and marshaled his thoughts before starting to explain in his deep and rumbling voice. "Glen Morillian was built by Barnabas Cedric, known to those outside of this valley as the Rebel Mage, to be the home of the Rangers. The Rangers were created to give cover and strength to the Keepers of the Royal Bloodline. One of the secrets entrusted to the Keeper is a vault hidden deep in the catacombs beneath this palace. It can be opened only by the Bearer of the Mark. I do not know what's inside that vault but I have often wondered if the Thinblade was thought to be lost because Mage Cedric had hidden it away for your arrival."

Even Emily was surprised. Clearly Hanlon had taken his oath of secrecy seriously.

Alexander stood. "Let's go have a look."

Hanlon motioned for him to sit. "It's late and we still have much to discuss. Anatoly told us how your home was attacked. Your father was a good friend of mine. I rode with him in the border wars and he saved my life on more than one occasion even though it was my sworn duty to protect him. I've dispatched a platoon of Rangers to ride to Valentine Manor in search of your parents. We believe that they would be on their way here if they survived the attack and I for one choose to believe that they did. Don't give up hope, Alexander. With any luck your parents will be here within a few weeks."

Alexander nodded, "Thank you, Hanlon. I believe they survived the attack as well. I hope to see them soon." He shared a heartfelt look of hope with his sister.

Wizard Kallentera leaned forward to ask another question, "How did you elude the nether wolves? Such creatures have not walked the Seven Isles since the Reishi War. They're said to be relentless hunters and supremely deadly in a fight."

"We didn't elude them, we killed them," Alexander said.

The wizard blinked. "Are you certain? They're said to fade into the ground with the coming of dawn only to rise again at dusk."

"Oh, that part's true," Alexander said. "But I'm also sure that all three are dead."

Erik leaned in and spoke next. "One died from a combined attack by Anatoly, Isabel, my brothers, Alexander, and me. The other was killed by Alexander with a little help from Isabel."

Alexander nodded, "The one I killed would have had me if Isabel hadn't stepped in front of its charge. She bought me the moment I needed to strike and it cost her a couple of broken ribs in the bargain."

Emily Alaric shot her only daughter a worried look. Hanlon and Erik smiled with pride. Isabel looked almost embarrassed to be the sudden focus of everyone's attention. "I'm all right, Mom," she said before Emily could get up to go check on her daughter. "Lucky fixed me up in no time. My ribs are good as new." She patted herself on the spot where she'd been hit to prove it.

"That's only two nether wolves," Wizard Kallentera said. "What of the third?" Alexander was starting to gather that Wizard Mason Kallentera was quite detail oriented.

"Anatoly just about cleaved one of the thing's hindquarters off. When it lashed out at him, I took its head off. Its bones are still on top of the gatehouse on the old plateau guard tower at the south edge of the forest."

Alexander was starting to get tired. He'd gotten most of his immediate questions answered and he needed time to think about what he'd learned.

"Wizard Kallentera, at some point I'd like to sit down with you and Lucky and have a long talk about magic, but not tonight." Alexander rubbed his eyes and tried unsuccessfully to stifle a yawn.

Mason Kallentera mused, "I suspected as much when you read my aura at the council table. I must say, I'm impressed. I've never met one who could cast such a spell without so much as a word."

All the fatigue that Alexander was feeling faded away in a rush. He stared at Wizard Kallentera for a moment, trying to decide what to ask first. "How did you know I was looking at your colors?" Alexander leaned forward, now completely alert and attentive. He'd had the ability to see colors since he was thirteen, but he never really thought of it as a spell. It was just something he could do. He'd always had questions about it.

Mason Kallentera smiled knowingly. "I've been a master wizard for many years. I have a number of spells that allow me to see magic being used around me and I make a habit of casting those spells every morning before I leave my chambers."

"You said that I cast a spell but I didn't," Alexander said. "I can just see colors when I relax my visual focus. I've been able to do it since I was thirteen. Are you saying that others can do the same thing with a spell?"

"Of course. I have such a spell, as do many other wizards," Mason explained. "It's a relatively basic, though very useful, spell. Typically, a novice wizard will learn this kind of magic before moving on to spells of more complexity and greater power. Normally, casting such a spell requires a set of exercises or incantations that take a minute or so of preparation. You say you were never taught this as a spell but that it just manifested as a natural ability when you were thirteen?"

Alexander nodded.

"That is somewhat troubling, but also very interesting. I've never heard of such a thing. If I may ask, do you have any other such abilities?"

"No, nothing," Alexander said. "I've always wondered about it. My parents just told me it was a gift, and it has been. It's saved my life on a number of occasions."

"Hanlon tells me your parents have both survived the mana fast. Have they taught you any spells?" Mason asked.

"No, they always told me I would have to attempt the mana fast before I could use magic and neither of them seemed too eager for me to choose that path."

Wizard Kallentera folded his hands carefully on the table. He spoke very deliberately. "Alexander, you are already a natural sorcerer. Your ability to read a living aura is proof of that fact. With training you could very likely master other magic. If you attempted the mana fast and survived, you would probably become a very powerful wizard. Natural sorcerers typically make the best candidates for the training and have the highest chance of survival. I am concerned, however, about the way you have manifested your talent."

"What do you mean?" Alexander asked.

"Your talent could be an anomaly that will never translate into an aptitude for deliberate manipulation of the firmament," Mason said, "in which case you would likely not survive the mana fast. Understand, I am only speculating. There are a number of other possibilities that could explain the way you're able to manifest magic. I'll do some research into the matter and let you know once I understand the situation more fully. Also, there are a number of spells I believe may shed some light on your ability if you'll permit me to cast them over you."

Alexander thought for a moment. "The more I know about magic, the better. What do I need to do?"

"Nothing at the moment. I'll make the necessary preparations. Once I'm ready, you must simply sit with me inside my Wizard's Circle. It will be painless and may reveal a great deal that could be of use to you."

Hanlon motioned to Wizard Kallentera to forestall any further discussion. "Alexander, tomorrow will likely be a trying day for you. It would be wise to be well rested."

Alexander looked at the Forest Warden with apprehension, "How so?"

"The nobles will wish to have a council meeting with you present. It will be tedious, take several hours, and will involve them posturing, preening, and speaking at length without saying very much at all." Hanlon held up his hands in mock surrender. "I know, I know, it's a waste of time, but actually it's not. The nobles effectively rule Glen Morillian and their support will be essential if you are to use this valley as a base of operations in the coming war. Mostly, they just want to feel important. If you give them that, they'll probably acquiesce to your rule. But if they feel that you've snubbed them, they can be all manner of difficult. In the long run, it'll be worth it to spend the morning listening to them blathering on.

"Then there's the matter of Mage Cedric's vault. I think you should open it tomorrow afternoon. If it contains items that can be of use, it may take some time for you to master them.

"Finally, tomorrow evening we'll be holding a formal banquet in your honor."

Alexander started to shake his head but Hanlon held up his hands beseeching Alexander to hear him out. "This is another function that the nobles, and the people, will expect. They'll be impossible to deal with if you don't give them their party. They seem to live for such events. If I never had to sit through another grand banquet I would be a happy man, but my wife," he smiled at Emily, "is another matter. She likes to entertain, and this will be one of the most-attended banquets of the year."

Emily smiled at Alexander. "I do enjoy a party, Alexander, but I promise you'll be able to slip away if you wish after the formalities are over."

Alexander eyed her with good-natured suspicion, "Exactly what sort of formalities?"

She leaned forward, eager to talk about the coming festivities. "Well, the evening starts with the arrival of the guests. Each guest is announced when they enter the ballroom. You will, of course, arrive last because you're the guest of honor and everyone will want to see your entrance. Dinner will be served shortly thereafter. I've been preparing since the riders from the fortress gate brought news of your arrival. After dinner, but before dessert, you'll be expected to recount your journey here and the circumstances of the mark you bear." She stopped, clearly expecting an objection on this count and she wasn't disappointed.

Alexander had been trying to put the events of the past two weeks behind him. There had been a lot of pain and fear. He didn't relish the thought of recounting the whole thing in front of a room full of strangers.

"Is that really necessary?" He was starting to feel a whole new kind of anxiety build in the pit of his stomach.

Emily nodded as she reached out and gave his forearm an affectionate squeeze. "I'm afraid it will be expected. More importantly, it will be your best opportunity to win over the nobles. If you regale them with a heroic story in a public setting, they'll look petty and small if they don't support you."

Alexander was starting to feel trapped. He had little experience at speaking in public and frankly preferred it that way. If he stammered and stuttered through his story, he would damage his cause. He could feel the heat rising in his face when Jack spoke up and offered him a lifeline.

"Lady Alaric, is it permissible for one to speak on Alexander's behalf?" Jack asked.

She nodded, "Yes, of course. In fact it's preferable. Most nobles believe it's a sign of greater importance to have another speak for them."

Jack smiled with relish and enthusiasm. "My Lord, it would be my honor and privilege if you would permit me to recount your exploits for the assembled guests."

Alexander stared at him with a mixture of incredulity and relief. "Are you serious? Of course!" Jack smiled with such pure joy that Alexander could only shake his head. "You're actually looking forward to standing up in front of all those people and telling them stories, aren't you?"

Jack nodded eagerly, still grinning like a schoolboy. "It is the calling of my life, the very reason I draw breath. To hold a crowd in thrall, hanging on my every word, is a power that no wizardry can match. I will do you proud, Alexander. By the time I'm done with them, you'll be every bit the hero they hope you are."

Jack turned his attention to Emily, "Lady Alaric, if I may, it will be important that Alexander has the proper attire for such an occasion. His travel clothes simply won't make the proper impression."

Emily was nodding, "Yes, of course, I've already made arrangements for you all to have a set of fine clothes fitted and ready by tomorrow evening. Our tailor will be by in the morning before breakfast to take measurements for the men and I was hoping Isabel would take Abigail to town for a dress. There are many fine shops that will make the necessary alterations on the spot." Abigail beamed. She didn't wear finery very often but she did enjoy it when the opportunity presented itself.

Alexander was starting to feel a little better about the evening. Jack's offer to speak in his place put him at ease. He'd heard Jack spin a tale and was confident that the crowd would be pleased. He marveled at how something as seemingly meaningless as a banquet could be so important. He remembered another bit from one of his father's lectures on strategy: "Battlefields come in all shapes and sizes. However they present themselves, you must always know the terrain and use it to your advantage to win the day." Alexander was starting to realize just how much he had to learn. He'd imagined that this war would be fought on the open plain in pitched battles with a clear enemy. He was coming to realize that he would have to look at each situation he encountered from this point forward as if it were a battlefield.

"Sounds like we have a busy day ahead of us. I could use some sleep," Alexander said as he stood.

Chapter 24

Apparently, everyone else had been shown to their quarters while Alexander and Isabel were in the bell tower, so Isabel offered to show him where he would be sleeping. He was happy to have her walk with him because he had something he needed to ask her. Before he could work up the nerve, she asked the question that was clearly weighing on her mind.

"Alexander, what do the colors tell you, in your magical vision?" She seemed almost nervous to hear the answer, as though he might have seen something in her that she wanted to protect.

He shrugged, "Different things in different people. I can usually see if someone is lying to me. I can tell a lot about a person's nature and it helps me see trouble coming in the dark because colors are visible to me even when it's too dark to see the person they belong to."

She seemed to worry over his answer for a few minutes while they walked through the palace to his quarters. Suddenly, she stopped and turned to him. "Have you looked at me? I mean, at my colors?"

He smiled gently and answered simply, "Yes."

She frowned as she worked up the nerve to ask the question that was really on her mind. "What did you see?" she said in a very small voice, almost as if she was afraid of the answer but had to know.

Alexander waited for a moment. When Isabel didn't look up at him, he reached out and gently raised her chin up so he could look into her eyes. "Your colors are clear and beautiful. You have a strength and goodness about you that is rare."

She smiled a little. When she felt her face start to flush, she turned and started down the hall again and didn't say anything else until she stopped in front of a large door.

"This is your room. If you need anything just pull the bell for the servant. Good night, Alexander," she said and then smiled up at him without making any move to leave.

His mouth went dry. The time had arrived for him to ask the question he'd been working over and over in his mind. He hesitated for only a moment before blurting it out, "Isabel, would you accompany me to the banquet tomorrow?" He held his breath.

Her face lit up with a smile and her eyes came alive. She actually curtsied. "It would be my honor," she giggled and added, "I was hoping you'd ask." She gave him a little kiss on the cheek and headed down the hall, calling out over her shoulder with laughter in her voice, "Sleep well, Alexander."

He watched her until she turned the corner, flashing him one last smile as she went. Only then did he realize he was standing outside the door to his room wearing a big dumb grin. He looked around quickly to make sure no one was watching before he entered his room.

It was much bigger than he expected. There was a well-dressed, older-looking gentleman standing in the middle of what looked like a sitting room. He was tall and thin with grey hair and a neatly trimmed silver mustache. The room was spacious and well decorated, carpeted from wall to wall in rich dark forest green. A low polished oak table sat in the center of the far end of the room with comfortable-looking couches on two sides and a pair of plush chairs on either end. Off to the right was a large stone fireplace with a cozy fire already burning and a set of four more comfortable-looking chairs facing the hearth, each separated from the other by a small table.

On the wall opposite the entrance was a set of ornate glass doors framed in rich dark green curtains pulled back with heavy gold-colored ropes ending in tassels. The doors opened out onto a balcony that had to be several dozen feet above the courtyard below. Over the fireplace hung a mirror easily as tall as Alexander; it was tilted down at just the right angle so he could see himself when he stood in the center of the room. On the left wall were two remarkably beautiful tapestries that hung from ceiling to floor, each depicting the Glen Morillian valley from a different angle. Between the tapestries was a heavy, polished oak door that stood open. All around the edge of the room were freestanding heavy brass oil lamps that cast a warm glow against the high white ceiling.

The well-dressed man bowed formally. "Your Majesty, I am Renwold. With your permission I will serve as your valet for the duration of your stay here at the palace."

Alexander was nearly speechless so he just stared at the man. Renwold took the silence as permission to continue. "I have turned down your bed for the evening, set out a selection of wine and banked the fire. If you find you are in need of anything at all, please just pull this cord and I will be along shortly." He walked over to a heavy, braided, gold-tasseled white rope hanging from a small hole in the ceiling.

"I will return at dawn with a hot beverage prior to the arrival of your tailor. If there isn't anything else, Your Majesty, I will withdraw."

When he didn't leave, Alexander blinked a few times before he found his voice, "Yes, of course, thank you, Renwold."

The valet bowed formally again and left, carefully closing the door on his way out. Alexander felt a great sense of relief to be alone. He bolted the door and did a quick search of his rooms. It was a suite of two rooms: the sitting room and a bedchamber with a small washroom. The bedchamber was richly furnished with a big feather bed against the center of the wall opposite the door. The large windows to the right of the door were covered with heavy, dark green curtains that were drawn closed. To either side of the bed was an identical nightstand, each with an ornately fashioned brass oil lamp burning brightly. A cushioned bench sat at the foot of the bed and a finely crafted mahogany armoire stood open on the wall to the left of the door. His pack, bedroll, and saddlebags were resting at the foot of the armoire but they hadn't been opened. Within the armoire were several sets of clothes that looked like they might actually fit him, as well as a rich, comfortable-looking robe.

Alexander was suddenly very tired. He went to the sitting room and extinguished all the lamps, checked the doors to the balcony to be sure they were locked, went into his bedroom and bolted the door. His final precaution was to put his long knife under his pillow before he undressed and climbed into the blissfully comfortable bed. Alexander had always preferred to be comfortable. He could sleep just fine on the ground if need be, but given the choice, he would rather have a warm soft bed.

He woke early, feeling well rested and ready for the day to come. While there were a number of things he wasn't looking forward to, he was looking forward to having Isabel on his arm at the banquet. While he lay in bed looking at the ceiling, he tried to imagine what she would look like in a dress. He decided that today was going to be a good day before he got up and threw open the curtains. The soft light of early dawn filled the room. He put on the robe and went into the sitting room. As he lit the second lamp, he heard a soft knock at the door.

It was Renwold with a tray of fresh-baked pastries and a pot of hot tea with honey and cream. Alexander stood out on the balcony looking over the courtyard below, eating a sweetbread and sipping his very hot tea when the second knock came. Renwold admitted the tailor, who, very respectfully and very professionally, took Alexander's measurements for his banquet finery. He enquired about Alexander's taste in clothing and about the colors that Alexander preferred.

Once he finished with the measurements, he selected a set of clothes from the armoire and insisted that Alexander try them on. At this point Alexander felt like he'd been whisked away by forces greater than himself so he simply agreed. The tailor expertly adjusted the fit of the clothes he'd picked out and Alexander had to admit that they fit quite well.

The tailor had selected a charcoal-grey long-sleeved shirt woven of finely spun soft wool; a broad, black leather belt; a pair of dark brown pants that matched the color of Alexander's boots; and a dark forest green vest with just a hint of gold filigree around the edges and a lining of black rabbit fur. And finally, a long brown leather cloak. Alexander was skeptical of the whole thing at first. He just figured it was easier to humor the man. If he looked ridiculous he could always change clothes once the man left but one look in the mirror changed his mind. The tailor knew his trade. Alexander was pleasantly surprised to see how good he actually looked in the outfit.

He supposed it was important to present himself well to the nobles during council so he decided to go with it. He reminded himself that different battlefields required different weapons. Perhaps appearance was one of those weapons when the battlefield was a council chamber filled with self-important nobles.

Once the tailor finished his work, Renwold announced that breakfast would be served in the family dining room and offered to escort Alexander through the maze of the palace. Before they left, Alexander tucked his long knife into the back of his belt and a smaller knife into his boot. He felt relatively safe here and it was pretty clear that the Alaric family was loyal to him. But he didn't trust the nobles; any one of them could easily sell out to Phane, and all it took was one well-placed blade.

He arrived at breakfast at the same time as Anatoly and Jack. It was obvious that a tailor had also paid them a visit. Anatoly was dressed in the court uniform of a Ranger, which looked very much like the field uniform except without the armor or weapons. Alexander could see that Anatoly had at least four knives tucked away in his new outfit and probably more if he knew the big man-at-arms at all. Jack was well dressed as well but not overly so. His look was professional but carefully crafted to present a sense of humility and service.

Hanlon, Emily, and Erik were already at the table when Alexander arrived. He took his seat and heard giggling from out in the hall a moment before Abigail and Isabel entered. Both were wearing simply cut yet elegant dresses. Abigail wore a shade of blue that almost perfectly matched her pale eyes and Isabel wore a vibrant green dress that matched her piercing green eyes. Alexander was torn between his surprise at seeing Abigail in a dress and his delight at seeing Isabel wearing one. Both were beautiful and both were beaming at the prospect of a day of shopping for clothes in the markets of Glen Morillian. Alexander couldn't help but smile. His sister had been through just as much as he had in the past couple of weeks and it lifted his spirits to see her happy. Then there was Isabel. She was beautiful in Rangers field armor. But to see her in a dress made Alexander's heart race.

Erik smiled up at his sister with pure mischief and asked, "Since when do you wear a dress?"

She shot him a look that would have stopped a charging bull dead in its tracks but couldn't help giggling with Abigail a moment later. She flashed Alexander a smile as she found her seat. Yes, today would be a good day.

The meal was simple but very good. Hanlon spent most of the time trying to prepare Alexander for the coming council meeting. It was clear that Hanlon didn't like the nobles much, nor did he find much value in the hours spent in council listening to self-important people go on about unimportant things, when everyone knew that the real decisions were made in private meetings anyway. But he assured Alexander that it was important to win over the nobles in order to gain the full support of Glen Morillian and that was enough to justify the meeting.

Jack asked to attend the council meeting for which Anatoly commended him on his bravery. Jack suggested that it would help him prepare for the evening banquet if he had a better understanding of the nobles. Alexander was happy to have the moral support.

Emily told them that their evening finery would be ready by midafternoon and that they needed to try it on early enough to give the tailors a chance to make any last-minute alterations. Hanlon smiled affectionately at how seriously she took the whole affair. His idea of dressing up was throwing his red sash on over his armor.

When they finished breakfast, it was time for the morning council meeting. Alexander felt the dread grow with each step toward the council chamber. It annoyed him how reassured Jack looked, and he couldn't help commenting about it.

"You actually look happy about this, Jack."

"I am in my element, Your Majesty." He stopped and faced Alexander. "I can't tell you how many times I felt the cold stark terror of near-certain death on our way here. In the face of all those dangers you carried the day. I know with the certainty of personal experience that Mage Cedric chose wisely. You are calm in the face of death. You keep your wits and make good decisions. If you are out of your element at court, then it is my humble honor to be your guide and champion, for in this arena there are few who can best me." He was the personification of confidence.

Alexander laughed and clapped him on the shoulder. "Champion away.

I'll take all the help I can get. And please, I'm open to any suggestions you might have for dealing with the nobles. Just remember, I've seen their colors. They're not to be trusted."

Jack chuckled, "One of the first things you learn at court is there are precious few people worthy of trust. Nobles tend to be far down the list. In many ways you have them at a disadvantage. Your ability to see their auras provides you with valuable insight that they are not aware you have. I would caution you to guard your talent jealously."

Hanlon agreed. "They're certainly not to be trusted and letting them know about your magical sight will only make them feel threatened. I know from experience how their behavior changes when Mason is in the council chamber. They're much more guarded and careful when they believe their agenda might be discovered through magical means."

Chapter 25

The big council chamber was full to capacity when they entered. Every chair lining the walls of the room was occupied, as was every chair at the big council table except for the head chair and the one immediately to the right, which had been reserved for Alexander and Hanlon.

As soon as they reached their chairs, Jack took a position to the right and a step behind Alexander and deliberately cleared his throat. The conversation in the room began to settle as everyone directed their attention toward Alexander.

Jack spoke clearly in a voice that easily filled the room but didn't sound at all strained. "Lords and ladies, in the name of the King of Ruatha, I call this council to order."

Alexander wasn't expecting that, but in light of the way it set every noble at the table back on their heels he decided to take full advantage of it.

The room fell silent. All eyes were on Alexander. He did his best to smile graciously before beginning. "At issue is whether the Council of Glen Morillian will recognize my claim to the throne of Ruatha." He remained standing as he unfastened his cloak and handed it to Jack. He wanted to make sure everyone in the room could see the mark burned into the side of his neck. "Please be seated." He remained standing while the nobles took their seats, all looking somewhat uncomfortable that Alexander did not.

"The world stands on the verge of war. Phane Reishi is loose in the Seven Isles and I have been marked as the one to stand against him. Prince Phane murdered my brother, burned my family home to the ground, sent men and netherworld beasts to hunt me, and he may have murdered my parents."

The room was deathly silent. Alexander paused and regarded the men seated around the table. He had their attention and they each looked to be taking him quite seriously.

"Phane fled two thousand years into the future to escape Mage Cedric. He has awakened from his long sleep to discover that the Rebel Mage made preparations to defend the world against him even to this very day. I stand at the heart of those preparations. I pledge to you that I will fight with all that I have and all that I am to preserve the Old Law and the people of Ruatha. All the world stands at a crossroads and only two courses lay before you. You can choose to serve the Old Law and stand with me, or you can choose to serve Phane. Choose wisely."

Alexander didn't sit but instead turned to Jack and took his cloak. He tossed it over his shoulders and stepped out from in front of his chair. "Warden Alaric, I have need of your assistance. Please have your Second preside over this council's deliberations." Without waiting for comment he strode purposefully for the door, followed closely by Jack. Once in the hall and out of earshot of the council room, he stopped to wait for Hanlon.

"How'd I do?" he asked Jack.

Jack smiled, shaking his head in wonder, "I thought you said you were out of your element. What I saw in that room was a king."

"I hope you weren't the only one," Alexander said.

Hanlon came out of the council chamber amid a cacophony of competing voices all vying to be heard over the next. He hurried up to Alexander and Jack with a grin that stretched from ear to ear.

"My Second is going to hate you for that. The nobles are all in an uproar but they don't dare go against you now. None of them can be seen to side with Phane." Hanlon chuckled and shook his head.

"That's my hope," Alexander said with a look of mischief. "Let's go find Lucky and take a walk down to the catacombs."

Hanlon led them through the maze of passageways, halls, and corridors that wound through the interior of the palace. Alexander tried to memorize the layout as best he could but it was still new enough that he found himself turned around more often than not.

The more he walked through the palace the more he came to appreciate the construction and decoration. Its grandeur was in the simple, elegant, and functional design, coupled with the fine craftsmanship, polished white marble floors, intricately carved oak furnishings, vividly colored tapestries, rich carpeting, and immaculate cleanliness. There was just enough ornamentation in the public areas to lend that essential air of authority necessary to any seat of power but without the ostentation and aggrandizement so often associated with a palace.

Soon they were walking through the service corridors that gave the palace staff access to every part of the place without having to carry the tools of their trades through the public areas. These passageways were made from simple cut granite and were purely functional. Alexander realized that the service access corridors formed a second set of passages that often paralleled the public halls.

After a convoluted series of twists and turns and a few flights of worn stone stairs, Hanlon came to a stop at a large oak door. He knocked three times before pulling on the heavy iron ring. The hinges creaked and groaned as the oversized door swung open. The room beyond was well lit despite the complete absence of windows. They were in the sub-basement and the air was somewhat stale and musty outside the room but smelled of incense within.

The door opened into a large room sixty feet long and forty feet wide with a high ceiling easily reaching ten feet overhead. The walls were lined with shelves from floor to ceiling and the interior of the room was filled with worktables of varied sizes. Every shelf was filled to the point of overflowing. There were books of all sorts. Some shelves held nothing but volumes with identical leather bindings. Others held all manner of books, tomes, folios, compendiums, and lexicons. Still others were stacked top to bottom with scroll tubes of wood, bone, or finely crafted silver.

The shelves that didn't hold books were filled with jars, pots, vials, decanters, canisters, bottles, bowls, hoppers, boxes, coffers, bags, and pouches. What was visible within the containers at a glance ranged from powders, ointments, and liquids of various colors and consistencies to leaves, herbs, and barks to eyeballs, feet, and teeth from a dizzying array of simple animals to magical creatures.

The tables that filled the interior of the room were equally occupied with such a variety of items that Alexander could only stare about in a vain effort to catalogue everything he saw. Several of the larger tables were covered with elaborate sets of glass beakers, vials, and basins of all shapes and sizes linked together with an intricate web of glass tubes, funnels, and coils of finely crafted copper piping. Some of the beakers and basins were filled with liquid while others looked to be carefully placed to catch the drippings from the mixture of liquids that ran through the pipes and tubes. A few of the tables were active with a number of small flames beneath a beaker here and a tube there providing the power that caused the entire arrangement to come to life, bubbling and steaming with rivulets of colored liquid running around carefully crafted spirals of clear glass tubing to deposit the product of the entire apparatus into a catch basin or heavy glass jar. Others were set up for processes that had not yet begun while still others had been used recently and were in need of disassembly and cleaning.

There were a few tables stacked with books in large piles of seemingly random placement and height. While still other tables had stacks of parchment, bottles of ink, and writing instruments as well as charcoal, pigments, colored chalk, and paints. One table toward the center stood out because it was slightly lower than the rest, sturdier looking, and perfectly circular. Its surface was completely clear of any of the clutter that was so evident elsewhere. Instead, the surface of the table was polished and smooth and the edge was inlaid with twin rings of gold wire, spaced about seven inches apart. Between the rings of gold was a series of intricate symbols also inlaid in gold.

Beneath most of the tables were cabinets, drawers, cupboards, and lockers. Not one of the tables was lined up with the walls; instead each seemed to be placed almost at random around the room, giving the place a feel of clutter and disarray. Fine crystalline chandeliers hung from the ceiling and tall, heavy brass lamp posts held finely wrought, mirrored oil lamps at uneven intervals all around the room, giving the place ample light.

Across the room directly opposite the door was a large fireplace with a set of five chairs arrayed before it. There were heavy, squat oak end tables separating the chairs; cushioned ottomans before each; and a broad, low table between the chairs and the fire.

Lucky and Mason were lounging comfortably before the well-stoked fire and talking quietly while sipping hot, honeyed tea. They waved when Alexander, Jack, and Hanlon entered the room.

As they threaded their way through the cluttered tables, Alexander did his best to take it all in. The character of the place reminded him of Lucky's little workshop only on a much larger scale.

Lucky smiled up at Alexander. "I don't get the chance to discuss the finer points of magic very often so I thought I'd take advantage of the opportunity."

"Looks like you'd be right at home here," Alexander said.

Lucky nodded almost wistfully as he looked around at the multitude of experiments and projects that appeared to be in progress all at once. "Indeed," he whispered before a frown creased his brow with a hint of concern. "Weren't you going to attend the council meeting this morning?"

"Already done." Both Hanlon and Jack smiled at that. "I wanted to go have a look at the vault in the catacombs and I was hoping you'd join us. You know a lot more about magic than I do," he added with a shrug.

"Yes, of course, but I am curious how the council meeting turned out.

Perhaps you could fill us in while we finish our tea? We just poured it, after all."
Lucky smiled up at Alexander unabashedly. He was always one for a good meal or
a hot beverage and he firmly believed that such important business should never
be rushed.

A grin spread across Alexander's face at his old tutor. "I guess some tea
couldn't hurt." He took a seat and poured steaming hot tea into one of the fine
porcelain, gold-rimmed cups on the silver tea service.

"As for the council, I couldn't tell you; they're still deliberating," he said
just before taking his first sip.

Hanlon chuckled, drawing looks from both Mason and Lucky, but it was
Jack who explained while Alexander sipped at his tea and sank back into the
comfortable chair.

"In just under five minutes, Alexander established his authority and gave
the nobles the option of siding with him and the Old Law or siding with Phane.
They're deliberating as we speak."

Mason nodded thoughtfully. "There is great power in belief. Oftentimes
you can force the outcome you desire by framing the question to allow for only
two choices, the one you wish and another that is unacceptable. It's important to
understand the converse. Never allow yourself to be limited by such a false choice.
The nobles are vulnerable to your tactic because they depend on the opinion of
their peers. They won't dare reframe the question for fear that you will counter
with a claim that they have chosen Phane. I'm confident that your ploy will work,
but be cautioned, there are liable to be a few of them who will resent you for this."

"I can live with that as long as I get the support of Glen Morillian. I'm
going to need it when I move to unite Ruatha," Alexander said with his eyes
closed.

He was looking ahead. Phane would be working to consolidate his power
and build an army. Alexander needed to do the same if he was going to have any
chance at all. That meant bringing the disparate rulers of the various Ruathan
territories together and forging one kingdom. The room fell silent. When he
opened his eyes, everyone was looking at him.

He shrugged, "As long as I have to wear this cursed mark, I'm going to
take my duties seriously. The fact is we're going to need an army, and a big one, if
we're going to have any chance against Phane because I guarantee he's building
one as we speak."

Alexander finished off his tea before taking a deep breath and getting to
his feet. Jack and Hanlon stood with him.

Lucky looked at Mason and sighed before he finished off his tea as well.
"The young are always in a hurry," he muttered as he got to his feet.

Chapter 26

The five of them wound their way down through the catacombs. The ancient corridors hadn't been used for years. Hanlon could just make out his footprints from the last time he'd been down into the bowels of the palace many years ago. They descended one flight of stairs after another as they made their way through countless crypts, corridors, and burial chambers. Some of the rooms were ornately decorated out of respect for the dead, while others were nothing more than rooms with nooks cut into the walls and filled front to back with bleached bones. Everywhere the dust was thick and the air was musty. The only noise was the echo of their footsteps and their breathing.

They lit their way with three handheld oil lamps from Mason's workshop, which provided more than enough light for Hanlon to navigate through the seemingly endless maze of passages. After an hour, Alexander became convinced that the only way he could find the way back would be to retrace their footprints in the heavy blanket of powder-fine dust on the floor.

Hanlon stopped abruptly and raised his lamp to take a closer look at the wall. He examined the footprints from the last time he'd been down here and found what he was looking for. He took hold of an empty sconce and pulled it away from the wall. A muffled metallic scraping followed by a click could be heard. He put both hands on the section of wall to the left of the sconce and gave it a shove. At first it didn't budge, but after a renewed effort a section of the wall about half again as wide as a normal door began to slide inward. The section of wall was made uneven on each side by the interlocking pattern of bricks that separated from their counterparts to the left and right. Once the section moved about a foot back from the wall face, it broke free and swung open on a set of hinges. Hanlon picked up his lantern and raised it to light the small square room beyond.

There was less dust in the unremarkable little room and only one visible exit: a single iron-banded oak door filling an oversized portal with a rounded arch at the top. The door was locked and looked quite sturdy despite long years of disuse.

Hanlon fished around in his shirt and withdrew a brass key on a chain around his neck. He handed Alexander the lantern, took the chain from around his neck, and slipped the key into the ancient lock.

"I have never opened this door and do not know what lies beyond. Each Keeper of the Royal Bloodline has been shown this place during his final initiation. The key to this door has been passed down through the generations since the first Keeper received it from Mage Cedric himself. Alexander, this is your door to open." Hanlon stepped back and held out his hand toward the door, motioning for Alexander to step forward.

Without a word, Alexander stepped up and turned the key. To his surprise it turned easily and the door glided open noiselessly with just a gentle push. The room that lay beyond was circular and domed. He stepped across the threshold and raised his lantern to light the room. It was a half sphere. The high point of the ceiling was about twenty feet from the smooth stone floor and the room was about forty feet across. The entire room was completely empty with the sole exception of a polished white marble mausoleum in the exact center. There wasn't even any dust.

The little marble building stood seven feet tall and seven feet on each side. It was a perfect cube with no adornment whatsoever, save for a band of writing delicately carved into the marble seven inches below the top edge and running the entire length of the side facing the door.

Alexander walked carefully around the little marble building, noting that the band of writing turned the corner and wrapped around the entire structure, starting and stopping above the outline of a doorway in the center of the far side. He looked closer at the symbol directly above the doorway and realized it was the mark that had been burned into the side of his neck. He felt a chill race up his spine. This vault had been placed here two thousand years ago expressly for him.

Centered in the outline of the door and about five feet up from the floor was the likeness of a man's right hand carved into the marble. Alexander raised his lantern to look more closely at the band of writing and discovered that it was in a language he was unfamiliar with.

"Lucky, do you know what language that writing is?" he asked.

Lucky shook his head but Mason Kallentera answered, "It's old Reishi." Silence descended on the domed room. Everyone turned to the court wizard.

"I have a number of ancient books written in old Reishi. It's the original language of the Reishi Wizards. Eventually it became a language taught only within the confines of the Reishi Wizards Guild. The last Reishi Sovereign made it a crime punishable by death to speak, read, or write it unless sanctioned by the Reishi." Mason raised his lantern and examined the arcane writing more closely. "I recognize a few of the characters from the circles of protection that ward this valley."

Alexander frowned, "Is that what that circular walk around the palace grounds is?"

Mason nodded, "This was Mage Cedric's home. During the war he placed a series of protection circles around the valley to ward against creatures of the netherworld. Some of the symbols found within those circles can also be seen here."

"Can you translate this?" Alexander asked in a whisper.

"Given enough time, I believe I can. I have exact translations of a number of the old Reishi volumes in my library. It will be a painstaking process but I agree that it may be useful." He started fishing around in his robes. "I'll need to make a rubbing so I can work on it in my library." He produced a bone tube and tapped out a roll of parchment, then found a piece of charcoal in another pocket and set to work carefully reproducing the series of ancient characters.

"Hanlon, does anyone else know of this place?" Alexander asked.

"Some know rumors of its existence, but I've never shown anyone the way down here, let alone which sconce opens the secret door."

"Good, I'd like to keep it that way," Alexander said. "Until we know what that writing says, I don't want to risk its message falling into the wrong hands."

Mason finished his rubbing of the entire message, rolled up his parchment and put it away.

Alexander stepped up to the outline of the door and placed his right hand on the handprint. It was cool to the touch and fit his hand perfectly but nothing happened. He expected the door to open. He looked up to the symbol over the door to verify that it was indeed the symbol burned into the right side of his neck. He pressed with more force but still nothing happened.

He turned back to the others who were watching silently while holding their breath. "Any suggestions?" he asked. They all stared blankly in response.

Lucky asked, "Does this place have a name? Was there a title given to this room by the one who brought you here?"

Hanlon nodded slowly as if dredging his memory. He spoke softly in his deep voice, "It's called a Bloodvault."

It all fell into place at once. Alexander was the heir to the royal bloodline. The Rebel Mage had to make sure the contents of this place were only accessible to the right person. Blood was the only way to be absolutely certain. Alexander drew the knife from his belt and sliced across his hand deeply enough to draw a line of bright red blood.

He placed his hand on the handprint again. Again nothing happened. He was just about to take his hand away in frustration when the marble began to grow warmer. Then, quite suddenly, points of scintillating bright white light appeared where each line outlining the door met the floor. The points of light flared for half a heartbeat before moving rapidly up along the outline of the door until they met at the apex. The door abruptly became transparent and Alexander's hand pushed through into the space beyond. With a sense of wonder, he walked through the now semi-visible door and stepped into a tiny room.

When he entered, the ceiling of the white marble room began to glow softly, filling the space with a warm, comfortable light. He looked back and saw his companions looking at the stone building with shocked disbelief. At once they rushed to the door and started feeling for a way to open it. He could see through the transparent door that they were yelling his name and becoming frantic in their efforts to gain access to the vault. He called out to them but they couldn't hear him.

He looked around and saw three shelves. The one on the left held a finely crafted ancient book with a locked leather strap binding it closed. The shelf on the right held an ornate coffer carved from the bone of some ancient and long-dead creature. The shelf opposite the door held a heavy gold ring set with a single black stone. Rolled up and slipped through the ring was a piece of parchment that looked as fresh and new as if it had been placed there yesterday.

The others were starting to become more concerned about his sudden disappearance into the little building and it looked like Mason was getting ready to start casting a spell in an effort to get him out.

He picked up the ring with the little note and slipped it into a pocket, stacked the book on top of the bone coffer and tucked them both under his arm, then turned and pushed through the transparent door with his bloody hand. It offered just the slightest bit of resistance. Hanlon leapt forward, seized Alexander by the wrist and pulled him through the door as if he was trying to save his life. Alexander stumbled when he came free of the door's slight resistance and would have fallen except Hanlon caught him and set him on his feet.

Everyone started talking at once. Alexander held up his bloody hand to quiet them so he could answer their questions.

"The door became transparent and insubstantial when I put my hand on it. I was able to push right through."

Mason looked at the Bloodvault, then back to Alexander. "It didn't become transparent to us. To all of us you simply fell through the stone wall and were gone. We tried to free you but couldn't even scratch the marble. This is a constructed spell of great power. I doubt anyone alive today could breach it, except possibly Phane."

Lucky was peering at the objects under Alexander's arm, "What have you found?"

"I'm not sure. These were each on a shelf," Alexander said as he set them down side by side.

Mason looked closely at the book and whistled, "This is a skillbook." He caressed the cover with a sense of awe and wonder. "These were constructed by the most powerful of wizards to impart a high level of skill in a given field within a relatively short period of time. Looks like Mage Cedric was serious about helping you defeat Phane."

Mason picked it up and examined it more closely. "It looks like a skillbook of the blade." He pointed out several little images of various bladed weapons on the four corners of the cover.

Alexander looked closer at the locking mechanism on the band around the book and saw that there wasn't a keyhole. "How do I open it? Is it a puzzle lock?"

Mason shook his head. "No, a skillbook can only impart the skill it contains to one person and it keys to that person by their blood. If you touch the lock right here with your bloody hand, it will open and key itself to you. I suggest you do so only when you're ready to study the book. Some skillbooks were said to lose their magic soon after they're opened."

"How long does it take to study the book and gain the skill?" Alexander asked.

"That's hard to say for certain," Mason said. "From what I've learned about skillbooks in my studies, I believe that a period of several hours of uninterrupted study is all that is required. But I should caution you, Alexander, I've never actually seen a skillbook before or even heard of one being discovered for several centuries. They are exceedingly rare."

"All right, I'll save that for later. Let's have a look in this box." He unlatched the lid on the bone coffer and carefully opened the little white box.

The inside was lined with red velvet. There were seven recesses formed to fit around the seven sealed crystal vials resting within. Each vial contained a clear liquid that looked like water except the contents glowed softly with the purest white light that Alexander had ever seen. It was like looking into the sun without the pain. The clarity, richness, and brilliance of the light was breathtaking. Alexander imagined that this was what a good person saw when they died and passed into the realm of light.

Mason and Lucky both stood and took a step back. Alexander looked up at them and the wonder on their faces.

He whispered, "What is this?"

Lucky and Mason spoke in unison, "Wizard's Dust."

He looked back at the vials of liquid. "It looks like glowing water to me."

Lucky tried to explain. "The wizards of old found that dissolving Wizard's Dust in purified and specially prepared spring water improved the odds of an apprentice surviving the mana fast. The process for this preparation has been lost for centuries."

Mason spoke next, "The contents of that case could buy a small kingdom. Wizard's Dust is so rare that most Wizards Guilds cannot initiate more than a handful of wizards every generation. Mage Cedric has given you the best chance you could get for becoming a wizard wrapped up neatly in this case."

Alexander looked again at the glowing vials of liquid magic and carefully closed the lid. "The only other thing in the room was this," he said as he withdrew the ring with the note from his pocket. He slipped the note out and unrolled it. The parchment was supple and crisp. The writing was clear and unfaded. All it said was: "Blackstone Keep is yours. Signed, Barnabas Cedric."

He read it and read it again, then handed the little note to Lucky. The moment the alchemist touched it, the paper faded, became brittle, and turned to dust.

"Huh, I guess it was meant for me," Alexander shrugged.

He slipped the ring on his right ring finger. It was a little too big at first, then the stone glowed faintly and the ring resized itself to fit his finger perfectly. He slipped the ring off just to make sure he could then put it back on.

"What's Blackstone Keep? The note said, 'Blackstone Keep is yours' and it was signed by Barnabas Cedric."

Mason tilted his head with a quizzical look. "May I see the ring?"

Alexander pulled it off and handed it to Hanlon's court wizard. Mason examined it carefully, then closed his eyes and spoke a few words in an arcane language. His eyes opened wide when the results of his simple divination spell flooded into his mind.

"This is the key ring for the ancient home of the Ruathan Wizards Guild at Blackstone Keep. It's been inaccessible for millennia." He handed Alexander the ancient ring. "Alexander, this is a treasure beyond imagining. Blackstone Keep is rumored to be a place of spectacular power. It has claimed the lives of countless wizards over the ages who attempted to gain access to its secrets."

Alexander slipped the ring back on his finger. "Where is it?"

"North of New Ruatha, but I've never been there myself," Mason replied.

Jack was standing quietly in the background as he usually did when his unique talents were not called for. He cleared his throat quietly before he spoke. "Alexander, I've seen Blackstone Keep from a distance. It is indeed a few days' travel due north from New Ruatha and it is most imposing. The Keep is carved out of the top of a mountain of black granite that juts up from the grasslands. It can be seen from the high places in New Ruatha and is a place that inspires awe and dread amongst those who live there. If you could openly claim Blackstone Keep as your own, it would force the Regent of New Ruatha to bow to your authority without question."

Alexander looked back down at the other two priceless items that Mage Cedric had hidden away to aid him in the fight against Phane. He couldn't risk losing either of them before he had the chance to use them. They were the tools that Mage Cedric had left him. He tucked them under his arm and walked back through the magical door of the Bloodvault. Once inside, he carefully placed the items on their respective shelves, then pushed his way back out through the door.

Chapter 27

He had Lucky tend to the gash across his hand and suggested that they head back up to the palace. Once everyone left the domed room, Alexander closed the door and locked it, then put the key around his neck. Before they left the little anteroom, Alexander stopped everyone.

"It's vital that this place and the contents of the Bloodvault remain secret. Do not tell anyone what we found here today. Mason, be extra cautious with the rubbings you took. Until we know what they say, we can't risk an agent of Phane's discovering them."

Once back in the hall, Alexander insisted that they head down the passage in the wrong direction to leave some additional tracks in the dust so it would be that much more difficult for anyone to find the hidden room.

They wound through the catacombs and found their way back up to the main levels of the palace. When they emerged into the light of day, Alexander realized they were all grey with the fine dust of the ages that blanketed the floor of every passage below like a new-fallen snow.

They did their best to make themselves look presentable before venturing out into the public areas of the palace. Even after brushing away the majority of the dust, they still drew a few looks from the early guests who were just starting to arrive for the banquet. Hanlon led them back to their quarters so they could wash up and change clothes. It was midafternoon by the time Alexander finally made it back to his room.

Renwold was standing in the center of the sitting room waiting for him to arrive. He had the curtains open, allowing the light of day to stream in through the big glass doors that opened out onto the balcony. The fireplace was filled with a roaring fire that snapped and popped as it threw off a warm orange glow and waves of heat. Sitting on the low table in the center of the room was a covered silver platter next to an ornate silver tea service.

"Your Majesty," Renwold said as he bowed. Alexander briefly wondered how Renwold knew when he was coming. "May I take your cloak?" the tall, thin, well-dressed valet offered without moving.

Alexander handed it to him and headed for the washroom. He filled the basin with warm water from a kettle that was sitting over a small flame and washed his hands and face. When he emerged, his cloak was nowhere to be seen but Renwold was standing in exactly the same place.

"Your Majesty, would you like some lunch and a cup of tea?"

Alexander was suddenly famished. He wondered idly what was under the cover on the serving tray so he took a seat at the low table and lifted the lid. Renwold looked somewhat uncomfortable at the prospect of Alexander serving himself. The large platter held a selection of sliced ham, turkey, roast beef, venison, sausages, cheeses of three different varieties, a selection of five different types of breads, crackers, biscuits, butter, honey, three types of jam, four types of sauces, and a covered silver tureen filled with a rich-looking, potato-and-sausage soup. Alexander looked up at Renwold in surprise.

The tall, lanky valet took his look completely wrong. "Your Majesty, if there is something else that you would prefer, I can have it made and brought up to you with haste. The kitchen is at your disposal." He actually looked a bit nervous, as if he thought Alexander was dissatisfied with his service.

Alexander laughed, "Renwold, there's enough food here for half a dozen people. Have a seat and eat something with me. I hate the idea of all this going to waste."

The color drained from Renwold's face. "Your Majesty, I'm sure I can't do such a thing. I am your valet. My duty is to serve you, not dine with you."

Alexander smiled up at him. "I promise I won't tell anyone if you won't. Now sit down and help me eat some of this."

Renwold did as he was commanded but was clearly uncomfortable with the prospect of eating at the same table as his charge. Alexander didn't care. He questioned him during the entire meal about the workings of the palace and the customs of Glen Morillian. Alexander was out of his element and he knew it. He needed to understand everything he could about the customs and expectations of the mountain community if he was to win the support of the people, not to mention the nobles.

Alexander found Renwold to be very knowledgeable about the traditions of the people and the nobility. Once he got the old valet talking, Renwold became much more comfortable sharing a meal with Alexander and even seemed to enjoy recounting all he knew about the traditions, beliefs, customs, folklore, and values of the people of Glen Morillian. Alexander found he rather liked Renwold once he was able to get through the stiff and proper façade that, no doubt, distinguished him as a valet worthy of a king. During the course of their lunch, Alexander learned a great deal.

Glen Morillian was established by Barnabas Cedric, who was more commonly known as the Rebel Mage. He had cast a spell calling up the impassable mountains from the forest floor to form a protective barrier around the entire valley. The idea was stunning to Alexander. He never imagined that such power could be wielded as to reshape the face of the world itself. Mage Cedric had literally made the mountain range that rose high into the sky all around.

As a result, the people of Glen Morillian felt safe and protected from the dangers of the outside world. Part of the bargain for the safety of the barrier mountain range was the oath of loyalty the nobles were required to take. They were required to swear an oath to uphold the Old Law and to support the Rangers of Glen Morillian before they became the heads of their respective houses. Their power and seat at the council table was contingent upon their fealty to the Old Law and their recognition that Glen Morillian existed for a purpose.

Over the generations, the story had been told over and over of how the one with the mark would one day come to seek the aid of Glen Morillian. The people of this little mountain community understood with the clarity of long tradition that they had enjoyed the protection of the barrier mountain range and the Rangers for the past two thousand years so they would be here to support the Marked One when he called on them. A little of the stiffness and formality returned to Renwold's demeanor when he stated flatly that Alexander was the subject of their greatest legend and the reason Mage Cedric had established the

Rangers.

It all felt so surreal. Alexander had grown up herding cows. He wasn't a king, at least not in his own mind, and he certainly wasn't a legend, yet here was a man who saw him as both. Not for anything he'd ever done himself, but for the things a long-dead wizard set in motion thousands of years ago. It was all so much bigger than Alexander. He didn't have any idea how he was going to measure up to the expectations that had been thrust upon him.

He looked at the heavy gold ring with the nondescript black stone on his hand. It was a beautiful piece of jewelry. Not in a million years would Alexander have chosen to wear such a ring. He'd never been one for finery or jewels. They just got in the way of what needed to be done. So much had changed in such a short time.

"I've enjoyed our lunch together, Renwold. I suspect that much of what you've told me will be helpful in the coming weeks."

Renwold stood, drawing a cloak of propriety and decorum around himself like a suit of armor.

"If you're ready, the tailor is prepared to present your evening attire," Renwold said.

Alexander grinned with a nod. Renwold was all business again. He cleared the tray and swept out of the room, sending the tailor in as he left.

The tailor was excited to present the set of clothes he'd fashioned for Alexander. He beamed while he opened his case and began removing his wares. Alexander was actually impressed. He was afraid that the tailor would make him a suit of fancy ruffled finery like those he'd seen the nobles wearing. He thought they looked ridiculous all dressed up and frilly. He was pleased to see that the tailor had better sense than that.

The tailor offered him a set of fine charcoal-black trousers with a matching long-sleeved shirt. Both were simple yet well made from the finest blend of woven wool. He presented a tunic made from a finely spun midnight-blue fabric with a fine silver filigree of ancient and arcane symbols sewn into the hem, collar, and cuffs; a set of polished, hard black leather boots that fit surprisingly well; and a wide black leather belt with a well-crafted silver buckle wrought to match the symbol burned into the right side of Alexander's neck. Finally, he presented a full-length cloak made from the same fabric as the tunic, with similar silver filigree sewn into the hem.

Once Alexander had the entire outfit on and took a look in the mirror, he was surprised at how like a king he actually looked. The outfit wasn't ostentatious or flashy but instead presented a subtle sense of command authority. In fact, Alexander decided, the lack of flash, frills, or ruffles added considerably to the air of nobility that his new set of clothes cloaked him in. He also noted that the mark on his neck was clearly visible. He thanked the tailor and commended the man on the quality of his work, especially on such short notice. The tailor beamed at his praise.

Renwold entered when the tailor left. "Your Majesty, Master Grace and Master Colton request an audience."

Alexander blinked. He thought this whole thing was starting to get out of hand. He didn't need a servant and he certainly didn't need a doorman.

"Of course, let them in."

Anatoly was dressed in the traditional dark-brown and forest-green dress uniform of the Rangers, and Jack was in a black coat and trousers with a fine white linen shirt.

Anatoly took a long look at Alexander and nodded his approval. "You might actually pull this off," he said, grinning ever so slightly.

His grin turned to a grimace, "If I'd known the ladies were going to press me into escorting them to town for their shopping spree, I would have gladly volunteered to go to that council meeting with you." The big man-at-arms shook his head. "I tell you what, Alexander, it was undignified. And then, to top it all off, your sister insisted that I accompany her to the banquet." He threw up his hands in mock dismay. "How am I supposed to slip out of the thing with her on my arm?"

Alexander innocently suggested, "I'm sure Master Colton would be happy to escort Abigail in your stead."

Jack didn't miss a beat, "I would indeed, and I'm gratified that you would entrust your sister to my humble care, but I'm afraid that my duties will not permit it."

"What duties?" Alexander asked.

"I will be announcing your arrival, of course," Jack replied. "Then there is the matter of recounting the story of your travels to Glen Morillian. I must be seen as an advisor and agent of the throne rather than a guest in order to effectively play my part. In addition to these duties, I will be much better suited to gather information about the results of this morning's council meeting if I have the freedom of movement expected of a functionary rather than the restriction of remaining at the table as is expected of a guest."

"I'm glad somebody's thought this all through. I just thought we were having a fancy dinner," Alexander said.

Anatoly nodded his agreement.

"Alexander, do you remember how you acted this morning at the council meeting when you delivered your ultimatum to the nobles?" Jack asked.

Alexander nodded with a frown, his mood darkening. The nobles made him want to check his money purse.

"Do that. You are the King of Ruatha. The nobles and their petty power struggles are of no consequence. You have the weight of the world on your shoulders. Do not request, do not ask—demand with perfect confidence that you will not be denied. Power is about perception. Present yourself as a leader and others will follow."

"You make it sound so simple." Alexander motioned for them to sit as he lowered himself into a comfortable chair.

"These people have been waiting for you for two thousand years," Jack said. "You have the loyalty of the Rangers without question. The people of Glen Morillian have lived their whole lives with the story of your arrival. You are a living legend. The only obstacle before you is the nobility. They are rich and comfortable and don't like the idea of being called on to give up any of what they have. They will try every way they can to weasel out of supporting your cause, short of open refusal. You must continue to force their hand as you did this morning at council and eventually they will fall in line."

"This all seems so frivolous and unnecessary. Phane is building his strength as we speak and we're going to a party. It doesn't seem quite right,"

Alexander said softly, shaking his head.

"Alexander, you *are* building the strength you need to prevail," Jack said. "This banquet is an important step. Once you have the commitment of the nobles, you can assume command of the Glen Morillian valley and begin assembling your army. Without the nobles, it will be a constant struggle to generate the food, manpower, and resources necessary to supply any military force. This is just a different kind of battlefield. Play the part of a king tonight and the nobles will fall in line by week's end." He seemed so certain.

"Alexander, I don't like this sort of thing any more than you do, but Jack's right," Anatoly said. "You need the resources the nobles bring to the table. Winning them over with a fancy party is far easier than fighting them."

Alexander felt like he was living a lie and that any moment now everyone around him was going to realize that he was really just a ranch hand. And yet, he knew that he couldn't let the nobles see his doubt or he was doomed.

Chapter 28

Renwold entered. "Your Majesty, gentlemen, the guests have assembled and I have just received word that the banquet is awaiting your arrival."

Renwold led them to an anteroom off the main corridor leading into the banquet hall. Abigail and Isabel were waiting for them there.

Alexander entered the room still worrying about the nobles, but when he saw Isabel he was struck speechless. Everything else faded away.

She looked even more beautiful than he'd expected. Her dress was made of deep-green satin that perfectly accented the vibrant green of her eyes. It was sleeveless and the neckline was cut low enough to be suggestive but not so low that it was revealing. It flowed along her natural curves down the length of her body until the waistline where it flared slightly and hung down to her ankles in elegant pleats. She wore her chestnut-brown hair tied up with a thin gold ribbon, leaving just a few strands loose to frame her face. Over her bare shoulders, she wore a rabbit-fur shawl the color of freshly fallen snow in sunlight.

Alexander blinked and had to remind himself to say something. He bowed, offering her his very best smile. "You look beautiful," was all he managed to say.

She smiled brilliantly and her face flushed slightly. Alexander noticed his sister smiling gently at the two of them. She wore a sky-blue dress trimmed in silver. Her long silvery blond hair was brushed straight and flowed down her back and over her left shoulder.

"Did you enjoy your shopping?" Alexander asked as he took in the two of them.

Abigail smiled brightly and nodded. "Looks like the tailor was able to make you look presentable," she said with an impish little grin.

Anatoly offered her his arm. "I guess it won't be such a chore escorting you this evening," he said with a smile. Abigail slapped his arm gently and rolled her eyes.

"Don't let him fool you, my lady. Master Grace will be the envy of nearly every man at the party," Jack said to Abigail with a wink that made her giggle like a schoolgirl.

Anatoly and Abigail left to make their entrance to the banquet hall, leaving Alexander and Isabel looking at each other and smiling.

After a few moments Jack cleared his throat, "Alexander, it's time."

He nodded without taking his eyes off Isabel, then offered her his arm and they followed Jack out of the anteroom.

Alexander hadn't been to the banquet hall, so he had no idea what to expect. Most of the palace was functional with just enough decoration and ornamentation to give the place a feel of authority. The banquet hall was something else altogether.

When they arrived at the entrance, Alexander saw that the room was huge, much bigger than any room he'd seen in the palace. The giant oak double doors stood open and there was a little podium on the right side of the threshold with a man standing before it dressed the same way Renwold always dressed. Alexander presumed the man had the duty of announcing the guests. When he saw Alexander and Isabel coming, preceded by Jack, he stepped away from the little podium to give Jack his place. Jack nodded courteously to the valet and stepped up to announce Alexander. He cleared his throat and a wave of silence spread through the assembled guests. Everyone turned to see Alexander enter.

He stepped up to the threshold of the room with Isabel on his arm and tried to take in the grandeur of the place. The ceiling easily soared fifty feet overhead supported by great stone arches. Half a dozen giant crystal chandeliers hung from brass chains in a row down the center of the hall, filling the place with a rich warm light. One end of the room was raised by three stairs, creating a level where the head table could sit higher than all the other tables. The head table was easily forty feet long and sat perpendicular to the length of the room with chairs lined up along the far side so those sitting there could face the room and be seen by all. It was draped with a bright white tablecloth that hung to the floor and was set with silver utensils and delicately crafted porcelain.

The main floor of the banquet hall was lined with rows of tables nearly as long as the head table but placed in alignment with the long axis of the giant room. On the wall at the other end of the long hall was a bar stocked with every possible type of wine, ale, and distilled spirits Alexander could imagine. Directly before the bar was an open dance floor with a small stage off to the side for the minstrels.

The walls were covered with a wide assortment of fine paintings and tapestries. Each looked like a masterwork and each offered a different piece of breathtaking scenery from the Glen Morillian valley. All along the walls rested oak benches carved with intricate patterns of trees, mountains, and animals.

The room was full. Not a seat was empty and it was clear that everyone was waiting for Alexander. He scanned the room and was able to pick out a few of the nobles from the council meeting. Hanlon, Emily, Erik, Lucky, Mason, Anatoly, and Abigail sat at the head table along with a few others that Alexander didn't know, including an attractive woman sitting next to Erik.

Jack surveyed the room calmly, allowing a sense of anticipation to build before speaking. "My lords and ladies, craftsmen and commoners, tradesmen and Rangers, Warden and Lady Alaric, it is my honor and privilege to present to you this night, his most excellent Majesty, Lord Alexander, bearer of the sacred Mark of Cedric, champion of the Old Law and rightful King of Ruatha, accompanied by the beautiful and brave Lady Isabel Alaric."

Alexander couldn't help feeling self-conscious. He thought Jack had gone way over the top and the assembled guests were sure to see through to the truth. He was quite surprised when every single person in the hall stood up, cheering and clapping in welcome.

He glanced at Isabel. She was pleased by the reception and smiled brightly. Alexander nodded his thanks to the guests and made for the head table and the only two vacant seats in the room. Everyone remained standing until he reached his chair. Instead of taking his seat, he picked up the wine glass from his place setting and raised it high. The room fell silent almost immediately.

"Tonight I raise my glass in gratitude to the people of Glen Morillian for your faithful allegiance to the Old Law and your unwavering loyalty to the duty

Mage Cedric charged you with so many years ago." He held his glass high in toast and the room burst into applause and cheers once again.

The moment Alexander took his seat, servants began to stream out of the various service entrances with all manner of trays, platters, boards, dishes, pots, pitchers, and bowls, each filled to overflowing with a dizzying variety of foods.

There were platters of sliced vegetables with bowls of sauce, large boards with ham, roasted duck, pheasant, quail, beef, venison, and elk. Others held assortments of cheeses of every variety imaginable and several that Alexander had never seen before. There were large bowls of fresh green salad; casseroles of potatoes sliced thin and baked with cheese; baskets lined with finely woven and very colorful towels filled to overflowing with hot loaves of bread; fine silver tureens filled with steaming hot soups and thick rich stews; boats with gravies and sauces; huge serving bowls heaping with pasta; platters filled with little bowls of butter, sauces, dips, mustards, jams, jellies, salsas, relishes, and dressings.

Alexander was astonished at the variety and quantity of the foods proudly presented to him by the serving staff. They took pleasure in offering each new dish and seemed to enjoy Alexander's pleasure as he sampled their offerings. Isabel didn't eat much of any one thing but she took great delight in trying a little of everything. When she found something she liked, she insisted that Alexander try it as well. He discovered that he rather enjoyed her attentions and her tastes were excellent. She didn't offer him anything that he didn't find delicious. He chuckled to himself at the dread he'd felt about this evening when he realized he was genuinely enjoying himself.

The food was excellent and soon Alexander was full. He looked out over the assembled guests. Everyone took advantage of the opportunity to sample as many of the fine dishes as they could. He was beginning to understand why these people were so eager to attend the palace banquets. As he scanned the crowd, he could pick out the nobles from their finery and entourages but the majority of the guests were simple farmers, craftsmen, ranchers, traders, miners, and shopkeepers. Such an event offered them the opportunity to enjoy a meal of rich variety and an evening of music, dancing, and fine wine.

There wasn't much chance for any real conversation during the meal because the serving staff was constantly bringing new dishes and trays, and what talk there was focused mostly on the food. Alexander offered his compliments and genuine gratitude to Emily for going to such great lengths in his honor. He didn't think she was going to stop smiling at his kind words.

Lucky was simply delighted. He tried each and every item that came to the table. He was unabashed in his pleasure and effusive in his praise for Emily and her staff. Even Anatoly seemed to be enjoying himself, although he was also keeping a wary eye on the guests. Alexander suspected that a room with this many people in it represented an inherent threat to the big man-at-arms.

As the meal wound down and the main courses began to be removed to make room for the desserts and pastries, conversation in the room began to build. Mostly, each table discussed among themselves the changes that were likely now that Alexander had come. It struck him as odd that this secluded little mountain valley had been waiting for him and preparing for his arrival for the past two thousand years. He still couldn't quite fathom the scope of Mage Cedric's preparations. The Rebel Mage must have been truly guilt stricken by his failure to permanently end the tyranny of the Reishi and the fact that Phane, perhaps the most dangerous of the Reishi line, had escaped into the future, far out of Mage Cedric's reach. These people were his legacy. He set this entire valley apart from the rest of the Seven Isles, protected from the inevitable political upheaval of the world, to await the time when the tyranny of the Reishi would awaken again to consume the lives and liberty of the innocent.

The burden of Alexander's duty settled once again on his shoulders when he saw Jack take a position at the left end of the head table. Jack did seem to have a masterful grasp of timing. The assembled guests were just starting to settle after the feast; most were picking at half-eaten plates of food while sipping glasses of wine, flagons of ale, or goblets of spirits. There was a natural lull in the flow of conversation and Jack stepped in to fill the void.

He caught Alexander's eye with a subtle motion and gave him a look as if asking permission to proceed. Alexander nodded. As much as he was enjoying the evening, he reminded himself that he had a purpose here. He had to win the support of the nobles and the best way to do that was to win over the people in this room. If the craftsmen, shopkeepers, and farmers gave him their allegiance, the nobles would have no choice but to lend their support as well. They couldn't afford to be seen hoarding their wealth when those who had far less gave their support so freely.

Jack took up a fine crystal chalice and a small silver spoon. He checked his position and cleared his throat. Alexander watched the young bard take a deep breath before raising his head and his glass. The clear chime of the crystal chalice brought the gathering to silent attention.

"My lords and ladies, craftsmen and shopkeepers, landholders and commoners, Warden and Lady Alaric, I stand before you this night to recount the journey of Lord Alexander which brought him here to your fine hall and your generous hospitality."

Jack set the glass and spoon on the edge of the table and clasped his hands easily behind his back. His voice carried to every corner of the hall with practiced ease but without sounding strained or overtaxed in the least.

"A fortnight ago, Alexander Valentine was hunting wolves in the north pasture of his family property with his brother and sister, when they were attacked by surprise. An agent of the Reishi Protectorate shot Darius Valentine through the chest with a poisoned arrow." Jack paused as the crowd gasped collectively. Alexander held his breath and his composure even as Isabel took his hand under the table. He glanced at Abigail and saw the tears brimming in her eyes.

"Lord Alexander was quick to respond with an arrow of his own, bringing the enemy's horse down with a single snap shot. He and his sister Abigail rode hard with their mortally wounded brother to seek the help and healing of their family alchemist, but the poison was too potent. Darius Valentine was the first life taken by the Reishi in two thousand years." Jack paused and looked down in deference for a moment. The room fell deathly silent.

"The night Darius Valentine died, Phane Reishi revealed himself to the world. You all heard him arrive. You all felt the magic of the warning spell cast so long ago by Mage Cedric. In that moment, as that wave of magic passed through the whole of the Seven Isles, the sacred Mark of Cedric was burned into the side of Alexander Valentine's neck."

Jack took a sip of water while whispers raced through the room. "Before dawn of the very next morning, Phane sent a zombie demon to attack Valentine Manor and kill Lord Alexander. His brave parents, Duncan and Bella Valentine, faced the netherworld beast to protect their children. To this day, Lord Alexander does not know if his very own mother and father survived that battle, but he does know that their unflinching sacrifice bought him his survival. The last time he looked at his childhood home, it was in flames."

Alexander held Isabel's hand for dear life as he struggled to maintain his composure. He was worried sick about his parents. The evening's festivities had taken his mind off the deadly serious nature of his curse and all that it had already cost him. He glanced again at Abigail and saw tears flowing quietly down her cheeks as Anatoly tried to console her. He reminded himself to be grateful for Jack. He wouldn't have been able to make this speech, even if someone had written it down for him.

"Lord Alexander and his sister Abigail fled to Southport with the protection of Anatoly Grace and Aluicious Alabrand. They made the journey quickly and quietly. The very next morning they woke to an attack by a platoon of Reishi mercenaries led by a fire wizard. It was in that inn just before the attack that I was offered the privilege of joining Lord Alexander's quest.

"We fought the soldiers even as the wizard doused the building with magical liquid fire. Lord Alexander killed the first of the enemy that day. We fled into the basement of the building and from there into the Southport underground where we made our way through the dark until we could find our way back to the surface.

"We dared not retrieve our horses for fear of being discovered, so we made our way on foot through the city until we reached a breach in the outer wall, where we encountered a squad of Southport city guard. They had been hired to kill Lord Alexander—reduced to common mercenaries by the corrupting influence of the Reishi. We fought them, and Lord Alexander felled three in that battle.

"We found shelter in a small farmhouse on the outskirts of town, gained horses and supplies, and set out the next morning for the forest. Knowing the road would be watched, we traveled across the open range. That night as we warmed ourselves around a small fire, we were visited by the ghost of Nicolai Atherton." There was a collective gasp as the room recoiled in a mixture of fear and disbelief.

"Lords and ladies, I must tell you, I would find such a thing hard to believe had I not seen it myself. This ghost warned us, indeed warned Lord Alexander, that Prince Phane had conjured a pack of nether wolves to stalk him in the night and rend the flesh from his very bones." The room fell deadly silent again. Every guest hung on Jack's next words.

"We were trapped. The Reishi were camped on the road ahead and beasts conjured from the darkness itself were stalking us from behind. Our horses were exhausted from a long day's travel and we knew it was only a matter of time before one of them came up lame. In the face of such a dilemma, Lord Alexander invented a new choice. One that few would have had the audacity to consider and fewer still would have had the courage and skill to accomplish." Jack smiled into the waiting silence and let the anticipation build within the crowd.

"Lord Alexander chose to steal the Reishi mercenaries' horses from their camp in the dead of night." He paused to let the whispers ripple through the room.

"His plan worked brilliantly. He and Master Grace slipped in under the cover of darkness. They strung together ten of the enemy horses and scattered the rest. Then, as they made good their escape, a lone man with a crossbow made a lucky shot from the dark and drove his barbed bolt into Lord Alexander's shoulder just inches from his heart." Again Jack paused and allowed the murmur of concern and fear to make its way through the room before he continued.

"From dawn to dusk we rode hard. We could all see the agony Lord Alexander was suffering. The barbed bolt was buried in his shoulder, its point scraping against bone with every stride of his horse. He did not falter, he did not waver, and he did not succumb to the torture of that awful day. With a platoon of Reishi mercenaries chasing us with all the speed they could muster, we made it to the old watchtower at the south edge of the forest just before dusk." Isabel squeezed Alexander's hand and gave him a worried look at the telling of how he'd been injured.

"On top of that plateau we made our stand. Master Alabrand, with the aid of his arcane arts, healed Lord Alexander's wound, and not a moment too soon, for the enemy had arrived and they were advancing. Six men came up the side of the plateau in the night, but we defended successfully and none made it to the top. The remaining Reishi mercenaries and the fire wizard made camp on the plain below to wait for reinforcements. We were trapped. Then we heard the howl." Jack took a sip of water while his audience collectively held its breath. "In all my years, I have never heard a sound so cold, so cruel, or so evil as the shriek of the dark beasts that stalked Lord Alexander that night.

"Nether wolves were loose in the world again for the first time since the Reishi War ... and they were coming. We spent most of the night trying to sleep while we awaited our fate. Lords and ladies, for my part, I am not ashamed to admit that the otherworldly howl of those dark beasts made my blood run cold. In truth, I did not believe that I would live to see the sunrise." Jack gave a little shudder. Alexander couldn't tell if it was real or simply stagecraft.

"During the darkest hour, just before dawn, their shriek of madness and hate shattered the night again. They were close. Moments later we found ourselves in a fight for our very lives. We hurled stones the size of a man's head at the beasts. Two of them took direct hits and fell from the path to the ground thirty feet below, only to bound back to their feet and renew their attack. Lord Alexander and Lady Abigail drove a dozen arrows into another of the foul monsters with nearly no effect. The creatures simply could not be killed, or so we began to think.

"They gained the top of the plateau. We were surrounded. We'd taken refuge atop the gatehouse, when one of the beasts bounded into the middle of us. In the brief but furious and desperate battle that followed, Master Grace cleaved the flank of the creature, distracting it for just an instant and taking the full force of a punishing attack for his effort. In that moment of opportunity, Lord Alexander struck." Jack paused again for dramatic effect. "The first of the three nether wolves fell as it lost its head to Lord Alexander's sure stroke." The crowd actually cheered. Alexander was torn between embarrassment at the embellished telling of the story and wonder at Jack's seemingly effortless ability to hold the crowd in thrall.

"I'm afraid our victory was short-lived." The bard shook his head to forestall their enthusiasm. "In the next few moments, the remaining two netherworld beasts were poised to kill two of the people that Lord Alexander loves most in this world: his faithful protector, teacher, and family man-at-arms, Master Anatoly Grace, and his beloved sister, Lady Abigail." Jack pointed out each in turn to put a face to the characters in his story.

"One nether wolf stood over the unconscious Master Grace, preparing to clamp its massive jaws around his head, while the other dark beast launched itself into the air in an arc that would bring the deadly monster crashing down on top of Lady Abigail." Once again Jack paused and casually took a sip of water. The whole banquet room fell quiet.

"At that very moment, when all seemed lost, dawn broke. It was as if the sun itself charged into battle flying Lord Alexander's banner. The clear light of dawn undid the foul beasts, leaving only a cloud of noxious black smoke where a moment before was a creature of bone and fang." Again the crowd breathed a sigh of relief and astonishment. Jack gave them a moment before resuming his story.

"But the beasts were not slain. No, they had simply taken refuge in the very ground itself to escape the light of the sun and would rise again to renew the hunt at dusk. And, the Reishi mercenaries and their wizard were still at the foot of the plateau. Only minutes later they launched their attack. The wizard called up liquid fire hot enough to burn the stone of the watchtower itself. Again and again he cast his magical fire up at us until Lord Alexander commanded that we make our attempt to reach the base of the plateau and engage the enemy. And his command came not a moment too soon, for the ancient watchtower that has stood for millennia crashed to the ground even as we fled down the narrow path to the plain below.

"When we rounded the corner and came into view of the wizard, he was conjuring yet another ball of liquid fire. His spell would have surely destroyed us all except for the brave and timely intervention of your own Rangers. The Alaric brothers, their sister Isabel, and Chase Covington drove the Reishi mercenaries off with their expert archery skills. You have reason to feel great pride for your Rangers. They proved their mettle that day and stood by their oath to protect the Ruathan bloodline." The room cheered again. Erik and Hanlon looked proud. Isabel blushed.

"The Reishi had reinforcements coming, so we rode hard all that day and covered a great distance. In the growing darkness under the shadow of the forest we took refuge in Falls Cave." There was a murmur amongst the guests as some of them confirmed that they knew the place. "We were successful in throwing the Reishi off our trail but had no such luck with the two remaining nether wolves. At dusk we heard their howls in the distance. None of us slept well that night.

"Well before dawn, the beasts found us. The battle that followed is mostly a blur. They came fast, faster than any horse can run. The first to reach us met Master Grace and his war axe. He knocked the beast off balance, giving Lord Alexander the opening he needed to deliver a mighty kick to the beast and send it toppling into the water. The second nether wolf leapt over a kill stroke leveled at it by Master Grace and landed squarely on Lord Alexander, sending him crashing into Lady Isabel, and then to the ground." There was another gasp. Emily gave Isabel a look that was at once worried and reproving.

"The dark creature reared up and drove its monstrous jaws forward for the kill strike, but Lord Alexander smashed it in the side of the head with the pommel of his sword, sending the creature snapping into the dirt. When it reared up to strike again, Lady Isabel drove her sword over Lord Alexander's shoulder and into the eye socket of the beast." Jack smiled in a knowing sort of way. "I'm here to tell you, it did not like that. The beast skittered backward off Lord Alexander, and the Alaric brothers, Chase Covington, and Master Grace hacked it to pieces." There was another collective sigh.

"Lord Alexander and Lady Isabel had scarcely regained their feet when the last nether wolf pulled itself from the water and renewed the attack. It charged straight for Lord Alexander and might have had him except for the unflinching bravery of Lady Isabel. She stepped right in front of the charging beast, sword raised and ready, but the nether wolf was just too quick. It crashed into her and sent her sprawling with broken ribs before it quickly turned and lunged at Lord Alexander. In the split second that Lady Isabel had given him with her incomprehensible courage, Lord Alexander gained the advantage that he needed. He spun to the side when the beast charged and brought his sword around with furious speed and took its head off with a single stroke." Another cheer filled the room. Several of the audience stood to clap. Alexander gave Isabel's hand a little squeeze. That had been a terrifying struggle and he knew without doubt that he would have died that day if not for her.

"We made our way to the main road and soon discovered that the Reishi had gained ground on us. They were now ahead of our position and lying in wait on Flat Top Rock." Again there were murmurs of acknowledgement by those in the room. Flat Top Rock was a well-known landmark to the people of Glen Morillian. "Rather than risk an engagement that we couldn't win, Lord Alexander did the next best thing. He led us through the forest on foot around Flat Top Rock." Jack chuckled, "And then, we stole the Reishi's horses for a second time in as many days." The room burst out in laughter and applause. Jack smiled and nodded as he beseeched the crowd to quiet down so he could continue. "I would pay good money to see the look on that wizard's face when he realized we had their horses … again." Laughter filled the room. This time Jack simply let it go until it started to die down on its own.

"We arrived at the fortress gate to Glen Morillian the next day. There are those who say that Lord Alexander is not the rightful heir to the Throne of Ruatha. I say he is. The mark burned into his neck by Mage Cedric's magic says he is. Warden Alaric says he is. Prince Phane Reishi says he is." Jack waited for a moment to let that last one sink in. "But you must decide for yourselves. Your free will is your own. I ask only that you consider this one question. Are these not the deeds of a king?"

Jack bowed and withdrew as the crowd stood to cheer and applaud.

Alexander wasn't sure if the enthusiasm was for him or for Jack's masterful rendition of their journey. Either way, the evening had been a success thus far so he decided to capitalize on it. He stood and took Isabel's hand. "Would you like to dance?"

Chapter 29

She smiled brilliantly even as her face flushed. Nodding in a giddy sort of way, she came to her feet in a rush and followed him out onto the dance floor. The minstrels filled the hall with music the moment they stepped onto the floor.

Holding her in his arms seemed to drown out everything else in the world. With all he had to worry about, he simply couldn't take his full and complete attention off of the woman he was dancing with. She captivated him in a way he didn't even know was possible. Her simple presence made the world sweeter, more vibrant, and filled with possibilities that he'd never even considered before. He'd seen the way his parents looked at each other from time to time, but never truly understood the bottomless well of joy that that simple look represented. It seemed like such a profound thing to simply hold her in his arms and share a dance with her. He realized in that moment that he had fallen in love with Isabel. That realization changed nothing of his circumstances but changed everything about the way he saw the threat he faced, the world, and his place in it.

What a precious and fragile thing love was. It was so worthy of protecting, of nurturing and sheltering. He wondered how many others had discovered this miraculous feeling within themselves. All in a rush of renewed terror, it dawned on him that this was what was at stake. Love would be the ultimate casualty of Phane's ambitions. The peace and security that every family in the Seven Isles depended on to survive and thrive was in jeopardy. And then, in a flash of stark horror, he imagined losing Isabel. The mere thought was agony itself. How many others would experience such unendurable pain if Phane prevailed?

The music stopped. Isabel's bright smile faded and a look of worry overtook her face. "What's wrong?" she asked.

Alexander pulled himself back from the darkness of what might be and anchored himself in the moment. He was still holding Isabel and looking down into her piercing green eyes. He shook his head slowly and let the joy of her presence back in with a smile. "Nothing. I just let the challenges ahead distract me for a moment."

The dance floor was clearing as the minstrels took a break. Isabel put her hand on his cheek. "It'll be all right, Alexander, you'll see." Then she smiled with mischief. "Come on," she said, taking his hand and leading him to the bar.

One of the young bartenders saw them coming and put off another customer politely so he could serve the guest of honor. Isabel smiled at him familiarly. "Hi Aaron, we'd like two chocolate swirls." He nodded and began to prepare two rather elaborate-looking concoctions involving warm cream, chocolate shavings, and some kind of syrupy liqueur. "These are my favorite," Isabel said with excitement.

Alexander marveled at her enthusiasm for simple pleasures. She was essentially a princess, yet she was as giddy as a schoolgirl at the prospect of sharing a confection with him. When the drinks were served, Alexander was actually impressed. They were delivered in large silver goblets wrapped in white linen napkins to protect against the heat of the drink. The rich chocolatey-looking contents had a swirl of white in the foamy topping and a sprinkle of chocolate shavings just resting on the surface of the foam.

Isabel sipped at hers and moaned softly. Alexander thought to himself that he could be happy simply watching her enjoyment. Then he tried his and understood. It was sweet, smooth, creamy, and chocolatey with just a hint of bite from the liqueur and a spicy aftertaste that only left him wanting another sip. He smiled at Isabel in surprised delight.

She giggled in return, "Told you."

They walked slowly back through the crowd toward the head table, nodding to a guest here and smiling to a guest there, when Rexius Truss stepped into their path. Alexander really didn't want to talk to the self-important little man, but thought it would be unwise to snub him. Isabel's hand tightened slightly on his arm.

"Your Majesty," Truss bowed ever so slightly. "That was quite a harrowing tale we heard tonight. Your proxy certainly has a flair for the dramatic." Isabel's grip tightened a little more.

"Yes, he does have a way with words." Alexander smiled agreeably. "I trust you are enjoying the generous hospitality of Lady Alaric."

"Yes, quite. I was wondering if I might have the pleasure of a dance with Lady Isabel here." His smile was almost as greasy as his slicked-back hair. Isabel's grip on his arm tightened further still.

Alexander leaned in so he could speak to Truss without being overheard. "I'm afraid that I managed to step on her foot and I think she would really like to sit down. We were just headed to our table. Perhaps another time," Alexander said with a look of embarrassment.

Isabel feigned a slight limp, leaning on his arm as they started around the little noble, but he stepped in front of them again.

"I'm terribly sorry to hear that, Lady Isabel. I do hope Lord Alexander hasn't seriously injured you." His look of concern was almost believable. "I would be happy to have my personal physician look at it for you if you like." He turned and waved to one of the men at his table.

"Oh, that won't be necessary, really, I just want to sit down." Isabel took another step to skirt Truss but he intervened again.

Before he could say anything more, Jack appeared from out of the crowd. "Duke Truss, I was wondering if I could have a moment of your time. I understand your vineyards are responsible for this vintage." He swirled the wine in his crystal goblet. "It has a most delightful character."

Truss turned to Jack with a much more genuine smile. "Ah, yes, this is one of the signature blends of my family estates." When he turned back Isabel and Alexander were nearly to the head table. Jack cleared his throat to draw him back into conversation. Truss indulged him for several minutes before returning to his table and his entourage with a somewhat sullen look.

Isabel laughed quietly to Alexander when they reached the head table. "You're my hero," she said, taking her seat. "Truss just won't take no for an answer."

"I'm sure he'll get the hint sooner or later."

Alexander scanned the banquet hall. Most of the guests were mingling amongst the tables or near the bar. Hanlon and Anatoly were telling stories of their time together in the border wars to an audience of half a dozen young men including Erik. Abigail was talking quietly with the attractive young woman who had accompanied Erik to the banquet. Jack was moving through the crowd from one talking circle to the next, and Lucky had dragged the chef from the kitchen, sat him down at a table, and was busy extracting recipes from him.

Alexander was about to suggest that he and Isabel take a walk on the ramparts when a group of three nobles, including Truss, approached and planted themselves across the table from him.

"Ah, Your Majesty, may I present Duke Covington and Duke Shivley," Truss said, looking down at Alexander past his sharp little nose.

"Pleasure to meet you, gentlemen." Alexander didn't stand. He really wasn't in the mood for politics. "Chase must be your son," he said to Duke Covington.

Duke Covington drew himself up proudly. "He is indeed."

"He's a good man. You have reason to be proud," Alexander said.

Covington beamed at the praise for his son. "You are very kind to say so, Your Majesty. We don't mean to trouble you this evening but we thought you should be aware that there are still some significant issues to be worked out at council before we can agree to support your claim to the throne."

Alexander felt his mood fall and his anger start to rise, but he kept his voice civil if not somewhat cold. "Really? What issues might those be?"

Truss jumped in before Covington could continue. "You must understand our lands and holdings have been in our families for many generations. We have a duty to our progeny to preserve our estates. We simply seek some assurances that our property will not be taken without fair compensation."

Alexander mused for a moment before replying. "Your lands are indeed yours, as the Old Law says. However, you must understand," he paused and looked hard at each in turn with his gold-flecked eyes, "the Seven Isles are about to be consumed by war. As I said at council, you have a choice to make. Side with me and lend what support you can to preserve the Old Law or side with Phane."

Truss tried unsuccessfully to smile. "There are those who would choose to abstain from the war you speak of. After all, we have much to lose and little to gain by such sacrifice." He spoke in such reasonable tones.

Alexander schooled his emotions while hot anger rose in his chest. He held Truss with his gaze, anger glittering in his golden-brown eyes. The other conversations at the table had fallen silent and all eyes were on him. When he spoke, he did not raise his voice but instead spoke with deliberate calm.

"My brother is dead. My home burned to the ground and my parents may be lost to me as well. Do not speak to me of sacrifice." Truss recoiled half a step and tried to backpedal but Alexander cut him off. "There will be no middle ground. For two thousand years, Glen Morillian has enjoyed the protection of the barrier mountains created by Mage Cedric. This place was created to lend support to my cause. You swore an oath to support my cause when you were granted title to your estate. If you choose to abstain from this war, then I will count you with Phane." Everyone at the table held their breath. Truss opened and closed his mouth like a fish searching for a response to the hard choice that had been placed before him. Shivley and Covington went pale and shifted ever so slightly away from Truss.

"That is hardly fair and certainly does nothing to respect the Old Law you claim to revere." Truss seemed to gain confidence as he spoke. "Our property is ours alone; you have no right to take it from us."

"I have no intention of taking your property. I expect you to offer what support you can to your king." Alexander tried to sound calm yet confident, both to establish his authority with the nobles and with the crowd of people who were gathering to watch the exchange.

Truss turned slightly crimson as his anger boiled over. "You are not our king unless and until we say you are." His arrogance was insufferable. "The Council of Glen Morillian has yet to recognize you and without the Thinblade, you have no legitimate claim to the throne. You have no right to demand anything from anyone."

The room fell deadly silent. Every guest in the banquet hall turned to watch Truss rail against Alexander's claim to power. Alexander regarded the petty little noble through glittering gold-flecked eyes for a moment while he calmly considered his options.

He stood slowly and pulled his collar aside so all in the hall could see the mark burned into the side of his neck. It was Jack who bailed him out of the tense confrontation. Standing in the very front of the gathered crowd of guests the smooth-tongued bard deliberately went to one knee and bowed to Alexander. There was a moment of hesitation, then, like a wave emanating from Jack Colton, the assembled guests all went to a knee and bowed their heads in fealty.

Alexander smiled at the little noble ever so slightly and motioned past him with his chin. The three nobles standing before him turned as one. Truss squeaked slightly and jumped at the sight of the entire hall bowing to Alexander. His head snapped back around to find Covington and Shivley on bended knee as well. He looked from side to side searching for support from any quarter, but found none. Shaking with rage, Duke Truss turned and fled.

"Rise," Alexander commanded in a clear voice. "Honored guests, I trust you will forgive the interruption. Please enjoy the evening. Lady Alaric has gone to such trouble to make this night memorable. I would hate to see her efforts wasted over a simple disagreement."

Alexander found Jack in the crowd and gave him a nod of thanks before addressing the remaining two nobles still standing in front of him. "Gentlemen, I trust this matter will be settled at council tomorrow morning." It was not a question.

Duke Covington actually smiled. "I assure you it will be, Your Majesty." He and Shivley bowed gracefully and melted back into the throng of guests.

Isabel leaned in and whispered in his ear. "That was magnificent." He felt a little thrill race up his spine at the feel of her warm breath on his neck.

"I'm glad you liked it," he whispered, looking toward the door Truss had left through. "I hope he comes around." Alexander was worried that Truss might yet prove to be trouble.

Isabel laughed. "After that, he'll have no choice. His supporters on the council will abandon him. By lunchtime tomorrow he'll be a laughing stock everywhere in Glen Morillian." She shook her head. "I doubt he'll even show for council tomorrow."

Alexander was still worried. He hoped the self-important little man wasn't fool enough to throw his lot in with Phane.

Hanlon and Anatoly stepped up to him. "Looks like you carried the day, Alexander," Hanlon said with a chuckle.

"I must say, Jack certainly surprised me today," Anatoly added, looking out over the crowd at the bard.

Alexander nodded with a smile, "He definitely has his strengths."

Alexander spent the rest of the evening with Isabel on his arm, chatting with his guests. He listened politely while people of all walks of life explained their trades and offered their services in the coming struggle. They all seemed to have a romantic view of what lay ahead and Alexander didn't have the heart to shatter that vision. He knew that the future held death and hardship but he needed these people. He needed what they had to offer and so he listened politely and offered his gratitude for their support. Most were nervous speaking to him and puffed up with pride when he acknowledged the value of their promised contribution. He spoke at more length with a few of the ranchers simply because he understood their business and could talk to them in terms they were familiar with. They were especially proud that their new king understood and valued their trade so well.

Eventually he found himself standing in a circle of nobles. Alexander felt somehow uncomfortable with them and it was obvious that after the events of the evening they were intimidated by him, but he knew he needed them so he made his best effort to be friendly. Conversation revolved around the types of goods each noble could offer to the war effort. Some had food while others had timber and still others steel. It was clear that they had come around to supporting Alexander as each tried to best the others in terms of the value of his contribution. Eventually talk came around to Alexander.

Lord Covington broached the subject. "Lord Alexander, if I may ask, how do you plan to proceed now that you have the support of the council, and Glen Morillian is set to formally recognize your claim to the throne?"

Alexander thought for only a moment. He had a pretty good idea what he was going to do, but he really didn't trust the members of the council enough to reveal the full extent of his plans. "I intend to build an army but I expect most of that will be done by Warden Alaric and his Rangers. As for me, I have some work to do with Wizard Kallentera and then I'll be leaving."

Isabel's hand tightened on his arm and she gave him a slightly worried look. Duke Shively asked, "Where will you go? You're safe here. Surely it would be wiser to remain here until the army is ready to move with you." There was a murmur of assent from the ring of nobles.

"It may well be safer here but I can't gain the support of the other territories from here. I need to get to New Ruatha and claim the throne so I can summon the territorial governors and demand their allegiance."

Alexander tried to sound calm even though he had no idea how he was going to accomplish such a thing. He didn't tell them about Blackstone Keep, which was his real destination. Nor did he tell them about the mana fast that he intended to undertake.

In the stunned silence that followed, Isabel's grip on his arm tightened a little more. Lord Covington broke the quiet. "That's quite a bold plan but it does put your safety in grave jeopardy. Surely you will take a sizeable force of Rangers as a royal guard."

Alexander shook his head, "The Rangers will be needed here to help Warden Alaric build and train the army. Besides, I have to move faster than a large unit can travel."

They all started speaking at once, mostly in protest.

Alexander held up his hand to silence them. "Ruatha must be reunited under one flag if we are to build the kind of army we need. Phane is gathering forces to himself at this very moment. Glen Morillian is a safe haven that can be easily defended, but we will not win this war by defense. I must find a way to strike at Phane, to put him on the defensive, to disrupt his plans, and undermine his allies. I can't do that behind the safety of these mountains. I must be visible if I am to draw the territories of Ruatha together again into one nation."

Duke Covington smiled approvingly, "I see your point and admire your courage. A lesser man would remain in the safety of our barrier mountains as long as possible. I do hope you will make adequate preparations for your safety."

"I certainly intend to. Now, gentlemen, if you'll excuse me, it's been a long day." Alexander bid them all a good evening and extracted himself with Isabel still on his arm from the circle of nobles, leaving them to discuss amongst themselves how to best build an army.

The banquet was winding down. The guests were starting to thin and the servants were clearing dishes and glasses from the tables. Alexander realized he was tired.

Once they were out of earshot, Isabel stopped and looked up at him with her piercing green eyes. She was so beautiful it made his heart ache. "You know I'm coming with you, right?" He could see she was ready to overpower any objection he might offer. "You're going to need a guide who knows the forest and Slyder gives me the ability to see the enemy coming a long way off. Face it, Alexander, you need me," she said with mock haughtiness and a defiant smile, daring him to refuse her.

Instead he gently brushed her hair back over her ear. "I wouldn't have it any other way," he whispered.

Her face flushed slightly at his touch. She blinked a few times as if she hadn't fully expected his response before smiling radiantly. They walked wordlessly from the banquet room and through the halls of the palace to Alexander's suite. There didn't seem to be any need for words. They each simply took comfort in the presence of the other.

He didn't say anything when they arrived at his door. Instead he simply took her in with his eyes before gently pulling her into his arms and kissing her softly yet passionately. She leaned into him and returned his kiss with abandon.

"Good night, Isabel. Sleep well," he whispered.

She sighed before giving him a look that made his heart race. "I doubt I'll sleep at all after that."

She left him standing outside his room with his heart pounding, his mind filled with possibility, and his soul soaring. It had been a much better night than he would have ever expected.

Chapter 30

Alexander slept like a baby. He woke early the next morning to the sound of loud banging on his outer door. He threw on a robe and opened the door to find Erik.

"Is she here?" It seemed as though Erik couldn't decide if he was angry or worried.

Alexander was still a bit groggy. "Who?"

"Isabel. Is she here? You left the banquet with her last night." He brushed past Alexander and went to the bedroom.

Alexander stood at the door and watched him while scratching his head and trying to stifle a yawn. Erik no sooner stepped into Alexander's bedchamber before he came out looking even more worried. Alexander started to feel a tingle of dread work its way up his spine.

"Erik, what's going on?" Alexander asked.

"Isabel is missing. She never came back to the family living quarters last night. Her room is empty, her bed hasn't been slept in, and the gown she wore last night isn't in her armoire. Slyder is gone, too. Isabel doesn't do this kind of thing. She always makes sure to tell someone where she's going." The words tumbled out of Erik's mouth as if he couldn't get them out fast enough.

Alexander was fully awake now. "Let me get dressed and I'll help you look for her." Alexander didn't take long. He strapped on his sword and long knife on his way out of his bedchamber.

Erik was pacing.

"I'm sorry, I thought, I mean I was just hoping…" Erik sputtered.

Alexander held up a hand to stop him.

"That's not important, Erik. Let's go find Isabel." He stepped into the hall. "The last I saw her she walked to the end of this hall and turned that corner."

Erik nodded, "That leads to the family living quarters."

"All right, let's trace her most likely path," Alexander said.

Erik was clearly agitated but seemed to be somewhat settled by Alexander's calm approach to the problem. He led the way down the hall and around the corner. The long hall that followed was interrupted here and there by doors to several other guestrooms.

Alexander stopped and relaxed his vision in the hopes that his second sight might reveal something, but it didn't. "Where do these doors lead?"

"Most are guestrooms, one is a cleaning closet, and that one at the end leads to a servants' access passage," Erik answered.

"Is anyone staying in any of these rooms?"

Erik thought for a moment before shaking his head. "The rest of your companions are on the other side of your room. These are all empty."

"Good."

Alexander marched to the first door and threw it open. It was much smaller than his suite and only offered one room rather than a sitting room and a bedchamber. The curtains were drawn back and tied open, the floors were clean, the fireplace was cold, and the linens were neatly folded on the foot of the bed. Alexander closed the door and went to the next while Erik opened the door across the hall.

They worked their way down the hall going door to door. Each room was clean, cold, and ready to be made up for the next guest.

The service corridor at the end of the hall opened onto the landing of a long staircase that led down several flights, broken by landings every twelve or fifteen steps. It was dimly lit with low-burning oil lamps at each landing, and it looked clean and well kept.

"Where does this lead?" Alexander asked.

"Down to the kitchen, prep rooms, and service quarters," Erik answered, looking past Alexander down the stairs.

Alexander was about to close the door when something caught his eye. He froze as he tried to peer through the gloomy light. When he bolted down the stairs, Erik followed right on his heels and nearly knocked him down the final flight of stairs when Alexander came to an abrupt halt on the second landing.

There, on the next step down, was Isabel's white fur shawl. He picked it up carefully, almost tenderly. When he turned it over and saw the lurid splotch of bright red blood, his legs nearly buckled. He steadied himself against the wall and handed Erik the shawl while fighting to keep the icy dread of the unthinkable from flooding into his mind and rendering him helpless.

He heard a low groan escape from Erik before he bounded down the remaining flight of stairs and raced down the hall. He stopped where the hall came to a tee and frantically looked back and forth down the hall for any further sign of Isabel. To his right, the corridor led to an outside exit. To his left, it led deeper into the palace. When he saw the puddle of red coming out from under the door, he felt the unthinkable push against his defenses. He dashed for the door and yanked it open.

There in the middle of the little storeroom lay a young man in a pool of cold and sticky blood. He had a wound in his gut from a single thrust of a blade that had apparently run him completely through. Next to the man, Alexander saw a footprint in the blood. He looked down the hall in the dim light and found what he expected. There was a blood trail leading from the outside door at the end of the corridor and a boot print in increasingly faded blood leading back to the door. When he opened the door to the service courtyard on the side of the palace, he saw where the young man had been killed. Blood mixed with dirt to form an ugly brown mud. Then he saw one of Isabel's shoes. As he picked it up, he swallowed hard.

"Take me to the nearest Ranger barracks," he commanded Erik, who nodded woodenly, his face ashen white.

Erik led him at a dead run around the courtyard and into a nondescript entrance to the low barracks room. The light of day was just overcoming the darkness and the Rangers were still sleeping. Alexander came to a halt just inside the door. There were rows of ten bunks on each side of the long room, each with a locker at the foot, and each with a man snoring under the covers.

"Everybody up!" Alexander boomed. A few came out of their bunks quickly, while a few rolled over and pulled their pillows over their heads.

"Everybody up, now!" he bellowed. "I am Lord Alexander and I expect every one of you dressed and ready to ride in five minutes. I will wait outside. Do not make me wait long."

Alexander felt a rising sense of sick panic in his belly and struggled to transform it into anger. He stalked from the barracks, allowing his anger to fester and boil.

"Erik, go tell your parents what's happened. Get Anatoly and Mason as well. I'm going to ride with the Rangers as soon as they're ready."

Erik nodded and dashed off.

Only a minute or two passed before the platoon leader emerged fully dressed. He was older than Alexander by several years and looked experienced by his bearing. His eyes were a deep brown and his hair was jet black and cropped short. He stood about Alexander's height and was only slightly heavier. Alexander could see the anger under his schooled demeanor. He strode up to Alexander, came smartly to attention and snapped a salute against his chest.

"Lord Alexander, I am Lieutenant Cross, leader of this platoon. If I may ask, what are our orders this fine morning?"

Alexander regarded the lieutenant calmly, deliberately nurturing his anger. "I will brief all of you at once, Lieutenant."

The Ranger regarded him somewhat more coolly and nodded once, "As you wish, My Lord."

Others were beginning to emerge from the barracks, first in a trickle, then in a steady stream until they all stood in formation behind their lieutenant.

"All present and accounted for, My Lord." Cross had reined in his anger and replaced it with the studied, detached professionalism of a soldier.

Alexander took a deep breath and held up Isabel's shoe. "Lady Isabel has been abducted." The lieutenant stiffened and his anger came back in a flash, only more fiercely. "I was the last to see her after the banquet last night. She was brought down the service passage from the guest quarters and out the door into the service courtyard around the corner there." Alexander pointed in the direction he and Erik had come from. "Erik and I also found a dead man in a small supply room just inside the outer door."

The entire platoon was standing at attention and looked ready for blood. Isabel was one of their own. Alexander could see the fierce loyalty they had for her and for her family.

"Lieutenant, you and your two best trackers will come with me while the rest of your men get horses for all of us and bring them around to the side courtyard." Alexander issued his commands with deliberate calm that masked his boiling rage, then turned and strode off toward the scene of the crime.

Lieutenant Cross started barking orders and was quickly following a step behind and to the right of Alexander with another two men in tow.

Alexander stopped short of the area in front of the door. "This is where they came out. I found her shoe right over there. I believe the young man was killed right there." Alexander pointed to the blood in the dirt. "Lieutenant, have your trackers examine the area and tell me what else they see."

The lieutenant nodded to the two men and they moved into the area very carefully, slowly, and deliberately so as not to disturb any tracks that might be there. One went inside while the other looked carefully at the ground in the surrounding area. Only a minute later, the two returned to the lieutenant and Alexander with their report.

"Lord Alexander, you say you and Erik came out of this door and found Isabel's shoe. Are these your tracks here?" The Ranger tracker pointed to the deep boot prints from Alexander and Erik.

Alexander nodded.

They looked at each other before one spoke. "There were two men here. One struggled briefly with the dead man in the storage room, killed him there where you thought, and then dragged him inside to conceal his body. Isabel was unconscious, loaded into a wagon or cart and taken in that direction. Presuming they remained in the cart and traveled all night, they are likely several miles ahead of us." He looked up at the sky. "Looks like a clear day ahead, so we should be able to track them well enough." The other nodded to confirm the report.

Moments later a herd of horses came around the corner bearing a platoon of angry Rangers bristling with spears, swords, and bows. Four men in the lead had the reins of an extra horse each. Alexander recognized his fine white mare with the brown splotch on its forehead and was pleased to see his bow and quiver were strapped to his saddle.

All four mounted up. Alexander raised his voice over the sound of anxious horses. "The trackers will take the lead. Do not get ahead of them and destroy the trail."

Everyone in the platoon nodded, some even looked a bit offended at the rather obvious command. Alexander didn't care.

They rode more slowly than Alexander wanted to. He was seething with anger and fighting to keep the unthinkable from overtaking his reason. The trackers were careful and thorough. On some stretches of road they were able to move quickly but on others they slowed to a crawl. Not an hour from the edge of town, they came to an intersection where three roads came together to form one larger road leading into the heart of Glen Morillian. The trackers stopped and dismounted. They spent several minutes going over the ground, even getting down on all fours and combing slowly through the dry dirt before agreeing on the road to take.

Half an hour later they came to a wide, shallow place in a small stream that served as a ford for road traffic. There was a small copse of trees hugging the opposite bank. The platoon let their horses drink from the crystal-clear water while the trackers dismounted on the far side. This time they didn't need to crawl but simply walked, heads down, right off the side of the road before stopping abruptly and pointing toward the stand of hardwoods that grew up along that section of the mountain stream.

Lieutenant Cross issued orders to his men with hand signals that they clearly understood perfectly. The platoon broke into four smaller units and spread out to approach the grove from several angles at once. When they entered the trees, they converged on a finely made four-wheeled cart. With practiced precision, the Rangers surrounded and enclosed the enemy position, half approaching with spears at the ready while the other half remained at range with arrows nocked.

The lead force called out to the lieutenant and Alexander, "It's empty. Looks like it's been abandoned."

Alexander dismounted, handing the reins of his horse to the nearest Ranger, and vaulted into the back of the cart. He found a blanket and some straw in the bed. His heart skipped a beat when he found a strip of cloth from Isabel's dress. She was leaving breadcrumbs. At the very least, she was alive when the cart was abandoned.

"Lieutenant, she was here. Search the area." He held up the little strip of cloth from her dress. With swift precision, the Rangers fanned out and did a quick but thorough search of the surrounding woods.

Within minutes, a Ranger called out from the bank of the stream, "Here, they brought her here."

Alexander, the lieutenant, and several others made their way to the bank.

The Ranger held up another little strip of cloth. "Looks like two men brought her here," he pointed to some tracks in the damp dirt. "They struggled and she went down here," he pointed out the place where Isabel had hit the ground. "Then they loaded her into a boat and cast off," he pointed to the overturned stones in the shallows along the bank and the indentation left in the soggy ground where the boat had been moored.

"This was planned," Alexander muttered to himself.

Lieutenant Cross agreed, "Whoever did this thought it through pretty carefully."

"Where does this stream lead?" Alexander asked.

The lieutenant looked in the direction the stream was flowing and frowned for a moment before he answered, "I believe it leads into the estates of Duke Covington."

Alexander tried to reason it out. Who would want to take Isabel and why? The only name that came to mind was Truss, but her abductors had clearly taken her downstream toward Covington's lands. It didn't make sense. When Alexander had looked at the nobles with his second sight, Covington was the most trustworthy.

"Lieutenant, search the area again. Make sure we haven't missed anything."

Cross issued orders to his men without hesitation. He was thorough, professional, and clearly had the respect and loyalty of his men. Alexander decided he liked him.

Minutes later they reported back. They'd found the horse that had drawn the cart wandering in the fields nearby and there were no other tracks. Isabel had been taken downstream in a small boat.

"Lieutenant, send a rider back to the palace to report to Warden Alaric, then split your force in half. I'll take one group and we'll work our way down this side of the stream while you work down the other side."

Again the lieutenant nodded to Alexander and issued his orders with precision and unmistakable command authority. His men obeyed without question.

Moving down the bank of the stream was slow going. The ground was uneven and muddy in many places and Alexander wanted to be sure that they didn't miss anything. He let the tracker set the pace and relied on his expertise to find where the abductors had come ashore. Close to noon, they came to a spot where the stream flowed into a wooded area, which slowed their progress even further. The trees were thick along the bank and the undergrowth hampered the horses. Alexander was becoming worried that they would lose the trail, when they came to a clearing where a horse trail crossed the stream along a little wooden bridge constructed of two logs lined on top with rough-cut boards.

Caught under the bridge was a simple little boat. It looked like the people who'd abducted Isabel had let the boat loose in the stream but neglected to ensure that it made it under the low bridge. The Ranger trackers made a quick search of the area. They quickly called Alexander and Lieutenant Cross over to a burned-out campfire.

"There was a single man waiting here with a team of four horses. The boat was brought ashore there," the tracker pointed to a spot on the bank of the little mountain stream. "Two sets of tracks lead here. One set is much deeper than the other so we believe one of the men was carrying Lady Isabel. He put her down here," he indicated an area of the grass that was crushed. "If you look closely you can see the print of a woman's bare foot." He squatted down with Alexander and the lieutenant and pointed out the faint impression Isabel had made on a soft place in the ground.

"From here she was walked by two men, one on each side, to here, where she mounted a horse. Looks like all four left that way along the trail," the tracker pointed into the trees.

"Good work. Take the lead and stay sharp," Alexander commanded as he returned to his horse.

They moved on into the woods along the narrow horse path. The trail wound around trees and was narrow enough that they rode single file. Not an hour later they emerged from the woods onto a well-traveled road. It was wide, travel-worn, and formed of hard packed dirt. The trackers spent nearly half an hour searching the road for any indication of which direction Isabel and her abductors had gone but found nothing among all the other horse and wagon tracks. As they searched, Alexander felt cold dread settling into the pit of his stomach. After the first few minutes, he knew they wouldn't find anything but he let them search without interruption in the hope that he was wrong.

"Lieutenant, where does this road lead?" he asked.

"That way takes us back to the road we were on when we stopped at the stream and then on to an intersection with another major road. That way takes us into Covington's estate," Lieutenant Cross said.

When Alexander could hold still no longer, he stopped the trackers and asked for their report. It was clear that they were miserable at having to tell him they'd lost the trail. Alexander fought quietly to maintain his hold on sanity and thought for a moment that he would fail right there in the middle of the road. The unthinkable closed in on him. He felt helpless and angry all at once. When he saw the telltale dust column of approaching riders, he calmed his emotions and reminded himself to be driven by emotion but ruled by reason. He told himself he would do all it took to find Isabel but that he must use reason and clear thought to accomplish his goals.

Chapter 31

He didn't have to wait long for the galloping horses to reach them. It was Hanlon, Emily, Anatoly, Abigail, and Erik, followed by a dozen or so Rangers. Alexander didn't know how he was going to tell them that he'd lost Isabel's trail. When they charged up, Hanlon spoke first.

"Lord Alexander, Isabel has been taken by Truss. He's offering her safe return in exchange for you." He reined in his horse beside Alexander, fished around inside his cloak and produced a letter, which he handed to Alexander.

Alexander looked hard at the Warden for a moment before unfolding the parchment. "You will meet my challenge by dusk three days hence on Flat Top Rock or Isabel dies. You will come alone or Isabel dies. Rexius Truss."

Alexander felt a flash of hot anger wash through him. The greasy little bastard had taken Isabel by force. She rejected him so he abducted her. A new unthinkable thought tried to invade his sanity but he shoved it away. He needed to think.

"Who delivered this letter?" he demanded.

Hanlon looked to Erik, whose face contorted in misery. "It was on her pillow. I didn't look because her bed was still made." He hung his head. "I thought she was with you, so I rushed out without seeing it."

Alexander nudged his horse up alongside Erik's and put his hand on the man's shoulder. Erik looked up with desolation in his eyes. Alexander leaned in so no one else could hear him. "I have a little sister too, Erik. I understand."

Erik nodded his thanks but the haunted look didn't leave his eyes.

Alexander turned to Hanlon. The Forest Warden's eyes were fraught with worry but also bottled rage. "It's about two days' ride to Flat Top Rock from the palace, right?"

"It is, but," Hanlon took a deep breath before speaking again, "you can't go."

Emily sobbed. She was dressed in Rangers' riding gear and wore tear streaks down her face in stripes through the travel dust.

Alexander felt his anger rise a notch in his belly. "What do you mean?" There was a hard edge to his voice.

Hanlon took another deep breath and sighed with anguish. When he spoke in his low, rumbling voice, Alexander could hear the sorrow of loss. "You cannot be risked, not even for my only daughter."

Emily fought, unsuccessfully, to hold back another sob.

Alexander looked at him hard. His words were deadly calm. "Warden Alaric, I'm going and the only way you will stop me is by killing me yourself."

The Rangers all stiffened. Hanlon looked like a man on the verge of an emotional breakdown.

Anatoly sidled up gently on his big chestnut mare. "You know this is a trap, right?" he asked Alexander.

Alexander looked at the big man-at-arms. Anatoly's eyes conveyed more sympathy than Alexander had expected.

He nodded slowly. "I can't just do nothing and let Isabel die. Her best chance, her only chance, is if I go and face Truss."

Erik shook his head, "You won't be facing just Truss. His master-at-arms is a very dangerous swordsman. I've seen him fight. He'll kill you, Alexander."

Alexander felt trapped. He had to do something but he had no way of knowing what he would be riding into. But to do nothing was to surrender to the unthinkable. He wasn't about to do that.

"We'll see about that." His gold-flecked eyes glittered with anger and determination. If he was going to face Truss and his henchmen, he needed an edge. He seized on the only edge he could get. "I have to get back to the palace." Alexander spurred his horse into a gallop. He didn't concern himself with the others. He knew what he had to do and he didn't have much time.

He raced back to the palace and didn't let up for a moment. He pushed his horse to its limits, but not past. He coaxed every bit of speed he could get without risking injury to the animal. He left everyone else strung out in a trail behind him. Anatoly and Abigail kept pace with him, but the rest fell behind a little more with every passing minute.

He thundered into the main courtyard past a platoon of Rangers drilling with wooden practice swords, rode right up to the palace entrance and leapt off his horse. Several Rangers raced up as he hit the ground.

"Lord Alexander, any word of Isabel?"

"She's been abducted by Truss," was all he offered before racing into the palace. Abigail and Anatoly were twenty feet behind him.

"Alexander," Abigail called out, "Where are you going?"

He slowed to a fast walk and Abigail and Anatoly came up on either side of him. "I'm going to get the skillbook." He stopped and tried to orient himself, looking back and forth down the broad marble hall, saw the door he wanted and headed for it.

Anatoly and Abigail looked at each other and followed. He navigated down into the basement of the palace and then to the door leading to the catacombs. He found a lamp and headed down into the dark without hesitation.

He remembered the way for the most part and where he was confused he followed the footprints in the heavy dust that covered everything. Anatoly and Abigail were right behind him, each with a lamp of their own. Alexander felt a sense of urgency driving him forward through the dark. Fine dust rose in little puffs with each step, leaving a cloud of dust in his wake that looked almost like fog in the dim light. Anatoly and Abigail started to take on the hue of ghosts trailing silently behind him. Finally, he reached the correct hallway. He slowed, lifted his lamp higher, and started examining the sconces on the wall, one by one. He would have missed it except that the one he wanted was missing the coating of thick dust worn by all the others.

Once inside the domed room he wasted no time. He slipped his long knife free and sliced the edge of his hand. Anatoly watched with resignation, Abigail with wonder as Alexander placed his bloody hand on the door. Again, bright points of light began at the base of the door's outline and raced up the doorframe to meet at the top of the arched door. Abigail gasped when Alexander pushed through the door and into the little room beyond. The skillbook and the Wizard's

Dust were right where he'd left them. He lifted the skillbook carefully to prevent any blood from coming in contact with the lock on the cover and tucked it under his arm before pushing back through the magical door.

He didn't even stop once he stepped out of the Bloodvault. He snatched up his lamp and headed for the exit, locking the door and securing the secret door behind him as he went. The dark corridors of the catacombs still held clouds of stirred-up dust that gave the place an eerie look as it swirled around them in the dim light of their lamps. When they emerged into the public halls of the palace, there were Rangers standing sentry at every intersection.

The first to see him called out, "Lord Alexander, Warden Alaric would speak with you."

Alexander didn't even stop for the man but brushed past him on his way to his quarters. "He'll have to wait."

In the light of the well-lit hallways, they looked pale and ashen from the coating of dust. At each intersection another Ranger informed him that Warden Alaric wished to speak to him, but Alexander ignored them all. When he reached his room and threw open the door, Renwold was standing right in the middle of the room in his customary place.

"Your Majesty, I have a plate of food and a pot of tea for you. May I lay out a set of clean clothes?" Renwold seemed totally unfazed by Alexander's appearance.

"Thank you, Renwold, but that won't be necessary," Alexander said. "I will be busy reading for the rest of the day. Please ensure that I am not disturbed for any reason. Also, I will be riding out tomorrow at dawn. Inform the stables that I will require two fast horses saddled and ready at first light. Have the kitchen prepare travel food for a week and see to it that a set of Lady Isabel's riding clothes and boots are packed in the saddlebags of one of my horses. Finally, wake me at first light and bring me a plate of food when you do. That will be all for now, and, Renwold, thank you."

"Of course, Your Majesty, I will see to it at once." Renwold bowed deeply and withdrew from the room closing the door behind himself.

Anatoly and Abigail stood looking at Alexander. He carefully placed the skillbook on one of the end tables next to a large chair in his sitting room and sat down in front of the covered platter of food. It was just as big as the last serving tray Renwold had brought him and was piled with meats, cheeses, fruit, and an assortment of breads. Alexander wasn't really hungry but he hadn't eaten all day and knew he should eat before he started studying or he would be distracted by hunger later. He motioned to Anatoly and Abigail to sit while he took a piece of bread and started piling meat and cheese on it for a quick sandwich.

Anatoly was silent but Abigail couldn't hold her tongue any longer. "Alexander, are you sure this is wise? They've set a trap for you and you're walking right into it."

He nodded while he chewed. "I know it's a trap but what are my choices?" he asked around a mouthful of food.

"Send me," Anatoly said calmly with a slight undercurrent of menace.

Alexander swallowed before responding. "The thought crossed my mind, but I can't risk it. The moment they realize it's not me, they'll kill her."

Anatoly replied quietly, "She may already be dead."

Alexander could see that the big man-at-arms didn't want to be pointing out the possibility but he clearly felt it must be said.

"I can't let myself believe that. Besides, Truss wants her for himself. I doubt he'll kill her without a good reason."

Alexander took another oversized bite of his hastily made sandwich when he heard voices arguing outside the door. A moment later Hanlon came striding in, trailed by his three sons and Chase. The Ranger at the door tried to apologize for the interruption but Alexander waved him away.

"Alexander, Chase and my sons have just returned. They passed Truss at the fortress gate. He was traveling with two men and a large wagon loaded with crates and boxes. I suspect Isabel was in one of them. I can order the gatekeeper to send a platoon after them and bring her back. You don't have to risk yourself."

Alexander could see that Hanlon didn't really believe such a plan would work but he was torn between his duty as Keeper of the Bloodline and his love for his daughter.

"No. He's demanded me and he will have his wish. That's Isabel's best chance. He'll no doubt have an ambush in place and his champion will be there to ensure I don't survive the encounter. I understand the risks and I accept them." Alexander pointed to the skillbook and then looked back at Hanlon. "I don't intend to go unprepared." He punctuated his statement by stuffing the rest of his sandwich into his mouth.

"Do you believe the magic in that book will be enough?" Hanlon asked.

Alexander shrugged as he chewed, swallowed hard, and then stood. "It's the only edge I can get on such short notice. Mage Cedric wouldn't have put it in the Bloodvault if it didn't contain powerful magic, so I can only hope it'll be enough. Either way, I ride for Flat Top Rock at daybreak tomorrow. Right now I need time to study the book undisturbed, so everyone out." He was past the point of being polite. He'd made up his mind. Now he just needed to execute his plan.

Hanlon nodded and motioned for his sons and Chase to file out of the room. "I'd like for Erik and his squad to ride out with you tomorrow. They'll hold a good distance from Flat Top Rock so you can make your approach alone but I want you to have some protection along the way there and back. Phane may have a surprise waiting for you on the other side of the fortress gate."

Alexander nodded with a small smile. "We'll bring Isabel back, Hanlon," he said as he put his hand on the Forest Warden's shoulder.

Hanlon couldn't muster any words. He looked at once grateful, distraught, and helpless to do anything but allow others to decide the fate of his daughter.

Once the room was empty, the bar placed on the door, a guard posted outside to prevent any disturbances, and his fire stoked, Alexander sat down with the skillbook in his lap and squeezed a drop or two of blood from the gash in his hand. He rubbed the blood around on his thumb and forefinger, then pressed his thumb against the lock plate of the skillbook. There was a slight humming for a moment and then the lock strap popped open with a loud click. Alexander cleaned his hand and rewrapped his bandage before carefully opening the book.

The first page was written in fine calligraphy and was in a language that Alexander couldn't read. He felt a little flutter of panic as he stared in disbelief at the unintelligible words on the page. Then, rather suddenly, the words shifted and

Alexander could read them. He wasn't sure what language they were in but he could understand the writing as if it were written in the common tongue he'd learned to read and write as a child.

The first page told him what he most wanted to know. He had feared that this might be a fool's errand and that he was just wasting time, but the introduction to the skillbook told him otherwise.

"This skillbook of the blade is intended for the one marked by the curse I cast on the Ruathan bloodline. I regret having placed such a terrible burden on your shoulders but I was called to take action in defense of future generations. If you are reading these words, then Phane walks the world again and all are in peril. This book is one of several items of great power that I have preserved within the Bloodvaults to aid you in your duty to defend the Old Law and the people of the Seven Isles from the evil of Phane Reishi. Use the power within wisely. Signed in my own hand, Mage Barnabas Cedric."

Alexander sat stunned for a moment before reading the passage again. The words had been written two thousand years ago, yet they were written expressly for him. He felt a little chill as he turned the page.

What followed was a treatise on fighting with bladed weapons. Alexander found that once he started reading, the words seemed to flow off the page and into his very soul. He saw vivid images within his mind of different bladed weapons and their best uses. He was caught up in visions of having practiced every thrust, stroke, parry, riposte, feint, stance, combination, and series of attacks and defenses he'd ever learned from Anatoly and many more that he'd never even heard of.

It was much more than reading about the techniques though. He felt like the wisdom, muscle memory, and skill of having practiced each movement for countless hours transferred into him as he read each passage. His understanding of combat with a blade broadened and deepened until he began to see the art with a sense of completeness.

He could remember practicing drills with every bladed weapon to the point of mastery and learning every blade-fighting technique ever proven on the battlefield. He came to understand the nature of a blade at a near spiritual level. A blade was an instrument of both life and death. It could preserve and protect and it could kill. The mastery of the blade that flowed from the pages of the skillbook into Alexander included a deep reverence for the value of a blade and the power it represented.

Then he came to a place in the book that described a series of actual battles that had taken place between two skilled blade masters. Each step was described and analyzed. The techniques, tactics, cadence and rhythm of each fight were examined. Alexander saw himself in each fight within his mind's eye with vivid detail. Each fight was as real as a memory. He could see the splatter of blood when his blade struck true. He could feel the rush of air when he spun to avoid his opponent's thrust. He could hear the sickening thud when his enemies fell to the ground and breathed their last.

He lived each fight and came to know the strengths and limits of his weapon in each one. He fought with a spear, a long sword, a short sword, a long knife, a pair of knives, two short swords at once, a long sword and a long knife at once, and finally throwing knives. Each weapon presented different opportunities and vulnerabilities. He came to know them all with the practiced ease of one who had lived a lifetime wielding his chosen blade.

Alexander was starting to feel his head ache as the new ideas swirled through his mind and took root in his heart and soul, sinew and bone. Then he came to the end of the section recounting each case study. What came next filled him with both hope and dread.

The last section of the skillbook dealt with the fighting style one should use when wielding the Thinblade. Alexander learned that the reason for the name of the sword was its physical dimensions. The Thinblade was so thin along its edge that it could cut nearly anything except another Thinblade. Alexander discovered that the techniques of fighting with a normal steel blade depended on the simple fact that steel could be stopped with steel. To claim victory with a normal blade you needed to circumvent the defenses of your opponent.

The Thinblade had no such limitations. If you faced an opponent with a steel shield, the most effective tactic was to slash down through the shield and your enemy's arm or more simply to thrust through the shield and into your enemy's heart. The Thinblade could cut through steel with ease. Alexander came to see the nearly unstoppable power of such a simple thing.

When he reached the section examining various actual fights between an Island Lord armed with a Thinblade and others armed with steel, he saw in his mind such carnage and devastation he was left feeling slightly ill. He watched himself wield the Thinblade against a dozen other men and cleave them into pieces with quick, deadly strokes. He saw in his mind's eye the raw power of the Thinblade and how unstoppable it was.

When Alexander reached the end of the skillbook, the sky outside his balcony doors was dark and his head was reeling. It felt full and throbbed with pain. He made his way to the washroom and filled the basin. He washed his face and went straight to his bed. He pulled off his boots but nothing else, fell into bed and wrapped a blanket around himself before slipping off into a deep and dreamless sleep.

Chapter 32

No sooner had he put his head on the pillow than he heard loud knocking at his door. With a struggle he opened his eyes and saw the light of dawn just beginning to peek through the cracks of his curtains. He emerged from his bedchamber into the sitting room and found the fire had died out but the oil lamps were still burning brightly. He made his way to the door, removed the bar, and drew it open while stifling a yawn.

Renwold stood at the door holding a platter of food. Anatoly and Abigail stood behind him; both were dressed for a fight. Alexander motioned for them to enter and went into his bedchamber to put on his boots and gather his pack and weapons. He felt a strange sense of heightened familiarity with his sword, as though he'd fought countless battles with it. It felt like a natural extension of his mind and body.

He came from his room dressed and ready. "I take it you're coming with me?" he asked as he sat down for a quick breakfast. He didn't really want to eat but he knew he had to. The next few days would be hard and he would need strength and energy.

"Of course," Abigail said as she sat down and took the lid off his breakfast tray. As expected, it was piled with more food than five people could eat. Abigail wasn't bashful; she selected a pastry and sat back on the couch with her breakfast.

Alexander motioned for Anatoly to sit and eat while he slathered butter on a biscuit. They ate quickly. Alexander wanted to be off soon. It was two days to Flat Top Rock and he didn't want to be late.

"Did you find the edge you were looking for?" Anatoly asked, motioning to the skillbook.

Alexander looked at the book for a moment before nodding slowly, "I believe I did. It's a strange feeling. I can remember battles I've never fought. I know techniques with a blade that I've never even heard of before."

"You sure you know how to make those techniques work? I mean it's one thing to read about something and another to actually do it." Abigail seemed skeptical.

"That's just it. I remember countless hours of practice. I remember fighting battles and killing enemies with blades that I've never even held." Alexander paused for a moment taking another look at the book.

"It taught me how to wield the Thinblade."

Anatoly and Abigail both sat up a little straighter.

"It's like I've actually held the thing, fought with it, killed with it. It's a powerful weapon. I can understand why people fear it," Alexander said.

When they emerged into the palace courtyard, Erik and his team were standing in a circle talking quietly near their picketed horses. They were all dressed in riding armor with swords strapped to their belts and bows with full quivers in riding cases on their horses.

Standing nearby were Hanlon, Jack, Mason, and Lucky. Alexander handed Anatoly his pack and walked over to the little group. "The skillbook is a thing of wonder. I believe that Truss and his master-at-arms will be surprised by my newfound ability with a blade."

Jack looked torn. "Alexander, I'll ride out with you if you wish but I believe I could better serve you by questioning those at Truss's estate to learn if there is more to his treachery. I've had dealings with men like him and their machinations are rarely confined to one plot or scheme."

"That sounds like a good idea. Just make sure you have an adequate force of Rangers to provide you with security," Alexander said.

"I've only seen Truss's master-at-arms once but I believe he is a battle wizard." Mason paused to fix Alexander with a very direct look. "Alexander, if I'm correct, he will be extremely dangerous. He will be fast, his weapons will be sharper than they should be, and his attacks will be driven by greater force than any normal man can muster."

Alexander didn't like the sound of that but he was committed to his course, no matter the risk. His brow drew down as he considered this new information. "I understand. I think the skillbook was drawn from the expertise of a battle wizard. I hope it'll give me the edge I need to win the day. I left it on the table in my room. I'd like you to take a look at it and see if you can figure out how it was made. If we could recreate such a thing it would give us a great advantage."

"I was hoping you would give me the chance to study it." Mason's eyes lit up at the opportunity.

"I've made a few things for you," Lucky said as he handed Alexander a leather belt pouch filled with four glass vials carefully packed inside.

He gave Lucky a questioning look.

"Owen arrived yesterday with my wagon so I was able to create a number of items for you during the night. The first vial is a healing draught. Drink it and you will succumb to sleep for half an hour and wake healed of most injuries. The second is a jar of healing salve. You already know from experience how that works. The third is a shatter vial of liquid fire. Throw it at your enemy and the contents will burst into flames on contact with the air. Be careful with that one, the fire burns very hot. The last vial is a potion of warding. Drink it before battle, and weapons will find it much harder to hit you. The potion creates a series of magical shields that will turn blades and arrows away. The weapon will not be stopped, just turned slightly so it will miss. The effects of the potion will last for about an hour."

"Thank you, Lucky," Alexander said and gave his old tutor a hug. He turned to Hanlon.

"The council ruled unanimously yesterday to recognize you as King of Ruatha." Hanlon sounded tired. It didn't look as though he'd slept at all since Isabel had been taken.

"Good. I'm appointing you Regent of Glen Morillian. Seize Truss's estates and break up his holdings. Distribute his lands to the citizens who have been working them and his holdings to members of his family who are found to be innocent of treachery. The rest is to go to the Rangers. Finally, send out the call for soldiers and start building an army. I want cavalry, infantry, and archers." He put his hand on Hanlon's shoulder. "I'm going to bring Isabel back home to you and

Emily, you have my word."

Hanlon nodded with his eyes closed but didn't try to speak.

Alexander strode to his horse and mounted up. The reins to his second horse were already tied to his saddle, and Anatoly had fastened Alexander's pack to the horse's rump. Everyone else was mounted and waiting.

They rode hard all morning, switching horses every couple of hours or so. It was another clear day but cold and dry. The air got progressively more frigid as they negotiated the switchbacks up the side of the barrier mountains on the road leading to the fortress gate. They reached the mountain stronghold by midday and made haste through to the other side, stopping only for a moment to explain the situation to the gatekeeper. He was angry that Truss had betrayed Glen Morillian, but he was furious that Truss had passed right under his nose with the Forest Warden's daughter in a box. He offered a platoon of Rangers to ride with them, but Alexander didn't want to be slowed or to give Truss any reason to kill Isabel so he politely declined the offer.

Once through the gate and on the road leading into the Great Forest, they again made good time. Alexander pushed on relentlessly until darkness simply made it too dangerous to continue. He was confident that they'd covered the majority of the distance to Flat Top Rock when they stopped to make camp.

There wasn't much talk around the fire that night. The brothers were all clearly worried sick about their sister. They alternated between anger and despair as they stared silently into the little cook fire. Alexander knew just how they felt. Rage had been boiling in the pit of his stomach since he'd discovered Isabel was missing and he feared that the only thing that would quench that rage was blood.

He meant to kill Truss for this.

He thought about the art of the blade. He would have reason to use it tomorrow. He thought about Isabel and her piercing green eyes in the moments before he fell asleep.

They were up at dawn and on the move after a quick, cold breakfast. The sky was filled with broken clouds, all white and fluffy, floating past on the breeze and casting their shadows across the world. It was warmer lower in the forest and Alexander was again taken by the beauty of the life all around them. He tried to focus on it to keep the unthinkable from invading his idle mind. It was late afternoon when Erik called a halt.

"This is as far as we can go with you, Alexander. Flat Top Rock will come into view just over that ridge. From there it's less than a quarter of an hour ride." Erik pulled a strange-looking arrow from his quiver and handed it to Alexander. "This is a whistler. Shoot it into the air and we'll come running."

Alexander took the arrow and slipped it into his quiver, noting the distinctive yellow feathers that set it apart from the other arrows he carried.

"You're walking into a trap, so be careful." Abigail came alongside her brother and gave his arm a squeeze. "Remember, there are three of them, so keep your eyes open."

He smiled his thanks and headed up the road. Sure enough he could see Flat Top Rock in the distance when he crested the rise. His heart started to beat a little faster. He checked his sword in its scabbard. At this range he couldn't see anyone but he didn't doubt they were there.

He rode on, but more slowly and cautiously. He expected an ambush, so he scanned the trees frequently with both normal vision and his second sight. When he reached the clearing where he'd stolen the Reishi's horses, he saw a wagon and several horses picketed but no sign of anyone. He expected the third man to be lying in wait for him.

He pushed on until he came to the path leading up the side of Flat Top Rock. It was a treacherous footpath not suitable for a horse, so Alexander dismounted and tethered his horses to a nearby tree. He checked his sword, long knife, boot knives, and the throwing knife he had strapped to the back of his belt. Each was where he wanted it to be and free in its sheath or scabbard. He took his bow and three arrows. He put two along the length of the bow itself and nocked the third, holding it in place with just a little tension on the string. Finally, he took the potion of warding from the little pouch, popped off the stopper and downed the sweet-tasting, syrupy liquid. It was warm going down but otherwise he felt nothing.

Alexander scanned his surroundings with his second sight and started up the steep and winding path to the top of the rocky prominence. He took his time, looking and listening for any threat. He expected an ambush at every moment so he moved with extreme caution. When he reached the top and cautiously peeked over the stone edge, his breath caught at the sight of her.

She was alive.

She still wore the beautiful dark-green gown she'd worn to the banquet, only now it was torn, tattered, and dirty.

Rexius Truss's henchmen had felled a tree against the side of Flat Top Rock and then chopped off the top twenty feet to create a couple of logs to sit on and provide wood for a fire. Isabel was sitting on one of the logs with her hands tied behind her back. Truss was on the other log, poking at the little fire with a stick. Leaning on a spear was another man dressed in a polished steel breastplate, greaves, and bracers. Resting on the log near his feet was a large round shield and a helmet. He had a sword strapped to his waist and looked to be perfectly comfortable wearing heavy armor. Alexander presumed that he was the master-at-arms Erik had warned him about.

He ducked back down to think about how he wanted to approach the enemy, when he caught the movement of a crossbow bolt coming at him fast. He turned just in time to see the bolt only feet from him. It was a clean shot. It was going to drive right through his chest ... except it didn't. Only a couple of feet away it suddenly veered to the side as if it had glanced off a steel shield and shattered against the stone wall he was crouching near. Alexander silently thanked Lucky and his potion.

He scanned the forest with his second sight and found his attacker. A man on a platform high up in the trees was looking at Alexander with disbelief. He'd fired a perfect shot and missed. Alexander drew his bow up quickly and smoothly. He got a clean sight on his target and loosed his arrow. It drove hard into the center of the man's chest and pinned him to the tree for a moment before he slumped forward off the platform, crashing through the trees to the ground below. One down.

He nocked a second arrow and quickly took the last few steps up to the top of Flat Top Rock. He sent his arrow at the master-at-arms but was a second too late. The man heard the crossbowman fall into the trees and had scooped up his shield just in time to bring it around and deflect the arrow. Alexander nocked his last arrow and sent it at Truss without a moment's hesitation. This one flew true. It stabbed straight through his right shoulder. Truss screamed in pain and then screamed again. The master-at-arms strapped his shield in place while chuckling at Truss's distress, then calmly pulled his helmet on and took up his spear.

Alexander dropped his bow. The master-at-arms was looking at him like a wolf eyes a calf. Alexander drew his sword and his long knife and advanced.

Truss was whimpering on the ground. He took a deep breath, reached over his shoulder, took hold of the bloody shaft and pulled it through with one mighty heave. He screamed again and squirmed around on the ground mewling in pain. Isabel laughed out loud with absolutely no humor.

Alexander and the master-at-arms engaged. The first clash happened much faster than Alexander had expected. The man seemed to move in a time all his own. One moment he was moving with the normal speed of a trained warrior, then, in the moment of the strike, he seemed to move in a blur with a kind of speed that no normal person could muster. His first strike would have killed Alexander had it not been turned aside by the potion of warding.

Alexander moved around the thrust in an effort to position himself between the enemy and Isabel. He remembered the technique from the skillbook but it was as if he'd learned it in theory and never actually practiced it. For a moment he worried that the skillbook hadn't actually imparted the skills he so desperately needed.

The master-at-arms paused and regarded Alexander for a moment. Alexander took that opportunity to slip his long knife back into his sheath, pull a boot knife and throw it into the log next to Isabel. A moment later the master-at-arms drove into him again, leading with an impossibly fast spear strike that again went just wide of running Alexander through. Instead, it sliced shallowly but painfully into his side. Alexander just barely spun out of the way when the enemy's shield came whipping past his head in a broad arc. He lashed out with his sword and felt the familiarity of a stroke that he'd never used before. It just missed. The master-at-arms spun full circle and whipped his spear around in a great arc using the broad-bladed weapon more like a sword than a spear.

In that moment of combat, thought faded and instinct assumed command. Alexander felt like something snapped into place. He knew where the spear would be a moment from now and where the enemy would move next. Everything about the dance of battle became clear. Alexander brought his blade up and parried the spear slash and counterattacked.

What followed was a blur of blade and steel. They fought for several minutes in a blinding cadence of attack and counter, thrust and parry. Alexander couldn't overcome his opponent's armor and the master-at-arms couldn't overcome Alexander's potion of warding. Each took several minor gashes from the other, but neither was able to deliver a kill strike. Alexander felt like he understood the intentions of the master-at-arms before they were formed in his enemy's mind but he simply could not match the man's inhuman speed. Had it not been for the potion of warding he would have fallen long ago. Had he not studied the skillbook he wouldn't have stood a chance against this man.

When they broke and separated to catch their breath, Alexander saw Truss laboring to climb down the tree and Isabel working with the knife to cut her bonds and free herself.

The master-at-arms stood a good fifteen feet from Alexander, casually leaning on his spear and looking at him now more in the way a wolf eyes another wolf from a different pack.

"You all right, Isabel?" Alexander called out over his shoulder without taking his eyes off his opponent.

"I am now," she said as she succeeded in cutting the leather bindings that held her hands behind her back.

The master-at-arms tilted his head. "You're not a battle wizard but you use techniques that I've never even seen before. I must say this has been a pleasure. I've learned more in the last five minutes than in the last five years. Shall we continue?"

He started to advance on Alexander, raising his shield and spear.

"I don't think so," Alexander said.

The master-at-arms gave him a disappointed look and replied with a deadly smile, "I'm afraid you don't really have a choice."

Alexander smiled back and hurled the shatter vial of liquid fire at his enemy. The battle wizard raised his shield and the vial exploded against it, bursting into flame. The liquid fire splattered over the top and all around the shield. Everywhere a drop fell, it stuck and burned brightly. In just moments the man was engulfed in flames. He screamed once in surprise and then again in terror before running madly right off the edge of Flat Top Rock, plummeting to his death on the road below.

A moment later Isabel raced into Alexander's arms and wept with relief. He held her tightly and let her cry on his shoulder. When she looked up into his eyes, all of his worry and fear melted away. She was battered and dirty, her hair was a mess, her face was streaked with tears, and she was beautiful. Maybe the most beautiful sight that Alexander had ever seen. She was alive and she was in his arms. Truss had escaped but Alexander didn't even care. He was filled with joy just standing there holding her.

They made their way down slowly and carefully. Once they reached their horses, Alexander sent the whistler arrow into the air. It streaked high overhead screaming with a high-pitched whistle that could be heard for miles around. Isabel sat on a rock looking tired and completely out of place in her torn and dirty gown.

"I thought you might want these," he said, handing her a set of her riding clothes and her boots all rolled up in a neat little ball.

She smiled up at him like the sunrise. "You're my hero," she whispered. "Now turn around," she added with a smile.

Once she was dressed, they mounted their horses and rode to the clearing where the wagon was still parked. Isabel dismounted in a hurry, went to the little wagon and started searching through its contents. A moment later she came up with a covered cage.

"They took Slyder before they kidnapped me so I couldn't use him to lead you to me." She popped open the cage, took her forest hawk out and gently tossed him into the air. He took to wing with enthusiasm. Isabel laughed with delight at seeing Slyder fly up into the trees.

Alexander and Isabel were sitting on the wagon applying healing salve to each other's injuries when Alexander's escort charged into the clearing. When

Isabel saw her brothers, she rushed to them, hugging each in turn. Anatoly and Abigail came to Alexander and listened to him recount the events of the fight and Truss's escape.

"Sound's like Lucky's magic decided the day," Anatoly offered with a slightly reproving look.

"You'll get no argument from me on that count. His potions saved my life and killed Truss's master-at-arms, no doubt about it. But, I did learn a bit about fighting with a blade. Once the magic of the skillbook actually sank in, I fought pretty well, just not as well as that battle wizard." Alexander shook his head. "That guy could move so fast it was scary. One moment he was fighting like a skilled warrior and the next he was driving his spear at me with blinding speed. I hope I never have to face another one of those."

Two days later they were back at the palace and having dinner in the private residence with the Alaric family.

Isabel told the entire story of her ordeal. Truss was indeed in league with Phane. His master-at-arms was a member of the Reishi Protectorate and he'd promised Truss quite a lot to lure Alexander out into the open. Truss's plan was sound given the prowess of his master-at-arms, but, thankfully, it played out quite differently than they anticipated. Hanlon and Emily were overwhelmed with relief at the safe return of their daughter.

As the evening wound down, Alexander maneuvered Hanlon out onto the balcony for a moment of private conversation. "Hanlon, I have a request of a personal nature."

"Name it." Hanlon didn't hesitate. He'd expressed his gratitude to Alexander when they returned and several more times during the evening but Alexander's request was quite a lot to ask.

Alexander took a deep breath and steadied his nerves. "I would like your permission and blessing to court Isabel." He held his breath.

Hanlon looked stunned for just a moment before grinning broadly and taking Alexander up in a giant bear hug. He set him back down and looked him square in the eye. "You have it. You've already risked the world for her and I've seen the way she looks at you. You have my permission and my heartfelt blessing, Alexander."

When he lay down to sleep that night he was exhausted but simply couldn't quiet his mind. There were too many possibilities swirling around inside his head. The threat was still out there but it seemed farther away and the reasons for fighting that threat seemed closer and more real. Alexander finally drifted off to sleep, feeling a sense of hope and optimism that he hadn't felt for a long time.

Chapter 33

Jataan P'Tal stepped off the gangplank onto the solid, unmoving boards of the Southport dock and breathed a sigh of relief. He hated the ocean. He believed that men should have firm ground underfoot. The solidity of it was reliable and predictable. When the very ground beneath your feet shifted and moved, you couldn't find firm footing and firm footing was the first part of being effective in battle.

Jataan P'Tal was a battle mage.

He was quite possibly the most deadly man alive in all the Seven Isles in any contest of blade or steel. He wasn't invincible, a fact he was all too aware of. He was just that good in a fight, another fact he was well aware of.

Battle wizards were rare. They had a unique connection to the firmament. Their power didn't flow from active visualization and concentrated will like most other wizards but instead was guided at a more basic, instinctual, and intrinsic level. A battle wizard's magic manifested in the moment of the fight. In that moment he moved with otherworldly speed and struck with inhuman force. In the moment of the fight a battle wizard saw time differently. His surroundings appeared to slow down. His perception and senses accelerated.

He had a different relationship with weapons as well. A battle wizard could hold a weapon and discern its strengths and weaknesses. He could know with a touch if an arrow would fly straight or if the haft of a spear was imperceptibly cracked or if a blade was made true. A powerful battle wizard could use his magic to repair a weapon or even make a flawed weapon straight. And in the moment of the fight, a battle wizard's magic flowed into his weapon and lent it a strength and sharpness uncommon to other blades.

In the last thousand years, Jataan P'Tal was the only battle wizard to rise to the level of mage. Jataan P'Tal was a very dangerous man. He had a calling and he was devoted to it with all his heart and soul. He was the General Commander of the Reishi Protectorate. His duty in life was to preserve the Reishi line. He had been raised from childhood to fulfill his duty to the Reishi. Now that he actually had a charge to protect, he felt a sense of exhilaration at his purpose taking on substance, mixed with a bit of apprehension at exactly the form his purpose had chosen to take.

He'd been taught every day of his life that the Reishi were responsible for creating the Old Law. They had brought the Seven Isles together and presided over a period of nearly two thousand years of peace, prosperity, and security. They had ushered in the greatest civilization ever known in the recorded history of the Seven Isles. And then they had been betrayed. Their secret had been stolen and released on an unsuspecting world. A world that had been ravaged by war and netherworld horrors until all was lost except for the sole surviving member of the Reishi Line: Prince Phane.

Jataan P'Tal had imagined living through this time since he was a child. He had stood guard over Phane's obelisk for hours hoping for a sign, hoping for the opportunity to help the Reishi rise again to tame a now broken and corrupt world. He wanted to be a part of that. He wanted to serve the noble cause of bringing the Old Law and the rightful and benevolent rule of the Reishi back to the world.

What he hadn't imagined was Phane. The man was not quite right. He had unseemly appetites. He called on creatures from the netherworld to do his bidding. Jataan P'Tal told himself that he was a soldier and Phane was a prince and the rightful heir to the Sovereign's throne, but still, he was troubled.

He took a deep breath of the ocean air that mingled with the smell of fish and livestock. The docks were busy. Jataan P'Tal stepped up on a crate to see over the crowd. He was a little man, standing only five and a half feet tall but stocky with just a slight paunch. His skin was swarthy, his close-cropped hair was jet black, and the irises of his eyes were black as night. He wore black pants and a black shirt of coarse cloth. His belt was cinched tight under his belly and he wore a black, fur-lined cloak over his shoulders. He didn't appear to be armed and he carried only a sack over his shoulder.

After just a moment on the crate, he saw his Second and marked his position in the crowd. Boaberous Grudge was a hard man to miss. As much as Jataan looked deceptively nonthreatening, Grudge looked dangerous and menacing. Men of courage gave him a wide berth and averted their eyes to avoid any hint of a challenge.

Boaberous Grudge stood over seven feet tall, weighed almost four hundred pounds, and was completely bald. By all accounts he was a giant. Jataan often wondered about the man's lineage. Despite his size, he was quick on his feet and agile as well. He was as strong as any three men together and had absolutely no fear of any man alive with the sole exception of Jataan P'Tal. He wore a large pack on his back, a huge breastplate, bracers and greaves. On his back, beside his pack, was an oversized quiver filled with a dozen javelins. Resting on his shoulder was a huge war hammer with a haft that was easily six feet long.

Boaberous was scanning around the crowd until he saw Jataan coming his way. They joined up without a word and set out into the streets of Southport. The blacksmith was Reishi Protectorate. That would be their first stop. They needed information, horses, and perhaps a few men to assist in their task.

The Rebel Mage had sent an assassin through the millennia to bring the Reishi line to an end for all time. Jataan P'Tal had a sacred duty to prevent Mage Cedric's assassin from succeeding. He'd always understood that the best defense was a good offense. He had come to kill Alexander Valentine before he had the chance to deliver Mage Cedric's final blow to civilization.

***

Phane sauntered casually into the council chamber of the Reishi Army Regency on Karth. His voyage had taken a day longer than he'd wanted but that didn't matter. He was here now. He looked each man in the eye as he moved closer to the table with each languid step.

The men at the table regarded him with a mixture of suspicion, fear, and anger. He shouldn't have been able to walk into their council chamber unchallenged and unannounced. Yet here he was and his demeanor was anything but expected.

They were all wearing armor adorned with an ornately stylized letter R emblazoned in gold on their polished steel breastplates. All nine of them were slightly overweight but each had clearly served his time in the field. Some bore scars. Others simply wore the grizzled look of a man who'd seen his share of death.

Phane flashed his best boyish smile at them, knowing that it would only chafe them further. He wore no armor, carried no weapon, and showed no respect. He regarded them casually for a brief moment before he reached across the table and took the wine goblet from the man in the center chair and hopped up on the table, sitting sideways so he could look over his shoulder at the man sitting in the seat of power, the center seat of the council table.

These men were the General Council of the Reishi Army Regency. They ruled half the island of Karth, with the House of Karth ruling the other half. They had been at war with each other, off and on, for the better part of the last two thousand years.

At the end of the Reishi War, a significant force of the Reishi Army had been trapped on Karth when the Reishi fell. Since the House of Karth had sided with the rebel forces against the Reishi, they were natural enemies. The war never really ended for the people of Karth. The island was governed by tyranny on both sides and the people bore the brunt of the burden.

Phane took a long drink from the goblet, draining it completely, then casually tossed it on the floor. When he flashed another of his boyish smiles at the man in the center seat, one of the other generals stood and drew his sword.

"How dare you? Guards!" he bellowed. When none came rushing in he frowned slightly and lunged at Phane, who simply slipped off the table and danced out of the way of the blade. He stopped just out of sword range and stood pointing at the man and laughing in mockery.

The man's face turned red and his mouth opened and closed in rage. Phane took another step backward and motioned with both hands to come for him, while wearing a big dopey grin and snickering at the grizzled old soldier.

The other men all wore masks of stone-cold anger but each held his seat at the table, staring at the intruder with a mixture of caution and disbelief. The man with the sword vaulted over the table but before he could hit the ground, while he was at the apex of his vault, Phane's smile contorted into a look of murderous glee. He thrust his hand out toward the man.

With one hand on the table and still in midair, the man simply burst apart as if a force of tremendous energy had struck him square in the chest hard enough to turn his body to pulp and splatter his parts around the room. The bulk of his mass smashed into the wall behind the table with such force that it liquefied on impact, squirting gore in every direction. One arm thudded onto the table as it came free of his torso at the shoulder. One of his legs spun end over end through the air and hit the edge of the table, leaving a lurid red splotch before flipping off onto the ground and settling in a pile of gore framed by a slowly expanding puddle of blood. His head skittered into the corner of the room and spun slowly to a stop, leaving a red circle painted on the floor around it.

The remaining eight men sat in stunned fear, splattered with the pulverized flesh, bone, blood, and guts of a man who only moments before had sat at their table. Phane giggled for a moment before his face took on the look of another murder waiting to happen. He drew himself up and deliberately cleared his throat.

"Gentlemen, I am Prince Phane Reishi." Their faces went white behind masks of splattered blood. "I am here to assume command of the Reishi Army Regency and deliver you victory over the traitorous House of Karth."

The blood-soaked men all looked back and forth at each other, little bits of viscera and bone falling from their hair when they moved their heads. The man in the center chair stood slowly and bowed stiffly, dripping blood on the table.

"Prince Phane, we are at your service." There was a slight tremor to his voice.

Phane flashed his most boyish smile. "Of course you are, General. You and your men can get cleaned up now, and do something with this mess." He gestured around at the table with a look of exaggerated disgust. "Then I would like to inspect my army." He turned and sauntered off, talking over his shoulder as he left the scene of carnage, "In the meantime, I'll make myself at home."

Chapter 34

Alexander screamed. He put his hands on either side of his head like he was trying to keep it from coming apart and screamed again. The pain was unbearable. He didn't know that anything could hurt so much. He slumped to his knees. The searing agony began to expand from the breathtaking torment in his head to the rest of his body. It felt like molten lead flowed slowly through his veins from his head into his torso and out to his extremities. He wanted to scream again but couldn't draw enough breath. He was on his knees slumped over with his forehead on the cold stone floor when a convulsion of tingling, burning misery tore through him. He fell over on his side and gasped for breath. His lungs simply wouldn't work. He felt them burn with need for air but couldn't make them draw breath. He shook in a paroxysm and imagined that this must be what it felt like to drown in liquid fire. His vision started to close down and he felt himself losing consciousness. He nearly panicked. He knew he would lose everything if he let himself succumb now. He had to endure the trial of pain, or perish.

Alexander had spent the week prior studying with Mason, learning about the mana fast and what he could expect. He worked hard and long to learn the mental concentration exercises and visualization techniques he would need to survive the ordeal and to control his access to the firmament once he succeeded.

Mason told him he wasn't ready. Most apprentice wizards spent years of daily study learning the strict mental discipline required of a wizard. Alexander had some training from Lucky disguised as simple thought exercises but without the rigor. He hadn't practiced the meditation and the careful, methodical creation of vivid and exacting images in his mind that was so necessary to a wizard.

Alexander had insisted. He needed the power that the mana fast represented if he was going to have any chance of stopping Phane. And he knew he needed to do this now, before he left for Blackstone Keep, or he might never get the chance again.

Isabel had asked him to wait. She begged him to put this off. It broke his heart to see the fear in her beautiful green eyes. She railed at him when begging didn't work. He took it without flinching. When that didn't work she fell into his arms and cried. He held her and promised her it would be all right. She stood at the door and watched with tears streaming down her face when he locked himself into the tower room to begin the ordeal.

Abigail had been angrier than Isabel but she knew her brother better and knew he wouldn't be swayed once he'd set his course. She told him she loved him and made him promise he would survive. She was standing next to Isabel when he secluded himself away for the fast.

Anatoly and Lucky hadn't tried to talk him out of it. Anatoly simply asked if he was sure he had to do this. When he saw the look of resolve on Alexander's face, he just nodded. Lucky gave him a few suggestions, pointers, and reminders of lessons past to help him with the trials that lay ahead. Alexander thanked them both for their support and promised he would survive and emerge stronger.

Mason had prepared the top room of his tower for Alexander. It was a round room just over thirty feet across, with a centered, twenty-foot magic circle inlaid in gold. Mason set up a cot, a small table, a meditation cushion, and a barrel of drinking water inside the circle for Alexander and cast the invocation that would protect the world outside the circle from the forces that Alexander might call forth. Until he completed the fast, he wouldn't be able to leave the circle. He had committed to his course. If he succeeded, he would live.

As the torment threatened to overwhelm his sanity he focused his mind on the pain itself. He embraced it and welcomed it into every part of his being. He felt like he was on fire but still he held onto the pain. Mason had told him that he had to face each trial directly in order to succeed. He had to become larger than the trial within his own mind. He had to master the challenge and learn to focus, concentrate, and control his mind and feelings in spite of the trial.

He lay on the floor all that night struggling for each breath, shuddering in unmitigated torment, occasionally convulsing when a wave of agony ripped through him. When dawn came he focused on the light from the tiny window and clung to the pain. He focused his will and looked for a place of clarity where he could find refuge from the gales of unrelenting agony that racked him down to the marrow of his being. He cast about within the confines of his consciousness for a place of safe harbor.

And then, after countless hours of torture, he found it: the eye of the storm. A tiny little part of his being that was held apart from the agony that so completely consumed him. He drew himself into that calm; took shelter in the stillness. For what seemed like a very long time, he just took refuge. But he knew that wasn't enough. He had to master the trial. He had to master the pain. He had to find a way to command his mind, his body, and his spirit in the face of the torture.

The eye of the storm was the key. He drew himself up from there and watched the pain wash through the rest of him. He detached his will from the suffering, detached his mind from the distraction of it. And then he began to gain command over his body. Bit by bit he was able to impose his will on his pain-racked body and bit by bit his body responded despite the crushing agony.

He made it to his feet with an effort that was beyond anything he'd ever exerted in his life before that moment. Once standing, the pain coursed through him as though it was rising to meet the challenge and maintain its supremacy over him. He bore down with his will. He allowed the pain to have full run of his body, looked it in the face and commanded his arms and legs to obey him anyway. And they did, slowly at first, but soon he was working through fighting sequences with an imaginary sword. Thrust, parry, advance, riposte, withdraw, and counterstrike. He could see the sequence of moves in his mind's eye and he commanded his body to perform the movements even through the blinding agony. He moved with jerking and halting steps. Each technique was forced and sloppy at first, but he kept at it.

He began to move more fluidly and cleanly. The pain was still there but he had control. He could act in spite of it. Like a dam breaking, the pain suddenly drained away. His nerves were raw and worn and he was exhausted, but the sudden absence of pain was one of the most sublime and uplifting feelings he'd ever experienced. A great wave of relief washed over his sweat-slick body as he collapsed onto his cot. The cool air felt soothing in his lungs and he felt lighter in spite of his fatigue.

It was midafternoon on the fourth day of the mana fast when Alexander passed the trial of pain. The first three days had been nothing more than meditating on an empty stomach and struggling with the solitude. The trial of pain came as suddenly as it faded away. He knew he needed sleep but he also knew he needed to drink the fourth vial of Wizard's Dust-infused water before he let himself drift off. Mason had impressed upon him the importance of drinking one vial each day without fail. He didn't say what would happen if he failed to do so but implied it would be very dangerous. Alexander rolled over and flipped open the lid to the little felt-lined case, removed the next vial, popped the sealed glass stopper off and downed the slightly sweet contents. He was asleep before his head hit the pillow.

He woke sometime in the middle of the night in terror. The fear was so palpable he could feel it closing in around him in the darkness. His heart hammered in his chest and he held his breath for fear of the darkness hearing him. He curled into a ball on his cot and whimpered. He didn't know what was out there but he knew it was horrible and it was coming for him.

He shivered in cold sweat while the dread coursed through him. He couldn't tell if he was asleep and caught up in a nightmare or awake and waiting for one of Phane's conjured beasts to rend him flesh from bone. He simply couldn't make his mind work right. The fear invaded every corner of his being and poisoned his reason with deep dark foreboding that ebbed and flowed like a tide, sometimes rising to the level of blind, paralyzing panic and other times receding into trembling trepidation.

When dawn came, he feared the light. In the light the things stalking in the recesses of his imagination could see him. There would be nowhere to hide. He found himself sitting in the middle of his cot, knees pulled up to his chest shivering in fear when he remembered that he had to face the trial to overcome it. But this time he already knew of a place where he could find shelter. He knew there was a refuge of stillness somewhere within him where he could stand apart from the stalking, formless fright that lurked on the edge of his awareness.

It took him quite some time to find it. He kept retreating away from it and, spooked by his own imagination, stumbling into a new and yet darker corner of his own mind. When he finally rediscovered the place of stillness where his own personal witness lived, he found the fear was distant there and no longer clouded his mind and corrupted his reason. He could watch it without feeling it. Gradually, slowly, he pushed the place of detachment from the little corner of his mind out into the rest of his consciousness. He almost felt foolish when the fear abruptly evaporated like darkness before the dawn. It had no substance except what he gave it. It had no power except what he permitted it to have. He had passed the trial of fear.

He drank the fifth vial at dusk and tried to sleep. To his surprise he slept quite well. He woke on the sixth day expecting that the final trial would accost him at any moment, but it didn't. He spent the whole day meditating. At dusk he drank the sixth vial and lay down on his cot. He started to doze off when it happened.

It felt like his awareness was ripped from his body and cast into the firmament itself. He saw the flow of time, space, and matter differently than he had ever imagined it before. It was one all-encompassing, living, breathing thing. It flowed inexorably forward. He could see all things as they came to be, but from behind the curtain, so to speak. He watched reality form like a wave in the firmament and crest in the moment of now, always moving, always in flux.

Then the wave of time sped up and he could see the future, or at least one possible future. Phane had conquered the whole of the Seven Isles. Alexander saw his parents, his sister, Lucky, Anatoly, and Isabel being tortured by Phane. The Reishi Prince cast powerful spells on them to keep them alive while he took perverse delight in their suffering.

Alexander was aghast at the magnitude of Phane's depravity. He was repulsed by the horror of what was being done to the ones he loved. He saw Phane cutting into Isabel and heard her call his name, beseeching his help, crying out in forlorn despair. As Phane maimed her, she lost that spark in her eye that so captivated Alexander. She lost hope and became despondent, no longer even interested in screaming at the ruinous things Phane did to her. Her will to live dimmed. The vibrancy of her spirit failed. She begged for death, pleaded for a quick end, but Phane pressed on. He took her past the limits of sanity and brought her to a place of total, abject, desperate anguish.

Alexander thought his soul would surely fail him. He wanted to cast himself into the infinity of the firmament itself and allow it to consume every trace of his being to escape the impossible horror of watching Isabel be so totally destroyed. When he thought it could get no worse, when he had seen every gruesome detail of each of his loved one's brutal and ruinous torture, Phane looked right at him as if he knew he was watching and giggled madly before he cast their souls into the pits of the netherworld.

Alexander followed into the darkness and watched helplessly while each of those he loved most was savaged in ways that made Phane's torture seem amateurish. The netherworld was a timeless place, so there was no end to their suffering. His loved ones were already dead, so they couldn't escape the unrelenting torture except by surrendering their sanity and all vestiges of their mind and will, leaving nothing that Alexander even recognized.

He witnessed these horrors and was powerless to stop them. He felt the despair threaten to overtake his reason and begin to insinuate its dark tendrils into the cracks in his sanity. He was to blame for their suffering. He had failed. Phane had cast the world into a thousand years of darkness and it was his fault.

He began to let go. He saw no point in remaining himself. The essence of his being was already adrift on the waves of the firmament, beneath reality itself. All he had to do was let go and he would cease to exist. The very fabric of his being would unravel and scatter into the stuff from which it was made. The despair would end. The knowledge of his loved ones suffering would be unmade and he would be no more.

But then he thought of Isabel. He couldn't let go of her. Her smile and the intelligence sparkling in her piercing green eyes were worth holding onto. He felt himself slipping away even as he clung to the memory of her.

Alexander suddenly felt a desperate need to live. Isabel would want him to fight. She would want him to live and he couldn't let her memory die. If she was truly gone, then she deserved to have someone remember her. As the raw despair began to fade with his determination to hold on, he remembered, ever so faintly at first, that he was facing the test of despair. He seized on that tiny scrap of reason in an ocean of hopelessness and nurtured it, fed it, and breathed life into it until it became a beacon he could see the truth by. He couldn't trust anything. Nothing in this place could be believed and so he resolved to believe in hope, whether his senses told him it made sense or not.

He pictured his family, his friends, and Isabel all alive and well. He focused on those thoughts even as wave after wave of horror from a very dark possible future crashed over him. He stood his ground and weathered the storm.

In the face of despair, he chose hope.

As abruptly as it had come, the despair receded.

Chapter 35

Alexander opened his eyes to see light streaming through the little window. He sat up carefully and looked around the room. He had passed each of the three tests and he still had one vial left. Mason had told him to drink all seven vials. He told Alexander that he would come on the morning of the eighth day to release the spell that kept him confined within the magic circle. Alexander drank the seventh and final vial of Wizard's Dust.

He spent the rest of the day in meditation. Just before dusk he felt his awareness slip from the confines of his body and flood out into the whole of the world, but this time there was no despair. He was detached and watched time unfold from the perspective of the whole of reality itself while still maintaining a distant awareness of his immediate surroundings. It only lasted for a moment before he came snapping back to his limited awareness delivered to him through his conventional senses, but in that moment he glimpsed the potential of magic. The firmament was everywhere all at once. To touch it was to touch the essence of reality. He spent the rest of the evening meditating on the possibilities that now lay before him.

When the next morning came and Mason opened the door, Alexander was dressed and sitting on the edge of his little cot. Mason entered the circular tower room and dispelled the magic circle with a word, walked to him and placed a hand on his forehead. He murmured arcane words under his breath and closed his eyes. A few moments later his eyes snapped open with a look of confusion and slight alarm. He flipped the lid of the case holding seven, now empty, crystal vials. He looked back to Alexander with a frown.

"You drank them all?" There was worry bordering on alarm in Mason's voice.

"Yes, one a day like you said I should," Alexander replied.

Mason's brow drew down even further and he looked deep in thought. He shook his head. "Did you experience pain, fear, and despair?"

Alexander nodded soberly, "More than I believed a person could, on all three counts."

Mason looked more perplexed now than worried. "That just doesn't make sense. Do you feel any different?"

"No, but I can see your colors now without shifting my vision. It's like my second sight has merged with my normal vision."

"Huh." Mason looked back and forth slowly as if he was searching for the answer to a question that he couldn't quite frame correctly. "Well, I guess it can wait. I'm sure you're hungry."

Alexander nodded emphatically, "Now that you mention it, I'm starving."

"I thought you would be. Hanlon's had a brunch prepared for you in the family dining room." Mason turned to lead him out of the tower but then turned back with a little grin. "Oh, and there's a surprise waiting for you down there." Mason walked out of the room with Alexander trailing behind.

"What kind of surprise?" he asked.

"The good kind, but I promised I wouldn't spoil it," was all Mason would say.

They made a detour by his room so he could wash up and change into some clean clothes, then hurried to the Alaric family dining room. Everyone was waiting there for him. All were anxious to see that he'd survived the mana fast. The surprise Mason had spoken of brought a lump to his throat.

His mom and dad were there.

They beamed at their son as he rushed into his mom's arms. His dad put a hand on his shoulder. For a long moment he just held his mother and struggled to keep from crying.

"I was so afraid you were dead," Alexander said. "The last thing I saw was the manor burning."

"We're fine, Son. We fled in the direction of Highlands Reach to throw any pursuers off your trail. That's why it took us so long to get here," Duncan said while Bella held her son out at arm's length and looked him up and down as if to make sure he wasn't broken.

She sniffed back tears and wiped her cheeks clean. "Come on, have something to eat. You look like you've lost some weight."

Alexander stopped and found Isabel with his eyes. She was looking at him but had been quiet. "There's something I have to do first."

He walked over to her and held out his hand. She took it and stood, looking a little confused but happy for his attentions just the same.

He looked at her with a sense of confidence and certainty that he'd never felt about anything in his whole life.

"Isabel Alaric, I love you. Will you marry me?"

She blinked, then her face flushed and she smiled radiantly as she threw herself into his arms and the room burst into applause.

He held her for a long moment. "You saved me again," he whispered for her ears alone.

"Mom, Dad, I'd like you to meet Isabel," he introduced his fiancé with an unabashed smile of pure joy.

They ate and then talked and then ate some more. Duncan and Bella recounted how they'd gone east away from Valentine Manor in an effort to lure the enemy after them. Their ploy worked almost too well. They'd been attacked and chased by something that prowled in the night. They hadn't even been able to identify the thing but they knew it was out there from the inhuman sounds it made. Bella kept it away with her magical light. When they discovered that it didn't like water, they were able to escape it by crossing a series of streams.

They made their way along the southern edge of the forest and encountered a squad of Rangers when they came to the forest road. They arrived a few days ago and had been worrying about Alexander since they learned what he was doing. Both Bella and Duncan had been through the mana fast. Both knew the dangers and the difficulties of the trials. Both were relieved to see him safely through the ordeal and both were proud of his accomplishment.

Erik reported that the Rangers from the fortress gate had scattered the Reishi hunting party. Most had been killed but both Wizard Rangle and Truss escaped. Alexander silently hoped that wolves had found them lost in the forest and had their way with them.

Alexander felt like he spent the bulk of the day eating. He hadn't eaten anything for a week and now he was making up for it. No sooner did he finish a meal and relax for a few minutes than he started to feel hungry again. The kitchen was more than happy to oblige him. His friends and family took the opportunity to tell stories of their recent experiences and generally enjoy each other's company. Alexander knew it would all end soon enough. He meant to set out for Blackstone Keep by way of New Ruatha within the week. He knew the journey would open him up to attack by Phane and his minions but it was a necessary risk. He'd accomplished most of what he could here in Glen Morillian. It was time to move on to the next challenge.

Late in the afternoon Mason handed him a slip of paper. It read: "Bloodvault one of three belongs to the one who is marked in service to Old Reishi Law. You have a right to your life because you are alive. You have a right to your liberty because you have free will. You have a right to your property because it is the product of your labor. You forfeit these rights when you take them from another."

Alexander read it and then read it again. "This is the writing on the Bloodvault?"

Mason nodded.

"It says 'Bloodvault one of three.' That means there are two more out there somewhere." He handed Isabel the piece of paper.

Mason nodded again with a knowing smile.

"There's another one at Blackstone Keep," Alexander whispered.

Even as he said it, he knew it had to be the truth. He felt a sense of urgency well up in the pit of his stomach. After reading the skillbook, he was nearly certain that the Thinblade was in one of the other two Bloodvaults. It only made sense. Why would Mage Cedric give him a skillbook that taught him how to wield the Thinblade if he hadn't preserved the ancient sword for him as well? When he looked at the heavy gold ring on his finger, he felt even more certain that he had to get to Blackstone Keep sooner rather than later.

Mason nodded yet again. "I suspect there is as well. The contents may prove quite useful. Blackstone Keep itself is a treasure. It's a near impregnable fortress with powerful constructed magic built into its walls."

Isabel was sitting next to Alexander, listening quietly. "So when do we leave?" she asked.

Alexander thought about it for a moment. "I'd like to have a few days with Mason to see what the mana fast did to me. After that, we should be on our way. I'd say by week's end."

There were little pockets of conversation around the room that all dwindled when they heard Alexander's plan. Alexander went to the table and took his seat. Everyone else joined him. For an hour before dinner was served they discussed their plans, evaluated their options, and explored the threats they knew were waiting beyond the barrier mountains of Glen Morillian. By the time dinner arrived, Alexander felt the sense of order he always got from having a plan. He knew what he intended to do for the foreseeable future and that was half the battle. Now all he had to do was go out and do it.

He spent the next several, very frustrating days working with his parents and Mason, trying to learn more about magic and his connection to the firmament. He attempted all of the mental exercises they taught him but was unable to make a reliable connection to the firmament. He read a few minor spell books that Mason offered him as starter spells but was unable to make them work at all. He didn't understand and, to make matters worse, no one else did either. Mason and his parents talked about how they worked with the firmament to manifest their desired outcome but when Alexander tried to follow their instructions, he got absolutely nowhere.

He was starting to wonder if the mana fast had been for nothing. It had been a trying ordeal. In some ways he felt like it had been a trauma but in other ways he felt like the experience of the trials had prepared him for what was coming. He had a better understanding of his limits and just how far he could actually push himself when he had to. If for no other reason, he was glad he'd endured the trials of the mana fast for the confidence he gained as a result.

Three days later when he'd all but given up on mastering the spells Mason had recommended, he was sitting on a cushion on his balcony just after sunset, practicing a meditation that his father suggested. It was supposed to hone a wizard's ability to visualize the outcome he wanted the firmament to manifest. But Alexander was tired and he let his concentration slip and allowed his mind to wander.

He thought about Phane and the struggle that lay ahead, wondering how he was going to face such a powerful wizard, let alone defeat him. Abruptly, he felt his awareness separate from his body. For a moment, it felt similar to the sensation he'd felt at the end of his mana fast. He was adrift in the firmament, experiencing the moment of now from every perspective all at once. It was disorienting and confusing. The cacophony of events, thoughts, and voices were too much to assimilate or understand.

But a moment later, he was rushing impossibly fast toward one point in the present moment. His awareness coalesced in one single location. His vision was free of his body. His eyes were closed but he could see as clear as day. He found his awareness floating near the ceiling in the corner of a strange room. He looked around and saw a long table with nine men sitting along the far side with their backs to a stone wall that was stained with a large dark splotch. Eight of the men wore armor with a gold-embossed, stylized letter R emblazoned on the breastplate. The man sitting in the center chair was dressed in a simple brown robe with delicate gold filigree lining the hem, collar, and sleeves that looked like writing in an ancient and arcane language. Alexander thought he recognized some of the symbols from the magical circle in Mason's tower room. The man's wavy brown hair was shoulder length and his face was almost too handsome. He looked perfectly proportioned in every way. But it was the eyes that caught Alexander's attention. They reminded him of the last time he looked in a mirror. They were soft brown with gold flecks glittering in the irises.

Alexander focused more intently on the scene and started to hear the voices of the men in the room. The men in armor were reporting to the man in the brown robes on the status of an army. He was listening politely while he sipped dark red wine from a fine crystal goblet.

The man to the right of the robed man was speaking. "We've set your plan in motion, My Prince. The attack will begin on the night of the new moon.

Karth will finally be ours!" He spoke emphatically and with enthusiasm as he made a triumphant fist with his gauntleted hand to punctuate his pronouncement.

The man in the robes smiled so honestly and with such genuine joy that Alexander began to think he would like him if he met him. Then the man suddenly stopped smiling, cocked his head for a moment like he was listening for some faint sound, turned and looked directly at Alexander.

Alexander's heart skipped a beat. The man in the brown robes stood abruptly and the look of murderous glee that ghosted across his face was enough to make Alexander's blood run cold.

He waved to Alexander as if to say "I see you" before he stepped up on the table and cocked his head with a smile. The men in armor were all standing and looking for the threat, but the man in the brown robes ignored them as he peered more closely at Alexander.

"I see my nether wolves have failed," he said. Alexander felt the icy tingle of cold dread flood into every recess of his soul. The man in the robes shrugged. "No matter, what I sent next will succeed." He chortled impishly and then a look of comprehension overtook his maleficent glee. A broad smile slowly spread across his face and he tipped his head back and laughed. Still smiling in pure joy, he pointed at Alexander. "You don't even know what you are," he guffawed again before his unwholesome elation turned to joyous malice, "but I do."

Chapter 36

Alexander's eyes snapped open. He was sitting on a meditation cushion on his balcony but he could still hear the laughter of the man in the brown robes. His heart hammered in terror. He reeled in confusion. It was so real. He felt like he was actually there in the same room with Prince Phane. He was certain beyond doubt that the man in the brown robes was Phane. Alexander focused on the experience, trying to recall every detail. He went to his sitting room and found a pen, some ink and a piece of parchment, and started writing every detail of the experience in rushed, hurried strokes. He played it back in his mind over and over, searching for anything he hadn't yet captured on paper.

Whatever the experience was, however it had happened, Alexander was sure the information he'd learned was valuable. He went over his notes again. When he was satisfied he'd recorded every salient fact, he put on his boots and headed for Mason's workshop. Alexander knew from the past few days that Wizard Kallentera slept very little and could usually be found in his chaotic-looking laboratory late in the evening working on something or other. The man was as bad as Lucky. He always had a dozen projects in progress and would flit from one to the next at a whim.

When Alexander entered in a rush, he found his parents and Lucky sitting around the fire with Mason, sipping tea and talking quietly. All turned at his unannounced entrance and stood quickly when they saw the look on his face.

"What's happened?" Duncan asked in his calm and reassuring way.

Alexander held up the scrap of parchment covered with his hastily scribbled notes. "I saw Phane," he said, hurrying across the room.

Everyone was speechless for just a fraction of a moment before they all started asking questions at once, then stopped talking just as abruptly.

Alexander took a seat and put his notes on the table in front of him. His mother poured him a cup of hot tea and stirred in a dollop of honey and a shot of cream just the way he liked it. He took a moment to gather his thoughts and slow his breathing.

"I was meditating like you suggested," he said to his father, "when my thoughts wandered off and I started wondering about Phane. Suddenly I was outside of my body, floating in the firmament. It was confusing and overwhelming. A moment later, I was just there in a room with Phane and eight men in armor."

Mason leaned in. "When you say you were there, how do you mean? Were you physically in the same room or were you just aware of the room?"

"I guess I was just aware of the room," Alexander said. "I could tell my body was still here on my balcony, but I could see the room and hear what the men were saying. It was like I was floating against the ceiling in the corner."

Mason nodded in thought.

Duncan took up the questioning. "What did you hear?"

"They were discussing an attack against Karth," Alexander said. "The men in armor were reporting to Phane on preparations for a battle. They seemed confident that they would win."

"It makes sense that Phane would go to the Reishi Army Regency," Lucky mused. "It's the largest standing army in the Seven Isles that still claims any loyalty to the Reishi line."

"Can you describe the armor they wore in greater detail?" Mason asked.

Alexander nodded and took up his notes. "It was polished silver with a big gold letter R on the breastplate. It looked ornate and well crafted like the men who wore it held high rank."

"That's the Reishi Army Regency, all right. Phane isn't wasting any time," Mason said.

"What else did they say, Son?" Duncan asked gently but intently.

"The men in armor didn't say anything else because Phane suddenly looked right at me." Looks of alarm passed all around the room before Alexander continued, "He said he could see that his nether wolves had failed but what he sent next would succeed. Then he started laughing maniacally and told me that I don't even know what I am, but he does. That's when I came back."

The room fell silent. Alexander tried to school the trembling in his gut with a sip of tea.

Duncan took a deep breath and let it out slowly. "All right, let's take this one item at a time. You had a clairvoyant experience without casting a clairvoyance spell, or even knowing how to cast a clairvoyance spell, for that matter. You saw the council chamber of the Reishi Army Regency in Karth and heard their battle plan to attack the House of Karth. Phane knows his nether wolves failed to kill you and he's sent something else to finish the job. And he knows what you are, but you don't."

Alexander nodded at his father's summation. Duncan Valentine was a man who valued facts. He often stated the facts of a problem as a starting point for discovering a solution. Alexander was familiar with his father's way of thinking and it set him at ease. Mason stood and started pacing in front of the fireplace.

"The claim that you don't know what you are may shed some light on your inability to learn any of the spells that Mason's had you study," Lucky offered. "There are many ways that a person can interact with the firmament. For example, I can't cast most spells to save my life, but I can imbue my concoctions with potent magic. Perhaps you have a more narrow connection to the firmament. So far, you've demonstrated an ability to see a living aura and you've just had a clairvoyant experience. Both of these things are acts of magic. Other wizards would have to cast a spell to accomplish either. You've demonstrated an ability to use aura reading and clairvoyance without using the normal process of spell casting."

"All things considered, I'm more concerned with whatever Phane has sent to kill my son." Bella was angry and frightened all at once.

"I agree, Bella, but Alexander should be safe behind the circles of protection guarding Glen Morillian. Nothing from the netherworld can get in here." Duncan tried to reassure his wife despite the look of grave concern clouding his own face.

Mason stopped pacing abruptly and turned to them. "Perhaps we can warn Karth." Before anyone could respond, he rushed off to one of his shelves and started looking for a book.

While everyone was watching Mason shuffle off to his books, Alexander refocused the conversation. "What do we know about Karth?"

The three looked at each other and Duncan nodded to Lucky. Lucky took a moment to order his thoughts before beginning his lecture. Alexander smiled slightly at his old tutor's familiar mannerism.

"The House of Karth sided with the rebellion during the Reishi War. Toward the end of the war, the bulk of the Reishi army was sent to Karth by the Reishi Sovereign to crush the House of Karth, but the Reishi fell shortly thereafter, stranding the Reishi army without support. They had nowhere to go and no way to get there, so the generals and wizards leading the force decided to conquer Karth and bring it under their rule. The House of Karth proved to be more difficult to subdue than they anticipated. They've been at war for the better part of the past two thousand years. The Reishi Army Regency rules over the southern half of the island while the House of Karth rules in the north. By all accounts, the place is a nightmare. Both sides rule their people with fear and violence and with no respect for the Old Law. The war flares periodically but both sides are pretty evenly matched, so the land holdings have remained more or less stable for many centuries."

"Phane just tipped the balance of power in favor of the Reishi Army Regency," Alexander said. "Once he consolidates his hold on Karth, it'll give him a base of operations and establish his credibility throughout the Seven Isles." Now Alexander stood and started pacing. "If we can stop him there, or at least slow him down, it'll give us more time."

"Agreed, but how can we do that?" Duncan asked.

"I don't know, but I think Mason might have an idea or two once he finds what he's looking for," Alexander answered. "Let's table that for the moment. I'd like to get back to the question of what I am. Lucky, you said there are many ways a person can interact with the firmament. Tell me about some of them."

"Elemental wizards are the most common. They deal in things like fire, water, and air. There are enchanters like my Guild Mage, Kelvin Gamaliel, and alchemists like me who imbue items with magic but wield very little influence on the firmament directly. There are conjurors who summon creatures to do their bidding. Necromancers deal in forces from the netherworld; they can summon creatures like the nether wolves and worse as well as wield dark powers directly. There are generalists who can wield magic from most of the different disciplines but cannot attain great levels of power in any one area, due in large part, to the general nature of their study. Generalists are often the most versatile wizards but they can't rise to the level of power wielded by a mage. There are those who specialize in divination, others who focus on evocation, and some few who practice transmutation. Then there are specialist wizards who have very narrow and specific ways of using their connection to the firmament. The battle wizard you fought is a good example. He had great power but it was limited by its narrow focus. Specialist wizards are very rare and often quite powerful within the confines of their abilities. Then, of course, there are witches. Women who have survived the mana fast like your mother. Witches tend to manipulate the firmament in very different ways than wizards, but that doesn't pertain to you."

"So what does that make me?" Alexander asked.

"If I had to say right now," Lucky mused for a moment, "I believe you are a specialist wizard but I couldn't say what type. In truth, you may have a unique connection to the firmament that has never been seen before. Whatever the case, I believe we can rule out the more common classifications because you've proven unable to master basic spells that would be easy for a novice wizard of a more common variety to learn. More importantly, you've demonstrated that your connection to the firmament is surprisingly powerful with the sheer range of your clairvoyant experience. Mason is a master wizard of significant power and experience. I doubt he could project a clairvoyance spell farther than a mile or so and then only with great effort and preparation. You looked across the ocean and into just the right room thousands of miles away, and you could hear what was said, as well. That is no small feat."

"So how do I control it? How do I use it to fight?" Alexander asked.

Lucky looked helpless as he shrugged and slowly shook his head. "I don't know, Alexander. Your abilities are different from any I've even heard of but perhaps Mage Gamaliel will know more."

"You're not still thinking about leaving Glen Morillian, are you?" Bella snapped.

Alexander looked at his mother with gentle determination and nodded.

"Alexander, you said yourself Phane has sent something else, something worse than nether wolves, to kill you. How can you leave? You must stay here where it's safe," she said in half plea and half command.

Alexander sat down with a sigh. He spoke quietly but with conviction. "Mom, during my mana fast, I saw what will happen to the world if Phane wins. I've been chosen to stop him. I didn't ask for it but the duty is mine nonetheless. If I hide here in the safety of Glen Morillian while he ravages the rest of the world and inflicts unspeakable suffering on thousands of innocent people, then I'm no better than he is. He's evil and he intends to impose his will on every living thing in all of the Seven Isles. I have to do everything I can to stop him, no matter the cost."

A tear slipped from her eye and she hastily brushed it from her cheek. "I'm very proud of you, Alexander, and I know what you say is right and true but I've already lost one child to this monster and I can't bear to lose another." Her voice trembled as she spoke and another tear slid down her face. Alexander took a seat next to his mother, put his arm around her and pulled her head gently to his shoulder. She cried quietly for a few moments in silence.

When she looked up, Alexander whispered softly, "I love you, Mom, but I have to do this."

She nodded, still wiping tears from her face.

Mason bustled up with excitement and exclaimed, "I've found it!"

Everyone turned to look at the court wizard. He held up a very old-looking book. "It's a dream-whisper spell. We may be able to use it to deliver a message to the House of Karth."

Alexander stood, suddenly quite interested, "How so?"

"I'll have to study the spell to see if it'll work and then I might need to make some preparations to adequately power it, but I believe I can send a message into the dreams of the King of Karth."

"Even over such a great distance?" Duncan asked.

"Distance matters much less in the realm of dreams," Mason said. "I have a projection spell but I can only throw my image for several hundred feet, so that would never work, but I may be able to reach him in his dreams."

"All right, then," Alexander said with renewed enthusiasm, "we'll still leave for New Ruatha as planned. Mason, when you figure out the dream-whisper spell, send the King of Karth this message: Lord Alexander, King of Ruatha, sends warning. Prince Phane has taken command of the Reishi Army Regency and they will attack you on the new moon."

Mason took a piece of parchment from a nearby table and copied the message. "I will send him your words," Mason said. "On another subject, I've studied the skillbook and I believe it might still be of great use to us. There are very clear instructions for fighting with a blade in ways that are probably not known by any in the Seven Isles, save a few. I could translate the basic instructions and use it as a basis for a training manual for our soldiers. It may better prepare them for the battle ahead."

"That sounds like a good idea. I'd like Hanlon and Anatoly to be the first to study it." Alexander paused for a moment. "Mason, I need to know how to use my connection to the firmament. I need to be able to control it and fight with it. Anything you can offer on the subject would be helpful."

Mason deflated slightly. "Alexander, I understand how important this is to you but I've searched my memory and my library for any insight into your abilities and found none. For now, trust your instincts. Take mental note of how you feel when you connect with the firmament and practice recreating those feelings. Your relationship to the firmament is unlike any I've encountered, but it also seems to have the potential for great power. Be open-minded as you try to master it; you might be surprised at what you're capable of."

Alexander spent the next few days trying to control his connection to the firmament without any luck at all. He could still see the living aura of everyone and everything around. His second sight had merged with his normal vision. At first, it took some getting used to, but it became normal and natural over the course of a few days. Other than that, he couldn't produce or cause any magical effects whatsoever. He tried to meditate the way he did the night of his clairvoyant experience but had no luck reproducing the effect, which only led to greater frustration.

Mason succeeded at sending a message to the King of Karth. At least he'd been confident that the message had been delivered. Unfortunately, there was no way to determine if it worked, if the king heard the message in his dreams, if he believed the message, or if he chose to act on it. Alexander consoled himself with the knowledge that they had done all they could and shifted his focus to more immediate concerns.

He was ready to be on his way. Lucky was working hard preparing potions and other concoctions for their journey. Abigail and Isabel were training with Hanlon and Anatoly in some of the new blade techniques from the skillbook. Alexander was trying without success to produce even the simplest magical effect. Jack had made friends with every cook, servant, valet, stableman, and groundskeeper in the entire palace. He was in his element at court. He knew how the place worked and played it like a fiddle.

What spare time Alexander had, he spent with his parents or Isabel but he was distracted and anxious. He felt like he was wasting time. He came to believe that his magic would come or it wouldn't. No amount of time spent trying to make it work seemed to have any effect. The day before they were set to leave, Alexander revealed his plan at breakfast.

"We'll be going on foot from the north fortress gate and traveling through the forest. I believe that's our best chance to avoid Phane's hunters. At the same time, I need Erik to take a hundred good Rangers and ride out from the eastern fortress gate to draw the enemy away."

Erik smiled proudly, "I'll make sure they see me."

Hanlon and Emily looked less enthusiastic about the assignment but they didn't object.

"Erik, this task will be very dangerous," Alexander said seriously. "I don't know what Phane's sent to hunt me but I'm certain it'll be deadly. I want you to ride fast. Take spare horses and don't let up. Do not engage unless you have no other choice. I want you to run from whatever is chasing you. Don't put yourself or your men at risk if you can help it."

Erik sobered slightly, "I understand."

Alexander considered for a moment before continuing. "I'd like Kevin and Duane to stay here." Both of Erik's younger brothers looked upset and started to object, but Alexander stopped them with a raised hand. "Your father will need you both to help him build and train the army."

Both looked disappointed but nodded their agreement. Emily looked a little relieved that at least two of her children would be safe for the time being. Alexander feared that wouldn't last. All too soon the world would be caught up in a war that no one anywhere would be able to escape.

"Our first stop will be the Wizards Guild in New Ruatha but I don't plan on staying there long. I want to talk to Mage Gamaliel to see if he can offer any suggestions or insight. My primary goal is to get to Blackstone Keep. I believe the second of the Bloodvaults is there. Whatever Mage Cedric left me there will be useful and we can use Blackstone Keep as a source of authority to help bring the territories under the banner of Ruatha and to house the army we're building.

"Erik, you'll ride straight to the base of Blackstone Keep and scout the area. Don't stay in one place long and keep your force intact as much as possible. Once I arrive, you'll help me secure the interior of the Keep and establish basic defenses. Hanlon, once you have a significant force assembled, I want you to secure the forest road. It's the main overland route from north to south and will provide us with a strategic advantage if some of the territories are reluctant to accept my leadership. After you have sufficient forces to control the road, begin assembling legion-sized units and sending them to Blackstone Keep but be sure to keep adequate forces to defend Glen Morillian."

Breakfast the next morning was somber. Everyone said their goodbyes and then Alexander and his companions were on their way to the north fortress gate. The ride was pleasant enough. Alexander's mind wandered while they meandered through rolling farmland, past herds of cattle. He wondered about his calling. It troubled him that he was so different from other wizards. He needed guidance but didn't know where to find it. He hoped that Mage Gamaliel would have the answers he needed, but for some reason that he couldn't quite define, he doubted it.

Most wizards could alter the nature of the world around them through a process of vivid visualization of the outcome they desired, coupled with a deliberate and controlled connection to the firmament. Alexander remembered how it felt to connect to the timeless realm beneath reality but he wasn't able to make it happen again. Most novice wizards were easily taught how to make that all-important connection. In fact, the biggest difficulty for most wizards was in controlling the degree of the connection. The firmament was virtually infinite and offered such an impossible variety of possibilities that wizards had been known to get lost. It was as if their consciousness, sentience, and even soul simply lost hold of their physical being. Those wizards died slowly.

Alexander couldn't seem to create a connection and yet his second sight had become a permanent fixture of his life. Now he could simply see the colors around all living things without effort or concentration. It troubled him because he knew that the source of his aura reading had to be a connection to the firmament but he couldn't feel it or control it. It was simply there. He didn't do anything to establish the connection and he couldn't stop it, yet he didn't feel any sense of risk. He didn't feel anything different at all except for the colors he could see.

Then there was his clairvoyant experience. Besides the unsettling encounter with Phane, he was bewildered by the fact that it happened at all. He tried over and over to recreate the experience but failed every time. He went over the feelings of the experience a hundred times, trying to identify exactly what it was that caused it to happen, but he couldn't seem to figure it out. When he took inventory of the things he could rely on for sure, he could only name his second sight and his newfound skill with a blade. He hoped it would be enough, but he knew that it wouldn't.

He needed to know what he was.

What troubled him most was that Phane did know. Alexander presumed he meant what type of wizard he was, what his magical calling was. He tried to reason through it and could only assume that Phane had encountered wizards like Alexander before. The idea that Phane knew more about his abilities and limitations than he did scared him. He knew at a basic level that the key to defeating an enemy was knowledge of their strengths and weaknesses. Phane was several steps ahead and gaining ground quickly, while Alexander was floundering.

He needed to get to Blackstone Keep. Mage Gamaliel might offer some insights but Alexander had the nagging sense that the real answers would be provided by Mage Cedric and his Bloodvaults. Blackstone Keep had been inaccessible for millennia. It stood to reason that it had been protected from the world all these years so it would be here for Alexander when the time came to fight the final battle of the Reishi War.

They reached the north fortress gate at midday. Alexander had been silent the entire ride. Once he was inside the mountain tunnel, he set aside his frustrations and brought his mind back to the task at hand. He didn't know if Phane would be able to see him leave from the north gate but Alexander believed it was his best chance of avoiding the Reishi.

He hoped Erik would be safe enough with a company of Rangers, but it nagged at him that he'd put Isabel's brother in harm's way. He'd read about command and leadership. He thought he understood it, but when the time came to make decisions that had very real consequences for other people, he found that the burden was much weightier than it ever seemed in the dry old history books.

He remembered times when he was unable to understand the hesitation or the indecision of a general or a commander in the accounts of battles fought long ago. He understood now. Those men made decisions about the lives of others. It was one thing to read about a battle that had been fought before you were even born and quite another to make decisions about one yet to be fought. The future was shrouded in shadow and mystery. Then there was the heavy responsibility of commanding others to risk their lives. Alexander was perfectly willing to risk his own life if the circumstances warranted it, but sending another out to face the enemy put a knot in his stomach. The feeling only deepened at the realization that he would likely send many men to their deaths before this war was over. How many lives would he command into the darkness?

A wave of disquiet washed over him as they came into a big chamber deep within the mountain. He looked around in the light of the massive chandeliers suspended from the ceiling and took in all of the men who worked and lived here. Some of these men would die in the coming battles. Some would die by his order and in his name. It was more authority and responsibility than any man should have. Why should he be able to cast away another's life with a word? What gave him that right? It was certainly more power than he ever wanted.

Then there was Phane. He was a man who clearly reveled in wielding power over the lives of others. Alexander wondered what caused a man to lust after that kind of power. He'd been raised to believe that life and liberty were sacred gifts. They were not to be taken from another without just cause. Phane clearly had no such restraint. From his brief encounter with Phane, Alexander got the impression that the Reishi Prince rather enjoyed watching others die on his word. How did that kind of darkness come to exist in a man?

Men came up to take the reins of their horses. The gatekeeper strode up with his administrator in tow and came to an abrupt halt, bowing formally to Alexander.

"Lord Alexander, we've been expecting you. I understand you wish to move through the gate today and be on your way immediately."

"The sooner we're on our way, the better," Alexander replied.

"If you'd like, the kitchen has a roasted pig on the spit. One last hot meal before your journey couldn't hurt," the gatekeeper offered.

Alexander felt a twinge of hunger at the prospect of a hot meal, and out of the corner of his eye, he saw Lucky perk up, so he agreed. They ate quickly, checked their packs and were through the gate within the hour. They still had a few hours of light left and Alexander wanted to cover as much ground as they could through the dense forest.

The north gate didn't have a road leading to it but a steep and winding trail instead; it was too treacherous for horses. Besides, they intended to travel through the forest to stay out of view of Phane's spies and mercenaries. It would be slower going but hopefully much safer. Alexander didn't want to fight if he didn't have to. He knew that killing a small band of mercenaries would have no effect on the greater conflict but could easily risk the lives of his friends or cost him his own. Engaging the enemy now was not wise. There was nothing to gain and much to lose. Moving quietly under the cover of the forest was the best strategy to get to New Ruatha. He had no doubt there would be enemy waiting for him there. By now Phane had probably alerted every agent of the Reishi Protectorate on the entire Isle of Ruatha. Alexander would be hunted wherever he went—best to move in the shadows.

Chapter 37

Isabel led the way through the forest with Slyder flying from treetop to treetop ahead of them. Alexander marveled at how she moved through the woods. She was silent and surefooted. She always seemed to know where to place her feet to find solid ground and to avoid crunching twigs and other forest debris underfoot. After a while, Alexander also began to notice that she left very little evidence of her passage. He felt clumsy by comparison. He could clearly see where he'd stepped and knew that he was making enough noise to alert every animal for miles around to their presence.

He started to emulate her. He stepped where she stepped and tried to move the way she moved. At first he didn't understand why she moved as she did, but after a while he started to see the advantages of her selection of foot placement and the path she took through the forest. There were times when she stopped and looked for the best way through the brush or a stand of trees. Sometimes Alexander thought he knew which way she would choose only to be surprised by her path. He never argued or questioned her; instead he took the opportunity to learn from her fluid, confident movement through the forest.

They made good time descending from the cold altitude of the fortress gate and into the warmer, thicker air of the forest floor in the foothills of the barrier mountains. Late in the evening, Isabel found a little clearing with a brook flowing past it and they made camp. She reported that Slyder saw no threat anywhere nearby so they built a little cook fire to prepare their evening meal.

As darkness fell, colors began to glow slightly brighter in Alexander's vision, illuminating the forest in a soft cacophony of living light. It was beautiful and haunting all at the same time. He'd never felt this kind of connection to the world around him before. With his second sight he could see the web of life and energy that penetrated and connected everything.

His view of the world began to subtly shift. He'd always been very much an individual but he was coming to see the connections between all living things. He watched his companions when they moved near large plants and trees and could see the colors of their living auras bend and flow into the surrounding aura as if their basic essence was somehow mingling. He felt a deep sense of peace and tranquility in the forest with all of the life surrounding him and wondered if the life energy of the plants all around were the cause of it.

After a quiet dinner, he rolled out his bedroll and lay down to look at the stars peeking through the meadow's gap in the forest canopy. Isabel tossed out her bedroll beside him and lay down. She looked at him for a long time while he stared into the sky, pondering the nature of his magic and his second sight.

"You've been quiet," she whispered softly. The others had already lain down for the night except Jack, who drew the first shift at guard duty. Lucky was already snoring softly.

Alexander turned on his side to look at her in the dim light of the fire and the stars. He could see her colors more clearly than he could see the features of her face.

"I've been thinking about magic and responsibility." He paused, almost afraid to ask the question. "Are you worried about Erik?" he whispered very quietly.

She was silent for a long moment. "Yes, but I know he's proud to do his part."

"I have no doubt of that, but I hate the fact that his life is in danger on my command. I never wanted this kind of responsibility. How can I even justify it? What right do I have to send others into battle?" He fell silent in frustration. The sound of the forest filled the void for a moment.

"I'm much more willing to follow a king who doesn't want power than one who does," Isabel said. "Truss would be king if he could. He would rule in his own self-interest. He would wield power to bolster his self-importance and he would use his power to inflict harm on the innocent for his amusement. Such a man shouldn't be trusted with power of any kind, but he wants it with all his twisted little heart and would gladly kill for it if the chance presented itself. I suspect Phane is no different. You've been given power that many men would kill for and you've had the weight of the world placed squarely on your shoulders in the bargain. You're being hunted by the most powerful mage to walk the Seven Isles in two thousand years and the concern you put words to is for the safety of my brother. Whether you want this responsibility or not, you have it, and I believe it's well placed." She spoke quietly but with firm conviction.

"I hope you're right," he said.

She reached out slowly and briefly touched his cheek. "I am," she whispered firmly. "And don't worry too much about my big brother. He can handle himself."

He took her hand and held onto it. Her presence calmed his mind and soon he was sleeping soundly.

The next few days passed without incident. They traveled through the woods moving as quickly as they could manage on foot through the dense underbrush. The few natural dangers they might have stumbled into were easily avoided. Isabel made a habit of scouting the area ahead through the eyes of her forest hawk. She stopped them at one point and warned of a bear about a mile ahead and then guided them around the area downwind of the bear to avoid any confrontation.

The forest was alive all around and Alexander made a deliberate effort to let the power of it sink into him. He felt invigorated by it and at times forgot what lay ahead and simply marveled at the ancient beauty of the place. He learned as much as he could from Isabel about the forest and tried to improve his ability to move more quietly. At dinner he quizzed her about the way she walked, how she chose her path, and the dangers inherent in the forest. Abigail and Anatoly listened intently and occasionally added questions of their own. Lucky seemed to be at home in the forest even though he looked totally out of place in his simple grey robes. Jack did his best to tolerate his surroundings and he never complained, but it was clear to Alexander that he was far more comfortable in the palace court than he ever would be out in the wilds.

Not long after breakfast on the third day from the north fortress gate, Lucky stopped excitedly and rushed off the path to a patch of odd-looking flowers.

"Alexander, Abigail, come look!"

He stood before a patch of strange-looking plants and smiled broadly. Each plant had a cluster of broad, bright green leaves at ground level with a single stalk jutting out of the center about a foot tall and as big around as a man's finger. The top three inches of each stalk was covered with dozens of dark little purple flowers all hanging by threadlike stems. There were probably a hundred plants in the patch.

Everyone came up alongside Lucky and looked somewhat dubiously at the flower patch. Alexander was studying the look of the aura around the flowers. It had a swirl of colors that gave him an uneasy feeling like they possessed a great but hidden power.

It was Jack who asked the question first, "What are they?"

"These are called deathwalker root. They are highly prized by alchemists. The leaves and flowers are important ingredients in a number of complex potions, but the root itself is the most valuable part. It's the main ingredient in healing potions and salve. In fact, the root can be prepared into a rudimentary healing salve fairly easily, but it must be done when it's fresh."

Lucky carefully grasped the stalk of one of the flowers and firmly but gently pulled it straight up out of the ground. The root was the diameter of man's thumb and about five or six inches long. It looked like a small white carrot.

"Help me gather about half the patch, working from the outside," Lucky said while pulling up another.

"Why only half?" Jack asked as he bent to remove a deathwalker root from the edge of the patch.

"These are rare and valuable. It's important to leave enough of the patch so that it can replenish itself. If we take them all, this patch will die. If we take half, it will remain for others to use in the future," Lucky explained.

They worked for several minutes, carefully pulling the odd-looking flowers up by their roots until they had a neat little pile. Lucky laid out a square cloth and set out two empty jars.

"Pluck the flowers one by one like this." Lucky used his fingernails to cut the threadlike stem of each flower without damaging the delicate little purple pouch. "Be careful not to burst the flower sack. The powder inside will make you sleepy, and it's the ingredient we want. Lay them on this cloth. Next, pluck the leaves at the base of the plant and put them in this jar. Finally snap off the root, brush off any remaining dirt and put them in this jar."

In minutes, Lucky had them organized and working. Alexander was always eager to learn and was so familiar with Lucky's teaching style that he didn't even think about the time lost. The fact that the deathwalker root could be used to make healing salve far outweighed any delay. Alexander had experienced the value of such magic firsthand. They worked quickly, with Lucky supervising their efforts. Once they were finished, they had a jar full of leaves, another full of the root itself, and a pile of delicate little deep-purple flowers on the cloth. Lucky carefully pulled the corners of the cloth into a pouch and tied a piece of string around it, then gently slipped it inside a metal canister.

"Once we make camp for the night, I'll show you how to cook the roots down into a healing salve," Lucky said. "It's not as effective as one I could make if I had a lab to work in but it'll do in a pinch and it can be made by anyone with the knowledge. The more powerful version requires a few other ingredients and preparation by an alchemist. The leaves are similar to numbweed but not quite as potent and they'll make you drowsy. The powder in the flower sacks is a potent sleeping agent. Mix the contents of one flower into a cup of hot tea and you'll soon fall deeply asleep and wake rested and refreshed eight or nine hours later. The contents of four to five flower sacks mixed into a tea are a deadly poison. With proper preparation by an alchemist, the powder of the deathwalker flower can also be made into a dust that can render a full-grown man unconscious in a matter of seconds if it's blown into his face."

The whole process took about an hour and then they were back on their way. Alexander made a mental note to look more closely at the aura of the plants he saw around him for that quality of color that made him uneasy. He was starting to develop a greater understanding of the subtleties of the living aura now that his second sight was a constant part of his vision. He'd long known how to tell if someone was lying or how to determine the basic nature of a person's character from the look of their colors, but he was starting to learn how the colors reflected a person's mood and emotions as well. He found that he could also tell when a plant was sick by the muddy look of the colors surrounding it or healthy by the clear bright nature of its aura.

He was also getting better at moving through the woods. Isabel had gracefully slipped into the role of instructor, offering her knowledge freely and without judgment. She was patient and exuberant all at once. She took delight in showing Alexander details about the forest. Abigail, Jack, and even Anatoly listened attentively to her brief lectures when she came to something of interest. One time it might be how to cross a patch of ground without leaving tracks, the next she might point out a plant to be avoided or kneel to inspect a set of animal tracks. Lucky occasionally nodded his approval at the information she offered and even added a detail or two, but never had cause to correct her. She was never offended at his additions but instead took the information as a gift and added it to her deep understanding of the forest.

Alexander was happy to be the student and discovered a deeper respect for Isabel with each piece of information she offered. He'd spent a great deal of time outdoors but most of it was out on the range with cattle. The forest was a whole different place. It was more three-dimensional. The trees above created a canopy of life that wrapped all around them. Isabel seemed to be much more aware of the three-dimensional nature of the forest than most due to her connection with Slyder. She often stopped to look through her hawk's eyes and it gave her a perspective of the terrain and their surroundings that was more complete. She was able to set a course that avoided difficult obstacles without having to backtrack because she could literally see them coming miles away.

They'd been pushing hard all afternoon and it was nearing dusk when Isabel stopped and closed her eyes while tilting her head back slightly in the way she did when she was looking through Slyder's eyes. Her eyes snapped open. She looked around quickly with a calm urgency that sent a tingle of warning racing through Alexander. He unslung his bow and nocked an arrow before she found what she was looking for. She pointed at a large tree with a few low-hanging limbs.

"There, make for that tree and climb quickly," she said.

"What comes?" Anatoly demanded, slipping his war axe free from the strap that held it across his back.

"Wild boar, over a dozen," she said over her shoulder as she headed for the tree.

Alexander heard the first squeal a few hundred feet through the brush. He didn't waste any time running for the tree. Anatoly was the last into the tree and he was just in time as a dozen wild boar charged through the woods squealing in fear or anger, Alexander couldn't tell which. They moved so much faster than Alexander would have thought and the bigger ones were easily four hundred pounds. He'd grown up around hogs on the farm, but they didn't move like this and they certainly didn't have five-inch tusks.

Isabel balanced herself between two branches like she'd done it before and smoothly loosed an arrow into a smallish-looking boar. Her shot drove cleanly through the boar's rib cage and into its heart. It squealed in pain and tumbled to a stop. The rest of the boar kept going into the brush.

Alexander gave her a quizzical look. They had plenty of food. He didn't understand why she would take down a boar. Then he heard a crashing noise coming toward them through the forest. Isabel's face went slightly white and she motioned urgently for silence. Everyone fell dead quiet as they waited for the noise coming toward them. Alexander broke out into a cold sweat and froze in place when he saw it.

It stood nine feet tall and weighed at least a thousand pounds. It had the head, barrel chest, and long powerful arms of a giant gorilla and the feet and tail of a large reptile. Its back was armored in grey scales and there was a row of eight-inch bone spikes running down its spine. Its belly and neck looked like the leathery skin of a reptile and was a leafy green, the color of new shoots in spring. As if the sheer size and power of the thing wasn't bad enough, Alexander could see in its colors an unnatural twisting of auras that looked like two creatures forced to coexist in one space. Its tortured colors stood out in stark contrast against the clear and vivid living aura of the forest all around.

It crashed through the brush and pounced on the dead boar, pinning the carcass to the ground with one of its clawed hind feet. It stopped and got very still, like it was listening for prey. Everyone in the tree froze, all eyes fixed on the beast.

Chapter 38

It tipped its head back and gave a strange noise that was not a growl or a scream but almost both at once. Off in the distance, the call was answered and then again from a different direction. The beast took the two-hundred-pound boar by the hind feet with one powerful hand and flipped it over its shoulder onto the row of eight-inch bone spikes, impaling it a half dozen times and holding it in place. Blood leaked from the carcass and ran down the sides of the beast. It held its prize by both hind feet with one giant hand and took off into the forest in the direction the rest of the boar had gone.

No one moved for a long moment. They just listened to the beast crashing through the forest and then to the squeal of another boar and then another.

"What was that thing?" Alexander whispered.

Isabel didn't answer. She was looking through Slyder's eyes.

Anatoly was the one who spoke. "That was a gorledon," he said quietly.

Isabel came back from her aerial scouting. "They're gone, and thankfully not in the direction we're headed." She started to climb down out of the tree.

Once back on the ground, Alexander was feeling decidedly less enthusiastic about the beauty of the forest. He looked around warily and knelt next to the very large lizard-like footprints left by the beast that had just carried away a two-hundred-pound boar at a dead run. Everyone was a bit shaken by the encounter. The thing was big and powerful, it moved very fast, and it seemed to hunt in a pack.

"Tell me more about that thing," Alexander commanded to no one in particular while he scanned the woods for other threats.

Lucky took up the mantle of the tutor. "The gorledon are unnatural, predatory creatures said to have been created by the wizards of Karth during the Reishi War. They took a large and very dangerous type of pack-hunting reptile and magically crossed it with the giant gorilla that inhabits their southern jungles. The result is a beast of fearsome capability. They run faster than a horse, climb better than a tree squirrel, hunt in packs of three, communicate with a sort of primitive language, have armored scales on their backs and sides that can easily turn aside an arrow, and they're strong enough to rip a man in two. They are very rare on Ruatha and have only been reported in the Great Forest."

Alexander looked over to Isabel. "Have you ever seen one before?"

She shook her head slowly. "I've seen paintings and drawings but I've never actually seen one before. They're said to be the most dangerous predator in the forest, except for a dragon, that is."

Alexander was speechless, but only for a moment. "What do you mean a dragon? Dragons are supposed to be just stories."

Again Isabel shook her head. "Far to the east, near the Pinnacles where the forest gets wild, there are said to be dragons. I've never seen one myself but I've heard stories of Rangers who have. It's been many years since a sighting, but then we don't go as far as the Pinnacles unless we have a very good reason to."

Alexander looked to Lucky and then to Anatoly, hoping that one of them would tell him that the fables and tales of dragons were nothing but stories.

"Alexander, every story has a basis in reality," Lucky said. "Often the truth of the story is much different than the tale, and dragons are no different. They are very rare and tend to keep to themselves, living in unpopulated and remote areas, but they do exist. I doubt you will ever see one and even if you do, it will probably be from very far away."

"Slowly but surely, everything I thought I knew about the world is being turned on its head." Alexander took a deep breath and centered himself. "I guess I won't bother worrying about dragons right now, but I am a little concerned about those gorledons. Will they be back?"

"I don't think so," Isabel said. "They got their kill for the day. Most likely, they'll go back to their lair and eat their boar."

"I guess that makes sense. Do they hunt at night?" he asked.

Isabel and Lucky both shook their heads in unison.

"Good, let's find a place to make camp. It looks like we have less than an hour of light left," Alexander said.

They found a large, jumbled pile of giant boulders not too far from the tree they'd taken refuge in. The huge rocks stood eight to ten feet high, were scattered haphazardly across the forest floor, and were covered on the north side with bright green moss. The boulders created a natural enclosure that was as defensible a place as they were going to find.

After a quick meal, Lucky took a few minutes to show everyone how to prepare the healing salve. It was a simple process. First he washed the roots, then smashed them into pulp and cooked them in water. After the pulp mixture began to boil, he poured off the water and used a fork to fish the fibers out of the remaining mush. The dark grey-green sludge that was left was the healing salve. It turned to a thick gelatinous salve when it cooled. Lucky scooped it up with a spoon and packed the thick ointment into three of his little jars. He handed one each to Alexander, Abigail, and Isabel.

"Apply directly to a wound and it will speed the healing process, but remember it will also make you sleepy. For more serious wounds, you will most likely lose consciousness if you apply a significant amount."

Everyone was still too much on edge to sleep so they stayed up for a while sitting around the little cook fire. It wasn't long before the conversation made its way around to New Ruatha. Alexander would have to claim the city as his seat of power if he was going to be recognized as King of Ruatha. The mark on his neck would be enough to persuade some, but certainly not all.

"Jack, you grew up in New Ruatha," Alexander said. "Tell me about the city and the Regent."

Jack took a moment to collect his thoughts. "The Regent of New Ruatha is named Danton Cery. He claims the title of first among equals on the Council of Ruatha but that title has little substance. The council is not so much a ruling body as a loose agreement among the rulers of the various territories of Ruatha. Each ruler claims a different title. Some call themselves kings, others governors, and a few have maintained the traditional hereditary title of baron or duke that has been attached to their territory since the time of the Reishi.

"Regent Cery is a capable administrator and a shrewd ruler. New Ruatha is a bit different in that the ruler is decided by the consent of the local council of petty nobles. Since the royal line has been absent for so long, the petty nobles in and around New Ruatha agreed long ago that the regent would be selected from among themselves once every ten years. Cery has been Regent for nearly fifteen years now, so he has firmly established his rule and made the necessary alliances to succeed in securing a second term as regent, which is actually quite an accomplishment since that hasn't happened in nearly a hundred years.

"In general, Cery is respected by the people for his fairness and evenhandedness. He understands his place is not to rule so much as to protect the lives and property of the people. He's been quite successful in protecting the people from the natural greed of the petty nobles while at the same time creating an environment where the nobles can thrive through legitimate commerce instead of outright usurpation of property.

"His constable has a well-defined role and does not overstep his authority. Most people in New Ruatha feel safe on the streets, even at night. All in all, the city itself is orderly and well maintained. Cery himself is not terribly ambitious. In fact, as my father tells it, he didn't even want the duty of regent initially. He was chosen because the two nobles vying for the position were not trusted by enough of the council to gain sufficient support. Cery was the only compromise choice that could gain the necessary backing. He even spoke in open council against being chosen, citing his duties to his house and holdings as his reason. It was said he gave an impassioned plea to choose someone else." Jack chuckled. "After his speech he had more support than before. He was appointed Regent against his will. Of course, some say it was simply a masterful deception that manipulated the council into selecting him but his behavior as Regent hasn't borne that out.

"He maintains a military force of sufficient size and capability to defend New Ruatha from any of her neighboring territories but not large enough to pose a credible threat to those territories. He doesn't want war and has carefully managed the affairs of the military to create a delicate balance of credible deterrent without overt threat. The forces he does have are well trained. Most are professional soldiers and many have served for their entire adult lives. He doesn't use his military for maintaining order within the city and he expects his soldiers to obey the laws just as any other citizen. As a result, his soldiers are well respected and generally trusted by the people.

"He has a friendly relationship with the Wizards Guild and the Bards Guild. The wizards reject any governance but their own and for good reason. They enjoy the sanctuary of New Ruatha and in turn provide service to the people in the form of healing and other magical assistance to mitigate the effects of natural disasters or to prevent damage to property or livestock. Cery welcomes bards into his court and has a standing invitation for any traveling bard to seek shelter in the palace. They seldom take advantage of the offer because the main guild house is located in New Ruatha and they generally prefer to stay there. I've appointed a court bard to the palace who is responsible to the Regent and acts as my emissary to the council of nobles. In general, his duties are dull and typically revolve around providing entertainment at palace functions. His real duty is to stay informed about the matters of state and report back to me. The last report I received three months ago was as mundane as ever. Cery maintains a smooth order that seems to run itself in the background without much management required."

Anatoly leaned in and gently interrupted Jack when he paused. "Are there any agents of the Reishi Protectorate in the city?"

"Yes, some of them are known to me while others are most likely not. The Reishi Protectorate is almost as capable of infiltrating an organization as my bards are. They have agents in a variety of places including the court, the military, various businesses around town, and most likely the Wizards and Bards Guilds. I know of two bards who are agents of the Reishi; however, I don't believe they're aware that I know of their true allegiance."

Abigail looked alarmed. "Why would you let them remain in the Bards Guild if they're loyal to the Reishi?"

Jack grinned with mischief. "Because they don't know that I know where their true loyalties lie. That makes them valuable assets. I can use them to provide information to the Reishi that the Reishi will believe is accurate. I suspect they'll become very valuable conduits of disinformation at some point in the near future. They're not a concern to me because, knowing their true allegiance, I can defend against any threat they may pose. I'm far more concerned that the two infiltrators I'm aware of are not the only ones within my organization. At the moment, the only one I trust absolutely is Owen. Which reminds me, I sent him to ride with Erik as far as New Ruatha. I wanted him to return to the guild house and begin the process of reestablishing my authority. I've been gone for several years and I suspect the housemaster has become too comfortable in his role as the acting leader of the Ruathan Bards Guild. Owen will remind him of his place and prepare the guild for my return as well as gather information about the current state of political affairs within New Ruatha.

"More importantly, Owen will begin to sow the seeds for the return of the Ruathan King. He will tell your story and build up awareness within the populace that will lend credibility to your claim to the throne, create anticipation of your arrival and define you in a way that will make your enemies at court fear you."

Alexander frowned, as did Anatoly. "Are you sure it's wise to alert the world and in particular the Reishi that Alexander will be coming to New Ruatha?" Anatoly was respectful to the bard with his question but also clearly concerned.

Jack nodded and turned to Alexander to explain. "The advantages outweigh the risks, I assure you. You must have the support of the people in order to gain the support of the Regent. If you suddenly appear at court without forewarning and without the knowledge of the people, it would be very easy for an agent of the Reishi or one of the petty nobles to make a move against you. With forewarning, the court will be forced to receive you and give you an opportunity to make your claim to the throne. The Regent will be bound by his own law to protect you while you're a guest at his court. In addition, the mystery and legend surrounding you will be enough to stay the hand of many would-be enemies. Finally, the Guild Mage will have an opportunity to make preparations for your arrival as well. His influence in New Ruatha is significant and his claim of loyalty to you will go a very long way toward establishing your credibility with the nobles and the people in general. As far as the risk goes, the Reishi know that you must go to New Ruatha to claim the throne. They'll be waiting for you there no matter how or when you come to the city."

"Isn't it likely that Phane's agents have already made a deal with the

Regent?" Alexander asked.

He was starting to feel on uneasy ground again, much like he had when he arrived at Glen Morillian. He was so unfamiliar with the inner workings and machinations of politics that he didn't really know what to believe except that Phane would probably be one step ahead of him.

"Phane has likely made contact with the Regent, but I doubt his emissary received anything more than a courtesy hearing," Jack said. "The Regent has been charged with protecting the throne since the time the Ruathan line fell. It's his most sacred duty and the basis for his claim to power and for the existence of the Regency in the first place. To go against that would undermine the foundation of governance for New Ruatha. Whatever else Cery is, he believes in stability and order. He wouldn't take an action that would undo that, and even if he would, the petty nobles of New Ruatha wouldn't support it. The Reishi are reviled in New Ruatha for their part in corrupting the Ruathan line during the Reishi War. The last Ruathan King sided with the Reishi out of fear and weakness, even when it was clear that the Reishi had lost all sense of morality or propriety. The House of Ruatha committed atrocities on the people and was cast down for it by Mage Cedric and his wizards. He spread the story far and wide that the Ruathan King had been corrupted by the Reishi and that one day a new king would arrive to redeem Ruatha and bring her back to her former glory. That story is still well known within New Ruatha even if it's seldom told elsewhere.

"You'll have some challenges establishing authority within New Ruatha but they'll be relatively easy to overcome. The real challenge will be in gaining the recognition, support, and loyalty of the rulers of the other territories. I suspect a few will be swayed by the mark on your neck but others will openly reject your claim."

Isabel drew a medallion from under her shirt and held it up to the firelight. "My father gave me this so that I may speak in his name at the Ruathan Council. You have the support of Glen Morillian already. We hold sway with both Northport and Southport because of our role in patrolling and maintaining the road through the forest. If need be, we can use the economic leverage of access to the road to force their allegiance."

"I'd much prefer to have their support without having to force it, but it's nice to know I have the option if I need it," Alexander said. "Hopefully they'll see the necessity of presenting a united front against Phane. That makes four territories, including New Ruatha. Jack, do you have any sense of the how the other territories are likely to react to my arrival?"

"Headwater will oppose you without question. Elred Rake, the Master of Headwater, is a ruffian and a thug who rules with fear and violence. His position on the Ruatha River and his control of the main road running east and west give him significant power over the economic fortunes of both Warrenton and Buckwold, so they're likely to support him. Highlands Reach is closely connected to Southport and will probably align with you."

Anatoly nodded. "I know the Governor of Highlands Reach, as does your father. He's a good man who believes in the Old Law. I suspect he'll support you without much resistance."

Jack continued, "As for Kai'Gorn, it's hard to say. They're so far to the south that they have more extensive trading ties with the Isle of Andalia than with most of Ruatha. I know little of their ruler except that he's said to be very independent-minded, preferring to keep his little part of the world held apart from the rest of Ruatha, especially after losing so much land during the border wars."

Anatoly agreed, "I wouldn't expect much from Kai'Gorn. They've withdrawn into themselves and severed many of the trading ties they used to have with Southport and Highlands Reach. The border wars cost them a great deal and they're still bitter about it. At this point, they have a substantial merchant fleet they use to trade with the northern cities of Andalia. I understand they still send an emissary to the Ruathan Council but he offers little input."

"It sounds like Headwater is going to be the main problem. If we can persuade Rake to support us, will Warrenton and Buckwold follow?" Alexander asked.

"I believe so but I doubt you have anything Rake wants more than he wants his autonomy. He's a petty tyrant who lives for power. You represent a limit to his authority. I suspect he'll side with Phane if he hasn't done so already," Jack offered.

"What kind of forces can he muster?" Abigail asked.

"Significant," Jack said. "He has a fairly large standing army that he uses to keep his petty nobles and his people in line. They're violent and lack uniform training but they fear Rake and will follow his orders no matter the cost or the risk. Rake is widely feared and justifiably so. He has a well-deserved reputation for ruthlessness."

"If Rake were eliminated would his army fall in line?" Alexander felt sort of odd asking such a brutal question with such calm nonchalance. He'd never considered killing another man in cold blood before, especially not for the sole purpose of political gain. The consequences of leadership in war were starting to sink in, and he didn't like how the demands of the situation made him so easily blur the line of morality. But when he weighed it against the alternative, the choice became clearer. He couldn't allow Rake to stand in the way of a unified Ruatha, especially if Rake was likely to side with Phane anyway.

"Warrenton and Buckwold are partners of necessity with Headwater," Jack said. "They need the road and the river to move their trade. They'll go where Headwater goes regardless of who's running the city."

Alexander nodded in thought. "Can you get us into New Ruatha and into the court quietly?"

"Sure. I know a number of routes into the city that are well concealed. We can show up in the palace as if we appeared by magic, if you like." Jack smiled with mischief again.

"That's exactly what I'd like," Alexander said. "I want the Regent to know that I'm coming but not when I'm due to arrive, only to have me suddenly be there right in front of him. I'd also like to keep everyone in New Ruatha off guard as much as possible for the duration of our stay."

Chapter 39

They were up and on their way just after dawn. Alexander was again feeling the urgency to get to New Ruatha and then to Blackstone Keep. He had so much to do and couldn't help worrying that time was running out. Phane was in Karth and had clearly taken command of the Reishi Army Regency. He appeared to be intent on taking command of the entire Isle of Karth. Once he had that secure, he would be able to consolidate his forces and have a good-sized army of battle-tested soldiers at his disposal. Alexander didn't know what Phane's next target would be, but he did know that eventually Phane would come to Ruatha and he wanted to be as ready as possible when that day came.

They moved more quickly than they had for the past few days. The encounter with the gorledons, coupled with Alexander's sense of urgency, made for a fast pace through the forest. It was midmorning when Isabel guided them up a rise and stopped to look out over the little valley below. She smiled broadly and motioned for Alexander to hurry.

He was speechless at the sight. The entire valley was filled with an ocean of trees covered with soft pink blossoms. After the greens and browns of the forest they'd been traveling through, it was a surprising sight. But more than that, it was breathtakingly beautiful. Alexander could only stare into the ocean of vibrant fluffy pink trees stretching out into the distance.

"It's called the Pink Forest. It blooms in late winter or early spring and then only for about three weeks. We just happen to be here at the right time." Isabel took in a deep breath and released it with a wistful sigh. "I remember this place from my childhood. I figured we might get lucky, so I took us this way."

Everyone else was standing in a row along the top of the bluff looking out over the pristine little valley. Alexander didn't say a word but instead simply took Isabel's hand and marveled at the stunning majesty of so many trees in full bloom.

They slowed their pace under the low canopy of the Pink Forest. The light that filtered through was shaded pink and the ground was littered with a spotty, almost polka-dotted covering of pink petals. Alexander didn't even really like pink as far as colors went but he couldn't help feeling his mood lift as he walked hand in hand with Isabel through the stand of trees in bloom. They came to a little hillock that jutted up forty feet out of the middle of the ocean of pink, like a lone island in a sea of color, and made their way to the top to stop for lunch. It was sheer rock on three sides with a steep little grassy patch on the fourth side that made for an easy path to the top. It stood just a few feet higher than the tops of the trees all around them.

"I never even imagined a place could be so pretty," Abigail said with a little bit of giddiness in her voice.

The stand of trees was three miles long and two miles wide at the widest point. A variety of evergreen trees stood all around it but within the borders of the Pink Forest there were only fluffy, pastel-pink, blooming trees packed in close together but not so close that each tree couldn't get ample light.

"I must say, while the forest is not my favorite place, I believe I could just sit here and look out over this particular patch of trees all afternoon," Jack said with a smile as he sat on his pack next to Abigail.

They spent the next hour preparing and eating lunch. As much as Alexander felt a sense of urgency, he didn't really want to leave this place. It was so soft and peaceful, calm and serene. He closed his eyes briefly and took a deep breath of the fragrant air. He released it slowly and felt a sense of calm soak into him. He took another breath and within moments he felt as if he were drifting on an ocean of infinity. He was no longer inside the limited confines of his body. He felt his essence extend to the farthest corners of the world and beyond.

With a start that nearly brought him out of his detached state, he realized that he'd felt this before. Twice in fact, once at the end of the mana fast and again when he'd seen Phane. He started to feel his awareness draw back into his physical body and with an odd kind of effort he let go of his thoughts, cleared his mind, and simply allowed the experience to happen for a few moments while formulating his real intent in the quiet recesses of his mind. It was a strange way of thinking. He had to keep his consciousness calm and undisturbed like the surface of a pond while carefully forming an image of his intent in the depths without causing so much as a ripple.

When he knew what he wanted to see, he simply willed his awareness to coalesce at the location of his chosen target rather than within his own body. Time and space didn't seem to matter here. There was no substance. All things for all time sprang from the singular, infinite nature of this place, and Alexander found that he could be where he wanted to be simply by willing himself to be there.

Sitting on his pack with his eyes closed, Alexander could see clearly, but his awareness was no longer in the Pink Forest. He was floating thirty feet above the road that ran through the Great Forest. On both sides he saw armed men hidden behind trees. Then he saw his target. Wizard Rangle was standing on a giant log near the road. Beside the log were three other men. Alexander recognized Truss immediately. The little rodent had apparently escaped intact and managed to join forces with Rangle and his men. The next man he saw made him uneasy. He had to be seven feet tall and easily weighed over three hundred pounds. His head was bald, his face was clean-shaven, and he wore a heavy metal breastplate. On his back was an oversized quiver filled with javelins and he was leaning against a giant war hammer with its spiked butt jammed into the ground. He looked bored.

The third man was even more unsettling but for different reasons. He was short and almost pudgy, but not quite. He wore all black and didn't appear to be carrying a weapon. The thing that most caught Alexander's attention was his aura. He could see in a glance that this man was a wizard of great and terrible power. Alexander had never seen a wizard such as this before. He had the color of focused and coiled power just waiting to be unleashed. Alexander had looked at wizards' auras before and he could always tell that they had a special connection to reality. He could see their relationship to the firmament but it was always tenuous, even with Mason who was a master wizard of significant power. All the wizards he'd ever looked at with his second sight had given him the sense that they could tap into the firmament but they were also guarded against it, as if they feared to stare openly into the vast infinity of possibility for fear of losing themselves to it.

The man in black had no such restraint about him. His colors told

Alexander that he had looked fully into the firmament and retained his sense of self. He was dangerous. Alexander suddenly wondered about Phane's aura but when he started to draw on his memories, he found his vision of the scene before him start to fade. He quickly let go of his thoughts again and simply allowed himself to float above the road, taking in his surroundings. It was a strange feeling to have his awareness separate from his body.

Then he heard horses coming up the road. He swung his point of view away from Rangle and his friends and looked down the road to see a company of Rangers riding fast. Erik was in the lead and he and his men were charging right into an ambush.

At the realization of what was happening, Alexander felt his awareness slam back into his body. He stood so fast that his feet came an inch or so off the ground. A dreadful, helpless fear for Erik and his men washed through him and left him with his knees trembling. He wanted to use his clairvoyance to go back and see the outcome of the ambush but didn't think he would be able to make it happen again. He stood there trying to breathe through the tightness in his chest.

Anatoly was up with his axe at the ready, looking around for the threat. "What is it?" he asked quietly but intently as he surveyed their surroundings for any possible enemy.

Alexander started pacing. He put his hand to his forehead and ran his fingers through his hair. By this time everyone was up and looking worried. It was Isabel that pulled Alexander to a stop and took him by the forearms to make him look at her.

"What is it, Alexander? What's wrong?"

He felt a wave of misery flood through him when he looked into her worried eyes. He could hardly make himself say the words. "It's Erik. He's riding into an ambush." His voice broke from guilt and helplessness.

He shut his eyes against the stricken look of desperate fear that filled her face. When she let go, he opened his eyes again. She stumbled back a step or two with a look of pure anguish. Alexander would have given anything in that moment to have not seen what he'd seen.

Then Lucky was there alongside him as Isabel sat down hard on her pack and put her face in her hands. "What did you see? Was it like the experience with Phane? Tell me everything, Alexander; the details are important."

He nodded while he fought back the sick feeling welling up in the pit of his gut. How could he be the one to send others to their deaths? Who was he to decide? How would Isabel ever forgive him if Erik was killed on his order?

"I was feeling a deep sense of peace." He snorted bitterly at the thought of how the beauty all around him had been the catalyst for his clairvoyance. "Then I felt myself adrift like I did at the end of the mana fast. I wasn't here anymore, I was everywhere at once and yet nowhere at the same time. For a few moments I just floated, trying to get a feeling for it. After a bit of a struggle, I decided I wanted to see Wizard Rangle. Everything came into sharp focus in an instant. I was floating over a road with men to either side waiting in the trees. Rangle was there and so was Truss." Isabel looked up at that. "There was another man who looked like a giant and then there was the one who scared me. He wasn't very big, but his colors were like nothing I've ever seen."

"How do you mean?" Lucky broke in.

"He was a wizard who was comfortable looking into the firmament without fear or restraint. The power pent up in that man was unnerving. Then I heard horses and I turned to look up the road. That's when I saw Erik and his company of Rangers riding hard right into the ambush. Then I was back here."

He looked at Isabel and saw the fear in her beautiful green eyes, and his blood started to boil at the thought of the pain she would endure if her brother fell. He knew the ongoing anguish it would bring her all too well. The thought of it kindled a rage within him that he'd never felt before.

Before anyone could speak again Jack called out, "There!" and pointed off in the distance.

Far to the east, across the Pink Forest and many miles farther, a plume of smoke rose into the sky. Alexander felt his heart sink.

Isabel looked toward the slowly rising smoke, then tipped her head back and closed her eyes. A moment later, Alexander heard the shrill call of a forest hawk as Slyder took to wing.

He wanted to go to her, to take her in his arms but he was responsible for the danger to her brother. He'd sent him into harm's way. He stood struggling with his rage, fear, and despair when Anatoly cried out in warning.

Chapter 40

The gorledon came fast. Alexander pushed Isabel to the side. The thing crashed into him and knocked him flat on his back. It took a step and pinned him to the ground with one giant clawed foot. He felt the crushing weight of the unnatural beast press the air out of him and the edges of his vision started to close down, when Anatoly's war axe caught the monster on the front of the leg it was using to pin Alexander to the ground.

The creature screamed in pain and backhanded Anatoly, sending him flying toward the edge of the sheer rock face of the hillock. He hit hard on his back, then somersaulted backwards, sending him sliding over the edge of the cliff. Just before his legs went over, he pulled a dagger free and buried it into the ground, stopping his slide toward a forty-foot fall. Jack scrambled to take hold of his arm and pull him to safety.

The gorledon lifted its foot slightly when Anatoly hit it, releasing Alexander just enough to roll quickly to the side. He found himself lying flat on his back between the feet of the giant monster. Anatoly's axe was buried to the bone and jutted at an awkward angle from the creature's knee. Blood flowed freely but the beast didn't look too concerned about it.

Everyone was scrambling. Abigail snatched up her bow, swung her quiver onto her back, and drew an arrow in one fluid movement, while backing away from the creature and circling to get a good angle. Isabel dove for her sword. Lucky snatched up his bag and got some distance from the beast even as he rummaged around for the potion he wanted. Jack was pulling Anatoly back from the brink of a deadly fall when the gorledon tipped its head back and let out a call that Alexander had heard before. It was a cross between a growl and a scream. Off in the distance, but not nearly far enough for Alexander's taste, he heard another and then another return the call. Gorledons always hunted in threes.

Alexander slipped his long knife free and drove it into the beast's leg just below the knee, then pulled down hard, cutting a deep gash into its lower leg. It leapt straight back a good ten feet with a terrifying scream of pain. Alexander scrambled to his feet, flipped his long knife to his left hand, and drew his sword. Calm settled on him when he felt the weight of the blade in his hand. The balance and purpose of the thing steadied his nerves and gave him focus. His troubles faded into the distance. Right here, right now, he was in a fight and he had a blade in his hand.

An arrow whizzed past him and sank deeply into the soft green underbelly of the beast right where its heart should be. In the distance, Alexander heard the other two beasts crashing through the forest. He made eye contact with the gorledon. In that instant, he saw the torment of the creature. It was a made thing, unnatural at the very essence of its being; an abomination created to serve the purpose of a long-dead wizard. Under different circumstances, Alexander would have felt sorry for it.

It lurched forward, hobbled by its injuries. Alexander charged, slipping easily under the wild swing of its powerful clawed hand, and drove the point of his blade into its underbelly, through the beast and up against the inside of the hard armored scales that lined its back, but he didn't stop there. He slipped to his left to give himself leverage. The moment the point of his sword slammed to a stop against the inside of its back plate, Alexander pulled to the side with all his might, ripping out the side of the beast as he rushed past. Viscera spilled out onto the ground. The gorledon gurgled in an attempt to call out to its hunting partners but couldn't manage more than a sputter. It wobbled slightly for a moment before crashing to the ground on top of a pile of its own entrails.

A moment later, Anatoly rushed up with his short sword in hand and drove his blade deep into the eye socket of the dying creature. Alexander remembered one of Anatoly's lectures from a time that seemed very far away. "Always confirm your kill," he had said. "Your enemy isn't dead until you make sure he's dead." Alexander was glad to see that Anatoly lived what he taught.

He was brought back to the present by the sudden appearance of two more gorledons at the base of the little hillock. Thoughts in the back of his mind mocked him. He'd found such peace here just moments ago and now he stood on a blood-soaked battlefield. Two nine-foot-tall, thousand-pound monsters that looked like the most dangerous parts of a giant gorilla and a giant lizard crammed together were rushing up the steep grassy ramp.

Alexander set his stance to meet the charge. An arrow sailed past him and sank deep into the throat of the oncoming gorledon on the right. The beast flinched and let out a yelp of surprise but didn't slow its charge.

A glass vial flew past Alexander on the left and broke against the arm of the other gorledon. The caustic black contents started to eat into the flesh with smoking and sputtering ferocity. The monster's charge faltered as it shook its arm in a desperate attempt to escape the pain of Lucky's acid vial. The contents of the vial worked quickly. Only moments after it shattered against the monster's elbow, it ate through the flesh and down to the bone. The beast howled in pain. The bone melted through and its arm flopped over at a sickeningly unnatural angle. Still the acid ate into its flesh until the forearm of the monster broke free and thudded to the ground, smoldering and sputtering as the caustic magical liquid continued to do its ugly work. The beast stopped in shock, pain, and confusion and rammed the stub of its arm into the ground in a frantic effort to stop the burning pain. When that didn't work, it turned and ran off into the trees, howling in pain and fear.

The other gorledon wasn't deterred, even when a second arrow from Abigail's bow found its mark. Anatoly came up on Alexander's left and Isabel on his right. The beast leapt impossibly high into the air in an arc that would bring it down right on top of Alexander. He dove forward under the deadly clawed feet and the creature passed overhead. He tried to tuck and roll, but the thing's heavy tail came down hard on his back and sent him sprawling face first onto the ground.

Anatoly leveled a mighty swing with his war axe but the gorledon saw it coming and turned its back to the blade, presenting its hard armored scales to take the brunt of the blow. The axe glanced off without so much as a scratch. Its turn brought it around to face Isabel. She darted in and stabbed into its softer, bright green underbelly. Her blade sank several inches before she withdrew and dodged the first swipe of the creature's heavy clawed hand. She wasn't able to avoid the back of its hand, though; it came around and knocked her flat.

Alexander scrambled to his feet to rejoin the battle. Anatoly spun his axe to use the long sharp spike on the back and swung again. This time the creature didn't see the attack coming and the spike drove through the softer scales on the beast's side. It flinched in shock and surprise, freeing the spike from its side in the process. At the same time, Abigail sank another arrow into its chest. It bellowed and lowered its head toward Abigail in preparation for a charge. Jack threw a knife with all his might. It flew true and buried itself into the side of the gorledon's neck. The creature flinched again and turned to face Jack. Alexander took the opportunity to slip around its other side and slice deeply into the flesh of its thigh. It wheeled back toward Alexander with a wild but powerful swing that passed only inches over his head, then came around with its other hand and caught him full in the chest with its oversized claws.

Alexander sailed back a dozen feet and landed flat on his back. The world spun. Blackness threatened to close in on him and he couldn't get his breath. He felt like a crushing weight was pressing down on his chest. As he struggled to breathe, he heard the beast roar again. He looked down at his chest and saw several deep gashes through his leather armor filling with bright red blood. He still couldn't draw breath. In a flash of panic, he reached into the little potion pouch Lucky had given him and pulled out the healing draught. He fought with the stopper, his hands slick with blood. Blackness was closing in. Finally, after what seemed like an hour of struggling, he got the vial open and frantically drank the contents. He was suffocating and his vision was going dark, yet he managed to smear a large dollop of healing salve into the wounds on his chest before darkness closed in and took him completely. For a moment, he felt like he was drifting. There was pain and panic all around, then the sweet oblivion of unconsciousness claimed him.

He woke late in the day. Isabel was sitting next to him, holding his hand. The first thing he noticed after seeing her was that he was breathing again, but when he tried to take a full breath, he felt a stab of pain in his chest. He groaned softly.

"He's awake," she called out.

Lucky came up next to him and put a reassuring hand on his shoulder. "Lie still, you took quite a hit. Your chest is still healing, so try to breathe shallowly." Lucky smiled down at him with a look of relief. "I feared the worst when you went down. It's good to see you on the mend."

Alexander gingerly looked around to see how the battle had turned out. The second gorledon was dead with an arrow buried to the feathers into its throat and sticking out the top of its head. Anatoly was lying flat on his back, looking over at Alexander. He looked to be under Lucky's care as well. Abigail was sitting next to him and gave Alexander a smile of relief and concern. Anatoly had dried blood on his lips and looked almost as badly beaten up as Alexander.

"Glad to see you awake. I was worried there for a few minutes, after I woke up, that is," Anatoly said softly and somewhat weakly.

"Glad to be awake. What happened?" Alexander asked.

Isabel recounted the rest of the fight while Lucky looked at the wounds on Alexander's chest.

"After you went down, Anatoly took out its other leg, which put the thing on its knees but not before it backhanded him in the chest again. I tried to stab it again but it just batted me out of the way like a rag doll. Since it couldn't get up, Abigail stayed just out of range and picked her shot. When it tipped its head back to roar in anger, she put an arrow neatly through its brain. Lucky gave Anatoly a potion that put him out for a few hours and we've all been waiting and worrying about the two of you since."

The thought slammed into Alexander like a lightning bolt. He felt the terrible dread flood into him again and almost lost the courage to ask. "What about Erik? Did Slyder see if he escaped?"

Isabel nodded with a mixture of relief, gratitude, and sadness. "He survived and made it through with over half his force. It looked like almost thirty Rangers fell in the fight, mostly from the liquid fire tossed into their midst by that wizard. I got the impression from the looks of things that Erik didn't stop to engage but just pushed through like you told him to." She stopped and looked down for a moment before continuing. Alexander knew the bad news was coming. "They captured two Rangers who were badly burned in the fight. Truss tortured them for a few minutes before he killed them." She looked angry and sad at the same time.

"I knew them both. They were good men," she whispered.

Alexander closed his eyes and gently squeezed her hand. "I wish I'd gone after Truss at Flat Top Rock. It was a mistake to let him go."

It was Anatoly who answered him. "That may be, Alexander, but that doesn't make you responsible for his actions. His free will is all his own and his choices are his to answer for. Don't fall into the trap of taking on the burden of responsibility for the actions of others, particularly others who have no conscience."

Alexander looked over at his old mentor. "Thirty men are dead on my order," he whispered as if saying it aloud proved his guilt.

Anatoly fixed him with his stern eyes and nodded slowly and deliberately. "That is the burden of command in war and this is only the beginning. There will be many more that die by your command before this is over. Just know that the alternative is far worse. At least those men died in service to life and liberty. If Phane gets his way, countless more will suffer and die to please his ego and his lust for power."

Alexander closed his eyes again and tried to push away the thought of thirty families grieving the loss of their sons, brothers, and husbands. He wanted to cry out. He wanted to shake the very Maker of the world until he explained how he could permit such evil to even exist. The idea of wanton murder and premeditated war for the sake of power alone was so alien to Alexander that he wondered how Phane could even be of the same species.

Alexander's childhood was so calm and peaceful, even blessedly boring. He had imagined being a great warrior fighting in the battles he read about in his studies. It always seemed so glorious. The pain of the wound in his chest wasn't glorious and the heartache he felt at the loss of thirty good men mocked the entire idea of glory in war. This was just sad and ugly. It made him hurt at the very root of his soul.

"Anatoly's right, Alexander," Isabel said. "You didn't send those men into harm's way out of a selfish desire for power, and not one went against his will. Erik stood before a whole battalion and asked for volunteers. Every last one of those men knew the purpose of the mission and the risks before they stepped forward. And Erik turned away a hundred more than he needed."

Isabel's words were all very reasonable and they were true as far as they went, but they didn't diminish the anguish of life lost for nothing but the lust for power. It was all so senseless. A part of Alexander simply couldn't grasp the concept of destroying other people's precious lives to further personal ambition. It just didn't make sense to him that some people were so broken and twisted inside that they could do such a thing, and yet it was so terrifyingly real.

He'd read stories about such evil but they were all very safe and cozy, tucked away on the page where they couldn't hurt anyone. In the past several weeks, he'd seen evil at work firsthand. Phane hunted him at a distance simply for being a potential threat to his ambitions. Truss abducted Isabel out of his desire to possess her and the value she represented as bait.

Alexander lay there holding Isabel's hand and tried to understand the kind of totally self-absorbed, self-important narcissism that must poison the souls of such people in order to motivate them to sever all ties with civil existence and embrace the savage within. What a cold and lonely way to live. What an empty and hateful way to see the world. How they must fear everyone else in the blindly selfish belief that others surely must see the world in the same way.

He wondered about the voice of conscience. It spoke to him often, that little voice in the back of his mind offering guidance about the morality of his choices. He always tried to listen. He knew the consequences of ignoring it. Alexander had never done anything that he considered evil, but he'd been less than kind to Abigail a time or two when they were children. The consequences were always a nagging feeling of remorse and guilt for mistreating her.

He wondered if evil people were haunted by the voice of their conscience or if they'd taught themselves to ignore it because it was an obstacle to their ambitions. Or worse yet, what if they simply didn't have that quiet, gentle voice of moral clarity at all? How could you reason with a person who didn't have a conscience? How could you ever trust him? How could you even turn your back on such a person?

What a cruel prank to play on the world to make a place where life and liberty were so immeasurably precious and then allow evil to exist. The very presence of which places an untenable moral burden on the innocent. They have a duty to themselves to protect their lives, liberty, and property, yet they have an obligation to their conscience to withhold violence against evil except in defense.

Alexander struggled with the question for a time before settling on his answer. He decided that evil had a right to exist until it acted to harm others. Once evil took life, liberty, or property from an innocent person, it forfeited the right to expect its life, liberty, or property to be respected.

He almost laughed when the words of the Old Reishi Law sprang into his mind: You have a right to your life because you are alive. You have a right to your liberty because you have free will. You have a right to your property because it is the product of your labor. In violating the natural rights of another, you forfeit your own.

Clearly, he was not the first to struggle with this question. Others had come to the same rational conclusion that he had, and they'd used it to build the greatest civilization ever seen on the Seven Isles. And that civilization had fallen only when it violated its own law. Perhaps the Old Law truly was a natural law, like gravity, with its own built-in enforcement mechanism that governed the fate of human society. Perhaps that was the balance to evil built into the world by its maker. Societies that respected the life, liberty, and property of all citizens would thrive and prosper, while those that allowed a tyrant or ruling class to abuse life, liberty, or property would fail to the detriment of all.

When he opened his eyes again it was nearing dusk. He realized that he'd dozed off again. Anatoly was sitting up and eating some camp stew Lucky had made over a little fire. Alexander slowly and gently took a breath. His chest was a bit tight but he could breathe deeply again. Lucky's healing potion was powerful magic. It had taken the better part of the afternoon but Alexander's chest was just about mended. Isabel noticed that he was awake and brought his pack over for him to lean against and helped him sit up. Abigail brought him a bowl of steaming hot stew, which he took gratefully. He ate slowly, even though his stomach was growling with hunger. After dinner he simply sat for a few minutes, looking out over the Pink Forest while the light of day faded. It was a beautiful place even with the two dead gorledons sprawled out not far from their fire.

Once his stomach was full, his nerves calmed, and his wounds mended, Alexander's mind began to wander back to the tasks that lay before him.

"I suspect they know we weren't with Erik," he said to no one in particular.

Anatoly nodded without a word.

Jack spoke softly, "Those Rangers were probably tortured for information about our plans."

Isabel nodded and looked down sadly. "It's a good bet they know we're coming through the forest on foot, but they won't know where or when. We still have a good chance of slipping past them, especially with Slyder keeping watch for us."

"It looks to me like the road is another day away at best. We might be able to slip across at night if we're careful," Jack suggested.

Alexander nodded in agreement but his mind was still processing the events of the afternoon. His wound was healed enough that he would be able to move tomorrow. Anatoly was mending even more quickly. Alexander was still playing out the basic struggle between good and evil in the back of his mind while trying to recall the details of his clairvoyance, both the specifics of what he'd seen as well as the state of mind he'd been in when it happened.

He was troubled by the colors of the man in black, which brought him back to the question of Phane and his aura. Alexander tried to replay his first clairvoyant experience. He didn't recall seeing anyone's aura, but then it was the first time it had happened, so maybe it was still a developing ability. When his second sight first started, it had taken a year or so before he was able to discern much of anything from the colors he saw. With time, practice, and experience, he'd come to understand how to read the aura of another person in a way that provided useful information and insight. He hoped his clairvoyance would also become more reliable and useful with time.

"We may be able to cross the road undetected, but I doubt it," Alexander said. "The man in black I saw with the Reishi is extremely dangerous. I suspect he was what Phane was referring to when he said I wouldn't survive what he sent next. He's dangerous in a way I can't adequately describe." He fell silent again.

"From your description of his aura, it sounds to me like he's a mage-level wizard," Lucky said. "If that's the case, then you're right about him being very dangerous. A mage can establish a connection with the firmament without restraint or limit. He has reached a place where he can maintain a firm hold on his identity and his will sufficiently that the firmament can no longer distract him from his purpose. A mage does not get lost in the firmament. As a result, the only real limits on what he can do are a function of his calling and his imagination."

Alexander frowned at a new question that presented itself. He found that was the way of things. Whenever one question was answered it inevitably led to others. "Then what's the distinction between a mage and an arch mage?"

Lucky nodded with a smile. It was the next logical question. "While a mage can establish a connection to the firmament and cause reality to bend to his will with awesome and frightening power, an arch mage is something else altogether. He has survived the second mana fast. In many ways he has transcended normal mortal existence. His will and consciousness are said to be fused with the firmament itself. An arch mage no longer needs to make a connection to the firmament because he has a permanent and ongoing connection to it already. It's said that an arch mage no longer casts spells per se but rather injects a vision of his desired outcome into the firmament and it becomes reality."

Alarm was building within Alexander as Lucky explained the scope of what he faced. "If Phane is so powerful, then why doesn't he just will me dead and be done with it?"

"Even the power of an arch mage has its limits." Lucky slipped easily into the familiar role of tutor. "First, every wizard has a calling which determines how his connection to the firmament functions. In order to reach the level of understanding necessary to fully connect to the firmament as a mage, one must focus on his calling. Such focus excludes other schools of magic. For example, I am a master alchemist. I have studied alchemy exclusively and one day I hope to gain the insight necessary to rise to the level of a mage alchemist. Mason Kallentera is a general wizard who has studied many areas of magic. He can do a great many things but, because he did not focus on his calling, he will never become a mage. An arch mage must first become a mage, which requires this kind of specialization, which, in turn, naturally constrains the scope of his abilities, while magnifying the level of power he can command within his chosen discipline.

"Second, every wizard is limited by his intelligence, imagination, and beliefs. If a wizard doesn't think of something, he cannot make it manifest. If he doesn't believe that something can be done, then he will not be able to cause it to happen no matter how powerful he is.

"Third, the firmament is like an ocean. The effects of a wizard's will may be able to cause great turbulence in the area immediately surrounding the wizard, but farther and farther away, the effects diminish in the same way the ripples of a stone cast into the water diminish as they get farther from the point of impact. I suspect that's why Phane summoned creatures to do his bidding. Once brought into this world, they can carry out his will where direct action by magic against you would have been beyond even his power because of the distances involved."

"Well, I guess it's good to know that Phane won't strike me dead any moment now," Alexander said more bitterly than he intended. "That just leaves a platoon of Reishi, Rangle, the man in black, and that giant I saw to deal with. No problem."

"Alexander." There was an edge to Anatoly's voice. "Complaining about the problems we face does no good. Focus on our goals and look for solutions." The admonition was an old refrain of Anatoly's teachings: Focus on the solution, not on the problem.

Alexander looked at his old mentor for a moment before nodding slightly. He cleared his mind and laid out the goals in his mind's eye: get to New Ruatha and then to Blackstone Keep. Then he laid out the obstacles that stood in their way: distance and a small but powerful contingent of Reishi led by at least two wizards.

After thinking about it for a moment, he realized that the enemy would be spread pretty thin on the road. In fact, they couldn't possibly have enough men to cover every crossing point. Unless they had some form of magic to alert them, Jack's plan of slipping by under cover of darkness might just work. More than that, he didn't see any viable alternative. He had to get across that road.

"All right, we move for the road at first light. We'll stop a mile or so short and wait until dark, then make our way across and push another mile into the forest before making camp. With any luck they won't even notice us."

Everyone nodded in agreement.

"We should probably douse the fire before it gets much darker or we'll risk being spotted," Anatoly offered.

Alexander drew last watch. He was sitting on his pack when the light of dawn broke over the horizon and washed over the sea of fluffy pink treetops. The golden fire of the sunrise deepened the color of the pink blossoms to a bright glowing reddish orange that was both beautiful and ominous. It looked to Alexander like he was on an island in a sea of fire that crackled and undulated in the gentle morning breeze.

The beauty of the colors all around stood out in stark contrast to the carnage of the two dead gorledons sprawled out in the middle of their camp. Lucky had clearly taken a few samples from the beasts including, from the looks of things, their hearts. Alexander shuddered at the sight of the monsters and the thought that he had come so close to death. He knew with certainty that his wound would have been fatal if not for Lucky's magic.

Chapter 41

Alexander was happy to be on the move again away from the ugliness of the battle on the little hillock. The morning sun cast a warm glow through the canopy and onto the floor of the Pink Forest. Alexander was becoming more aware of the forest and the little details that Isabel had patiently taught him over the past few days. He could see why she felt so alive here. He let his mind wander as they made their way into the evergreen trees at the border of the Pink Forest. They'd lost a lot of altitude since leaving Glen Morillian and the air was warmer and thicker. New shoots of bright green leaves were beginning to sprout, giving the forest a dappled look of dark green and brown speckled with the new growth all around. It was beautiful with just the evergreen trees and shrubs, but the explosion of new growth that the early spring was causing added a whole new dimension to it. On top of the vibrancy of the new growth, the colors of the living aura surrounding those little shoots screamed of life to Alexander's second sight. Almost as if by osmosis, he started to feel more optimistic.

They reached their stopping point a few hours before dusk. Isabel reported that the road was about a mile away. She had Slyder fly down into the tall canopy and flit through the trees to scout the road for several miles in each direction.

"There are soldiers on horseback riding patrol for miles in each direction of where we'll come to the road. It looks like they've cast a wide net to see if they can catch us when we cross," she reported.

"They must have some way of warning the others," Anatoly observed. "Otherwise, I suspect they would employ a different strategy."

Alexander nodded. "Makes sense, but even if they can warn the others, we'll be far enough into the forest on the other side of the road before they can respond. Once we're into the trees, they can only follow on foot. We stick to the plan. An hour after dark we'll move."

Even with Alexander's second sight, the forest was hard to navigate in the dark. More than once he became entangled in dead branches that snapped loudly when they broke. They moved painfully slowly in an effort to be silent but still made it to the road in good time. Alexander scanned the forest for any sign of a living aura but saw none, other than the forest itself. It looked like their plan would work. The road was just too long to patrol effectively with such a small force.

Once Alexander was satisfied that they were in the clear, he whispered the order to go. All six of them raced across the road at the same time. Alexander's head swiveled back and forth searching for threats as they crossed the danger area. He saw none.

Then, just when his foot landed on the centerline of the road, he discovered his mistake. The ground ignited beneath his boot. Heat flared up through his leg and sent him sprawling face first onto the ground. From the point of his footfall, fire rose up in a line stretching down the center of the road. The flare of magical flame raced away in each direction, leaving only a charred, smoldering line. The pain in Alexander's foot faded quickly. It was a shock and surprise but did no damage. No sooner had the realization of the spell's intent become clear than a whistler arrow streaked up through the trees not a mile from their position. Then another went up from the other direction. The enemy had their position and was on the hunt.

They abandoned stealth and crashed into the forest, moving as fast as they could through the darkness. The branches scratched and clawed at them while they ran. Once they were several hundred feet off the road they slowed to a quick walk, being careful to stay together. They could hear shouting in the distance as the soldiers of the Reishi gathered where they had crossed the road.

It was slow and dangerous but Alexander pushed on through the night trying to gain distance from his pursuers. The feeling of being hunted was becoming all too familiar. He could feel his senses becoming more alert as the night wore on. Every noise and every shadow represented a threat. By dawn his nerves were frazzled, he was exhausted, and his mind was tired. He just hoped that the night's travel had bought them the distance they needed to stay ahead of the enemy. He knew that their trail from moving through the forest in the dark would be easy to follow, so he started looking for opportunities to leave a less trackable trail in the hopes that he could slow or even lose his hunters altogether.

Isabel took the lead. She knew the forest much better than he did and she knew how to move without leaving a trace. Alexander suspected that if she were alone she could easily lose the Reishi, but with the six of them it would be a much more difficult task. She led them to little streams and used them as pathways to cover their tracks even though she said any experienced tracker would see the evidence of their passage in the streambed. She searched for rocky areas and helped them move through without marking the mosses that covered some of the stones. She found fallen trees and carefully walked the length of the tree to avoid marking the bark. Her path was not direct but instead meandered in a course that would make little sense to a tracker.

After an hour of carefully concealing their tracks, she set out in a straight line to gain more distance only to repeat the process again a few hours later when they came to a rocky patch or a stream that presented an opportunity to disguise their trail.

She reported that a dozen Reishi including the man in black and Rangle were following on foot about three miles behind while the rest had gone north along the road on horseback, led by the giant and Truss.

"It looks like they're having a hard time finding our trail after we left that little boulder field. They're losing ground on us," she said when she opened her eyes and broke her connection with Slyder.

She kept her forest hawk in the trees around the hunting party. So far it was clear that the trackers they had were no match for the forest knowledge of a Ranger. Alexander began to feel a little better about their situation even though he knew they would likely face a fight once they left the cover of the forest. The Reishi, no doubt, knew they were headed for New Ruatha and the giant and the soldiers under his command would probably be waiting for them on the plains between the northern edge of the forest and the city.

Alexander tried to put the thought out of his mind for the time being. It was a problem he would have to face when it presented itself. For now, he just wanted to gain as much ground on the man in black as he could. They started moving more quickly as the afternoon wore on, and Isabel reported that their hunters were still fumbling around looking for a trail. Alexander was exhausted. He could see that everyone else was at least as tired as he was but no one complained about the pace. If they could gain enough distance they would be able to sleep without fear that the Reishi could make up the ground in the dark.

It was grueling. They fast walked until darkness brought them to a halt in a little clearing. There was no sense pushing on. It was too dark to cover much distance and they needed rest and a meal. They would be traveling hard all day tomorrow and they wouldn't get far if they didn't get some sleep. Their meal was cold. No one spoke much. They drew for watch and went to sleep. Alexander felt like he'd just put his head down to sleep when Anatoly gently shook him awake for his watch. It was the dead of night and the forest was dark and eerily silent.

Alexander stretched as he sat up and pulled his cloak around him. He fumbled with his boots and carefully made his way to a nearby log to sit down while he kept watch over his sleeping friends. He fought to stay awake. He was tired and the night was so dark. To keep his mind active, he tried to work through all of the challenges he faced. Toward the end of his watch, he looked up with a start when he saw a light in the distance through the trees. It was just a flash but it had the quality of real light and not the gentle, colorful glow of an aura seen with his second sight. He focused and caught another flash of light. It looked like it was coming toward them. His blood ran cold when he realized it looked like torches coming through the forest.

He woke Anatoly. "Looks like we have company," he whispered. The big man-at-arms sat up and looked in the direction Alexander pointed. After only a moment he nodded and started strapping on his breastplate. Alexander woke everyone else in turn. They quietly made ready for the coming threat. When the lights got closer, it looked to be about half a dozen men with torches. Alexander reminded himself that there could be considerably more than that if only a few were carrying light.

They decided they would have a better chance if they caught the enemy by surprise in the dark rather than try to flee through the forest at night. They spread out and waited with weapons ready. When the enemy got closer, Lucky stood up abruptly. Alexander could see the sense of alarm in his colors.

"Those aren't soldiers, they're night wisps. Quickly, gather wood for torches and a fire."

Chapter 42

Lucky didn't often get excited and he rarely commanded anyone to do anything. It just wasn't in his nature. He was far more likely to gently suggest a course of action or ask questions designed to lead others to a conclusion.

Alexander didn't hesitate. He had no idea what a night wisp was, but the fear in Lucky's voice was enough to send a shiver up his spine. He started gathering sticks and small branches. Everyone else joined him quickly. Lucky was busy clearing an area for a fire pit and setting a few stones in place.

Alexander dumped the first load of twigs and sticks into the little circle of stones and went back to work finding more. A moment later the stack of kindling he'd given Lucky whooshed into a bright fire, casting light and shadows into the surrounding forest. Alexander worried that the Reishi might see the flames but decided that whatever the night wisps were, they were a more imminent threat than the Reishi, who'd made camp a few miles back under the watchful eye of Slyder.

As the fire grew and more wood was brought to the little circle, Lucky called out, "Look for branches that would make good torches." Then he started rummaging around in his bag.

A few moments later he called out again, "They're almost here. Quickly, everyone into the firelight."

They all gathered around the little fire just before the night wisps floated out of the woods and into the clearing. Each was about a foot in diameter and looked like nothing more than a pale glowing orb of light. They bobbed and flitted about erratically, sometimes moving slowly like a soap bubble on a gentle breeze, other times moving with startling quickness, easily covering the space of a dozen feet in the blink of an eye. They floated, bobbed, weaved, and flitted into the clearing, coming right for the six of them. When they reached the glow of the fire, they abruptly recoiled out of range of the firelight.

"Light, fire, and magic can harm them. Your weapons are useless. Steel has no effect," Lucky said as he wrapped lengths of burlap around the ends of the torch sticks and then drizzled them with oil. He lit one and handed it to Anatoly, who was looking irritable that his axe had just been pronounced useless.

He took the torch and held it up high. The night wisps shied away from the brightness. Once everyone was armed with a torch, it became clear that they would run out of firewood before dawn.

Anatoly, Isabel, and Alexander held their torches high and escorted Jack into the brush to look for more firewood. The night wisps floated closer but stayed just outside of the glow of the torchlight. Jack was able to gather another load of wood but it was a nerve-racking process. The strange glowing orbs looked so calm and quiet. There was no ferocity or snarling to them at all, yet they conveyed a sense of menace that made Alexander shudder.

They worked for the next hour to keep the fire stoked and burning brightly, but the firewood was becoming scarce near the clearing and they had to

venture farther into the darkness to find the wood they needed. The brightness of
the torches was not enough to keep the creatures very far away.

Jack found a dead limb and managed to break off a hefty piece, when one
of the night wisps darted forward into the dim light of the torches and passed right
through Alexander's left shoulder. It felt like the touch of death itself. He was
grateful that the creature hit his left side because he would have surely dropped the
torch if it had hit his right shoulder. Numbing cold stabbed through him where the
creature had passed, while at the same time a deep, penetrating fatigue flooded
into him that left him almost too tired to stay on his feet. The little orb of light
glowed more brightly just after passing through him, as though it had taken
something from him and gained strength for it.

Anatoly struck the thing squarely with his torch. It hissed and backed
away, then slowly dropped toward the ground.

When they made it back to the safety of the ring of firelight, Alexander
sat down heavily under the exhaustion and sudden fatigue. The prickly sensation
of pins and needles danced across his flesh as the cold slowly seeped away and he
started to regain some use of his left arm.

When he looked out into the forest, there were only five of the dangerous
little lights left. But the light of Lucky's fire was starting to fade. The wisp
Anatoly had stabbed with his torch had fallen to the ground and faded out. Another
wisp darted into the edge of the firelight toward Jack and was met by both
Abigail's and Isabel's torches. They both hit it squarely and sent it tumbling down
toward the forest floor, where it faded and went dark.

In the commotion, the torches dimmed and the fire sputtered. The
remaining four wisps took advantage of the sudden moment of darkness and
darted in so fast that no one could even try to stop them. Jack, Abigail, and
Anatoly were each hit. All three went to their knees from the numbing cold of the
little monsters.

Lucky poured a flask of oil on the fire, bringing it roaring back to life.
The night wisps retreated well away from the ring of firelight. Three of the
remaining four night wisps glowed more brightly as if they'd grown stronger after
passing through a living being. They bobbled in the darkness for a moment, then
each of the three slowly separated into two little glowing orbs each.

Now there were seven.

Anatoly tried to stand but couldn't muster the strength. Jack and Abigail
stayed on their knees, trying to overcome the agony of the deathly cold that shot
through them. The seven night wisps hovered in the periphery of the little clearing,
keeping to the shadows. Isabel handed her torch to Lucky and snapped up her
bow. She tore a cloth strip from the hem of her shirt, wrapped it around the tip of
an arrow, then held it in the fire. She took careful aim and loosed her flaming
arrow. It passed right through the center of one of the little floating orbs and stuck,
still burning, into the side of a tree. The wisp slowly floated to the ground and
went dark, as the dry moss on the tree caught fire. The flames licked the dead, dry
branches above and soon the side of the tree was ablaze. The wisps moved away,
farther into the forest to escape the light. The flames on the tree burned brightly
for several minutes until all of the lower dead wood was burnt, but the fire failed
to ignite the live branches and the needles of the boughs higher up.

Alexander stood, finally able to muster some strength, and found his bow.

He made a flaming arrow of his own and targeted another wisp in the trees. It was far enough away that he missed but his burning arrow managed to catch the lower dead wood of another tree on fire.

Then Alexander noticed the light of dawn dimming the stars above.

It seemed that the wisps also noticed the coming dawn, because they started to move away into the forest.

Lucky started ministering to the wounded and found that mostly they were just cold to the core and too tired to get up. Isabel and Lucky built up the fire in the growing light and put water on to boil for hot tea. They cooked breakfast while the four who'd been hit by the night wisps tried to recover some of their strength.

Lucky gave them each a steaming mug of tea laced with potent-smelling herbs. Alexander didn't care about the bitter taste; he just wanted the warmth of it. They all drank their tea too quickly but felt better for it even if it did burn their tongues a bit.

"Looks like the Reishi are on the move and they're headed right for us. I'd say they're about three miles off," Isabel reported after her first cup of tea.

Alexander shook his head. "I wish we could slow them down somehow. We're not going to make very good time today with everyone feeling like they could sleep for a week."

Abigail nodded her agreement with a grimace.

The night wisps had robbed them of a much-needed night's sleep and had added to their fatigue by draining vital energy with their attacks. The fire had no doubt alerted the Reishi to their position, undoing all of the hard work Isabel had done the day before to lose their pursuers.

"I may have something that can help," Lucky said as he began rummaging through his bag. "Ah, here it is." Smiling broadly, he held up a little canister.

Anatoly looked skeptical, "What's it do?"

"The Reishi will no doubt find our campground here," Lucky motioned to the little clearing. "When they do, the powder in this container will make their lives miserable for a few hours."

Anatoly wasn't convinced. He'd seen Lucky's concoctions work and he'd also seen them fail miserably. He wanted to be sure this one would work. "How so?" he asked.

Lucky smiled again at his old friend, "I'm glad you asked." Anatoly rolled his eyes. "I'll sprinkle a bit around the camp and cast the activating spell when we're a good distance away. Then, the next time anyone sets foot in the area, thousands of tiny little slivers no bigger than a hair and no longer than an eyelash will lift up off the ground and swarm the intruders. The sharp little slivers will embed themselves in their clothing and cause such itching and irritation that they'll just about have to stop and thoroughly clean out their clothes. The alternative is to be literally rubbed raw. Left unattended, the slivers will work themselves into a person's skin and cause all sorts of sores and infections. Really quite nasty." Lucky punctuated his explanation with another broad smile.

Anatoly just chuckled and shook his head.

"If we can strike back at them, even if it is with high-grade itching powder, I'm all for it," Alexander said, packing up his bedroll in the growing light.

While the others packed, Lucky went to the dead night wisps and carefully scraped up the little puddles of clear-looking slime that remained. "Night-wisp ectoplasm is a powerful substance," he muttered almost to himself, while he carefully filled several little vials with the strange-looking stuff.

Soon they were on their way and moving as fast as they could given their fatigue. They made no attempt to cover their trail for the duration of the morning and stopped for lunch in a field of boulders on the slope of a little hill in the forest. When they finished eating, Isabel took a look through Slyder's eyes. He was waiting at the site of their camp to see how Lucky's delaying tactic worked. When she started laughing out loud, Alexander figured it had worked well.

"Lucky, you're a genius," Isabel said. "They're all running around trying to get away from their own clothes. It's like watching a dog chase its tail." She giggled again at the sight. "Looks like they're going to be a while. The guy in black doesn't look happy about it and neither does Rangle."

By this time, those who had fallen prey to the night wisps had regained much of their strength. They were all still tired, but the penetrating fatigue brought on by the night wisps' attack had faded. They moved for speed as much as possible, only occasionally choosing a course for the purpose of hiding their trail. About midafternoon, it started to drizzle, and as the afternoon wore on, it turned into the kind of steady light rain that soaked into everything.

Isabel reported that the Reishi had managed to clean their clothes enough to start moving again but they looked quite uncomfortable. They moved more slowly and were constantly scratching some spot or other. She giggled mischievously to herself every time she looked through Slyder's eyes.

Alexander was just happy they were outpacing their pursuers. When evening began to fall, he started to worry about the night wisps. With the steady light rain, it would be difficult to build a fire and keep it going. Without fire, they would be helpless against the menacing little creatures.

They found a rock outcropping in the forest that provided some cover from the rain, and built a makeshift shelter over the exposed side with fir boughs. Unfortunately, they couldn't find enough dry wood to keep a fire going all night, so they stacked what they could and made a few torches and a few more fire arrows. Alexander knew it wouldn't be enough, but it was all they could do with what they had.

More than anything, they needed a good night's sleep. He drew second watch; it was quiet except for the steady fall of light rain and the sporadic cacophony of drops falling from the tree limbs when the wind blew through. He went back to his bedroll after his watch, hopeful that the night would pass quietly.

He woke at dawn feeling rested and ready for another day's travel. After a quick breakfast, Isabel took a look at the Reishi through Slyder's eyes.

"Huh, the night wisps attacked the Reishi last night. I saw at least three dead and a number of scorch marks where Rangle apparently used his fire to ward off the wisps." She smiled at Alexander, "Looks like we caught a break."

He couldn't help but feel good at the news, and her smile always lifted his spirits. Everyone was in much better shape after a full night's sleep and a good meal. They would make good time even with the steady rain that showed no signs of letting up. Alexander pulled the hood of his cloak up before stepping out into the weather.

For the next two days they made steady progress heading east. Isabel led the way through seemingly endless tracts of fir trees, winding through the brush to make their trail difficult to follow. She kept Slyder near the Reishi and looked in on them often. They were losing ground and struggling to stay on the trail. In two days, they'd fallen about five miles behind.

The rain had been falling steadily and the forest was wet. Alexander and his companions were soggy and cold. In the back of his mind, he worried about the night wisps. Now that the forest was thoroughly soaked, they couldn't build a decent fire if they wanted to, even with the little bit of oil that Lucky had left. Without fire, the night wisps could easily be the end of them. He reminded himself to stop wasting energy on problems that hadn't happened yet. He had more than enough real problems to worry about without fretting over potential dangers.

The next morning the rain broke and the sky showed signs of clearing. The monotone, flat-grey cloud cover gave way to big grey puffball clouds that scudded across the sky like they were marching toward a distant enemy. The sun peeked through here and there, casting bright rays of light down to the ground through the thick, moist air. The day was warmer than the past few, but the wind had picked up so it felt colder in the shade of the forest.

Isabel turned them north about midday. She said they should reach the northern edge of the forest by evening of the next day. The Reishi were still a good distance behind and steadily losing ground. The rain was making it even harder for them to follow Isabel's circuitous trail. She led them in a straight line until the terrain presented an opportunity to confuse the Reishi, then she led them in unpredictable and almost bizarre patterns, sometimes turning abruptly for no apparent reason and other times walking in large circles so their tracks would intersect and create a confusing maze of trails to follow. Where they found flowing water or stone, she used it to conceal their path. Other times she stopped and brushed out their footprints with fir boughs to make it look as if they had simply vanished.

She knew an experienced tracker would find the trail eventually, but it would take much more time to find it than it took her to obscure it. Every tactic she employed was designed more to delay their enemy than to lose them outright, and her efforts worked. She frequently looked at the enemy's progress through Slyder's eyes and saw them walking in circles looking for some sign or mark on the ground. She kept Slyder high in the trees and was careful to ensure that he was never seen. She knew all too well that the value of a spy diminished greatly if the enemy knew they were being watched.

True to her word, Isabel led them to the northern edge of the forest in the late afternoon of the next day. Alexander could see the city off in the distance. It was bigger than he had expected. He'd only seen Southport, Highlands Reach, and Glen Morillian in his whole life. Each was a fair-sized city but none was close to the size of New Ruatha. Even at this distance, he could see the sprawl of the houses and buildings stretching out onto the plains all around, but the thing that caught his eye and captured his imagination was the multi-tiered plateau in the center of the city. It was still two hours until dusk and he could already see the seemingly endless lights glittering over every part of it.

Chapter 43

Jack smiled at the sight. "It's been a long time since I've looked on the Glittering City. It's good to be home." He sighed somewhat wistfully and then said more sardonically, "I only hope my guild is still in order. Bards can be an unruly bunch when left unsupervised for so long."

Alexander grinned at the mixture of joy and mischief that danced across Jack's face.

"I've missed New Ruatha, too," Lucky said with fondness. "It's been many years since I studied at the Wizards Guild. I hope Mage Gamaliel is well. It will be good to see him."

They stood well back into the wood line and looked out across the high grass of the plains. It looked like they could make the edge of the city by dark, but Alexander wasn't sure he was judging the distance correctly. "How far away is it?" he asked.

"It's more than half a day's walk," Jack smiled knowingly. "Looks closer, doesn't it?"

Alexander nodded thoughtfully, "Where do we enter the passages you spoke of?"

Jack pointed to the eastern edge of the city. "There, where the river flows in. We can enter the underground passages and make our way right into the central plateau without ever setting foot on the streets."

Alexander looked at the sky and the position of the setting sun. "We still have a couple of hours of light left. Let's make the best of it and move farther east so we have as little ground to cover as possible out in the open."

They started moving through the forest only a hundred feet or so inside the tree line. Alexander knew there were probably Reishi patrolling the grasslands between the forest and the city, and he wanted to avoid them if at all possible. Isabel said the majority of the Reishi had gone north along the road on horseback. They would have easily made it to New Ruatha a few days ago and were probably looking for them at this very moment. Even as that thought entered his mind, Alexander felt a strange sensation well up in his head almost like pressure building behind his forehead.

He stopped and focused on the sensation. The moment he did he was swept up into the firmament. His awareness was no longer confined to his body but spanned the whole of existence. It was a jarring sensation that flooded his consciousness with more information than he could possibly process. It was all a jumble of tangled and disjointed events cascading through his mind.

Then, abruptly, he was floating beneath the present moment, beneath the firmament itself. He no longer saw the impossibly vast cacophony of events in the world but instead looked up at the wave of time from beneath, where it was calm and quiet. He could see where it crested into the world of reality and created the moment of existence that every living thing shared. It was a whole new sensation, like being within the ocean of the firmament rather than spread across the place where it crested into the moment of creation.

And then it sped up.

It was so beyond anything that Alexander had even imagined that he couldn't quite grasp what was happening. The point in time where the firmament touched reality moved forward just a minute or so. Not long, but Alexander knew with awed certainty that he was seeing into the future, or at least one possible future. His awareness narrowed down to the place inside the tree line where he and his friends were. He saw himself and his friends moving through the forest. Then he saw Truss leading more than a dozen mounted Reishi mercenaries around a thicket on the edge of the forest. Next he saw a hail of crossbow bolts crash into his friends. Isabel was hit. Lucky was hit. Jack was hit. Truss laughed.

Alexander slammed back into his mind and the present moment with such force that he nearly lost his balance. Scarcely a heartbeat had passed and yet his vision felt like it took several minutes. He looked up and saw the thicket that Truss would be charging around not fifty feet ahead.

"Take cover!" he commanded quietly as he whipped his bow off his shoulder and nocked an arrow.

Everyone except Anatoly hesitated for just a moment. Anatoly quickly and fluidly slipped behind a big tree while unslinging his war axe. A moment later everyone else scrambled to get behind a tree, when a dozen horses came around the thicket. The enemy saw them in the thin woods of the forest's edge and wheeled toward them.

A dozen crossbow bolts zipped past them, peppering the trees they were hiding behind, but none hit home. Alexander's mind reeled at the implications. He'd seen the future and yet he hadn't because the future he'd seen didn't happen. He couldn't quite make sense of it and he clearly didn't have time to try. The enemy was fifty feet away and coming fast.

Alexander counted fifteen soldiers. They were mounted, well armed, and wearing light armor. He tried to touch the firmament again to see if he could use his magic to help in the fight but felt nothing, so he fell back on old reliable skills. He rolled around the tree, bringing his bow up and the string back, took quick but careful aim and let his arrow go. The first kill of the fight was his. The mercenary toppled off the back of his charging horse with an arrow buried through his breastplate and into his chest.

A moment later, Isabel and Abigail imitated him and dropped a soldier each. Still the enemy charged. The next volley of arrows from Alexander, Isabel, and Abigail leapt from their bows only feet before the enemy reached their position. Three more fell, but the remaining nine enemy soldiers crashed past the trees and spun quickly. Truss was shouting commands from a distance of thirty feet or so behind his force of mercenaries.

Alexander felt time slow down. He surveyed the scene quickly but calmly. Abigail scrambled onto a large fallen log that was too big for a horse to leap and drew another arrow.

From his hiding place behind a giant cedar, Jack swung a broken tree branch at the legs of a horse rushing past, sending it crashing face first into the dirt. Anatoly employed a similar tactic, except his axe took the horse's legs off at the knees and sent the animal into the ground, squealing in pain. Both soldiers tumbled off their mounts and landed hard. Lucky was sitting with his back to a large tree, rummaging around in his bag. Isabel dropped her bow and drew her sword.

The enemy was all around them, pulling their horses to a halt so they could converge on Alexander and his companions. They were armed with spears and long swords. Each had a crossbow but they'd all been fired. Alexander leaned his bow against the tree with one hand while drawing his sword with the other.

He felt a sense of calm focus settle on him. He was in a fight and he had a blade in his hand. The timeless experience imparted on him by the skillbook gave him a feeling of familiarity and certainty.

He stood away from the tree in a clear challenge to the first soldier who brought his horse around for an attack. When the horse rushed, Alexander calmly took a couple of steps in front of its headlong charge. His quick move put the enemy's spear on the other side of the animal's neck, protecting Alexander from its sharp tip. At the same time, he brought the tip of his blade around and caught the enemy soldier on the outside of his thigh just above the knee. The momentum of the horse did the rest. The blade drove through muscle from front to back, then sliced out the side. The man screamed in agony and slipped off the side of his still-charging horse.

Isabel dodged a charging horseman by circling around the trunk of a fir tree only to run into the attack of another. With her back to a tree, she traded sword thrusts with the mounted man. Abigail killed another with her bow. She stood, feet planted squarely, on top of the old log and calmly drew another arrow. Anatoly ducked under the slashing attack of a horseman and swept the legs out from under the horse with the blade of his axe, unhorsing yet another enemy soldier. Jack carefully moved from one downed soldier to the next with his now bloody knife.

Two mercenaries came at Alexander just after he met the first charge. He easily parried the sword of the first but it put him in position for the second's attack. He deflected the spear enough to prevent being run through and instead escaped with a gash on top of his left shoulder. As the spear rode over his shoulder, he thrust the point of his blade up into the abdomen of the horseman, lifting him off the horse, over his head, and bringing him crashing down onto the forest floor.

Isabel cried out when the soldier she was fighting slashed her across the chest only inches below her throat. From where Alexander was, it didn't look deep, but it was bleeding freely. A second later, the man who had cut Isabel stiffened when an arrow from Abigail's bow sprouted from his chest.

The soldier who'd missed a moment before wheeled to face Alexander again, slashing with his sword. Alexander calmly used his sword to stop and trap the enemy's blade against the horse's neck, while drawing his long knife and burying it into the rider's hip. The enemy screamed in pain before toppling off his horse.

The battle lasted only a few seconds. Just as the last man fell with Alexander's long knife buried in his hip, Lucky stood up with a strange-looking little bone whistle. When he realized that he'd missed the fight, he looked almost disappointed and kind of sheepish.

Seeing his men all fall very quickly, Truss wheeled his horse and spurred it into a gallop toward the plains. Lucky broke into a broad grin and blew the whistle. At the silent sound, all the horses immediately started bucking in sudden, startled pain. Truss lost control and toppled off his horse but got tangled up in the stirrup. Alexander watched the petty little noble get dragged off into the distance by his panicked horse.

Lucky chuckled, "Handy little whistle." He held up the old carved-bone whistle that looked like a tiny wild stallion. "I'm sure Truss agrees," he added with a grin. He slipped it into his pocket and picked up his bag. "Now, let's have a look at those wounds."

"Take a look at Isabel first," Alexander said. "Abigail, Anatoly, help me round up some horses. We might as well ride."

Chapter 44

They skirted around the edge of town in the darkness. Alexander didn't want to risk another encounter. Truss would no doubt look for any chance to make trouble and the man in black was still somewhere behind them. Alexander had no interest in meeting him face to face. He was alert and wary. This city was hostile territory as far as he was concerned, at least until the Regent accepted his authority.

The thing that weighed heaviest on his mind was how to approach the palace and the current government. Jack seemed to think that the Regent would accept his authority on the strength of the mark on his neck and the legend that the line of Ruatha would be remade. Alexander was less sure. He did know for certain that the manner of his introduction to the people, the nobles, and the Regent of New Ruatha would have a great deal of impact on how he would be received. Alexander realized that he was looking at the situation like a fight: thrust, parry, riposte. He had the initiative. His objective was clear. He decided to act like a king and brazenly take his throne rather than ask for it. He wasn't sure about the arena of politics, but he knew that in a fight, showing weakness was the surest path to defeat.

His plan was risky. If the Regent had already made a deal, or if he decided to deny Alexander his claim, he'd have to fight his way out of the palace. Not a prospect with good odds of success. But the alternative seemed sure to fail. If he went to the Wizards Guild first and then to the palace it would look like he didn't believe his claim to the throne was valid. Perception was key. Everyone had to know with certainty that Alexander had no doubt about his rightful place as the King of Ruatha. Any doubt he showed would infect the populace with uncertainty.

Alexander had just convinced himself that the risk was worth it, when they came to the east road leading into the city. A flyer pinned to a post caught his eye. He moved up next to it and tore the parchment from where it hung. It was a sketch drawing of him and Abigail. There was a reward for their capture, dead or alive, in the amount of a thousand gold sovereigns. The bounty notice went on to claim that they were traitors to the Sovereign of the Seven Isles, Phane Reishi. It listed a whole litany of crimes including the murder of their parents, horse theft, and was finally punctuated with a charge of incest. Alexander's blood boiled. This was likely the work of Truss.

He handed the flyer to Anatoly while he fumed, trying to find reason through his anger. Did this change his plan or was it just a distraction? He needed the power the throne would give him to raise an army. Without a united Ruathan army, Phane would pick off one territory at a time and Alexander would fail.

Anatoly frowned at the wanted poster. "This could be a problem. Even if the Regent doesn't buy into these charges, there are likely to be opportunists who will take a shot at you just for the gold." Anatoly handed it to Jack.

Jack looked it over quickly. "Huh, it'll take some doing, but I can have this made into a lie by the end of the week."

Abigail took it out of his hands when she saw her likeness on the page. She stared in disbelief at the list of charges. "Who would do such a thing? These are all lies," Abigail raged a little more loudly than Alexander would have liked.

Jack motioned for her to keep her voice down. "Of course they're lies. Lies are the stock in trade of our enemies. But they're amateurs when it comes to swaying public opinion. They seek to buy loyalty, which is an appeal to the baser nature of people. Some will respond to such an offer but they will not speak openly of it. Our enemies fail to grasp the true yearning in the hearts of men. People want to believe in ideals that make their souls sing. They want the feeling of being a part of something great and noble.

"By the end of the week every minstrel and bard in all of New Ruatha will be singing the song of Lord Alexander and his triumphant return to redeem the Ruathan royal line and to save the people of our fair city from the scourge of Prince Phane." Jack smiled and tapped his coat pocket. "I've already got the first verses written. A few hours of polish and practice and I can start teaching my bards the story and the music. By this time tomorrow, every bar, inn, ale house, public house, tavern, and town square will be filled with your song. Within a few days, these flyers will all be torn down and ripped to scrap by angry citizens who want to believe in the promise you represent."

Alexander shook his head. "Do you really think it will be that simple?"

Jack laughed. "Simple? No, not at all. Propaganda is a fine art, but it's more powerful than magic when properly employed. It can move the masses to believe in something. In the end, large numbers of people who are willing to die for a cause they fervently believe in will always carry the day. And, it doesn't hurt that you actually do stand for principles worthy of their loyalty."

Anatoly, ever the pragmatist, asked, "So what do we do between now and then? The way it looks to me, Alexander's likely to be slapped in irons the first time a city guard lays eyes on him."

Alexander's rage settled into a low boil in the pit of his stomach but he didn't try to extinguish it; instead, he fed it. He wanted to be mad. He would need the anger before the night was through.

"We take the throne room."

Everyone looked at him like he was a bit crazy.

"Lucky, I want you to go to the Wizards Guild and tell the Guild Mage that I respectfully request his presence in the throne room. Tell him to bring a handful of trusted wizards and come ready for a fight."

He took the poster from Abigail and folded it into quarters, then pulled his long knife, sliced the edge of his hand to draw blood and smeared it on the parchment. He let it dry just slightly while he wrapped his hand and then pressed the parchment to the scarred mark on his neck. When he held it up to the light the effect was exactly what he wanted: his mark in blood on the back of a wanted poster. He handed it to Lucky.

"Give him this," Alexander said. "Once you arrive, ask him to send a messenger to Owen at the Bards Guild. I want as many bards as he can round up to come to me in the throne room as well."

Jack took out his little tablet and quickly scrawled a note telling Owen just what was needed and handed the scrap of paper to Lucky. Lucky tucked it into a pocket and gave Alexander a clap on the shoulder and a smile before trotting off into the city.

"Jack, we need to get into the palace without being discovered," Alexander said.

Jack bowed at the waist with a little grin, "By your command, My Lord."

Jack led them into the city, using small side streets that didn't look very well traveled. For all the lights on the central plateau and the main streets, the path Jack took was dark and shadowy. They made their way down alleys behind buildings and only rarely encountered people. They wound up on a little dock that ran along the riverfront with water on the right and a ten-foot stone wall on the left. It wasn't long before they came to an iron grate that covered a sewer drain in the side of the sea wall. Jack stopped and dismounted. He fiddled with the lock for only a moment or two and it came open. Alexander frowned. He'd never actually seen anyone pick a lock before and he was astonished to see just how quickly it could be done.

"I'm afraid the path isn't very pleasant, but it will get us where we want to go," Jack said before he entered the dark and foul-smelling passage.

They wandered through the underground of the city for hours by torchlight before coming to a series of stairs. Periodically, they were slowed by locked grates but Jack was able to open them relatively quickly each time. Stairs took them upwards into the bowels of the central plateau until they came to an entirely different level of passageways that ran under the palace. Jack navigated without hesitation or error and finally brought them to a ladder.

"The hatch at the top of this ladder will open to the palace servants' passageways. From there the throne room is not far. It will probably not be guarded, since it's rarely used. We should be able to slip in before anyone knows we're here." Jack paused and cleared his throat. "May I ask what your plan is once we reach the throne room?" Anatoly nodded to echo Jack's question.

Anger was still slowly bubbling in the pit of Alexander's stomach. Anger at the burden of duty and responsibility that had been placed on his life, anger at the cost to his family, anger at the very existence of Prince Phane and all that he stood for. Alexander set his pack down and took out the finery he'd worn at the banquet in Glen Morillian. He took off his traveling tunic and cloak and donned the midnight blue tunic and cloak with the fine silver filigree. Then he checked his sword to make sure it was loose in its scabbard. Only after he'd changed clothes and cinched the straps of his pack did he answer. His companions were all watching him when he stood and faced them.

"I plan to take the authority that has been so rudely thrust upon me," he said quietly but with intensity and an undercurrent of anger. "I plan to claim the throne. I plan to demand that the Regent bow to my authority and kiss my ring."

Anatoly raised an eyebrow. The old man-at-arms understood anger. He could see it dancing in Alexander's gold-flecked eyes. He was also his protector and he had a duty to question decisions made in anger. "If the Regent refuses?" he asked.

Alexander smiled with absolutely no humor. "You'd better be ready to fight." He held Anatoly's eyes for just long enough to see that his old mentor understood his resolve before turning to Jack. "And you'd better be ready to talk." Jack nodded.

He looked to his sister and Isabel. "Are you with me?"

Abigail snorted derisively as she slung her bow across her back. "What do you think?"

Isabel put her hand on his chest and looked him in the eye without a word. Her eyes were so beautiful, so filled with intelligence, and so fierce all at once. He gently took her hand and kissed the inside of her wrist before turning to the ladder and starting his ascent.

It was a long climb, easily forty feet or more. At the top was a little platform off to the side with a much shorter ladder leading up to the trapdoor. He didn't hesitate. When he lifted the heavy wooden door, he saw that it opened in the floor of a long, dimly lit, bare stone corridor. He raised the door farther and climbed into the hall, carefully laying the door onto the floor to avoid making any noise. The hall looked to be exactly what Jack said it was. It was unadorned and purely functional, yet clean and frequently used.

In short order, they were all up the ladder and into the little passageway. Jack took only a moment to orient himself before leading the way down the hall. He led them around a few twists and turns before stopping at a large door.

"Here we are. This is one of the servants' entrances to the throne room. From the looks of it, the room is dark," Jack said, lifting a taper from the glass-enclosed candle sconce on the wall next to the door. He eased the door open gently to a quiet room that had the look and feel of a place that hadn't been used in a long time.

Jack held the candle high and strolled in. The room was big, probably fifty feet wide and a hundred feet long. The arched ceiling was easily fifty feet high at the apex. At one end was a raised dais of white marble shot through with black. Each of the five steps was a half circle that met the back wall. In the center of the dais was a large, ornately carved, jewel-encrusted, gold throne. To each side was a chair of lesser size but equal ornamentation. Behind the throne was a heavy, red velvet curtain that hung from a brass rail twenty feet up on the wall. Sewn into the curtain in gold thread was the crest of Ruatha.

High-backed, heavy wooden chairs lined the long sides of the room with ornate brass sconces holding finely crafted oil lamps above them. Between each sconce hung a rich and vibrantly colored tapestry depicting scenes from the distant past. The floor was pure white marble polished to a mirror shine and covered with a thin layer of dust. Running from the base of the dais down the center of the room to the large double doors at the far end was a plush, deep-red carpet with gold embroidery along the edges. All in all, it was about what Alexander expected a throne room to look like.

Jack began lighting the lamps along the wall with his taper. As the lamps brightened the room, the colors of the tapestries stood out in contrast to the simple white of the floor.

"All right, we probably don't have much time. Isabel, I want you in the chair to the right of the throne, and make sure that medallion your father gave you is visible. Abigail, you take the chair to the left. Both of you keep your bows handy. Anatoly, I want you to stand just to the left of Abigail. Jack, you will be just to the right of Isabel."

Alexander strode to the throne and inspected the area. He looked behind the heavy red and gold curtain and saw that it hung a good three feet from the wall and concealed a door as well as a heavy iron bar leaning against the wall. He dropped the bar into place to prevent anyone from entering the room through that door. That left the double doors at the other end of the room and the servants' doors in the middle of each long wall.

When he saw the heavy, red, rope pull cord that blended in with the curtain, he almost laughed. "Jack, is this a bell?"

Jack nodded, "It sounds the bell in the palace tower to put all on notice that the King is in court and will hear the petitions of the people. That bell hasn't tolled in a very long time."

"Huh, I was wondering how I was going to get the Regent to come to me," Alexander said as Jack lit the last lamp. The room was now brightly lit and even with the thin coating of dust on every surface, the place looked important.

Alexander slapped the dust from the thick red cushion on his new throne and took a seat. Isabel and Abigail were a little more hesitant.

"Alexander, I'm not royalty," Isabel said a little uncertainly. "It's not right for me to sit on the queen's throne. Maybe it would be best if I stood."

Alexander shook his head. "No. I need you to sit and I need you to look like it's the most natural thing in the world. You are a Princess of Glen Morillian by birth and my betrothed, are you not?"

Isabel looked a little flustered. "Glen Morillian doesn't have princesses," her face reddened a little, "but I have accepted your courtship," she said with a genuine smile.

"Then you will be the Queen of Ruatha. Take your throne," Alexander commanded gently but seriously.

Her eyes widened at the realization of everything her feelings for Alexander actually meant. She started to say something but thought better of it and nervously sat down on the queen's throne.

Abigail stood looking at her brother with a look that said he was getting into trouble again.

"Well, what are you waiting for?" He motioned for his sister to take the throne on his left.

"I'm not royalty. I'll stand, thank you very much." She was looking less and less enthusiastic about this whole plan.

Alexander smiled at his sister's discomfort. It took a lot to rattle Abigail, and Alexander had no intention of letting her off so easily. "You are Lady Abigail Ruatha, Princess of the Isle of Ruatha by blood." He smiled broadly at the look of dismay that spread across her face.

"I am not!" she said hotly. "Just because you've got that mark on your neck doesn't make me the princess of anything."

Jack interceded gently, "I'm afraid it does, Abigail. Alexander is the rightful King of Ruatha. As his sister, you are Princess." He shrugged apologetically at the glare she directed his way.

"See, you're a princess, so sit on the throne and try to look royal." Alexander gave her his best "gotcha" smile. She returned a look that said the conversation wasn't over but took her seat, anyway.

Alexander let all mirth drain away and found the anger that he'd been saving for this moment. When he spoke next he was deadly serious.

"When those doors open, you are the Queen of Ruatha," he said to Isabel. She nodded almost imperceptibly. "And you are the Princess of Ruatha," he said to his sister. She held his gaze without flinching. "Abigail, even if you don't believe it, whoever comes through that door has to believe it or we're all dead." Her gaze faltered a little.

"We have to convince the whole world that we are the rightful rulers of Ruatha. If we can't do that, then everything is lost and Phane will win." He looked at Abigail for her buy-in.

She pursed her lips and nodded. Then she unbraided her long silvery hair, fished a brush out of her bag and started brushing out the trail dirt. "If I'm going to be a princess, I might as well try to look like one."

Isabel frowned a little and followed her lead. She seemed a bit flustered, but offered Alexander a warm smile just the same when he put his hand on her shoulder to comfort her while she worked the knots out of her rich chestnut-brown hair.

"Looks like we're about ready. Jack, would you do the honors?" Alexander asked, motioning to the bell pull that hadn't been pulled in so very long.

Jack took hold of the heavy red rope and looked to Alexander for one last confirmation. He nodded. Jack took a deep breath and held it as he pulled hard. The peal of the bell reverberated through the stone of the palace. Jack pulled again and then again. The bell rang out loud and clear, sending the message to everyone in the city of New Ruatha that the King had returned.

Chapter 45

The ringing of the bell faded slowly, leaving only deathly silence behind. Alexander held his breath and strained to listen for the sound of people approaching. For just a moment his courage began to falter. He knew he was trapped if things didn't go well. If they had to fight, they might not survive. Then he thought of Darius, and the anger he'd been nursing all night blossomed within him. He grabbed hold of it with his mind and held onto it for the courage it gave him. He breathed slowly and deeply, trying to remain calm while keeping his anger-fueled courage in force.

He heard the sound of boots in the distance, and the calm of having a set course washed over him. It was a surreal feeling. He sat on the throne of Ruatha, his sword leaning against the right armrest, and waited. He could feel the tension. Even Anatoly seemed nervous but he stood his ground, leaning on his war axe.

Alexander had been thinking about his magic while they traveled through the dark of the underground passages beneath the palace. He'd come to believe that it would provide him with the strength he needed to meet any challenge. His experience at the edge of the forest had given him a sense of faith in it. He didn't understand how to use it yet but it had provided the warning that saved their lives. Alexander felt an all-encompassing confidence settle over him. If there was a fight over the throne, he did not fear it. His magic would provide the edge he needed.

As he voiced his newfound certainty within his own mind and felt the sureness of true faith, a subtle change came over him, like a piece of a puzzle snapping into place. His awareness of the room became clearer, more intimate, and more detailed. Things that he couldn't see with his eyes, he could clearly see in his mind's eye. On the screen of his mind he could discern every detail. He could focus his attention on any point in the room and see the details clearly but without taking anything away from his normal vision or his second sight. The sensation was so unexpected and new that he almost forgot where he was and what he was doing.

He sent his awareness into the nooks and crannies of the room to see what he could see. He was surprised to discover the balconies high on each side wall that looked down on the throne room. They were concealed in the darkness. He looked closely at the small places and found details that he made a note to check on later, a scratch on the leg of a chair here and a missing nail there. He had to be sure he could trust his strange new way of seeing and a test was the best way he knew to verify what he saw.

It wasn't like normal vision. It was more like the scene from a daydream, but vivid and clear. He had little doubt the things he was seeing were real. He closed his eyes and still his mind's eye saw clearly wherever he directed his attention. He relaxed the focus of his mind's eye, and the daydream visions faded but the general awareness of the room and the objects and space all around him were still very clear in the background of his awareness. It was as if his mind had aligned itself with the manifestation of the firmament in the immediate area and he could see reality at a deeper and more exacting level than his senses could ever perceive. He noted that he had none of the sensations he'd been told to beware of when looking into the firmament. Other wizards had to be careful when they accessed the firmament lest they become lost in the infinite possibilities it represented. Alexander felt none of that. He simply saw more of his surroundings with his magic than he could with his senses.

The sounds of boots were coming closer. With his mind, he reached out past the door and saw the hallway. A dozen palace guards were running toward the throne room, followed by a smaller group of men in robes. One was clearly the Regent; the others looked like advisors. At least one was a wizard. Alexander realized that he could still see a person's colors through his new vision.

He took a hard look at Regent Cery. The man was just as Jack had described him, competent but not ambitious. He was a man who would rather not have power but didn't trust those around him to wield it with wisdom and fairness. He saw his station as a duty with privileges, not as a right or an entitlement. Alexander felt a weight lift at seeing Cery's colors. His plan hinged on the Regent being an honorable man.

Alexander brought his focus back when the soldiers approached the door. He pulled his cloak collar down a little to expose the mark on his neck and checked his sword. He could see the tension in Isabel but also the firm resolve. Her bow was leaning, string down, against the left side of her throne and her quiver was leaning against the right armrest along with her sword. In just a few minutes she had managed to brush her hair into a lustrous chestnut brown that made her look regal even in Rangers' leather armor.

He smiled a little at the twist of fate that had brought her into his life. Of all the things that had happened to him since that awful day when his brother was murdered, meeting Isabel was the one point of light in a very dark period of his life. The more time he spent with her, the more he loved her. She was strong and smart but those weren't the qualities that most captivated him. She was beautiful in a stunning sort of way. He had to admit that that didn't hurt, but the essential goodness of her nature was what he found almost humbling. She was tough and capable but she was also beautiful at heart. He was drawn helplessly toward that quality most of all.

When the door burst open and a dozen heavily armed men stormed in, Alexander snapped back to the present and the task at hand.

He sat on his throne, leaning his face on his left fist, with his right hand stretched out on the armrest not inches from the hilt of his sword. Both Isabel and Abigail sat straight backed, looking for all the world like they belonged there. All the tension had drained from Anatoly at the very real possibility of a fight. He stood leaning lightly on the hilt of his axe.

The guards flowed in, fanned out into a battle line, and began their approach toward the dais. Alexander watched them come, trying to look disinterested while cataloging their armor and weapons. They wore chain mail, carried small round shields strapped to their left arms, and held spears in their right hands. Each had a sword on his belt. By the way they moved, Alexander knew they had training in the use of their weapons but little actual experience. They advanced to within ten feet of the dais and stopped before their commander stepped forward.

Alexander scanned their colors. Mostly, they were just men doing a job. The commander was unsure of himself but put on a good show of authority. He was even more unsure of Alexander.

"In the name of the Regent of New Ruatha, I command you to surrender and stand trial for trespass." The guard commander spoke forcefully but with an undercurrent of nervousness.

Alexander ignored him and studied the men just entering the room. He could tell that the first was Regent Cery. He was an average-looking man about six feet tall. He wasn't fat but he wasn't slender either. His hair was receding and his neatly cropped beard was white. He wore relatively simple robes and no jewelry except for a heavy medallion with the crest of Ruatha etched in gold on its face.

His retinue consisted of two functionaries, a high-ranking soldier, and a wizard. It was clear from his colors that the wizard had already cast a spell or two, but Alexander couldn't discern the purpose of his magic.

The palace guard stood aside when the Regent approached. He stopped at the base of the dais and just looked at Alexander and his companions with incredulity. It looked like he was trying to make up his mind what to do. Alexander said nothing but gently cleared his throat.

Jack deliberately cleared his throat on cue and bowed slightly to the Regent. A look of recognition creased the Regent's brow at seeing Jack.

"Regent Cery, I am Guild Master Jack Colton, Bard of New Ruatha. It is my great honor to present Lord Alexander, King of Ruatha."

The Regent flinched. His eyes snapped to Alexander while confusion and doubt danced across his face, but Alexander thought he saw something more. He thought he saw hope.

"It has long been foretold that the line of Ruatha would be remade. Lord Alexander has arrived to fulfill that promise. Let it be known far and wide, the King of Ruatha has returned," Jack pronounced in a tone that gave weight to the words.

Alexander held the Regent's eyes. Cery was struggling. New Ruatha had been founded on the promise that the line of Ruatha would one day be remade, but those stories were so old that they had become just stories. Alexander sat up and pulled the collar of his cloak down to give the Regent a good look at the mark burned into his neck.

Regent Cery's eyes got a little wider. The soldiers started to murmur amongst themselves.

"Regent Cery," Isabel said. He had a hard time pulling his eyes away from Alexander. When he looked her way, she tapped the medallion of Glen Morillian hanging around her neck. "My father sends his regards and has authorized me to speak on his behalf. Lord Alexander is recognized as King of Ruatha by the Council of Glen Morillian and the Warden of the Forest. Mage Cedric's promise has been fulfilled."

Cery's doubt was beginning to fade. He looked back to Alexander and studied him for a long moment. He nodded ever so slightly when he made his decision.

"If you truly are the King, then I welcome you home." The Regent spoke with the confidence of long practice at command. "However, I must have unequivocal proof before I will accede to your authority. You are marked as the

legend says you would be, and you have the word of the Forest Warden to support
your claim. These are sufficient cause to welcome you into the palace as an
honored guest but I see that your sword is not the Thinblade. The legend is clear.
The one who will remake the line of Ruatha will wield the Thinblade."

"Master Colton told me you were a cautious man," Alexander said.
"Given my recent experiences, I'm coming to respect caution more and more.
We've been hunted by agents of Prince Phane. The journey has been long and
hard. Your offer of hospitality is most welcome but I must warn you, our enemies
are close on our heels and quite determined. Once they realize that we're here,
they will find a way to attack."

"I see." The Regent took a thoughtful breath and nodded to himself
before turning to his advisors. "General Markos, secure the palace. Assign an
honor guard to our guest and his companions. Handpick your best and most
trustworthy men. Minister Savio, see to the preparation of the guest suite in the
north wing. Coordinate with the general to ensure the entire wing is secure."

Both men nodded, then bowed to Alexander before turning and leaving
the room.

"Perhaps we should adjourn to a nearby meeting chamber," Regent Cery
suggested. "Your rooms will be a few minutes before they're ready and I would be
interested to hear any news you might bring."

"Thank you, Regent," Alexander said as he stood.

His new sight was still alive in the back of his mind. He could still see all
around in his mind's eye while seeing through his normal vision at the same time.
It was a sensation that was going to take some getting used to. Isabel and Abigail
stood with him.

Jack cleared his throat to draw the Regent's attention. "Regent Cery, I
would like to introduce Lady Isabel Alaric, Lord Alexander's betrothed; Lady
Abigail Ruatha, Lord Alexander's sister; and Master Anatoly Grace, Lord
Alexander's champion." Anatoly gave Jack a smirk at the title of champion but the
Regent bowed respectfully to each in turn.

"You are all most welcome. If you have need of anything, please do not
hesitate to ask. Our staff pride themselves on impeccable service and attention to
our guests."

Before he could continue, there was a commotion from the door just
before a large group entered the chamber. The man in the lead could only be the
Guild Mage. Lucky was at his right, with another wizard at his left. Behind them
by only a few paces were a dozen bards led by a broadly smiling Owen.

Mage Kelvin Gamaliel stood a good six and a half feet tall and easily
weighed two hundred and fifty pounds. He was barrel-chested and heavily
muscled with swarthy skin, large powerful hands, and coarse, closely cropped
black hair with a touch of grey starting to show. He wore finely crafted black plate
armor that showed just a hint of red when the light was right and carried the
biggest war hammer Alexander had ever seen. The man to his left was the
quintessential-looking wizard, dressed in ordinary grey robes and walking with a
finely made oak staff shod in silver. Lucky smiled broadly as he entered with the
Mage.

Owen was dressed in the same simple earth tones that he always wore.
His troupe of bards all dressed a little differently and each was distinct. Some wore

finery as if it was their normal attire, while others dressed more simply. Some carried instruments, while others didn't. All of them looked intelligent and inquisitive as they looked around at the details of the throne room, no doubt cataloging everything they saw so they could enrich their stories and songs with intimate detail.

Regent Cery looked resigned at the new arrivals, yet not in the least surprised. The King's Bell had not rung in many centuries. Everyone in New Ruatha would have heard it and would want to know what it meant.

The Guild Mage fixed Alexander with his piercing grey eyes. Alexander could feel the scrutiny as the wizard evaluated him. He didn't waver. He stood his ground and met the Mage with his own gold-flecked golden-brown eyes. The Mage's colors radiated power in a way that Alexander had only seen once before: the man in black. He was now certain that the enemy pursuing him was a mage as well. That knowledge answered one question and replaced it with a more definite threat.

The biggest difference Alexander saw when he looked at Mage Gamaliel was the confluence of different auras. His armor gave off an aura all its own, much less complicated and dynamic than a living aura, but visible nonetheless. His giant war hammer also radiated a clear reddish color. Then there were a number of other items that produced colors all their own. Alexander remembered Lucky telling him that Kelvin Gamaliel was an enchanter. He was a master craftsman who could imbue items with magic. Each item of power he possessed revealed itself to Alexander in the colors it produced. Alexander filed that piece of information away for later use.

A quick survey of the rest of the approaching visitors revealed only the other wizard's staff to be magical in nature. It glowed brightly with a clear soft-blue aura.

Mage Gamaliel took his eyes off Alexander just long enough to nod to Regent Cery. "Good evening, Regent," he said.

Cery smiled politely to the Guild Mage and nodded slightly when the Mage passed and came to the foot of the dais.

He stopped and looked at Alexander very deliberately. Alexander could see the aura of the amulet he wore pulse while the Mage scrutinized him. The room had fallen silent. The tension returned to Anatoly who was equal to the Mage in size but not in power.

"Tell me, Mage Gamaliel, what do you see?" Alexander decided to be bold. Audacity had served him well today.

Realization flickered across the Mage's face ever so slightly. "I would not answer such a question in public." He was not angry or disrespectful but simply matter-of-fact. "May I look more closely at the mark on your neck?" he asked.

Alexander nodded and pulled his cloak collar down to reveal the scar burned into his flesh on the night this ordeal had begun.

Mage Gamaliel strode up to the fourth stair of the dais and leaned over to look at Alexander's neck. "May I?" he asked, quietly requesting permission to touch the mark.

Alexander nodded.

The Mage whispered words in an old and arcane language that Alexander had never heard spoken before, while he placed two fingers on the mark and closed his eyes. A long moment passed. The Mage's eyes snapped open and he looked Alexander in the eye for just a moment before nodding once slightly and turning to face the crowd.

"He bears the Mark of Mage Cedric. The stories of legend are coming to pass."

The room fell silent at his pronouncement. Alexander looked out over the crowd of expectant people. He felt the burden of his duty weigh even heavier under the eyes of so many whose futures depended on his success. It looked to him like they were expecting him to speak but he didn't know what to say. He decided to suggest that they move to a council room, when he caught movement out of the corner of his mind's eye.

It was an odd sensation to see that which he could not have seen. To be aware of things beyond his senses felt unnatural. There was a man on the balcony above and he had a crossbow. He was moving in a crouch and was almost to the low stone wall that served as a railing. From there he would be in position to take his shot.

Chapter 46

Almost in the same instant, Alexander slipped beneath the firmament and saw the play of time in the coming seconds. His awareness floated beneath the surface of the infinite ocean of possibility and watched the firmament unfold into the future. He saw the crossbowman fire, saw the bolt strike him in the chest, and watched himself die. He wound time back in his mind's eye and stepped out of the way. The bolt killed Abigail instead. He wound it back again and saw how time played out in each possible branch of the immediate future. Then he found the only course that would win the day. With a jolt, his awareness returned to the present.

He caught the Mage by surprise or his plan would never have worked. With his left hand he shoved the Mage hard toward his sister. Mage Gamaliel tried to catch his step, but he tripped on the top stair of the dais and fell forward into Abigail, sprawling on top of her. Alexander pulled a knife from the back of his belt and leapt for the floor at the base of the dais. The crossbow bolt missed him by inches and hit hard against the back plate of Mage Gamaliel's enchanted armor. The glass tip of the bolt shattered, releasing a pungent-smelling liquid that did little more than leave a spot on the Mage's reddish-black plate armor.

Everything became clear and simple to Alexander in that moment. He was in a fight and he had a blade in his hand. His focus narrowed down. Everything else in the world fell away. There was only the enemy and the blade. Alexander knew the perfect clarity of a singular purpose.

Sailing through the air, he hurled his knife at the enemy only he could see in the darkness of the balcony above. The blade struck home and the enemy fell backward before Alexander hit the ground. A moment later the crossbow crashed onto one of the chairs lining the wall and clattered to the floor.

The Mage was up quickly, hammer held high and scanning the room with his penetrating vision. Alexander could see the magic of the amulet concealed beneath his armor glowing brightly. The wizard with the staff spoke a word, and a ball of bright bluish-white light streaked from the tip of his staff to the arched ceiling, where it stopped and hovered, brightly illuminating the entire room.

One of the soldiers picked up the fallen crossbow. He looked at it closely for only a moment before turning to the Regent. "Palace issue," he said.

The Regent took a quick breath. He turned to the commander of the guard detail. "Secure the balconies and summon a platoon at once." The commander snapped orders to his subordinates and men started moving.

The Mage was apparently satisfied that the threat was past. He lowered his hammer and held out his hand for Abigail who was still flat on her back and somewhat shaken at having the huge Mage fall on top of her.

"Are you hurt?" Despite his size he spoke gently.

She rubbed her shoulder and winced while she regained her feet. "Nothing that won't mend." She hadn't seen the crossbow or the enemy above and she was mad at being knocked to the floor. "You'd better have a good explanation,

Big Brother," she turned her ire on Alexander.

Before Alexander could defend himself, Mage Gamaliel answered for him. "He does. There was an assassin in the balcony." He pointed to the position the enemy had fired from and then cast about and found the crossbow bolt on the floor. He picked it up, showing Abigail the blunt wooden tip with the remnants of glass affixed to it. "Glass-tipped and filled with poison. You can probably smell it on my armor. In reality, your brother saved your life. By some means that I do not yet understand," he gave Alexander a meaningful look, "Lord Alexander saw the enemy coming. Clearly, he could have simply evaded the attack, but in doing so, the trajectory of the bolt would have carried it into you, so he pushed me into the path, assuming that my armor would protect me." He looked at Alexander again. "Fortunately, his assumptions were correct."

Alexander was astonished. The Mage was observant at a level of detail that Alexander couldn't quite understand and his power of reason was quick and spot on. He understood immediately why Lucky held this man in such high regard.

"Have I missed anything, Lord Alexander?" he asked.

"No. Your account of the attack is correct in every detail, save one. I made no assumptions. I knew with certainty that your armor would hold. I would have found another way had I believed otherwise."

"Later, I would like you to explain how you knew these things." The Mage turned to Regent Cery, who was standing stone still and clearly angry at the breach of security in his palace. "Regent, may we find a more secure location?" he asked gently.

They made their way to a large room with only one door and no windows. The lamps were already lit and platters of breads, cold meat and cheeses with a variety of sauces were already on the table. Clearly the serving staff was quick and efficient.

Alexander took the chair at the head of the table to reinforce his claim to the throne. He knew the Regent would have normally sat there but Alexander wasn't about to show any sign of weakness. He needed this too much. Once everyone was seated at the table, with a few bards sitting in chairs along the walls, Alexander began.

"Regent Cery, Mage Gamaliel, war is coming. Prince Phane is on the march and he intends to consume the whole of the Seven Isles. If he succeeds, the world will fall into darkness and there will be suffering on an unimaginable scale. I have witnessed firsthand the netherworld beasts that are allied with Phane and I know from personal experience that he is without conscience. Life is a toy to him to be trifled with. I've come here to claim the throne of New Ruatha and to unite the Isle of Ruatha under my rule so that I can build an army capable of withstanding the forces Phane will bring to bear against those who love life and freedom."

Alexander had a hundred questions he wanted to ask the Mage but now was not the time. He had too big an audience. Now was the time for broad strokes and sweeping rhetoric.

"I can't fight this enemy alone. I call on all who would see their children grow up free to stand with me. Can I count on your support?" He looked at the Mage first.

Mage Gamaliel looked at him for a moment as if weighing the content of his soul. He spoke softly, yet his voice carried clearly to every corner of the room. "My order has waited for this day for two millennia. The Wizards Guild of New Ruatha was founded by Mage Cedric for the purpose of serving this cause. You are the one he has marked to lead us in this fight. I pledge my support and that of my guild."

"Thank you." Alexander had never meant any two words more. The Mage was a formidable ally. With his backing, Alexander was one very large step closer to reuniting the territories of Ruatha into a nation capable of fielding a real army. He looked to Regent Cery next.

The Regent looked a bit uncomfortable, but he was a man used to making decisions even when he didn't like the options. "Mage Gamaliel has verified the mark and Glen Morillian has recognized your claim to the throne. I will recognize your authority but you must understand that I only speak for New Ruatha and the surrounding lands. Many of those who govern other territories in Ruatha will not recognize you unless you can present the Thinblade. Even then, I doubt Headwater will bow to your claim."

"Thank you, Regent Cery. I will deal with Headwater another day. I would have you retain the duties of Regent of New Ruatha. I don't have time to govern and you are clearly far more capable of it than I. I have only two instructions for the time being. Secure the palace and begin raising an army."

The Regent nodded as an aid came up and whispered in his ear, while placing a knife on the table. "It seems that you killed the assassin. Your knife pierced his heart." Regent Cery handed the knife to Alexander. "Also, your suites are ready."

Alexander felt dead tired. It was well into the morning and he wanted to be clear-headed when he sat down with the Mage. He had so many questions.

Alexander stood. "We'll talk more tomorrow." He turned to the aid. "Please show us to our quarters."

In spite of his fatigue, Alexander couldn't help but feel slightly awed at the magnificent construction and design of the palace as he walked through the labyrinthine hallways. The floors were polished marble in many of the larger halls. Others were covered with rich, thick, artfully woven heavy carpets. Still others were inlaid with thousands of tiny one-inch, multicolored square tiles fitted together so closely that the grout between them wasn't even visible. The tiles spread out in complex patterns or beautifully designed scenes of the city. The walls were adorned with rich colorful tapestries, remarkably detailed paintings that were clearly ancient yet held their vibrant colors flawlessly, and expertly carved woodwork either polished to a sheen or gilded in gold.

Ornate benches, chairs, and small sitting tables were placed along the walls at convenient locations. Elaborate yet functional chandeliers hung from the ceilings of the larger rooms and halls, while polished brass sconces held fine crystal oil lamps along the walls in those passageways where the ceilings were too low to accommodate hanging lamps.

Many of the arched ceilings were adorned with colorful frescos. The ceiling of one hall was painted to appear open to a partly cloudy sky in midspring. Big fluffy clouds broke the light blue of the background and the lamps were placed to make it look as though the clouds moved on the breeze as Alexander walked down the hall. It was a remarkable effect. Another hall's ceiling was done in polished black tile with points of mirror to create the effect of a night sky overhead.

Everything was well kept, in good repair, and brightly polished. Alexander thought the palace must employ an army of servants just to keep it clean. It was much bigger than the palace in Glen Morillian and much more elaborately decorated.

The north wing was the set of quarters reserved for visiting heads of state and it was secured by providing only one entrance. Alexander and his companions made their way up a flight of stairs that opened onto a stone bridge leading across an artificial chasm built into the palace. The bridge ran the fifty or sixty feet across a fall of easily a hundred feet to the courtyards below and it was enclosed in an arched wrought-iron cage set with crystal-clear panes of glass. The lamps lining the glass tunnel were all glowing brightly.

Alexander stopped for a moment to take in the sight. When he looked around, he noticed that there were six guards on a platform just behind the opening in the floor where the stairs came through. All were armed with crossbows and they had a number of long pikes that could easily reach the staircase below. When he looked to the other end of the glowing crystal tunnel, he saw another six guards standing watch over big double doors.

He marveled at the artistry of the enclosed bridge. He could see the lights of the city all around and the stars overhead as he walked down the softly glowing bridge. He took Isabel's hand and she gave him a warm smile while she too marveled at the beauty around her.

When they reached the doors, a young, burly-looking guard with markings of rank on his breastplate bowed to Alexander. "I am Captain Sava, commander of your guard force, Lord Alexander."

Alexander looked at his colors and liked what he saw, so he offered the man his hand. Captain Sava was a little surprised but took it enthusiastically.

"Captain Sava, thank you for taking this duty. I have enemies who are ruthless and cunning. I urge you to take great care in your duty. The enemy will not hesitate to kill your men to get to me. My companions may come and go from these quarters as they please without question or challenge. The Regent and Mage Gamaliel are welcome without invitation. Stop all others who wish to pass and obtain permission for them to enter before allowing them to cross this threshold."

The burly captain bowed. "As you command, My Lord." Then he stood straight and proud and nodded to his men to open the doors.

The suite of rooms was more than Alexander would have expected or ever asked for. The heavy, brass-bound, engraved oak doors opened to a large oval receiving room with a high vaulted ceiling and a brass-railed semicircular staircase winding up along the left wall of the room to the level above and ending in the railed balcony of an open hallway. A giant crystal chandelier hung from heavy chains in the center of the arched ceiling forty feet overhead and filled the room with warm clear light. Large arched passageways led out to the left and right and an even larger archway straight ahead passed under the balcony above. Along the right wall of the oval room were three large, ornately engraved, brass-inlaid armoires each with a cushioned bench resting before it. The floor was a mural of inlaid tiles, each of a different shape and color and each fitted perfectly in an impossibly complex puzzle that produced an image of the Ruathan coat of arms.

The Regent's aid stopped in the middle of the floor. "On your left is a dining room with the servants' entrance. Your staff is quartered in the levels below. There are six trusted servants, all of whom have served in the court for their entire lives. The servant and food preparation areas for this wing are entirely self-contained. The only way for them to leave is through the main door. The door leading to the quarters below can be locked and barred to ensure privacy and security.

"On your right is a council chamber with a meeting table and several writing desks complete with lamps, parchment, ink, quills, and sealing wax for any correspondence you may wish to send. Directly ahead is a sitting room and lounge area with a balcony overlooking the square below. Eight bedchambers line the hall on the second floor. The chamber at the end of the hall to the right has been prepared for you, Lord Alexander. Each chamber has its own water closet with a bath and each has a direct line from the heated cistern in the main palace so our guests can have hot water whenever they like. If you need or want anything, use the pull cord in each chamber to summon the serving staff. If they are unable to fulfill your needs, please make your request to the security staff just outside the door and they will see to it that your wishes are met. May I be of any further assistance?" Minister Savio asked.

"No, thank you, you've been very helpful. Please convey my gratitude to the Regent for his hospitality." Alexander wanted to be polite but more than anything he wanted to sleep.

The aid bowed and left the large entry hall, closing the door on his way out.

Anatoly grunted as he looked around. He put the heavy bar in place on the double doors and set the locking pins into the floor, then gave the door a tug to be sure it was secure. "I'm going to have a look around before we settle in for the night," he said before he went about securing the already very secure suite of chambers.

Alexander wearily climbed the stairs and went down the hall to his room, saying good night over his shoulder. His room was actually two rooms: a sitting room that doubled as an entry room, and a bedchamber. Alexander barred the door and took a quick look around to make sure he was alone before undressing and quickly washing the trail grime away. He was asleep before his head hit the very fluffy goose-down pillow.

Chapter 47

He woke to daylight peeking through the cracks around the edges of the heavy curtains. He got up and dressed in his full finery. He didn't really like the expensive clothes. They weren't more comfortable than his traveling clothes, but they did convey authority and he still needed to win the loyalty of the people of New Ruatha if they were going to respond favorably to his call to arms.

When he came down the staircase, he heard voices coming from the dining room and found everyone else was up and at the table. The middle-aged serving woman looked nervous when he entered. She'd already brought food for everyone and they were all eating without waiting for Alexander. He smiled to reassure her.

"Good morning," he said around a yawn as he took a seat at the table.

The serving woman bustled up quickly to pour him a hot cup of tea. "Lord Alexander, what would you like for breakfast? The chef can make just about anything you wish."

She seemed eager to please, but Alexander was already surveying the food on the table. There was a platter of fresh-sliced ham, link sausages, and strips of bacon. A large bowl full of steaming scrambled eggs, baskets of hot biscuits, a loaf of bread on a cutting board, and pitchers of juice and milk. It looked like a veritable feast after days of trail rations.

He smiled up at her and her eagerness to please. "What's your name?"

She blinked before answering. "Mrs. Bree, at your service, My Lord," she curtsied.

"Mrs. Bree, what is your first name?" Alexander asked pleasantly.

She stammered a bit before she answered. "Adele, My Lord."

"Adele, this is a wonderful-looking breakfast just the way it is. Please convey my compliments and thanks to the chef."

She beamed at his praise. "I will, My Lord, he will be most pleased. If there is anything else, you have only to ring."

"Thank you, Adele, I'm sure we'll be fine for now." He smiled at her again before she hurried off to deliver his compliments.

Alexander ate his fill. When he finished, Lucky was still eating biscuits with butter and jam. Everyone else was sitting in the big high-backed chairs, sipping tea and talking quietly about the grandeur of the palace. Isabel had found a simple off-white dress and a green ribbon for her hair. Abigail was wearing a similarly cut powder-blue dress. From the clean luster of their hair, both had clearly taken advantage of the hot bath in their rooms.

Alexander looked at his sister and considered teasing her. She didn't usually wear a dress. He knew she was much more comfortable in riding gear or simple work clothes. When she saw the mischief in his eyes, she beat him to it.

"You're the one who said I have to pretend to be a princess," Abigail said. "I might as well look the part. Besides, the serving staff was kind enough to stock my room with a number of dresses that fit quite well. I wouldn't want to disappoint them."

Alexander just smiled. He was glad to see that she could still be lighthearted and enjoy the moment, even after the terrible ordeal of losing their brother and their home and their quiet life on the ranch.

He turned to Isabel and took in her simple beauty. He couldn't decide if the fabric of her dress had a hint of green woven into it or if it was just the vibrant color of her eyes that created the effect. Either way, she was stunning. He took her hand and allowed himself to get lost in her piercing green eyes for a moment.

"You look amazing," he whispered softly. He pulled his attention away from her with an effort but kept hold of her hand.

"We have a lot to do before we leave for Blackstone Keep. I feel like I've slept away half the day," he said to the rest of the table.

"That's because you have," Abigail said teasingly.

He gave her a look in return but couldn't help smiling just a little at the jibe.

"We've accomplished the most important objectives I had for coming here," Alexander went on. "The Regent has recognized me as King, and Mage Gamaliel has pledged his support. I still need to talk with him about my magical calling and I'd like to confer with the Regent about the state of his military and what we can expect going forward. What else should we try to do before we leave?"

"We should have riders take word of your arrival to all of the territories and demand their allegiance. Some will comply on the strength of your claim and the legend alone. Others will resist, but at least we'll know where we stand," Anatoly offered.

"I can also send out bards to tell your story, but I'll need to spend some time with a number of my best to teach them the story and the songs I've written," Jack suggested. "I was hoping to do that this afternoon."

Alexander nodded his agreement. "Good, the sooner we spread the word, the sooner we can be ready for Phane."

Isabel squeezed his hand to get his attention. "The man in black and his giant friend have arrived in New Ruatha with Rangle," she said. "I've had Slyder watching them for most of the morning. It looks like they're making inquiries about your whereabouts but they've stayed well clear of Guild Row. It seems that they don't want the attention of the wizards or the bards."

"Phane seems to think that guy is more dangerous than a pack of nether wolves," Alexander said. "He makes me nervous. Keep an eye on him for me?"

Isabel nodded just as there was a loud knock at the door. Anatoly stood with his axe in hand. Alexander hadn't noticed the big man-at-arms' war axe leaning against the wall behind his chair, but it didn't surprise him.

"I'll get it," he said, taking his axe with him and heading for the door.

Anatoly came back from the entry hall with Regent Cery and Mage Gamaliel.

Alexander stood to greet them. "Good morning. We were just discussing our next moves. Please sit. If you're hungry, we have more food than we could possibly eat."

Regent Cery smiled at that and nodded with satisfaction. "I'm happy to see my staff is taking good care of you," he said, taking a chair.

Mage Gamaliel sat across from Lucky. "Looks like Master Alabrand is pleased with the food as well. High praise to your chef, Regent."

Lucky smiled through a mouthful of biscuit at his mentor and nodded happily. Alexander always marveled at how content Lucky was when presented with a good meal.

He took a deep breath and collected his thoughts. "We have much to discuss and a number of important things to do before we're on our way."

The Regent looked startled. "Where would you be going? You've only just arrived and you say your enemies are hunting you. Wouldn't you be safer here?"

Alexander nodded. "Possibly, but there are things I must do and sooner would be better than later." He deliberately withheld their ultimate destination. He felt he could trust the Regent but he was learning the value of caution. Information was power and the less others knew about his plans, the less chance the enemy had of discovering them.

"Regent, I'd like for Master Grace to look over your military and talk with your commanders. I need to assess your military strength, organization, and capability. Anatoly has far more insight into the workings of an army than I do and I trust his judgment."

"Of course, I will instruct General Markos to provide Master Grace with anything he requires."

"Master Colton needs a place to meet with his bards." Alexander wanted to get his plan in motion. His urgency to get to Blackstone Keep was building. "Can you have your aids make arrangements for a secure location, preferably out of anyone's earshot?"

Cery nodded again. "Minister Savio will see to your needs, Master Colton."

Alexander took a deep breath before he began with his chief concern. "Phane is currently in Karth. He's taken command of the Reishi Army Regency and is waging war on the House of Karth. When he's done there, he'll likely solidify his hold on Karth and consolidate his army. At that point, I expect he'll send envoys to all of the islands and demand their surrender. Some will bow to his demands out of fear or greed. Those that do will bolster his army's numbers. Those that don't will become his next targets. He knows I'm here and he fears me, or at least he fears what Mage Cedric has set in motion through me. I suspect he'll attack Ruatha next. I intend to draft letters to each of the Ruathan territories and demand their allegiance, so I'll need couriers to carry those messages."

"You'll have them," Regent Cery assured Alexander.

Alexander leaned forward a little. "Can you tell me anything about the man I killed last night?"

The Regent looked a bit uncomfortable at the question but he answered forthrightly. "He was a member of the palace guard and has been for many years. We tried to find his wife and two children to question them but their quarters were empty. I personally questioned his captain. He had no explanation for the attack and we could not determine where he got the glass arrowhead filled with poison. I must admit, the whole incident is quite troubling and somewhat of a mystery to me."

Alexander sat back, taking a deep breath as he thought about the news. "I suspect the enemy has his family. Redouble your efforts to find them and be gentle when you do. If the man did what he did to preserve the lives of his wife and children, then I want you to make sure they're provided for."

"But he betrayed the palace and tried to kill you. The palace guard must know such a thing is inexcusable." Regent Cery was clearly angry about the betrayal.

"The man who attacked me is dead," Alexander said. "That's punishment enough. If his family was abducted and used for leverage, then they bear no guilt for his crime. I will not have them punished for being held hostage and losing their father and husband. If and when you find them, I wish to speak with them. They may have information about the enemy that could be useful."

"As you wish, Lord Alexander, but you are far more generous than many others would be under similar circumstances," the Regent said.

"Perhaps, but the way I see it, these people and I have something in common. We've both lost someone we love to the enemy." Alexander held the Regent with his glittering, gold-flecked eyes for a moment to drive home the point. When the Regent nodded, Alexander took a deep breath and changed the subject. "I think that's everything we needed to get done for the moment. Right now I need to speak with Mage Gamaliel." Alexander looked around the room.

"Actually, there are a couple of other items we need to discuss," Regent Cery said. "The local council of petty nobles will expect you to address them before they agree to support your claim to the throne. Technically, I speak for New Ruatha but on matters of such importance, they will want to have a say, even if only for show. As you can imagine, your presence has created quite a stir in the ranks of the politically minded. Many fear you will diminish their power. Others believe that the best course is negotiation with Phane. Yet others are skeptical of your claim to the throne. The first step to securing their allegiance will be to address the council and present your expectations of them and your intentions going forward."

Alexander sighed. He hated formal settings and wanted nothing to do with a council meeting, but he understood the necessity of winning over the petty nobles. "Very well, I'll meet with them later this afternoon. You spoke of something else?"

The Regent and the Mage shared a look before the Regent spoke. "Yes, a large number of people have gathered outside your balcony. They are awaiting your appearance and I suspect they will remain until you show yourself."

Alexander frowned. He chided himself for not anticipating something like this. These people had lived with the legend of his arrival their whole lives. His presence, especially after the warning spell alerting everyone to the awakening of Phane, was bound to draw attention. And he hadn't been terribly subtle in the throne room.

He sighed as he stood up. "All right, I should go make my appearance so we can get to work."

Alexander stepped out onto the balcony from the large, very plush sitting room and saw the black granite mountain off in the distance that was Blackstone Keep. He'd never seen the old home of the wizards before and the sight made his heart beat a little faster. It was a long way off but even at this distance he could see it was a magnificent fortress that could only have been wrought with magic.

He took a step toward the low stone wall that served as the railing for the balcony and his heart began to beat even faster when he saw the throng below. He reached the railing and looked down a hundred feet to the large square and was shocked speechless. He'd never seen so many people all in one place in his whole life. There must have been thousands. A ripple of excitement coursed through the crowd, followed by a hush that made Alexander start to sweat. All these people were here to see him. The full weight of his burden settled squarely on his shoulders. Every soul in the square below expected him to protect them from Phane and the war he was bringing to the Seven Isles. Alexander almost faltered at the thought of all these people's futures hinging on his decisions and actions. He had to remind himself to breathe. The Regent came up on his left and the Mage on his right.

"Slip this on your finger and the crowd will be able to hear you clearly, even from here." Mage Gamaliel held out a simple gold ring. "It's a little trinket I created to help my voice carry in large gatherings." He shrugged, "Comes in handy from time to time."

Alexander swallowed hard and slipped the ring on his finger. He felt a tingle of magic race over him. The Mage nodded for him to begin.

"Prince Phane Reishi has returned to wage war on the Seven Isles." He paused for a moment to let the ripple of apprehension that flowed through the crowd die down. "Mage Cedric made preparations for this day. One of those preparations was to place the Ruathan bloodline into hiding so that an heir to the throne could step forward and lead you in this fight. Today, I stand before you to fulfill his promise." When he paused, a cheer rose from the mass of people below. The stories they had grown up with were coming alive right before them.

Once the noise died down, Alexander continued. "The days and months ahead will be marked by hardship and sacrifice. As we speak, Phane is waging war on the House of Karth. When he has consolidated his forces, he will likely come here. We must be ready. I call on the people of Ruatha to unite in common cause against Phane. If he succeeds, your children will never know the taste of freedom."

The crowd had grown quiet in rapt attention.

"I have instructed the Regent to begin assembling an army. Before this is over, we will need every soldier we can get to fight this war. Do not think you will be able to leave the sacrifice to others. Everyone in the Seven Isles will become entangled in this conflict before the future is decided. If we do not stand together, then the future is lost."

Alexander paused again and surveyed the crowd. They were as silent as a graveyard. He had just pronounced a sentence on their lives. The trepidation and uncertainty was palpable.

"I give you this pledge: I will give everything that I have and everything that I am to protect you and yours." He waved to the crowd, then turned away from the railing, walked back into the sitting room and handed Mage Gamaliel his ring.

Jack nodded thoughtfully. "Not bad. You sowed the seeds of a call to action that I can definitely work with."

Alexander was three steps into the plush sitting room when the crowd erupted in a roar. The sound was deafening. It swelled up from the square below and washed into the room and over Alexander like a force of nature. He could feel the reverberations of thousands of voices raised to their peak in unison, every one of them proclaiming solidarity with his cause and purpose. He remembered Jack's words: A mass of people united in a common purpose was more powerful than magic. He hadn't quite understood that before now. He turned to look over his shoulder at the bard. Jack gave him a knowing wink and a nod as he stood in the wake of the fading roar, soaking it in and reveling in the unrestrained power of it. He had an odd, wistful smile on his lips as if something long hoped for and much dreamed about had come to pass.

He walked past Alexander and gave him a friendly clap on the shoulder, whistling as he went. "I'll be with my bards." There was a renewed spring in his step.

Chapter 48

"I agree with Master Colton, Lord Alexander," Regent Cery said. "Your speech was well done. The people now have hope and direction. It's what they need for the moment. Since Phane awoke, there's been fear and uncertainty in the streets. Your words have gone a long way to turn their feelings into resolve and determination. I suspect Master Colton will use your words as a basis for his songs and stories. Within a few days all will know what you have said here today."

Alexander didn't react at first. He felt the burden weigh even heavier now that he had thousands of people entrusting their future to him. "If I gave them what they needed today, then I am glad for that, but my words won't win this war. There will come a time, all too soon I fear, when their enthusiasm will be dampened by blood." He slumped down onto a comfortable couch with the sound of the crowd far below murmuring in the background as they discussed the momentous events of the day.

"Regent, if there's nothing else too pressing, I'd like a chance to speak with the Mage. Please make the necessary arrangements for Anatoly and Abigail to see your military."

Regent Cery bowed slightly, "Of course, Your Majesty."

There was that title again. It always felt like he should look over his shoulder for someone wearing a crown when he heard it. What cruel tricks the world could play.

Mage Gamaliel took a big chair opposite the couch. Isabel sat next to Alexander while Lucky closed the doors to the balcony to shut out the noise of the people outside.

Isabel looked at him for just a moment before she kissed him on the cheek and whispered in his ear, "You did a good thing for the family of that guard who tried to kill you. I'm proud of you."

He gave her a smile in return and took her hand as Lucky settled comfortably into the chair next to the Guild Mage.

"Lord Alexander," Mage Gamaliel began, but Alexander cut him off with an upraised hand.

"Just Alexander, please. Titles are useful for getting nobles to do as they should, but little else."

Mage Gamaliel paused for a moment before a broad smile spread across his face and then he laughed from his belly. "Very good, I'm Kelvin," he said. "Since we've met, you've used your magic twice. The first time you saw that I was looking at you with the power of my amulet of seeing." From inside his shirt, he withdrew the beautifully crafted amulet made of gold and platinum wrought in the likeness of a human eye and held it out for Alexander to see. "The second time you saw a threat before it could be seen. Yet I did not see you cast a spell in either instance."

Alexander had waited for this moment for a long time. He had so many questions that he didn't know where to start, so he decided to start at the beginning. "Since I was a child, I've been able to see the living aura of people, animals, even plants. Before the mana fast, I had to concentrate to make it happen. Now it's just a part of my vision. Magic also produces an aura that I can see. When you entered the throne room, I saw the aura of your enchanted items, and when you looked at me with your amulet, its aura pulsed with power."

Kelvin leaned forward with interest. "You say your ability to see a living aura is constant?"

Alexander nodded.

"You didn't cast a spell to bring the effect about?" Kelvin asked.

Alexander shook his head. "In fact, that's one of the things I wanted to talk to you about. I can't seem to cast even the simplest spells. I worked with Mason Kallentera and with my parents but I was unable to even establish a connection to the firmament in the way they instructed me."

This was the crux of the matter. If he was to have any chance against Phane, he needed to understand his calling. He needed to be able to wield magic.

"Yet you're able to sustain a constant aura-reading spell." Kelvin mused as he sat back in his chair looking up in thought.

Alexander sat forward expectantly but didn't interrupt the Mage. He had to remind himself to breathe.

"I have never encountered a wizard such as you. You took the mana fast recently, yes?" Kelvin asked.

"At Glen Morillian. Mage Cedric left Wizard's Dust for me in the Bloodvault," Alexander replied.

Kelvin looked a bit startled but recovered quickly. "We'll come back to the Bloodvault later. Did you feel a connection to the firmament at the completion of the fast?"

"I suppose so. It was like my awareness and the firmament became one and the same for just a moment and then I was back in my body again."

"That's odd. Most wizards describe the moment when they first look into the firmament as a vast void of limitless, unformed possibility that is distinctly separate from their consciousness. I've never heard anyone describe his initial connection to the firmament the way you have. Aside from the aura reading, have you experienced any other manifestations of magic?"

"Yes. I've had two instances of clairvoyance. Twice, I've seen a few moments into the future, and I can also see anywhere nearby me with my mind's eye," he said matter-of-factly and without embellishment.

Isabel's hand tightened on his. The Mage looked astonished and Lucky sat forward at hearing the news. The room fell silent for a moment before Lucky spoke.

"You've seen into the future? When did these instances happen? What did you see?" Lucky asked.

"The first time was in the woods when Truss attacked. I had the sensation that I was floating beneath the firmament, watching reality unfold. Then time sped up and I saw what was going to happen. I saw Truss and his men come around the thicket and attack with a volley of crossbow bolts. We were caught in the open. The battle didn't go well for us in my vision. When I snapped back to the present, I called out for everyone to take cover and we avoided the crossbow volley."

"I wondered how you knew the enemy was upon us, but I didn't think to ask at the time. The ramifications of your vision into the future are a thing to ponder. You say it happened a second time?" Lucky asked.

The Mage was sitting on the edge of his seat again.

"The second time was in the throne room. That was when the all around sight first manifested. I found that I could send my vision to any place nearby and see true detail clearly in my mind's eye. I discovered that when I relax this new vision I can see all around me as if my peripheral vision was impossibly extended. It was with this new vision that I first saw the guard on the balcony.

"Before I could react, I slipped beneath the firmament and watched the coming moments unfold. I could see the outcome of his attack. It's like time doesn't pass there and I can control the flow of things, so I played out the next few moments a number of times. I tried to dodge the bolt and saw it kill Abby. I held my ground, and it killed me. I tried to deflect it, and it killed me again. Over and over I played out the coming attack in my mind until I found the course of action that I took. That's how I knew the arrow wouldn't penetrate Kelvin's armor. It was like imagining the future, only with a terrifying sense of certainty that I was seeing the actual flow of events rather than just the product of my imagination."

Again the room fell deadly silent. Lucky and the Mage stared at Alexander with awe and disbelief.

"I…" Kelvin began and stopped. He looked out the window for a moment before taking a deep breath. "I'm not often rendered speechless." He shook his head. "Alexander, I've never heard of such a thing," Kelvin said when he found his voice. "I don't doubt you, but I'm not sure I can help you either." He closed his eyes as if trying to assimilate his new understanding of reality and finding it difficult to reconcile with all he'd known his whole life.

"Let me begin by restating the facts. You've been able to read a living aura since you were a child but it required concentration. Once you survived the mana fast, the ability became a constant part of your vision. You've had two clairvoyant experiences. You've had two precognitive experiences, and you can see your surroundings in your mind's eye at will." He looked to Alexander for confirmation.

Alexander nodded. It reminded him of how his father always started solving a problem by stating the facts.

"What did you see with your clairvoyance?" Kelvin asked.

"The first time, I saw Phane in the council chamber of the Reishi Army Regency in Karth. The second time, I saw the road through the forest at the point of an ambush set for me by the Reishi."

Again Kelvin was speechless, but only for a moment. "How can you know it was Phane you saw? And how do you know it was Karth?"

"I described the crests on the breastplates of the eight military leaders in the room to Wizard Kallentera and he said it was the crest of the Reishi Army Regency. As for knowing it was Phane," Alexander shrugged, "he saw me there. He said he could see that the nether wolves he'd sent to kill me had failed, but what he sent next would succeed. That's when I came back."

Mage Gamaliel looked alarmed. "Did he say anything else? Anything at all?"

"He said, 'You don't even know what you are, but I do,' and then he laughed," Alexander replied.

Kelvin took a deep breath and let it out slowly. "When you touch the firmament, do you feel a sense of boundless rapture and infinite possibility?"

Alexander shook his head. "I don't feel rapture. I don't feel like I'm going to get lost in it like I've been told I'm supposed to feel. When I'm there, I'm in complete control, like the firmament is just an extension of my mind and consciousness."

Kelvin sat back and closed his eyes again. When he opened them, Alexander could see he was at a loss.

"Other wizards have created spells that would let them see a living aura, see at a distance and even see into the future, but they were all very accomplished wizards who'd spent their lives in pursuit of knowledge and mastery of the firmament. The sheer distance of Karth is beyond any clairvoyance spell I've ever heard of, and a precognition spell is virtually worthless because it takes a great deal of time to cast in exchange for a glimpse of only moments into the future. Most wizards don't even bother learning such a thing. All around sight is a known spell as well, but it also takes several minutes to cast and only lasts for a few minutes at best. It seems you have power like nothing else I've ever heard of and yet you can't consciously make contact with the firmament or cast even the simplest novice spells." He shook his head. "I will assign every scholar in my guild to research every book in the library for any hint or mention of one such as you. If Phane knows of your calling, then others may as well. There's bound to be some mention in the old records."

Alexander felt deflated and tired. He had hoped that the Mage would be able to reveal how his calling worked and how he could put his magic to use, but it was just as much of a mystery to him as it was to Alexander.

"Thank you, Kelvin. Anything you learn on the subject would be of interest to me."

Kelvin frowned. "Be cautious. Your calling has not manifested in a way that I'm familiar with, but there can be no question that the power at your disposal is great. Practice those capabilities you are aware of with deliberate intention. Keep a journal of your progress. Any time you experience something new, go slowly. Record everything you can recall about the experience: your mindset at the time, the circumstances surrounding you at the moment, your mood and feelings, everything. Details are important. Pay special attention to your feelings. Control of emotion is one of the things a wizard must spend a great deal of time mastering in order to withstand the allure of the firmament. People are motivated by emotion and that is where the firmament becomes so dangerous. It can flood our senses with such intense feeling that we lose our grasp on reason. Just because you haven't had this kind of connection to the firmament doesn't mean you can't or won't."

That was a possibility that Alexander hadn't considered. It hit him like a slap in the face. He was so worried that his calling was different from other wizards and now, suddenly, he was afraid that the firmament might represent the danger he'd always been warned about. Alexander felt doubt and confusion swirl through him. He needed the magic desperately, yet it was just out of reach in the murkiness of the unknown. For one terrifying, fleeting moment, he felt all certainty slip away and leave him with nothing but doubt and ambiguity. He nodded numbly, only dimly aware that he was doing so as he groped for something of substance, something solid and real that he could be sure of. Isabel squeezed his hand and leaned forward in concern at the glazed look in his eyes.

He snapped back to the present, leaving those things he could not be certain of in the dark recesses of his mind and filling his consciousness with things he knew to be real. Isabel was real. The look of loving concern in her piercing, crystal-clear green eyes was real. His duty, although unasked for, was real as well. Magic or not, he had to find a way to protect the future from Phane.

He gave Isabel's hand a gentle squeeze in return and offered a slightly forced smile for her concern. With grim resolve he accepted the facts of reality. He had to deal with the truth of the situation and make do with that. His magic was unreliable and there was no one who could teach him how to make it useful, except himself. No amount of wishing for the world to be different would cause it to miraculously change. He had to deal in what is.

Alexander stood and walked to the balcony doors to stare out at the charcoal-black silhouette of Blackstone Keep in the distance. He hadn't found everything he was looking for in New Ruatha but he'd done well enough for now. He reminded himself that this was just a stop on the way to his real goal—the dark and foreboding fortress mountain looming over the horizon.

"We'll be leaving tomorrow," he said when he turned back to face his silent observers.

Kelvin nodded thoughtfully. "Many wizards have tried to enter Blackstone Keep. None have returned, but then none of them had Mage Cedric's ring, either. Was that also in the Bloodvault?"

"Yes, along with a skillbook of the blade and a letter telling me that Blackstone Keep is mine." Alexander paused, considering how much to tell the Mage. "I believe there's another Bloodvault in Blackstone Keep and I believe it contains the Thinblade. I need that sword if I'm going to have any chance of uniting Ruatha."

"What makes you so sure the Thinblade is there?" Kelvin asked. "It's been lost for thousands of years. Some legends say it was destroyed during the Reishi War."

"The skillbook contained a section on fighting with the Thinblade," Alexander answered. "Mage Cedric wouldn't have included that if he didn't intend for me to have the Thinblade as well. The fact that it's been lost for so long makes sense. If Cedric did mean for me to have it, then he would have placed it beyond the reach of anyone looking for it. What better place than his Keep?"

"Your reasoning is sound," Kelvin said. "A skillbook with a chapter on the sword of kings, that is an astonishing find. I never knew such a book existed. May I see it?"

"I left it with Mason and Hanlon. They're going to use the blade techniques in the book as the basis for training the Ranger army that they're building."

Kelvin smiled and nodded his approval. "Good, I'm sure I'll have a chance to study the book another time. Mason will know I'd like to see it and will bring it when he comes with the main force of the Rangers. I have long searched for the secret to enchanting a skillbook; perhaps I can learn something from this one. Have you had a chance to test your new skills?"

"Unfortunately, I have," Alexander said somberly. "I'm very confident in my ability with a blade."

Isabel had been quiet during the entire conversation, but she offered her confirmation. "Alexander saved me from Truss and his battle wizard. I saw him fight and I can say with certainty that there isn't a Ranger alive who could best him in single combat."

"You faced off against a battle wizard? With a blade?" Kelvin looked incredulous, then he shook his head. "You do have a lot to learn about magic. One lesson you almost learned the hard way is never, ever fight a battle wizard on his terms. They're just too fast. How is it that you survived the fight anyway?"

Alexander shrugged. "Lucky's potions. Just before the fight, I drank a potion of warding that kept the battle wizard's spear from hitting me cleanly. Even with that, he was still more than I could handle, especially with his armor and shield, so I tossed a fire potion at him. When he caught on fire, he ran off the cliff."

"You got lucky," Kelvin said sternly. "Battle wizards are a whole different kind of dangerous. If you ever come up against one again, don't chance a fight. Head-to-head in the open, there simply isn't a more deadly kind of wizard."

"I'll keep that in mind," Alexander said. "At the time, I didn't have much choice and, thanks to Lucky, everything worked out, but I understand that he was beyond me even with the power of the skillbook. It was like he had a different relationship to time. When he struck, he moved faster than any man can move."

"That's one of the primary effects of their magic," Kelvin confirmed. "They also strike harder and can make their weapons perform better. Combat is the focus of their magic."

"Are they rare?" Alexander asked.

"Quite, there are only a handful in the entire Seven Isles and only one that I know of has risen to the level of mage. I met him once. He's the General Commander of the Reishi Protectorate." Kelvin paused, giving Alexander a meaningful look. "It's likely that you'll encounter him at some point."

Alexander felt a bead of cold sweat run down his back.

"Describe him."

Kelvin shrugged. "He's not much to look at. He stands about five and a half feet tall, kind of pudgy with a bit of a belly, swarthy complexion with jet-black hair and dark eyes. What I remember most is his reserved confidence. He carried himself like nothing and no one was his equal, not arrogant or egotistical, but like a man who knew he was beyond those around him."

A little of the color drained from Alexander's face. "The man in black. He's here in the city right now. He's what Phane sent when the nether wolves failed. He's been following us since we crossed the road in the forest." Alexander suddenly felt very vulnerable.

Isabel tipped her head back slightly and closed her eyes.

Chapter 49

"Dear Maker! He's outside in the square, looking up at our balcony right now," Isabel said urgently as she stood and hurried to the armoires that held their weapons.

Kelvin was on his feet as well. "How does she know he's here?"

"Her bird. She can see through its eyes when she wants to. I asked her to keep an eye on the people hunting me. We wouldn't have made it here if it wasn't for Isabel and Slyder." Alexander leaned a little to see Isabel around the wall of the archway that led to the entry hall.

She was rushing back into the sitting room with her bow and quiver. She looked so at odds with herself. She was wearing a simple dress that only served to accentuate her natural beauty, but she had a quiver over her shoulder and she was nocking an arrow as she headed for the balcony with a look of grim determination.

Alexander couldn't help smiling at the sight. He'd known Isabel for a relatively short time but he felt such a deep connection to her. He was more at ease in her presence than he would have ever thought possible. Beauty had always flustered him a bit, but she was so much more than beautiful. The nature of her character, the clarity of her mind, and her simple human compassion easily overshadowed her physical beauty.

Kelvin looked alarmed. "What's your intention?" His voice was a bit more forceful than Alexander had heard before.

She didn't stop until she reached the door to the balcony. "I intend to kill him," she tossed the words over her shoulder like the matter was settled. Alexander could see she was looking through Slyder's eyes one more time to fix the enemy's position.

Kelvin took a few quick steps to the door and put his hand against the frame. She looked up at the big Mage with such fierce intensity that he actually took a step back.

"This guy has been chasing us since we left Glen Morillian. He ambushed my brother's company of Rangers and killed a number of good people, many of whom were my friends. He needs to be dealt with and sooner is better than later." She tried to open the door, but Kelvin stopped her again.

"Lady Isabel," Kelvin said, "you will not succeed against this man. Your attack will only serve to alert him to our location. When you attack, he will come for Alexander and we are not prepared to defend against him. Please, do not act rashly."

Isabel faced him defiantly. "He's right out there, standing in the center of the square looking up at this balcony. He already knows we're here. I can get a shot off quickly enough that he won't have a chance and even if I don't get him, I want that bastard to know we're trying to kill him, too!"

Alexander hadn't seen her this angry before. He watched the confrontation for a moment, simply enjoying the intensity of her passion and marveling at her courage. She stood her ground against a mage without batting an eye, all the while demanding that he stand aside so she could pick a fight with another mage.

"Hang on for a second, Isabel," Alexander said before he headed into the entry hall.

He could see with his all around sight that she was looking at him with confused anger while he trotted into the other room. He went to the door first. Six guards scrambled to their feet when he opened it. A young sergeant was commanding the guard detail.

"Send a message to your commander immediately. I want this guard detail doubled at once."

He didn't bother to wait for a response. He closed the door, dropped the bar in place, and went to the armoires. He strapped on his sword and slung his quiver before taking up his bow and nocking an arrow. He locked eyes with Isabel when he entered the sitting room. She gave him a look of such fierce passion that he had to remind himself to breathe.

Kelvin shook his head. "This is unwise. He can only guess at your location for the moment. If you show yourself, he will attack as soon as he can make preparations."

"I've doubled our guard. He'll have to get through two dozen men just to get to our quarters and that's if we don't kill him right now." He looked at Isabel. "We'll move quickly to the balcony, staying low, come up as we draw, take aim and shoot."

She nodded. Determination sparkled in her green eyes.

Kelvin sighed and looked to Lucky for support. Lucky just shrugged and spread his hands. "He's always been stubborn once he's made up his mind."

Kelvin looked helpless. He snorted, then shook his head again. "Very well, but I would have come much better prepared if I'd known you were going to pick a fight with a battle mage. I can't talk you out of this?"

Alexander and Isabel spoke in unison. "No."

Kelvin took a deep breath and let it out slowly. "Very well, let me see your arrow heads," he commanded. When they raised the arrows, he placed a hand on each and spoke softly in a strange language. The spell didn't take long to cast, and Alexander would have doubted that anything had happened if he hadn't seen the way Kelvin's colors swelled and deepened as he spoke.

"This enchantment will make your arrows penetrate most types of armor." He stood looking at them with disapproval but said nothing more.

Alexander and Isabel opened the door just enough to get out and stayed low as they moved to the balcony.

Isabel whispered, "Stay low for a moment. Let me take another look." A few moments later, she nodded. "He and the giant are still standing in the center of the square, looking up at us. Should be an easy shot at this height."

Alexander nodded and they stood in unison, fluidly drawing their bows and taking aim. They released their arrows at the same moment. The shafts sailed through the air and down into the square. They were both on target. Alexander watched the arrows travel to their mark. Only a heartbeat passed, but the man in black stepped aside more quickly than should have been possible. Each arrow passed through the empty space where his torso should have been and drove several inches into the flagstone of the square.

Jataan P'Tal stood with his hands behind his back, looking up at Alexander like he was measuring his worth as an opponent. The big man beside him hadn't flinched or even paid much attention to the two arrows that just missed him by a couple of feet. Instead, the giant smoothly drew a javelin from the extra-large quiver on his back, took a couple of hop steps and hurled the weapon.

Alexander grabbed Isabel and spun out of the way only a moment before the javelin hurtled over the balcony wall and buried into the top of the doorframe.

Alexander and Isabel both drew a second arrow and sent it at the man in black with practiced ease. Again they missed; this time both arrows skittered across the square. And again the giant returned a javelin thrown with such tremendous force that it stuck eight inches into the stone of the wall behind the balcony, just missing Alexander.

"Stick the giant," Alexander said as he drew a third arrow.

Isabel nodded, following his lead. They crouched and moved along the balcony a few feet so they could pop up in a different place from where they'd ducked. When they stood, they saw that their enemies were standing at the edge of the square, well out of arrow range.

The man in black offered a salute to Alexander before he turned and walked casually down one of the streets that led out of the square.

Kelvin came up alongside them with Lucky.

"Well, it looks like you won his respect." The Mage paused, staring down onto the now mostly empty square. "He's still going to try to kill you, though. I'll summon a wizard or two to augment the guard force. Two dozen men aren't enough to stop him."

Alexander looked at him. "You really think he can make it through two dozen men in a confined space like the glass bridge?"

For a long moment, Kelvin didn't answer. "He can kill all of your guards without difficulty. Alexander, I don't think you understand the nature of a battle wizard's power. He's lethal in a fight. If he'd had a ranged weapon, he may well have killed you right here on this balcony."

Alexander thought about how easily the man in black had sidestepped the arrows that would have killed any other man. It was almost as if he could see a moment into the future. He turned and went back inside to the armoire and replaced his bow and quiver but kept his sword. Everyone followed him into the entry hall.

"With your permission, I will accompany you to Blackstone Keep," Kelvin offered.

"I was hoping you would. I'm sure I'll need some help figuring the place out. Kelvin, I want you to know that I don't take your counsel lightly." Alexander motioned toward the balcony and the square beyond, "That may have been ... unwise, but I learned a thing or two about my enemy. We'll leave first thing tomorrow morning and we'll slip out quietly. I'll ask the Regent to announce a banquet in my honor for tomorrow evening to throw off ... what did you say his name is?"

"Jataan P'Tal, General Commander of the Reishi Protectorate."

Alexander smiled at the memory of his childhood lessons. "My father taught me that deception is one of the most effective weapons in existence. Perhaps I can't beat Commander P'Tal in a straight fight, but that doesn't mean I can't outsmart the man. With any luck, we'll be a day ahead of him before he realizes we're gone."

There was a knock at the door. Kelvin was immediately alert and tense. He wheeled on the door and looked intently. Alexander watched the aura of his amulet of seeing pulse with magic as Kelvin looked through the door. He relaxed.

"It's Regent Cery and your friends," he said before he lifted the heavy bar from the door and opened it.

The hall was filled with men. There were groups of six at either end and two more groups of six spaced a third of the way inside each end of the glass-encased bridge. They were all armed with crossbows, short swords, and short spears with long, flat-bladed heads that made them look more like a long knife on the end of a staff than a typical spear.

Regent Cery was accompanied by his court wizard Izar, General Markos, and Minister Savio. Anatoly, Jack, and Abigail were with him. Anatoly looked concerned at seeing so many guards.

"Why the increased security?" he asked.

Isabel answered before Alexander could. Anatoly had been one of his teachers and he'd learned to choose his words precisely when answering Anatoly's questions. The old man-at-arms dealt in reality as it is. He had no time for anything else and wasn't afraid to say what he thought, especially to Alexander and Abigail. More than that, Alexander wanted his mentor to respect him, so he always took care to be precise and accurate, which usually meant taking a moment to choose his words before answering him. Isabel had no such concerns.

"The man in black who's been chasing us is here in the city. He was out in the square a few minutes ago so Alexander and I took a shot at him." She reported the facts calmly and succinctly like she was addressing her commanding officer.

Anatoly stiffened a bit at the news. "I take it you didn't hit him," he said.

This time Alexander answered. "No. Apparently he's a battle mage named Jataan P'Tal and he's the General Commander of the Reishi Protectorate."

Anatoly's face lost a little color. More than anything else, seeing the look on Anatoly's face at the mention of Jataan P'Tal's name frightened Alexander.

"I know who he is," Anatoly said. "If he's here, then we must leave. I've seen the man fight. He fought in the service of Kai'Gorn during the border wars as part of an agreement to allow several operatives of the Reishi Protectorate to serve in a number of important offices in the city. I watched him wade into our forces with nothing but a sword. He killed thirty-four men in just minutes. It broke the spirit of our unit, and the commander ordered a retreat. I've never seen a man move so quickly or with such sudden violence. When he struck, men fell. Alexander, you can't stay here."

"I know," Alexander said. "We're leaving tomorrow morning, first thing. Mage Gamaliel will be coming with us." A bit of the tension eased from Anatoly's face. He nodded his approval.

Alexander turned to the Regent and said, "Regent Cery, I'd like you to announce a banquet in my honor for tomorrow evening as a ruse. Cancel it at the last minute with my apologies."

"Of course, Lord Alexander," Regent Cery said. "I was planning a formal banquet anyway a few days from now. I'll just move some of the preparation up a bit. There is still the matter of the council meeting. The local petty nobles will be assembling in less than an hour. I would strongly advise you to attend. Your presence will solidify your claim to the throne."

The council meeting was about what Alexander expected, a bunch of self-important petty nobles preening and posturing for each other and for Alexander. Each of them tried to sound important without saying anything of consequence and without making any firm commitments. Alexander listened politely for about an hour while each noble pledged his support to him provided he could produce the Thinblade. It seemed that none of them believed he would be able to, so they could be gracious and offer their support while secretly thinking that they would never have to deliver on their promises. He studied their auras and remained impassive while they spoke. He didn't call them out when they lied to him or made conditional promises he knew they had no intention of keeping. Instead, he gave them rope.

He made a mental note of every promise offered and every claim of loyalty to the Ruathan bloodline. He didn't offer anything himself, but simply listened to their long-winded speeches that strung one word after the other without any meaning.

These men lived in a world where the meaning of words was fluid, where there were no absolutes. Everything was a matter of interpretation or opinion. Truth and fact mattered little to them. Power was their stock in trade and it was clear after the meeting that most of them didn't care much how they acquired it. Alexander reminded himself that Phane was more than happy to play off such desires and was in a position to offer these men a great deal in exchange for their allegiance.

By the end of the meeting, he better understood Regent Cery. He was a man who simply wanted a stable and consistent world to live in, and having found others unable or unwilling to provide such a place, took it upon himself to do so for his community.

Alexander could just make out the silhouette of Blackstone Keep through the twilight when he returned to his quarters. He was comforted by the presence of a wizard and two dozen well-armed soldiers guarding the glass bridge.

Isabel and Jack had accompanied him to the meeting while the rest of his party had stayed in their quarters preparing for their journey.

Adele was waiting in the foyer when they entered. "Lord Alexander," she said with a bow, "if you're hungry, dinner can be served any time you like."

Alexander suddenly realized he was famished. He smiled graciously even though he was still a bit irritable from listening to a dozen liars talk for what seemed like hours.

"Adele, that would be wonderful, I'm starving."

She beamed. "I'll begin at once," she said with another bow and hurried off.

Alexander could hear the bustle of a small serving staff bringing food and dishes into the dining room as he took a chair in the sitting room with Anatoly, Lucky, and Abigail.

Abigail smiled with mischief. "How were the nobles?"

He gave her a smirk, "Less than noble."

She chuckled, "Better you than me, Big Brother."

Lucky cracked the shell of a nut from the bowl on the low table in the middle of the room and popped the meat of it into his mouth. "Did you learn anything?"

It was a question that Lucky had asked him countless times during his childhood. Alexander had discovered that upon reflection he could usually pinpoint some detail or element of any experience that broadened his understanding in some way or another. He thought for just a moment before nodding.

"Regent Cery is the right man for the job. None of the other petty nobles in the territory of New Ruatha can be trusted."

Anatoly grunted, "Not surprising."

"How'd your inspection of the military go?" Alexander asked while he fished a nut from the bowl.

"They have about ten thousand heavy cavalry, twenty thousand infantry, and another twenty thousand archers. They're well trained and organized. General Markos is a good commanding officer. His men respect him and he knows his business. Precious few have any battle experience and their equipment is a bit old and worn, but all in all, they'll be a good addition to our forces. I'd like a little time to train them and improve their equipment before sending them into a fight, though." True to form, Anatoly delivered his report succinctly and clearly, without embellishment.

Abigail picked up when he stopped. "I was impressed by their archers. They have a larger bow than I've ever used. It's no good for riding, but on foot it can send an arrow about twice as far as my bow with three times the force. The thing stands a few inches taller than me and the arrows they use are a good six inches longer than the ones we're used to."

"Huh, that could be useful. Are the raw materials to make more readily available?" Alexander asked.

"Yep," she said. "We walked through the trees they use to make them in the northern edge of the forest. I talked to the head bowyer, and he said he could make a thousand a month if he had a hundred men to help him."

"Good, the more the better. I'll talk to the Regent and ask him to make the arrangements to start stockpiling weapons."

Alexander turned his attention to Jack. "How'd it go with your bards?"

"Quite well, actually, they took to the lyrics and music quickly and with enthusiasm. I guess it's to be expected given that this is the biggest story to be told in millennia. I also told them about the wanted posters. Those will be discredited and torn down by week's end," Jack said confidently.

"Sounds like we've accomplished everything we needed to. If we can just lose Commander P'Tal, we'll be in good shape," Alexander mused.

Adele entered tentatively. "Lord Alexander, dinner is served."

Alexander and Lucky stood in unison, both with a smile.

"Thank you, Adele. It smells wonderful, even from here."

They enjoyed a leisurely meal while they discussed strategy and politics. Alexander knew he could win some of the territories over for a time without the Thinblade, but he would need the ancient badge of office that the magical sword represented if he was going to have any chance of uniting the whole island of Ruatha. That meant Blackstone Keep. He started to feel anxious to be on the road again. He felt safe enough here with the heavy guard and the palace secured against any unfamiliar visitors, but he knew it was only a matter of time before the enemy attacked. When they did, there would be death. The best way to prevent that was to deprive them of their target.

After dinner, he walked Isabel to her room and kissed her goodnight. They shared a look of longing and desire. They had agreed to wait until they were married, but sometimes they both regretted that decision.

Alexander looked into her eyes for a long moment. "We'll have all the time in the world," he whispered before kissing her on the forehead.

Her hand slipped from his as he turned and willed himself to put one foot in front of the other. He dared not look back. Once he was in his room, he closed the door and leaned against it like he was holding it shut against an irresistible force.

Chapter 50

He sat down to meditate for a few minutes before bed. He'd decided that he needed to explore the magic available to him more fully. He put a heavy pillow on the floor and got comfortable, sitting cross-legged with his back straight, hands folded in his lap, and eyes closed in the dim candlelight of his sitting room.

He began the deep breathing that Mason had taught him and allowed the tension and stress to drain away. Once he was relaxed, he began the process of quieting his mind. As each thought, worry, or concern intruded, he recognized it, observed it without emotion for a moment, and then dismissed it. Soon his mind was quiet. He drifted in the simple peace of meditation for a time and then found himself adrift in the firmament. He had no location, no point of awareness, and no form. He was one with all.

At first, he felt overwhelming confusion at the cacophony of thoughts and events that inundated him. It felt like the whole of reality was taking place within the theatre of his mind. It was far more than he could see, hear, or understand at one time, so he just observed. He took the mindset of the witness. There was no involvement, no attachment, no emotion, only awareness.

Gradually the flurry of the countless events occurring everywhere at once faded into the background. He started to see the firmament as a whole. A great, living, breathing, dynamic ocean of potential with a wave moving through it that manifested the present moment where it crested. It was constantly moving, shifting, and changing. And it was beautiful, not so much for what it was itself, but for the moment of now that it created and all of the beauty, love, and life that took place in that one precious moment.

Alexander simply observed for a while. His awareness floated on the firmament like an oil slick spread impossibly thin across the whole ocean of potential. The crest of the wave faded into a background music of impossible complexity and beauty. It made his heart soar with the possibilities it represented. And then, quite suddenly, he felt a jolt of fear. Was this the rapture he'd been warned about? Had he lost himself to the endless potential of the firmament?

His awareness slammed back into his body with such force that he lost his balance on the cushion. He stood and paced for a few minutes, trying to remember every detail of the experience. Then he thought of his journal and spent the next several minutes writing. He wasn't sure what value the experience represented but he knew with certainty that he had accessed the firmament.

After giving it some thought, he sat down again and tried to repeat the process. This time it was easier. Only five or ten minutes passed before he again found himself drifting pleasantly in the limitless ocean of potential. This time he had an objective: Phane.

Alexander's awareness was all encompassing and spread out across the firmament. At the moment he focused on Phane, he felt impossible motion and a sensation of shrinking. His point of focus went from the impossibly large to a single point on the crest of the wave that was reality.

He was floating high in the air above the central square of a large city. Fires burned everywhere. Soldiers moved in squads from door to door, dragging the inhabitants out into the street and setting their homes ablaze. He could hear cries of desperation from the victims and righteous shouts of command from the soldiers.

He looked around for Phane. The Reishi Prince was standing on top of a flat-topped pyramid in the center of the giant flagstone square in the middle of the city. On either side of him stood a creature that made Alexander shudder with fear and disbelief. Each had two arms and two legs and a head like a man but that was where the similarities ended. The creatures stood eight feet tall, were exquisitely muscled, and had skin that was a smooth shiny black like obsidian or the surface of oil. Their faces were without eyes, nose, or mouth. Instead, they simply had indentations where their eyes and mouths should have been and bumps where their noses should have been. They had no hair or genitals. Their knees were those of a canine and their large feet were those of a raptor. They had oversized hands, and each of their six fingers ended in a three-inch-long, razor-sharp talon. Alexander could see the darkness of their auras and knew at a glance that they were from the netherworld.

He took a moment to study Phane's aura. The Reishi Prince had dark and angry colors that were murky and opaque but glowed brightly and extended farther from his body than any aura Alexander had ever seen. The power of the man was clear. His connection to the firmament was intense.

A few steps down the side of the pyramid stood a cordon of soldiers wearing the plate armor and crest of the Reishi Army Regency. Alexander looked around and saw fires burning all around the city. Phane watched, while the hopes and dreams of hundreds of thousands of people died by his command.

Alexander realized he was seeing Karth. The capital city had fallen, and quickly. There was still a bit of fighting here and there, but Phane stood in the center of the city for all to see. The message was clear. Karth was his. Resistance was pointless.

Alexander let go of his focus and returned to himself more gently this time. He opened his eyes and looked around his room. It was hard to imagine the scale of suffering he'd just witnessed. Karth was a large city, almost as big as New Ruatha, and it was being systematically destroyed, leaving its inhabitants to suffer the loss of homes, loved ones, and their very lives. He felt helpless in the face of such suffering and angry at his helplessness. Worse, Alexander knew with certainty that any who stood against Phane would suffer a similar fate if he failed.

For the first time since he'd received the mark on his neck, he was fiercely grateful for it.

The scope of the loss he'd witnessed staggered him. He'd been chosen to protect his people from the kind of loss suffered in Karth. Then it occurred to him that perhaps he wasn't just supposed to protect Ruatha but the whole of the Seven Isles. How many countless lives had been lost or crippled this night in Karth? How many more would fall if he didn't protect them?

He'd been committed to his inherited duty ever since he realized the significance of the threat, but now it was much more real. There was more substance to the enemy and greater proof of his evil. Alexander felt a smoldering anger in the pit of his stomach. He was glad the task of ridding this perversion from the world had fallen to him. He still had no idea how he was going to accomplish such a thing, but he knew now more than ever that he had to find a way. Phane must die, and sooner would be better than later.

He paced for a few minutes before going to bed, the scenes of destruction and carnage still vivid in his mind. He stepped back from his emotions, and with ruthless severity he quenched his anger and forced himself to go to sleep. As much as he wanted to nurse his feelings and dwell on the injustice of his enemy, he knew the most important thing he could do was to find the Thinblade. That meant he would need to be well rested for tomorrow's journey.

He woke just before light the next morning and dressed in his riding clothes. He came down the stairs to a quiet entry hall with his pack ready to go. He took a moment to inspect his weapons and rest them on his pack against the wall next to one of the armoires. He saw a light in the sitting room and found Lucky and Anatoly talking quietly over a cup of tea.

Lucky poured him a cup and added a dollop of honey and a shot of cream. Alexander took it with a smile and sipped carefully. The first sip was always his favorite. He loved the pungent aroma and the feeling of the heat flowing into his body. He savored the sensation for a moment before lowering the cup into his lap.

"Karth has fallen," he whispered.

Lucky and Anatoly looked at each other, then at Alexander. Lucky began the inevitable string of questions that Alexander knew his statement would provoke.

"Did you have another clairvoyant experience?"

Alexander nodded, then took another sip of his tea. He always liked this time of the morning just before daybreak when everything was quiet and undisturbed. He spoke softly. "This time I had much more control. I think I've figured out how to make it happen when I want it to and how to control where I direct my vision. I saw a large city with a pyramid in the middle of the central square. Phane was on top of the pyramid with two creatures from the netherworld that I never want to see up close." He shuddered at the memory of the terrifying-looking monsters. "Karth was being razed by the Reishi Army Regency. The whole city was on fire." Alexander looked down into his tea.

"I was hoping Karth would keep him occupied for a bit longer," Anatoly said before finishing off his tea.

"Can you describe how you entered the firmament?" Lucky asked, leaning forward with interest.

Alexander recounted the experience in as much detail as he could remember. Lucky listened intently without interrupting. When Alexander finished, Lucky sat back and looked up at the ceiling for a few moments.

"That is entirely different from my own experience with the firmament and from the descriptions of other wizards' experiences. Typically, a wizard describes the firmament as a vast and endless potential that is entirely apart from the wizard. It beckons with the promise of your greatest desire made manifest and plays on emotion with intensity. No wizard to my knowledge has ever experienced being spread across the firmament ... except ..." Lucky stopped and looked off into the distance, lost in his own thoughts.

Alexander waited patiently. He knew from long hours of study under the tutelage of the master alchemist that Lucky could tune the world out and search the recesses of his mind for an obscure fact or memory and that it was best to leave him to it.

Several moments later, Lucky's eyes refocused and he looked at Alexander. "I recall reading an account of the experiences of an ancient Reishi arch mage. He lived during the era of the third Reishi Sovereign, maybe three thousand years ago. If memory serves, this mage described his experiences with the firmament much the way you do. As if he became part of it and could listen to the music it made. He did talk of the rapture that was a constant tug against his reason and took great pains to express just how much effort it took to avoid losing himself in it, so his experiences are different in that regard. I'll ask Kelvin to see if he can find the volume. It may contain information that I don't remember or that I didn't understand at the time."

Abigail, Jack, and Isabel came into the sitting room, each dressed for travel. Alexander poured Isabel a cup of tea as she sat on the couch next to him. She smiled her thanks.

Anatoly took the opportunity to change the subject. The fall of Karth was not a good note to begin their journey on. "The stables will have our horses ready with supplies for our trip. I spoke with the stable master yesterday. He's a gruff old man but he knows his trade. He showed me the horses he has for us and I must say I'm impressed. We should make good time."

Adele came in somewhat timidly. Light was just beginning to show on the edge of the sky outside the balcony doors. "Forgive the intrusion, Lord Alexander. Would you like breakfast now?"

Alexander looked up and gave the middle-aged serving woman a smile. "Yes, thank you, Adele." She looked pleased and hurried off.

There was a knock at the door. Anatoly rose to answer it while Alexander closed his eyes and focused on his mind's eye. He sent his vision to the door and tried to push through to the other side but found that it was too far away to see clearly. The door seemed to create a barrier to his vision at this distance. He made a note to himself. He'd decided to experiment with his magic when the opportunity presented itself. He knew his all around sight had a limited range that allowed him to see things in his mind's eye, while his clairvoyance was like seeing through his own eyes as if he were actually there.

He backed off and watched Anatoly lift the bar and open the heavy door to admit Kelvin and the two assistants he had in tow. They were each carrying a large bag. Kelvin was wearing his red-hued black plate armor and had his giant war hammer. Before the door closed, Alexander sent his vision down the hallway. The farther he went, the darker it got and the less clearly he could see details. Halfway down the hall, he was as blind as if he was simply remembering what the hall looked like. When the door closed, he opened his eyes and felt a moment of disorientation before his real vision took over for his magical sight.

Kelvin had his assistants place the bags on the low table in the middle of the sitting room before he walked them back to the door issuing instructions. Lucky followed and requested that they search the library for the tome describing the account of a wizard who experienced the firmament similarly to the way Alexander had described.

Kelvin returned smiling broadly, with Lucky trailing behind. "I come bearing gifts." He took a seat in front of the two large bags. "My magical calling is enchantment. I'm not very skilled at casting spells, but I can imbue items with magic better than anyone alive." He made the statement matter-of-factly without hubris or conceit. "My calling has led me to become a master craftsman, since only items of the finest quality and materials can withstand the powerful energies involved in the enchantment process. As such, I am always making or acquiring items of fine quality and I have amassed quite a collection over the years. I've brought some of these items to offer as gifts today."

Everyone was surprised, except Lucky who looked like he knew this was coming. "Kelvin's work is known far and wide," he said. "Kings and nobles regularly petition him to make items of power for them. These gifts will help us succeed against Phane, so accept them in the spirit in which they are given."

He gave Alexander a look that forestalled any protest. Lucky knew Alexander was uncomfortable receiving gifts of great value, especially when he had nothing to give in return.

Kelvin faced Alexander. "Many years ago I visited the central Island of Tyr and struck a bargain with an ancient dragon who lives there named Bragador. She's a magnificent creature." He smiled almost wistfully at the memory. "Dragons view time and life a bit differently than people do. They do not die of age. Instead they grow stronger, wiser, and more powerful with every year. She has lived for nearly twelve hundred years. Bragador tested me in ways I did not believe I could endure but I survived her trials. Once she was satisfied that I was worthy of her acquaintance, she allowed me to offer her a bargain. In that bargain I acquired a load of shed dragon scales. Within each scale is a core sheet of dragon steel." He tapped his breastplate. "I made this suit of armor from those plates. Dragon steel is many times harder than the finest steel and much lighter. It requires magical fire to work because normal fire has no effect on it. With the remaining dragon steel, I made this." Kelvin lifted a flat-black shirt of finely wrought chain armor that had just a hint of red to it. It was made of metal rings so fine that Alexander had to lean closer to actually see the tiny little rings all linked together.

Kelvin handed the shirt to Alexander, who took it with a look of wonder. The metal shirt was cool to the touch and weighed only a couple of ounces, but it felt durable in a way that Alexander couldn't quite explain. It had a feel of permanence and a timeless quality to it.

"Kelvin, thank you, but this must be priceless. I can't possibly …" Alexander started to say.

Kelvin cut him off with a raised hand. "You can and you will. I made this mail shirt years ago and it has sat in my vaults because I couldn't find someone worthy of wearing it, until now. Mage Cedric chose you. You lead our struggle against a very dark future. This shirt will protect you. If you wish to repay me for this gift, then be victorious." He gave Alexander a very direct look. "I cannot defeat Phane. I know of no wizard who can match him. If you do not succeed, then darkness will consume our world. You are our only chance at a future worth having."

Alexander was humbled. He looked Mage Gamaliel in the eye. "If it's within my power, then I will succeed," he said quietly and solemnly, as if making an unbreakable oath to an unquestioned authority.

Kelvin nodded his satisfaction and turned to Abigail. "Lucky tells me you are an accomplished archer." She glanced at Lucky and looked back to Kelvin, wide-eyed. He took a beautifully crafted, medium-sized composite bow from one of the bags. "This bow should be just the right size for you. It's not too big to use effectively on horseback and will send an arrow farther, harder, and straighter than most any other bow. I crafted it to be very powerful, even without any magic. Before I enchanted it, I wasn't strong enough to pull the string all the way back and therein lies the magic I have invested in this bow. My enchantment makes it easy to draw. The natural power of the bow and your skill at archery will do the rest." He handed it to Abigail with both hands.

She took it with a look of delight. "Thank you." She looked at the well-crafted bow and tested the draw. It pulled back with ease. Her look of wonder turned to a smile. "This is wonderful. I can hardly wait to try it out." She got up and kissed the Mage on the cheek.

Kelvin smiled broadly. "You are most welcome. I trust it will serve you well."

He turned to face Isabel. "I'm told you have a familiar. A forest hawk named Slyder. It takes a remarkable individual to attract a familiar without having survived the mana fast."

Isabel smiled. "He was a gift from my parents when I was little. They had Mason cast the spell to call him to me, although I remember that he doubted it would work. I'm glad it did. Slyder is one of my best friends."

"You have a natural affinity for animals or it would not have worked. That is why I believe this is the perfect gift for you. It was made before the Reishi War and enchanted by a wizard of great power. I acquired it many years ago and have saved it for just the right person." Kelvin removed a jewelry case from the bag and opened it to reveal a necklace made from sturdy links of silver with a tiny gold figurine of an animal attached every inch or so along the front of the chain. There were a total of seven animals: bear, wolf, horse, hawk, ferret, mountain lion, and deer.

"It's beautiful." Isabel's eyes sparkled with delight as she carefully lifted the exquisitely crafted necklace from the case.

"And oh so much more," Kelvin said with a knowing smile. "When you wear it, you will be able to commune with animals. Most animals will be friendly to you and you will be able to talk to them within your mind. Remember, animals are not as intelligent as people and they have very different concerns than we do, but they can be helpful in many circumstances and will often provide invaluable information."

Isabel blinked in surprise, then hugged the Mage. "Thank you," she whispered. "I love it."

Alexander smiled at her delight and was more than happy to help her put it around her delicate neck. Kelvin smiled in satisfaction when Alexander closed the clasp.

He turned to Anatoly, who frowned in near alarm. If Alexander was uncomfortable accepting gifts, Anatoly was almost hostile to the notion.

"Lucky told me you would not want anything, but I have an item that I think will assist you in your duty to protect Alexander. It's only in that spirit that I offer you this gift." He took a broad, heavy leather belt from his bag. "I made this from the leather of a wyvern and enchanted it myself. When you wear it, you will have the strength of three men." He handed the belt to Anatoly, who took it reluctantly.

"Thank you, Mage. I will take great care with this and return it to you when Alexander has finished with this business," Anatoly said.

Kelvin chuckled. "If that is your wish, then I will honor it, but know that I give this in the spirit of a gift."

He turned to Lucky who looked genuinely surprised. "I acquired this item several years ago from a traveling merchant. He claimed it was made by a master craftsman on the Isle of Ithilian. It was of such fine quality that I bought it simply because I value quality workmanship. When I heard you were coming, I took the time to enchant it for you."

It was a sturdy leather bag, much like the one Lucky always carried, but with a wide strap that fit easily across his chest and over his shoulder.

"I know how much of a pack rat you are and I've seen how many things you're able to carry in that bag of yours, so I thought you might like to have a bigger bag—bigger on the inside, anyway." Kelvin smiled at the startled look on Lucky's face.

"I believe you will find that it holds much more than it looks like it could and the weight of the contents will not affect the weight of the bag. It should make traveling a bit easier and allow you to carry most of your concoctions without fear of breakage or damage."

"Kelvin, this is wonderful. Thank you."

Finally, Kelvin turned to Jack. "Master Colton, I haven't forgotten about you." He took a dull grey-colored cloak from the bag. "In the swamps of southern Karth lives a large lizard that is able to blend in with its surroundings. This cloak is made from the leather of such a creature and then enchanted to retain the natural ability of the beast. When you wear it, you will be able to hide in plain sight by simply willing the cloak to blend in." He handed it to Jack, who stood to receive it. He held it up inspecting the workmanship, then threw it over his shoulders with a flourish, tossed up the hood, and promptly faded into the background.

Alexander could see where he was if he focused, and of course his aura was still visible. But for anyone with normal vision, it would be hard to tell that Jack was standing there.

Jack removed the hood, and the cloak returned to its normal grey. He bowed formally. "Mage Gamaliel, you do me honor. I will wear this cloak with pride and use its power in service to Alexander and the Old Law. Thank you."

Kelvin chuckled, "Well spoken, as usual."

He stood up. "These items are given in the hopes that they will help protect the world from Phane. Use their power well. Now, I think I smell food."

Lucky stood, grinning. "Indeed you do."

Just then Adele stepped to the threshold of the room. "Lord Alexander, breakfast is served."

Alexander stood up and gave the serving woman a warm smile. She was always so eager to please and worked hard to do a good job. Alexander liked her even though he'd just met her only two days ago. He reminded himself that she was one of the people he was fighting to protect. If he failed, she would come to a bad end along with countless others.

"Thank you, Adele," Alexander said, heading for the dining room with the rest of his friends. "It smells delicious."

And it was. Adele and her staff had produced a huge spread of bacon, sausages, eggs, potatoes, biscuits, and juice. Alexander ate his fill and savored every bite. He knew he would be eating travel rations for the foreseeable future and wanted to enjoy his last good meal before he left. He always admired Lucky's simple, unabashed pleasure at good food and sought to emulate his old tutor in that regard. The meal was over all too soon. Adele appeared almost as if by magic when Alexander pushed his plate away.

"Lord Alexander, are you leaving? I … I only ask because you're dressed for travel and I've noticed your packs are lined up in the foyer." She looked a little timid at having asked a question that she had no real right to ask.

Alexander offered her a smile of reassurance. "We are leaving, Adele, but I hope to be back in a week or two."

"Oh, I do hope you hurry back. I've so enjoyed having you here. You're very friendly, if I may say so. Most guests in this wing of the palace are too important to even notice my staff and me. You've been so nice, and well, I just want to say thank you." She stopped short to cut off her rambling.

Alexander's smile broadened. "You've been a delight and your service has been impeccable. Thank you for taking the time and making the effort to do your work well."

She blushed at the praise. "I took the liberty of preparing some food for your journey. When I saw your packs I thought you might like something to take with you. I'll be right back up." She hurried off to retrieve bundles of bread, fruit, dried meats, and sausages.

Alexander and his companions were in the foyer and had gathered their equipment and strapped on their weapons when Adele came bustling into the entry hall carrying a basket full of cloth-wrapped bundles of food. She had one for each of them and started handing them out quickly.

Alexander took his with a smile and slipped it into a pocket on the outside of his pack. "This is very thoughtful, Adele. Thank you again."

The moment he stood back up, the faint glow coming through the balcony windows in the sitting room changed from the pale blue of a new dawn to the orange red of a furnace fire. Half a heartbeat later, a wave of heat washed through the archway and into the foyer as a ball of liquid fire burst against the outside of the balcony doors, setting them ablaze in a wall of flame.

Chapter 51

Alexander grabbed his pack and his bow and quiver. His friends wasted no time either. They heard commotion out in the hall a moment later, followed by a volley of arrows from the square below that shattered the glass of the balcony doors and allowed the wall of liquid fire to spill onto the carpets of the plush sitting room and ignite the floor and drapes.

Alexander threw the door open to the glass bridge. What he saw stunned him to the core.

The man in black was standing in the middle of the bridge. He held nothing but a knife. There was a trail of broken bodies crumpled in pools of crimson littering the hall behind him. Commander P'Tal stood at the center of the bridge with his knife buried into the heart of the wizard that had been standing watch with the guards. Jataan P'Tal pulled the knife free and started walking toward the dozen troops standing between him and his target. He wore no armor, had no shield, and wielded only the medium-sized knife for a weapon.

The remaining guard force was divided into two squads of six. The squad nearest the door held its position. The men down the hall fired a volley of crossbow bolts at the lone advancing enemy. Alexander saw Jataan P'Tal's magic flare brightly. He contorted himself almost impossibly and the six crossbow bolts passed him by without so much as a scratch. He walked briskly but not overly hurried, like a man on his way to an important meeting.

The six men rushed to the attack with spears and swords. Jataan P'Tal met the attack with practiced ease. He seemed to know what his enemy would do before they did. When their attack came he was simply not in the way of the strike but had moved to a position where he could counterstrike with deadly effect.

The first guard thrust with his spear. P'Tal stepped at an angle just outside the thrust and slipped his blade over the top of the thrusting arm, slicing to the bone across the inside of the man's upper arm. Blood sprayed across the guard's chest and his spear clattered to the floor. Jataan P'Tal was already past the dying man. The next guard slashed with his sword. P'Tal stopped cold in his tracks and the blade whistled past just inches from his belly. A moment later he lunged with impossible speed and drove the point of his blade through the leather breastplate, under the lower edge of the ribcage, and into the man's heart. He pushed the man off his blade and into another advancing soldier, then caught the haft of the third man's spear thrust, pushing it down and to the left and casually slashed the man's throat with the tip of his knife. More quickly than any man should be able to move, he rolled around the man he'd just killed and drove his knife into the ribs on the left side of the fourth guard, grabbed him by the throat before he could fall, and pivoted his body into the path of the spear being driven at him by the fifth man. He slipped past the man whose spear was now impaling a dead man, ducked low to dodge the blade of the sixth guard, and sliced the inside of his thigh to the bone. The fifth man let go of his spear, drew his sword and spun with a powerful slash. The blade missed Jataan P'Tal's throat by mere inches, while he stood stock-still, waiting for the attack to pass. When it did, he smoothly moved into the man's now open guard and drove his blade into his heart. He'd killed all six men in the space of four heartbeats, but it would take a few minutes more for some of them to die as their lives literally drained out of them in angry red pools staining the floor.

Alexander was shocked at the precision of the violence. Everyone stood almost mesmerized by the spectacle. When Jataan P'Tal began to casually walk toward them without missing a beat, their trance broke. Abigail was first to respond with an arrow from her new bow. When she released it, her target was his heart. It leapt from the bow with more speed, power, and deadly purpose than any arrow Alexander had ever seen, but Jataan P'Tal turned sideways and the arrow passed within a fraction of an inch of his chest. He gave Abigail a look of curiosity. It wasn't anger or indignation but respect. She had come close and he seemed to give her a slight nod even as he came to kill them. The remaining six guards fired another volley of crossbow bolts. He dodged them with a kind of speed and intuition that Alexander knew with icy certainty was driven by deep and powerful magic. In that moment he understood why Mage Gamaliel knew it was unwise to engage this man.

Behind them, another ball of liquid fire hit the lip of the balcony wall and sprayed a wave of flame through the now shattered balcony doors and into the already burning sitting room. Alexander could hardly believe how quickly the attack had taken place.

Anatoly barked an order to retreat at the remaining six guards. They obeyed with unusual quickness. Once they were safely in the foyer, Kelvin took one step forward with his great battle hammer and swung a mighty overhead stroke down on the abutment of the glass-encased bridge. The floor beneath them shuddered and the floor of the bridge cracked and split. Jataan P'Tal staggered as the floor of the bridge reverberated under his feet. Glass shattered for twenty feet from the point of impact, sending countless shards raining to the ground below, followed first by one small chunk of the floor, then another, and finally a six-foot section of the bridge fell away, leaving only the trusses below to keep the entire bridge from collapsing and crashing to the ground.

As he regained his footing, Jataan P'Tal picked up a spear and, in a blinding flash, hurled it at Alexander. It was like nothing Alexander had ever seen or could even imagine. No one could move that fast. The short spear hurtled in a straight line with impossible speed and terrible force. It struck home before Alexander could blink: a clean, direct hit just slightly left of center in the middle of his chest. The impact of the spear tip against the dragon-steel chain knocked Alexander clear off his feet and sent him tumbling across the floor, while the haft of the spear shattered from the rebounded force of the sudden stop.

Pain shot through Alexander with suffocating intensity. Surely he was dying; no one could survive such violence. He felt his chest and found, to his surprise, that there wasn't an inch-thick spear haft protruding from it. Once he realized he might not be dying, he started to struggle for breath but it felt like a horse had kicked him.

He could hear activity in the distance but it sounded very far away and unimportant in the face of the darkness slowly threatening to swallow him. He looked in the direction of the door just as Lucky tossed a glass orb filled with angry-looking liquid fire onto the bridge. In the same moment, Abigail and Isabel both sent arrows toward the enemy. P'Tal dodged them without much effort. The orb shattered against the ceiling of what was left of the glass tunnel and burst into flames that dripped down across the passageway as if a curtain of fire had been drawn across it.

Jataan P'Tal stopped and picked up a sword. With one stroke, he cut a gaping gash through the fine wrought-iron web of glasswork that enclosed the bridge and deftly climbed up on top of the bridge to avoid the fire.

Anatoly and Jack slammed the heavy bound doors shut, dropped the bar in place, and jammed the floor and ceiling pins home. The conflagration coming from the sitting room was growing quickly and sending waves of heat into the foyer.

Darkness closed in on Alexander's vision. At last, with great effort, he took a breath. The hot fury of the gasp sent shock waves of pain through him. He rolled onto his side and saw the spear tip of the weapon that was meant to kill him. It was curled over as if a man with impossible strength had driven it against a heavy plate of hardened steel. The first three inches of the blade were neatly curled around and around into a tight little circle. He closed his eyes and steeled himself for another breath. The shock of the pain was lessened only by the anticipation of it. Alexander retreated into the place within his mind that he'd found during the mana fast: the place where the witness lived, where there was no feeling, consequence, or importance attached to any event. From there he observed his pain with ruthless detachment. He accepted it and focused his will. He needed to act. The enemy would be here soon and he needed to move. With an act of sheer stubbornness, he drew another breath and sat up. Fire ignited within his chest anew.

Lucky knelt beside him and raised Alexander's shirt to reveal the clean and unblemished surface of the dragon-steel chain armor he'd been given only an hour earlier. Lucky nodded in grim satisfaction and permitted only the briefest glance of gratitude to Kelvin before digging into his bag for a jar of healing salve. He took a big dollop of the thick ointment and pulled up the chain and Alexander's undershirt, revealing the red, swollen, and bruised spot just over his heart. Lucky examined the wound for only a moment before slathering the enchanted ointment over the whole area. Next, he dug a couple of numbweed leaves from his bag and unceremoniously stuffed them into Alexander's mouth.

Alexander took another breath just as a thunderous jolt shook the door and doorframe. Cracks spread out from the center of the double doors. He started to get up in spite of the waves of pain, but was unable to lift his own weight and that of the pack still strapped on his back. Isabel and Lucky each offered a hand and helped him regain his feet.

Jack was talking to Adele. "Do your quarters have a balcony or a window?" She nodded quickly, with a look of shock and disbelief at the sudden turn of events.

Kelvin turned to Anatoly. "Go! I'll hold this ground and give you time to escape."

Anatoly looked the Guild Mage in the eye and nodded with the battle-tested resolve of a hardened soldier. He barked a command to the remaining six guards. "Stand with the Guild Mage! Hold this ground!"

The door shuddered against greater force than it could bear. The cracks widened. The heavy oak bar started to splinter and the locking pins in the floor and ceiling sheered off.

Alexander steadied himself and drew another breath. He could feel the numbweed working. The pain was becoming distant and less urgent. He followed Jack and Adele into the dining room, through the door to the serving quarters, and down the stairs to the level below. With each step his breathing came more easily and the pain receded a little bit more. The injury wasn't severe, mostly bruising and a few cracked ribs, but it still hurt.

Adele led the way past the kitchen and a number of startled cooks and scullions to a comfortable but simple-looking sitting room with a little balcony about fifty feet up on the side of the detached palace wing.

Jack went out and looked down. He turned back to Adele. "Do you have a rope?" he asked urgently.

She looked flustered for a moment before answering, "Just the one in the well that the kitchen uses for water."

"Show me," Jack commanded.

They rushed off and Alexander took the opportunity to sit down and focus on breathing. He drew breath to the limit of his endurance and released it slowly in an effort to keep the bruised muscles of his chest from tightening. The numbness had set in and the drowsiness that always accompanied the healing salve was settling in as well. He was in no danger of losing consciousness but he was starting to get tired. In the distance, they heard another loud thud followed by the cracking and splintering of the doors as they burst open, swung wide, and crashed into the walls. A moment later the whole structure shook violently. Alexander heard shouting followed quickly by the cries of men in battle. He hoped Kelvin would survive the fight.

Jack returned with a rope. The building shuddered again. Alexander heard a groan followed by a loud cracking noise. The structural integrity of the entire building began to fail from the repeated hammer blows of the Guild Mage. Jack ignored the battle raging upstairs and deftly tied one end of the rope around a couch and tossed the other end over the balcony railing. He pushed the couch up to the doorframe to secure the rope and turned to Alexander.

"Can you make it down?" he asked.

Alexander nodded through the pain. "Send Adele and her staff down first. This place isn't going to hold for long."

Jack started to protest but stopped short at the look Alexander gave him. Adele was scared of the rope descent but she was more frightened of the fire and battle raging upstairs. She and her staff obeyed their instructions without much fuss and were quickly on the ground. Isabel and Abigail went next, followed by Lucky and then Alexander. He came down too quickly and hit the ground hard, sending him onto his back as the weight of his pack pulled him over. He rolled out of the way for Jack and Anatoly who followed closely behind. There were people in the street looking and pointing at the wing of the palace now half engulfed in flames.

Another great and terrible shock reverberated through the building and into the ground beneath, followed by an ear-splitting crack as the building started to fail. Adele and her staff scattered. Alexander and his companions ran toward the square to get some distance from the building. He knew even as he ran that the enemy waited in the square, but it was the only option. The other three sides of the building were too close to the outer walls of the palace. If the structure collapsed, those roads would be buried with stone and debris.

Even before they reached the end of the road and entered the square, Alexander had drawn his sword. It gave him focus and cleared his mind. Everything else receded from his awareness, even the pain. Right now, he was in a fight and he had a blade in his hand.

They rounded the corner and saw at least twenty men surrounding Wizard Rangle and the giant. The enemy was easily seventy-five feet away and looking up at the burning structure, but they noticed Alexander almost immediately. Even if they hadn't, they would have in the next moment when Abigail's first arrow drove cleanly through one of the soldiers and skittered across the flagstone square, trailing blood behind it. The middle of the square was empty with the exception of the enemy, but citizens of New Ruatha stood in clusters all around the square's edge watching the spectacle.

The enemy turned as one and loosed a volley of crossbow bolts at them. They were close enough to the corner of the building to retreat behind it to avoid the deadly rain. Alexander cast about for an escape route. The square was mostly shopfronts with a few roads leading out here and there, but the closest road was a hundred feet away.

The building shuddered again and the side opposite them started to crumble. It was slow at first as if the building was reluctant to let go of its life and form, then it accelerated in a great rumbling, crashing cacophony. Alexander stole a look around the corner and saw that the enemy was distracted by the collapse of the building and the rising dust cloud. He shouted, "Now!" and ran for the road.

They were almost there when Alexander heard the giant command his troops to give chase. He glanced and saw Rangle creating another ball of liquid fire between his outstretched hands. The undulating bubble filled with angry-looking orange-red liquid. He looked back to his sister. She was running with an arrow already nocked. Alexander pointed at Rangle and shouted, "Abby!"

She spun, saw the threat, and drew just as Rangle released the ball of liquid fire. She brought up her aim a bit and let her arrow go. It leapt from the bow and streaked to the ball of fire sailing toward them. Arrow and magic met in the sky above a cluster of charging troops. The arrow entered the bubble whole and exited as a spray of char and fire. The bubble burst, showering liquid fire down onto the mercenaries below.

Alexander heard Anatoly in the background shout, "Well done!" to Abigail.

They made it to the edge of the square and raced into the street with the sound of screaming in the distance and footfalls somewhat closer. There were at least ten men still chasing them, followed by the giant and Rangle. They ran to the first turn and rounded the corner when Alexander stopped. His chest ached and his lungs burned. He'd had enough of running and was starting to feel an implacable anger at the injustice of Phane and everything he stood for well up inside of him again. They all stopped with him, looking for a place to escape.

"We stand," he said. "Right here. Isabel, Abigail, take positions over there and kill that wizard if he rounds this corner." Alexander pointed to a wagon parked without its team across the street and forty feet or so from the corner.

"Anatoly, are you tired of running?" Alexander asked his old mentor.

Anatoly set his face and nodded slowly as he hefted his axe onto his shoulder.

They could hear the fall of boots approaching quickly. Alexander shrugged off his pack, bow, and quiver. Anatoly tossed his pack aside, too. Jack pulled up his hood and vanished against the pattern of the wall, while Lucky backed off a dozen feet or so down the sidewalk and pulled a vial from his bag.

The moment the first three men rounded the corner, the ground shook from the collapse of the remaining part of the north wing of the palace. The men were distracted just enough by the huge crash that they were totally surprised to find Alexander and Anatoly standing there waiting for them.

Anatoly struck first. A great downward diagonal stroke with his war axe caught the first man on the left shoulder and cleaved him clear through to the right hip. Alexander caught the next man on the point of his sword and drove the blade through his heart and out his back before swiftly drawing it out, stepping past the dying man who hadn't yet slumped to the ground, and deftly chopping off the arm of the next man with a swift downward stroke.

The rest of the men poured around the corner and something snapped into place in Alexander's mind. He released all thought. An icy calm flooded into him. He found himself in the singular moment of the now. There was nothing but him, the enemy, and his blade.

He whirled, slashed, and thrust with precision and economy of motion, no longer driven by thought or calculation but by instinct and magic. When he struck, the enemy fell. When they struck, he simply wasn't in the path of their attack. Their blades fell on empty space while his unerringly found its mark with ruinous precision. He felt the melding of his blade skill and his all around sight. He found that he didn't need to see with his eyes because his mind's eye saw more quickly and more accurately. Anatoly fought with the discipline of a trained soldier. Jack could be seen flickering into view and lashing out with his knife. Alexander saw the giant coming and altered his course through the enemy to meet the new attack, but Anatoly was closer.

Anatoly and the giant met head-on and crashed into each other with fury. Their battle was a contest of strength, mass, and anger. Their collision drove them both to the ground where they lost hold of their weapons and resorted to grappling. The giant was a good six inches taller than Anatoly and at least a hundred pounds heavier, but Anatoly was wearing the belt that Kelvin had given him. Alexander calmly, almost routinely, killed the last of the charging guards while Anatoly gained his feet with one of the giant's hands in his vice-like grip. He spun around once, then twice, and tossed the giant through the air and into the window of a shopfront across the street.

Alexander turned to see Rangle standing thirty feet away preparing another ball of liquid fire. He didn't waste a moment. He tossed his sword into his off hand, slipped a knife from his boot and threw it with clean precision at the fire wizard. Rangle saw it coming and did the only thing he could, the only thing that would save him. He interrupted the casting of his spell, causing the magic to dissipate and the liquid fire to evaporate before it could fully manifest. The alternative was to allow Alexander's knife to break the bubble as it formed and have his own liquid fire splash all over him. Alexander's knife drove into Rangle's shoulder instead. Alexander steeled himself with grim determination. He was going to kill Rangle and he was going to do it right now. He started toward the wizard until the giant rose from the rubble of the shop and hurled a javelin at him. Without his all around sight he would have been too late to avoid it. As it was, the javelin missed him by just inches.

Rangle was casting another spell but this time it came out much more quickly. A plane of reddish heat formed before him, blocking Alexander's path. Two arrows zipped by Alexander from behind but turned to ash when they passed through the wall of heat. The giant was preparing to throw another javelin when Abigail and Isabel turned their arrows on him. Each of them loosed an arrow, causing his javelin to go wide. Isabel's arrow bounced harmlessly off his breastplate, but Abigail's arrow drove through the steel breastplate and an inch into his chest over his right lung. He cried out in rage and surprise.

Both turned and fled, Rangle retreating back into the square toward the rubble of the collapsed palace wing and the giant into the storefront he'd just demolished. Alexander wanted to pursue them but he reminded himself that the battle mage may well have survived the confrontation with Kelvin and could still be coming for him. Alexander gave one last look toward the burning mound of broken stone and timber that only minutes ago had been his lavish quarters and silently asked the Maker to deliver Kelvin alive and whole from the rubble. He turned without a word and found his pack.

Chapter 52

"Let's go."

Alexander headed off down the street, drawing stares from the people he passed. It wasn't five minutes before he heard the sound of galloping horses. He started looking for a way off the road when a platoon of palace guards rounded the corner and headed straight for him. The commander was Captain Sava.

"To the King!" he shouted fiercely to his men at the sight of Alexander.

Only moments later Alexander and his friends were surrounded by a protective cordon of loyal soldiers.

Captain Sava dismounted and saluted crisply, fist to heart. "Lord Alexander, we feared the worst when the north wing collapsed. The Regent has ordered ..."

Alexander cut him off. "Have six of your men dismount. We need their horses. Six men will provide escort to the stables. The rest will begin searching for a giant about seven feet tall and maybe three hundred and fifty pounds, a wizard dressed in brown robes with a knife sticking out of his right shoulder, and another wizard about five and a half feet tall and dressed in black. Engage with superior numbers using archers or crossbows. They're all extremely dangerous, especially the one in black. Finally, the Guild Mage may be buried in the rubble of the visitors' wing. Summon what men you need to dig him out."

Captain Sava didn't hesitate. He ordered the nearest six men to dismount. Without taking a breath, he started assigning duties to the rest of his men. Only moments later Alexander and his companions were on horseback and racing through the streets of the city toward the stables. They arrived quickly with Captain Sava in the lead. The captain called out orders to make Alexander's horses ready immediately. The stable master was a competent man who understood an occasional need for urgency. He didn't ask questions but instead started barking commands to his stable hands and had Alexander's group mounted on well-bred, well-trained steeds in minutes.

"Captain Sava, see that the Regent is aware of the events of this morning. I will return soon." Alexander offered the man his hand.

Captain Sava took it with pride. "I will see to it myself. Safe journey, Lord Alexander."

Jack led the way down the winding roads away from the central plateau and into the less affluent neighborhoods below. People stopped to look when they passed and whispered or pointed at Alexander. He didn't pay any attention to them; instead he scanned for threats. He didn't know what Phane might throw at him next and wanted to be sure that he saw it coming, whatever it was.

Soon they were out of the city and on the plains to the north of New Ruatha, riding hard toward the looming black mountain on the horizon that was Blackstone Keep. The road they followed looked as though it had once been well traveled but had long ago fallen into disuse and disrepair. An hour out of the city they slowed their pace to rest the horses. Blackstone Keep was a two-day ride even if it looked like it was only a few hours away. He had to assume that his enemies would be coming after him, so he felt a sense of urgency to cover more ground, to keep running, but he had to protect the horses. If they lost even one, it would slow them down more than anything else.

He was lost in thought when he heard Slyder overhead. He looked up to see the small-framed forest hawk circling high above. Isabel tipped her head back slightly and closed her eyes. Her shoulders tensed in alarm even before her piercing green eyes snapped open.

"Enemy to the north, maybe an hour's ride. Looks like troops from Headwater. They're spread out in a watch line for miles in each direction."

Alexander reined in his horse and brought the big chestnut stallion to a stop, patting the side of his neck to reassure him.

"How thin is the line?" he asked.

"Squads of four every mile or so," Isabel answered. "Just close enough to see the next link in the chain."

Alexander was tired of running. He was tired of being hunted. And he was angry. The simple injustice of it gnawed at him. Phane wanted to rule the world, not to help make it a better place, not to heal people or bring nations together, not to prevent war or establish stability through just and moral law. He wanted to rule the world to placate his ego. He wanted to be more important than everybody else and he wanted everyone alive to know it. Petty ego. Self-aggrandizement. Narcissism.

Alexander stared at the silhouette of Blackstone Keep while his blood boiled at a low simmer. When the thought occurred to him, he almost laughed.

"Have you tried talking to your horse yet?" he asked Isabel.

She looked almost startled.

"No. In the excitement I forgot all about it," she said. Her hand came up to the finely crafted animal-charm necklace around her neck.

"Give it a try. Ask your horse how she's feeling. In fact, ask them all, if you can," Alexander suggested.

She gave him a blank look for a moment. "I'm not sure how it works but I'll try." She placed her hand on the neck of her horse and closed her eyes. Alexander could see the aura of the necklace swell with the flow of magic.

When Isabel opened her eyes, she had a strange look on her face. "The mind of a horse is much different than the mind of a bird. I always felt some of Slyder's cravings, instincts, and impulses when I was connected to him. It's similar with the horses only they want entirely different things for completely different reasons. They're all feeling fine and are good for several miles at a gallop, except they would like a drink of water sometime soon."

Alexander smiled. "Good. Let's find them some water and then we're going to run that watch line. Isabel, call Slyder down here, please. I'd like him to carry a message north to Erik and his men. They should be in the vicinity of Blackstone Keep by now and I think we could use their help. How many men did it look like the enemy had in total?"

"I'd estimate almost a hundred, all on horseback and well armed," she answered.

Alexander nodded in thought as he looked out over the desolate grassland. The last of winter was still hanging on here and the new starts hadn't yet ventured forth, leaving the place looking bereft of life or purpose. The sky was a dull, monotone grey that looked like it went on in every direction forever. The position of the sun could not be discerned nor the fact that a sun even existed, for that matter. The daylight was even and lifeless through the indifference of the cloud cover. The air was still and just a few degrees below comfortable. The day matched Alexander's mood.

"When we run the line, take what opportunity you get to kill any enemy you can without slowing to fight them. Once we're through, we run for Blackstone Keep. Isabel, I need you to talk to the horses and tell them our plan. Let them know we're going to need all of their speed and stamina. Also, while we ride, check on them from time to time to make sure we aren't injuring any of them."

She nodded and closed her eyes to talk to the animals. Slyder landed on her shoulder, looking at her quizzically.

Jack eased his horse forward and handed Alexander a note. "I took the liberty. Is there anything you'd like to add?"

Alexander read the note: "Being pursued—come south along road with haste to assist. Alexander Ruatha." He nodded approval, rolled the slip of paper tightly and handed it to Isabel. She tied it to Slyder's leg and sent him on his way. He gave one shriek when he took to wing and grew smaller against the grey backdrop as he ascended toward the clouds.

"We'll walk our horses until we see the watch line, then we charge them." Everyone nodded agreement. "Once we're through and have some distance, we'll slow to a steady gallop. When darkness falls, we'll walk in the night along the road. The enemy probably knows we're headed for Blackstone Keep. They also know we'll be much harder to attack once we're there. I doubt they'll stop for dark tonight."

It was midday when they crested a small rise in the low rolling grasslands and saw the squad not a mile away. Alexander urged his horse into a gallop. He saw the enemy become aware of them and heard a whistler arrow streak into the sky. To his left and right in the distance, he thought he could just see the stirrings of other men mounting up to give chase. He led his charge straight ahead. He was tired of being the defender. He knew from long hours of study that battle is decided by attack, not defense, that life itself is action, not passivity. He meant to take action. He meant to attack.

The four-man squad, seeing the charge, chose to meet it head-on. They came in a line at Alexander and his companions. Anatoly pulled up alongside Alexander and barked orders to Abigail and Isabel to form the second rank of a wedge formation and then to Lucky and Jack to form the third.

"At close bow range, break away from us and flank them," he shouted.

They thundered across the rolling plain toward the four soldiers wielding long spears. Alexander drew his sword, and everything else faded away. The world narrowed to this moment. He was in a fight and he had a blade in his hand. Nothing else mattered.

He could hear the pounding of his heart even over the roar of the galloping horses and the rush of wind. When they closed the distance to thirty feet, Abigail and Jack on one side and Isabel and Lucky on the other broke away from Anatoly and Alexander, veering off at forty-five degree angles. Alexander fixed on his opponent. He could see the stubble on the man's face and the grime in his

stringy hair. The men on the left and right of the charging line simultaneously
pitched backward off their horses with arrows protruding from their chests; Isabel
and Abigail had drawn first blood.

Alexander smiled grimly at the look of uncertainty that ghosted across his
opponent's face. He didn't give the fourth man a moment's attention; he belonged
to Anatoly, and Alexander knew that the man's fate was already decided.

The space closed between them. The enemy's spear came up for the
strike. The battle spanned the moment of a blink. Alexander's opponent thrust
forward with his spear. Alexander swept his sword vertically across his body from
left to right, catching the blade of the enemy spear and driving the point past his
right shoulder, tipped his blade over the haft of the spear just before his opponent
passed on the right, then brought his blade horizontally at the level of the man's
neck and thrust forward hard. The man's head came free and spun idly, forehead
over neck nape. The corpse rode out from under its severed head before it
remembered gravity's pull and thudded to the ground.

Anatoly held his war axe in his right hand with the haft running down the
side of his horse. He flipped it sideways just before the enemy struck, causing the
point of the enemy's spear to strike the side of the axe blade and glance wide
across his body. The impact turned the spike on the back of Anatoly's axe
forward, bringing it into perfect position for a quick thrust into the man's chest.
Without missing a step, Anatoly lifted the man up and off his horse, then casually
tipped his axe forward to let the man slide off the spike.

Alexander and his companions continued running toward Blackstone
Keep. More whistler arrows rose into the sky shrieking the alarm to all of the
soldiers stretched out along the watch line.

By midafternoon, the enemy had fully regrouped and were pursuing with
reckless abandon. They didn't seem to be concerned for their horses. Like a man
in a footrace pours every last scrap of energy into the final stretch, the enemy ran
their horses like tomorrow wouldn't matter, but Alexander knew it would.

He kept a measured and steady pace, checking with Isabel regularly about
the condition of the animals. They were still strong and eager to run, but
Alexander knew that just one wrong step and they would be facing far too many
enemy soldiers to defeat in a fight. He rode as cautiously as he could while still
keeping the gap between them from closing too quickly.

When he looked back he imagined that the enemy force numbered at least
a hundred. They were maybe twenty minutes behind and gaining slowly. He told
himself he just had to make it until dark. Once they had the cover of night they
would all have to slow to a walk at best or risk hobbling their horses. He knew the
enemy wouldn't stop. They could see their quarry. They had them on the run and
they smelled blood. They would ride through the night but they didn't have
Alexander's vision. He could see them coming. He could fight them at night like a
man who can see fights the blind, with unfair advantage.

He chuckled at the thought of fairness in relation to a fight, remembering
another lesson his father had taught him: The only fair fight is one you live to walk
away from. There were no rules in the realm of violence except the most basic
moral laws that governed the conditions under which violence was acceptable.

Once the threshold was reached, once it was decided that force was
necessary to protect life, liberty, or property, then half measures and restraint were

imaginary concepts best left to childish fantasy. Violence was a contest with death. The stakes were life itself. There were no rules worthy of being taken seriously in such a contest, only the singular, primordial command to survive.

Alexander rode, feeling the rhythmic motion of his big powerful horse beneath him, and focused on that most basic purpose, survival. He knew he would not win his future with force but with thought. His mind was his only weapon. Everything else was a tool to be wielded by his free will. His ability to choose, to act, was his power.

He discarded his assumptions and looked at the situation facing him with fresh eyes. He knew little of the political reality of the other islands. Since the fall of the Reishi, the Seven Isles had become little more than a collection of disparate territories, each vying for its own interests by whatever means was convenient. There were still areas where the principles of the Old Law held and men could count on justice from their neighbors, but there were many places where the only rule was brute force and intimidation, or worse, a stifling morass of regulation and bureaucracy masquerading as justice. Even on Ruatha, every extreme could be found from the basic fairness and justice enforced in New Ruatha to the endless political machinations of Headwater to the outright rule by force in Kai'Gorn.

He considered the reality of the world and it occurred to him that he would need much more than a sword to bring Ruatha under the rule of the Old Law once again. The Thinblade was the hereditary badge of office of the Island Kings, but in the end, it was just a sword. Those who chose not to respect the authority it represented would have to be persuaded to stand against Phane by other means. A part of him wanted to force it on them, but he knew at a deep and basic level that he could not and would not follow that course. That was the way of Phane. He needed to find another way, one that respected the free will of the people.

They rode through the day staying just minutes ahead of the enemy and slowly losing ground. When Alexander looked back, he thought that the enemy had purchased speed at the cost of numbers. They were pushing their horses beyond their limits and a number of them had fallen by the wayside. Still, there were more than fifty men behind them, more than enough to put an abrupt end to his hopes for the future.

Darkness came slowly but inexorably, bringing a sense of relief as it descended. Alexander slowed their pace. Isabel reported that the horses were tired and thirsty but still healthy. They rode until it was fully dark. Alexander could see the light of the enemy torches in the distance. Their pursuers were farther off than they had been all afternoon but they were still coming. When they came to a little stream, Alexander stopped for a break. He scanned all around while the horses drank their fill and was satisfied with the emptiness of the darkness.

They made slow progress during the night and it seemed that the enemy was gaining on them by the light of their torches, but then it started to rain. It was cold and miserable and Alexander was profoundly grateful for it. It wasn't long before the torches were no longer visible and all he could see of the enemy was the dull smudge of their living auras off in the distance.

By morning, they were all tired. The horses were exhausted and needed a rest, but Alexander knew that he couldn't give them one. He held out hope that they wouldn't lose one to injury even as he urged a faster pace. The rain let up just before dawn and the slate-grey clouds showed signs of breaking up under the morning sun.

The imposing onyx-black silhouette of Blackstone Keep was looming impossibly large in the distance. Details of the battlements and towers started to become visible, but the thing that suddenly struck Alexander like a lightning bolt was the faint outline of an aura that surrounded the entire mountain. He'd heard the story that the mountain itself had been called up out of the ground by the command of some ancient and terrible magic but he hadn't really believed it until now. The ramifications staggered him. If magic could do this, then what could it not do? There seemed to be virtually no limit in the face of such a magnificent accomplishment.

The morning wore on and the enemy gained ground at the cost of dwindling numbers. Alexander knew he couldn't keep this pace. The horses were beginning to complain to Isabel of exhaustion and pain. They wouldn't reach Blackstone Keep before they lost a horse and if they slowed, the enemy would catch up. Either way, they would have to fight too many soldiers.

He agonized over the decision before finally choosing to stop and fight in the belief that it was better to choose the battlefield rather than allow a hobbled horse to do it for him. Then he heard the shriek of a hawk overhead. It was Slyder. He looked to the north and saw a cloud of dust rising in the distance. Erik had received the message.

He whispered, "Not much longer," to his horse and nudged him into a gallop toward the company of Rangers heading to reinforce him. They would even the odds considerably. If he had to fight, he much preferred a fight he had some chance of winning. Erik and his Rangers gave him that chance.

He just needed to make it a little farther. It was hard to judge distance across the plain. He couldn't tell who was closer, the enemy or Erik, but it was clear that the horses were spent. His anger boiled over and the decision came to him easily.

"We fight!" he called out.

Anatoly looked over at him, saw his resolve and nodded, reining in his horse and wheeling about. Isabel slowed her horse as well. Alexander slipped off his exhausted horse to face the enemy on firm ground. Isabel sent Slyder to urge her brother to hurry, while Alexander slung his quiver and checked his sword in its scabbard. He stood, arrow nocked, and waited for the enemy to arrive. Only moments ago it felt like they were coming with unyielding speed, now it felt like time itself had slowed down as he counted the heartbeats until the battle was joined.

It was Jack who dismounted next. "This is unwise, Alexander. We're hopelessly outnumbered. Erik will not arrive in time. We should run."

Alexander shook his head. "No. The horses are spent. If we keep running it's only a matter of time before one of them falls. We make our stand here and hope Erik arrives in time to save us."

Jack looked at him with a strange little grin. "Well, I guess it'll make for a great verse in my next song."

Alexander laughed.

"Spread out. Stay mounted as long as possible," he called out to his companions. He could hear the enemy now, almost feel the thunder of the hoof beats in the ground beneath his feet. Before they were even within the realm of bow range, Abigail sent an arrow toward them in a high arc. It fell well short but still covered more ground than Alexander would have thought possible. When he looked at her, she shrugged.

"I wanted to know the range of my new bow," she said, nocking another arrow.

The enemy numbered at least forty. Only another minute now. Abigail shot again. This time one of the enemy soldiers toppled off his horse. She smiled fiercely as she smoothly drew, aimed, and released another arrow. Alexander waited until they entered the range of his bow and joined her in the fight. She had three down before he scored his first kill. Isabel was next. They killed a dozen before Alexander tossed his bow to the ground, shrugged off his quiver, and drew his sword.

The enemy hurtled toward him like a wave of flesh and steel intent on grinding his life out of existence. He stood calmly and waited for the charge. Jack tossed up the hood of his cloak and faded out of sight. Lucky threw a glass vial of liquid fire twenty feet out in front of Alexander. It burst into a patch of flame ten feet across that rose eight feet into the air. Still the enemy came. When they reached the fire they split like a wave washing around a tree. Anatoly charged to the right side of the fire, leaving the left side to Alexander. Isabel and Abigail moved off to the sides of the charging enemy and sent a steady stream of arrows into them.

Alexander dodged the first enemy spear. Then he was surrounded and fighting for his life. They passed him quickly, stabbing with their spears, then wheeling to come around for another attack. He dodged and parried, thrust and slashed as they swarmed around him. Anatoly was at his back, still mounted, and swinging in great deadly arcs with his big war axe. Jack was to his side, still less than visible, using the element of surprise that his cloak afforded him to lash out at any enemy that got close enough.

Alexander stabbed a passing soldier. Another charged through the puddle of liquid fire and caught him on the back of his shoulder with the tip of his spear. The strike would have cut deep if it hadn't been for his armor. The force of it drove him to his knees, giving the next horseman an opening. His spear point drove down hard into the middle of Alexander's back and sent him to the ground, gasping for breath.

A soldier dismounted quickly and approached Alexander for the kill. Alexander was on his knees trying to regain his feet when he looked up at the advancing soldier and saw his face go white in shock and pain from Jack's knife in his back. Alexander stumbled to his feet and clumsily parried away another attack when a horse crashed into him and sent him tumbling to the ground again. He struggled to gain his breath and shake off the stunned feeling. He was in a fight and needed to act. He could see the enemy closing in from all directions but he couldn't seem to get his focus back. A soldier came up over him and raised his spear for a kill strike. Alexander saw an arrow point appear in the soldier's chest and a look of confusion and shock wash over his face before he fell over right on top of him. Alexander struggled to roll the dead man off his chest and regain his feet, when another force crashed into the fight.

Erik had arrived.

The battle ended quickly. The enemy found themselves outnumbered and facing a superior force in both equipment and training. Erik had divided his force into three parts. Half charged into the fray wielding spears while the other half split in two and moved to Abigail's and Isabel's positions on either side of the battle to provide archery support. Alexander regained his feet and scanned the battlefield. Many of the enemy had fallen. Anatoly was bruised and battered but not seriously hurt. Jack was next to him and still nearly invisible. Alexander heard the command for retreat. His head snapped to the location of the voice. It was Truss with another man that Alexander had never seen before. He vowed to himself that he would kill Rexius Truss before this war was over but for now it was enough to live through the day.

Erik had just over half of his company left, fifty-seven men in total. He'd left Glen Morillian with a hundred. The ambush meant for Alexander had cost Eric dearly, but he carried out his mission and now stood before Alexander with grime coating his face and blood staining his armor.

"We got here as fast as we could," he said.

"Your timing was perfect." Alexander shook his hand. "How are your men and horses? Can you ride?"

"We can. I have nine more horses than men. Your animals look in need of rest." Erik was all business.

Before Alexander could answer, Isabel crashed into her brother and gave him a big hug. "I was so worried when you ran into that ambush," she said. "I'm sorry they killed so many of your Rangers, but I'm grateful you're all right."

"Me too, on both counts." He looked off toward the enemy. "Looks like they've stopped to regroup. We should be on our way."

"Agreed," Alexander said. "Isabel, can you see who's coming in the distance? I can't tell if it's just stragglers or more men."

She looked through Slyder's eyes and inhaled sharply. "It's that giant-sized man and Wizard Rangle with a group of soldiers from Headwater."

Alexander nodded to himself, rubbing his shoulder. "This is getting a bit old. Sooner or later we're going to have to stop running and make a stand."

"Can we do that from a more defensible position?" Anatoly asked pointedly.

Alexander gave him a look and a grin, "Wouldn't be a bad idea."

One of Erik's men brought a fresh horse for Alexander and they mounted up. The enemy didn't try to give chase. Instead they regrouped and consolidated their forces, giving Alexander the time he needed to get to the base of Blackstone Keep.

Chapter 53

It was unlike any mountain he'd ever seen. It jutted abruptly from the grassland in a dull black granite wall and rose nearly straight up from the floor of the plain into the sky. The place radiated power. Alexander could see the magic permeating it and flowing through its ancient foundation.

Erik led them around the base of the artificial mountain to the only road leading up to the entrance. The steeply rising road was only twenty feet wide and had little in the way of a railing. They guided their horses slowly and steadily in single file close to the inside wall. The road wrapped around the enormous base of the mountain once, then again, rising many thousands of feet over the plain below before turning onto a spur that led to a much smaller peak jutting up from the side of the central mountain. The road continued around the smaller peak, wrapping around it again and again, winding steeply toward the top.

They reached the top of the second peak by midafternoon. The view of the plain all around was spectacular. The plateau of the central city in New Ruatha could be seen clearly in the distance. The mountains to the north were visible as well and the southern horizon was tinted green from the Great Forest.

The top of the secondary peak was a square platform, easily a thousand feet across and enclosed on all sides with a four-foot-high stone wall carved out of the black granite of the mountain itself. The road led onto the platform in the middle of the south side. Blackstone Keep loomed over them to the east. The only other exit from the platform appeared to be through an archway on the east side facing the Keep, but there was no bridge.

Alexander stood looking at the archway, which led to an abutment of stone that stretched out just ten feet over a chasm that fell two thousand feet to the road below. The abutment ended abruptly in cleanly cut stone as though it was meant to end there. The chasm was easily five hundred feet across. He could see another arched opening leading into an open area of the Keep beyond, but without wings he had no hope of getting there.

Yet he could also vaguely see a bridge even though it wasn't really there. An aura of magic ran across the empty sky like a ribbon of color almost too faint to see, even with his magical vision. The more he looked, the more certain he became, although the span had no substance. It was not in this world but some other—a place that occupied the same space yet did not exist here at all.

Anatoly stood on the edge of the abutment looking down.

"Quite a defense."

Lucky agreed. "The old stories tell of the vanishing bridge of Blackstone Keep. The Keep Master is supposed to command the bridge into and out of this world. In one state it's as solid as stone and in the other it doesn't even exist. The secret of such a powerful constructed spell has been lost since the fall of the Reishi."

Erik ran up. "I've secured the platform and posted sentries. The enemy is approaching in greater numbers. Looks like more than a hundred. At their present pace they'll be here by dark." He gave the report in crisp statements of fact without any emotion or judgment. "Might be a tough fight if we get cornered up here."

"We won't. Cedric wouldn't have sent me here without a way in." Alexander looked around at the stonework of the arch and abutment. It was the same dull black granite that the rest of the Keep was made of. It looked just like the stone in his ring. "I just have to find it," he said absently.

Alexander searched meticulously. He ran his hand over every square inch of the arch that he could reach. He looked at the stonework in the vicinity with methodical care. He expected to find some mechanism to operate the bridge but found none. As the afternoon wore on, he began to feel doubts. Reports of the enemy's progress came to him every hour, each one chipping away at his certainty. He was sure that Mage Cedric's ring was the key. The note had said as much, but it hadn't given any detail or instruction that could help him and time was running out. Once the enemy reached the road, the only choices left to him were to find a way across the bridge or to stand and fight.

When the report came that the enemy had reached the road, he started to worry that he'd doomed himself and his friends. He'd looked for a physical mechanism for hours but found nothing. When all avenues of inquiry failed, he decided that the only path left to him was magic. Perhaps that was the key. The ring and the Keep were the products of magic; maybe magic was necessary to unlock them. As he thought about it, he felt more certain that his theory was right but he had no idea how to make it work.

"Lucky, is it possible that this ring is activated by magic?" he asked.

Lucky nodded slowly at the question. "Yes, it's even probable. Mage Cedric would have wanted to make sure that only a wizard could access the Keep."

"So how do I use my magic to make it work?"

"That I cannot tell you," Lucky said. "Some items have activation spells while others simply require a connection to the firmament and a wizard's will directed into the item."

Alexander frowned. "I doubt it requires a spell. If it did, Cedric would have left it for me with the ring." He took a deep breath and released it slowly, then sat down cross-legged on the abutment of the bridge, facing the Keep.

He started with the breathing exercises he'd learned in Glen Morillian, slowly relaxing his body and clearing his mind. He tried to focus on nothing, as he had in the past when he'd experienced clairvoyance, but he was too distracted by the urgent need of the current situation. He needed to gain control over his own thoughts and direct his mind and feelings if he was going to have any chance of making a connection with the firmament, let alone activate the power of the ring. He just couldn't seem to drive the thoughts of the advancing enemy from his mind. The more he tried the more insistent the thoughts became. He opened his eyes and brought his attention back to the moment, trying to clear his head before starting the process again.

Again he was plagued with worry about the enemy and his desperate need for urgency. The more he struggled to focus his mind away from those thoughts, the more difficult it became to push them out of his consciousness. Finally, he stood up with a feeling of hopelessness and anxiety.

He looked around to see his worried friends all watching him. The burden settled on him once again. Lives were in his hands. Their futures depended on him.

Erik approached the edge of the abutment carefully and looked down. "The enemy has reached the spur. They'll be here in half an hour."

Again his report was without emotion but Alexander could see the concern on his face. There were more than a hundred men and he could just make out the oversized frame of the giant with them. That probably meant Rangle was with them as well and might even mean Jataan P'Tal was there, too.

Alexander knew that even with over fifty Rangers and the high ground they would not survive this fight. He felt the first hint of panic start to push against his mind from the darkness of his imagination. The future of the world rested squarely on his shoulders. If he failed here, nothing else would matter. His panic threatened to step out of the darkness and make itself known, but he pushed it away with an effort of will.

Isabel took his hand and gently turned him away from the chasm below. She looked him straight in the eye with her clear, intelligent green eyes and he found something he'd momentarily lost.

He found faith.

"Alexander, I believe in you. You can do this." She held him with her gaze until the shadow of doubt faded from his golden-brown eyes. For a moment, there was nothing else except the two of them. In that moment, he felt peace and clarity. He nodded with a smile of gratitude, turned back to face the Keep and sat down.

This time he didn't fight against the thought of the coming enemy. Instead he started with that thought and faced it fully before releasing it from his awareness. Once he'd accepted the truth of it without fear or worry, it faded away. He cleared the field of his mind with gentle firmness, looking at each thought that came to him with complete acceptance and awareness before dismissing it with the knowledge that he had seen it and it required no further attention. Soon he was in the state of empty-mindedness where thoughts did not intrude. He was an observer in his own mind.

Then he was drifting on the firmament. His awareness expanded beyond his body and filled the whole of the world. All things became a part of his awareness and yet no one thing was clear enough to see with certainty. The past was a shadow of the present moment, no longer possessing substance and yet fixed and permanent. The future was a potential, a collection of probabilities and possibilities that may yet come to pass. The moment of now was an impossibly vast number of thoughts, feelings, and happenings, all jumbled together in his mind. He had no location, no identity, and no point of focus. He was everywhere at once and yet nowhere. He focused on his awareness and drew it closer to his physical body without returning to it.

After a moment of struggle, the whole of the world rushed past as his focus narrowed and shrank to the place just above and behind the arch he was sitting under. He could see the Rangers posted all around. Erik was making ready for battle. Anatoly was walking with him, inspecting their preparations. Isabel and Abigail sat behind him on their packs, looking both anxious and slightly worried.

He heard a shout from the forward scout that the enemy was near. With focused will he moved his point of awareness around in front of his body and directed his attention toward the ring. He could see the aura of its magic only faintly, like it was dormant and waiting. With the equivalent of a mental shrug, he thrust his awareness into it. In the distance he heard the first sounds of battle across the large square platform.

He found a place of stillness within the ring. At first, it was very dark but even through the darkness he could discern form and purpose all around him. Slowly, he began to see. It was like watching the lights of a city wink into existence from a hilltop as the light of day fades. He watched the ring slowly come alive and found to his surprise that his mind did not inhabit the ring but the Keep itself. In this place they were one and the same. He sent his awareness out through the enormous Keep. For just a moment he was almost lost in his own curiosity. There were so many rooms and so many things of interest. He wanted to examine them all, but in the faraway distance he could hear the sounds of battle growing closer.

He redoubled his effort and directed his focus with ruthless precision to the bridge. Once his mind was there, it was such a simple thing—without effort he willed the bridge to become real. It came into existence with a slight shimmer and then solidified as though it had been built of immovable stone and had stood in this place for all these years.

When he opened his eyes and snapped back into his body, he felt a faint and unbroken connection to the Keep like it had become an extension of his body, a part of his mind. His awareness of the place was complete even though he didn't understand much of what he could now see. He sat looking at the solid bridge with a feeling of satisfaction for just a moment until an arrow passed over his shoulder and bounced on the bridge once before sailing out into the open sky. He spun to his feet and saw a pitched battle taking place before him. The enemy was advancing with the giant in the middle of the fray. When Alexander saw Rangle step up on a rock wall and start casting a spell, he called out.

"Retreat! Across the bridge! Quickly!"

No one had seen the bridge come into existence because they'd been too busy fighting for their lives.

Alexander snatched up his bow and sent an arrow at Rangle. He missed but came close enough to disrupt the spell and convince the fire wizard to take cover.

What followed was a fighting retreat. The bridge was twenty feet wide and five hundred feet long without any railing or even a curb. The first squad of Rangers peeled away from the formation on Erik's command and raced past Alexander in single file. Abigail and Lucky trailed behind them. Anatoly came next with Jack and Isabel close behind him. He slowed his approach just enough to pull Alexander up onto his horse, then raced across the thin ribbon of black stone.

Alexander felt like he was charging across the sky itself. An arrow glanced off his back and tore his shirt. Once again he silently thanked Kelvin for the gift that had saved his life every day he had worn it.

They reached the other side, and Alexander dismounted quickly to turn with his bow and give cover to the rest of the retreating Rangers. Some of the enemy soldiers were armed with crossbows but hadn't had time to reload after their initial attack.

The bridge ended in another archway made of the same black stone as the rest of the Keep. On either side, the arch flowed into a four-foot-high, one-foot-thick stone wall that ran across the west end of a grassy paddock cut into the side of the mountain. The paddock was easily two hundred feet across and three hundred feet from the bridge to the stone wall at the back. The grassy field ended abruptly with sheer stone walls rising high above on three sides.

Alexander looked up and saw a number of bridges spanning across at different levels and noticed several arched hallways leading from the paddock at ground level. The long-ruined remnants of stable fences and a few buildings where horses had been housed long ago were scattered around the empty field. The simple wooden structures were now little more than mounds of rotted wood overgrown with grass and weeds.

He took a position just to the right of the arch behind the cover of the low wall. Isabel and Abigail lined up next to him with bows at the ready. Chase ordered the Rangers who'd already made it across to take positions along the wall as well.

The bridge looked so small and insubstantial. The remaining Rangers of Erik's company retreated in haste with a force easily numbering fifty men pursuing like wolves chasing a wounded deer; they had the smell of blood and they wanted their kill. Alexander knew their recklessness would be their end. For a fleeting moment he almost felt sorry for the men who were about to die by his command but the feeling was quickly replaced with a righteous anger.

Abigail loosed an arrow at the pursuing enemy. It arched gracefully over the heads of Erik and his men and killed the first enemy soldier charging across the bridge. He tumbled off the back of his horse and crashed onto the bridge just in front of the horse behind him, causing that horse to stumble as its rider pulled his reins hard to the right. The horse tried to regain its footing but veered off too sharply and wasn't able to stop before its front feet slipped over the edge of the bridge and it pitched forward into the sky.

The rest of the enemy slowed to avoid becoming entangled with the dead man, which gave Erik and his men greater distance from them. Alexander surveyed the scene. The soldiers from Headwater were charging across with abandon, but on the other side he could see the giant, Rangle, and Truss with a handful of other men still standing safely on the bridge abutment just under the far arch. Alexander frowned. He was hoping to get them, too.

He waited. Abigail killed another with a clean shot. The enemy tried to raise their shields when they saw the first volley from the Rangers come their way but it was no use. Erik crossed under the arch and into the paddock. He was the last of the Rangers. All that remained on the bridge were enemy. It looked like forty men or more. After all this time, it almost seemed too easy to Alexander. He watched a dozen arrows reach the apex of their path toward the enemy and then raised his hand to Chase.

"Cease fire."

Chase looked a bit confused but obeyed the command and ordered his men to hold.

Alexander reached into the ring with his mind. Now that he'd established a connection, it was as if the ring, or more accurately, the Keep, was an extension of his own body. He could feel the span of the bridge with his mind. It was as easy as scratching an itch on his face. He willed the bridge into its place outside of this world. There was a moment of hesitation, like the Keep was asking if he was sure, then with a flicker, it faded from existence, leaving the enemy two thousand feet up in the empty sky. Alexander felt a twinge of guilt for the horses as they plunged to their deaths.

The enemy tumbled through the air, screaming until they were too far away to be heard anymore. Alexander looked across at Rangle and watched the wizard send a bubble of liquid fire streaking across the chasm. It was too late to retreat. Abigail tried to burst it with an arrow but missed. The bubble came right for the top of the stone arch. When it hit, the angry orange-red liquid fire within would burst forth, showering everyone with droplets of death and pain.

Even as it came toward them, Alexander felt the awareness of the Keep linked to his own mind and he knew that they were safe. Men scattered away from the arch but Alexander stood and watched. The bubble of fire burst twenty feet from the side of the Keep as though it had hit a wall of glass. It sprayed out over the chasm but not a drop crossed the plane of that invisible magic shield. It was a magical Keep after all. Alexander was coming to understand the truth of that statement.

Alexander waved to Rangle before turning back to his friends. "Looks like we made it." He leaned his bow against the wall and walked out into the midst of the Rangers and stepped up on a pile of rocks that had once served as a fence corner.

"We're safe from the enemy out there," he pointed toward Rangle and the giant far across the chasm. "But we don't know what lies within the Keep. This is a place of profound magic. We must be cautious until we know what to expect and what is safe."

All of the Rangers nodded their agreement. Blackstone Keep was a place of legend. Not a single wizard in two thousand years who entered the Keep had returned. Alexander was almost certain that he could control the magical protections of the ancient structure, but he didn't want to take any chances.

"Erik, secure the paddock. Do not enter the Keep. Set two men at every entrance to the Keep and another two men to watch the bridge arch. Make camp and tend to the horses." Erik saluted, fist to heart, and started giving his Rangers their orders.

There were forty-seven Rangers left from Erik's company of one hundred. They had paid a heavy price for the mission that Alexander had assigned them. Many of the Rangers had lost close friends in the past two weeks. They were sad and angry at the same time. Dinner that evening was quiet and somber.

The giant and Rangle were camped on the far side of the bridge with only a few men left. Alexander wanted to finish them off but knew it wasn't worth the risk. He had more important business within the Keep, and his enemy was powerless to harm him here.

He spoke to the Rangers after dinner, expressing his gratitude for their loyalty, admiration for their valor, and sorrow for their losses. After a brief and heartfelt speech, he made a point of going to each squad of Rangers to sit with them for a time and listen to the stories they told of their fallen. The personal details of the people who died by his order brought a lump to his throat and heaviness to his heart. Each one of the fallen Rangers was a person with hopes and dreams for the future, with families and loved ones.

Isabel stayed beside him, listening wordlessly to the stories of friends she knew and had lost. He could see the glistening sorrow in her green eyes. She didn't try to hide it. She loved many of these people, grew up training to become a Ranger with some and had lifelong friendships with others.

Alexander did his best to simply listen to those who remained. He did it more for himself than for the Rangers. They didn't know it. They thought he was trying to comfort them, and he was. But he was also burning the memory of each person who died by his word into his heart and mind. They were gone because he asked them to risk their lives. He knew with terrible clarity that these would not be the last to fall by his command and he wanted to make sure that he understood the full consequence of what he was going to ask of others. He never wanted to forget. He didn't ever want it to become easy to send good people to their deaths.

Each and every life was precious and priceless beyond measure. Each death was a tragedy that would eat a giant hole right out of the center of many other people's lives. He knew his purpose was just and worthy of such sacrifice. He knew that these Rangers had volunteered for this risk with open eyes. And he knew that he never, ever wanted it to become easy to send men into harm's way. Hearing their stories seared the pain of their loss into him with exactly the ruthless severity that he wanted.

His soul was marked by it, just as it should be.

He slept soundly that night and woke after full light the next morning feeling an air of expectancy. The enemy still occupied the bridge platform across the chasm but they were powerless to reach the paddock. Abigail took a shot across the chasm just to see if her new bow could reach that far. It was close but fell just short. She wrinkled her nose with a frown.

"I want that wizard. He's been nothing but a nuisance since Southport." She looked up at the walls rising on each side of the paddock and picked out a few places where passages opened to platforms jutting out of the sheer rock face. "I bet I could reach if I had a little more altitude." She pointed to a platform two hundred feet up that wrapped around the corner of the wall, looking down to the paddock on one side and the chasm on the other. "I could get him from there."

"I bet you could," Alexander said, looking up to the place she was pointing at. "Maybe we'll see if we can find our way up there later, but I have something else I need to do first."

After breakfast, Alexander told Erik to maintain a secure perimeter and to stay out of the Keep.

There were three tunnels leading from the paddock, one in each of the three walls enclosing the broad grassy field. The place was amazing. The Keep itself looked to have been carved from the mountain of black stone by a master sculptor who simply removed the excess material to create spires, towers, bridges, rooms, halls, and chambers. It was the most impressive building that Alexander had ever seen.

He went to one of the walls of the paddock. It was made of black granite with faint grey speckling that he had to look closely to see. It looked like the giant block of stone that should have filled the space the paddock occupied had been cut away and discarded, although Alexander couldn't imagine where they had put it because it would have been enormous, at least two hundred feet wide by three hundred feet long by another five hundred feet high. He realized that the builders had cut this section of the mountain away to bring the place where he stood down to the same level as the bridge platform across the chasm.

He put his hand on the cold stone of the wall and closed his eyes as he focused on the ring, and the Keep came alive in his mind. He could see a three-dimensional map of the entire place, in all of its impossibly intricate detail, floating within his consciousness. There was so much to see, so many rooms and halls to explore, and so many secrets to discover. Some areas of the Keep looked like they were off-limits or dangerous. He couldn't quite describe how he knew they were dangerous but he knew with certainty that those areas should only be explored with caution.

The place was vast. There were hundreds of towers and buildings on the top of the mountain and thousands of rooms, chambers, galleries, halls, corridors, staircases, quarters, laboratories, and libraries cut into the interior. Whole wings looked to be devoted to the study of magic in all of its varied manifestations. Other sections looked like barracks and still others were quarters and living areas. There were halls organized like marketplaces, and other areas opened to the sky and provided places for fresh food to be grown, while still others looked like training grounds for soldiers. The place was bigger than most cities. There were countless levels, from towers that rose thousands of feet above the level of the paddock to passages that delved down into the bowels of the mountain and even beneath the level of the ground far below. Alexander could hardly grasp the complexity or the immensity of the place. He knew that a person could easily get lost within and never find their way out if they weren't careful.

He could see that sections of the Keep could be magically shielded and that some corridors could be sealed to prevent access. The place had been built with the purpose of war and security, first and foremost. The more he explored the image in his mind's eye, the more aware he became of the undercurrent of deadly magic that pervaded the fortress. The Keep itself could kill unwelcome guests. Some areas were open and accessible, while others were severely limited to those with expressly granted access.

Alexander searched for the one place he needed most and found it easily. When he focused on the small, dome-shaped chamber with a little building in the center of it, he found that it lay in a room off the central stairway that wound up through the central tower: The wizard's tower. He could see the way there. It would be a long walk.

Chapter 54

They took lightweight packs and set out for their ultimate goal. Alexander led them into the central tunnel that cut right into the heart of the mountain. The floors were not made of stone block but of smooth black granite. The walls were not brick or plaster but more of the same cleanly cut, seamless black stone.

The light faded when they moved farther inside the twenty-foot-wide, twenty-foot-high arched tunnel.

"Ah, I was hoping for an opportunity to try my latest acquisition." Lucky rummaged around in his new bag and pulled out a small pouch. Bright, clean white light spilled out when he opened it. He removed three heavy glass vials filled with a brightly luminescent substance. "These are the remains of the night wisps we killed in the forest. If you let the gelatinous goop that's left over when they die dry out in the sunlight, it turns into a brightly glowing powder that's ideal for producing light in dark places. It's almost as if it absorbs the sunlight for later use," he said with a satisfied smile as he handed one vial to Alexander and another to Jack. The vials cast a bright yet soft light that filled the tunnel with illumination for several dozen feet in every direction.

The tunnel ran straight and level into the side of the mountain for several hundred feet without any hint of a door or passage until it opened into a giant room, five hundred feet square and at least two hundred feet tall. Huge support pillars stood every fifty feet or so, and a maze of bridges and stairways ran all through the chamber. On every wall were numerous doors and hallways, some opening onto the main floor while others opened onto the many bridges that crisscrossed overhead. Some of the passages looked big enough to carry wagon traffic, while others were clearly meant for foot traffic alone.

"This is the entry hall. Each passage takes you to a different part of the Keep. We need to go this way," Alexander said, pointing off across the giant room. Each step sent eerie echoes bouncing around in the ancient, abandoned Keep.

He stopped abruptly at the sight of a skeleton lying on the floor. Its owner was long dead. What remained of his clothing was just a dusty stain on the floor. The man's staff had rotted into nothing more than a line of color on the black stone where it had fallen. The bones looked brittle and desiccated and no flesh remained, not even scraps of dried sinew. Alexander knew that wizards had tried to enter the Keep over the years and none had ever returned. He wondered if he was looking at one of those who had tried and failed. More importantly, he wondered what killed him. There was no sign of a struggle and no apparent reason for his death. Alexander reminded himself that caution was still in order.

The place was dark, foreboding, and ominous while at the same time it was the most magnificent achievement Alexander had ever seen. The walls and floors were so precise and exacting that he was convinced that the construction tool of choice was magic. No hammer or chisel had cut these halls. The stonework was simple, clean, and utilitarian.

Alexander led them across the giant entry hall and took a staircase up to the first level of bridges, then found an open passageway along one wall. He led them through passages, halls, and chambers on his way to his destination. They moved steadily upward through the belly of the mountain-sized Keep. Once deep inside, the silence was almost oppressive.

Abigail whispered, "Are you sure you know where you're going?"

Alexander chuckled, "Why are you whispering?"

She frowned a little and spoke in a voice just above a whisper. "It's so quiet. It doesn't feel right to disturb the silence."

"I guess I can see what you mean." He pointed down the hall. "We're almost there, just a few more minutes."

They walked on. When they rounded a corner, Alexander suddenly stopped dead in his tracks. He could see the colors of a plane of magical force that guarded the hall. Even if he couldn't have seen it, he could feel the hair on his arms standing on end.

"Can you see that?" he asked no one in particular.

"See what?" Abigail said.

"Do you feel any kind of magic? Like the air just became dangerous?" he asked.

Jack spoke up this time. "Now that you mention it, I did feel a bit of strangeness just after we turned this corner."

"I believe it's a magical shield," Lucky said. "We should be cautious."

Alexander closed his eyes and touched the magic of the ring. He could see the whole Keep floating before him but it was so complex and huge that he couldn't see the detail he needed. With an effort of will he focused on the place where he stood, and that area became clear and magnified while the rest faded out of view. In the vision of the hallway created by the Keep Master's ring, there was a shield barring the path that led to the area reserved for the wizard's laboratories, libraries, and workrooms. It was a low-level shield meant to protect the inner chambers from those without magic. He focused on the shield for a moment before he understood the nature of its operation and then approached slowly, hand outstretched. At first touch he felt a little thrill of magic race through him like the shield was testing him. It offered only faint resistance before allowing him to push through.

"Anatoly, I'd like you to try and pass," Alexander said. "Approach slowly with your hand out."

Anatoly frowned a little but did as requested. His hand met the shield and stopped. He pushed harder but still couldn't pass. He shook his head in wonder.

"It's like there's a solid stone wall right here that I can't see," Anatoly said with his hand on the invisible barrier. "Except, I did feel a little tingle the moment I touched it, and then the thought that I wouldn't be able to pass came immediately into my head. I'm not sure I like this, Alexander."

"I'm just trying to figure this place out," Alexander said. "I think I can lower the shield but I want to try something first. Lucky, see if you can pass."

Lucky shrugged and walked through the shield like it wasn't even there. "Ah ... it appears to be keyed to the magic within a person."

Alexander nodded. "This is the core of the Keep where the wizards studied, experimented, and created their spells. Looks like it was off-limits to everyone else."

He closed his eyes and found the shield again in his mind and willed it away. There was a shimmer along the plane where it had stood only a moment before, and Anatoly's hand, which was still resting on the barrier, fell forward.

"Huh," Anatoly said, stepping through quickly, as though that place in the hall was dangerous.

They passed many stout, ironbound oak doors spaced at long intervals along the hall. Surprisingly, the wood of the doors looked solid and sturdy. There was no hint of decay, although they did look old and well used.

Lucky looked around with excitement. "What's behind these doors?" he asked.

"I think they're libraries and laboratories. Most of the rooms are pretty big." Alexander didn't stop.

Lucky smiled with anticipation. He stood in the home of the wizards of old and was eager to explore, but he kept up with Alexander and the others just the same.

There were many side halls that jutted off the main corridor, but Alexander stayed his course. The passage was long and straight, driving through the heart of the mountain. The ceiling was high overhead and the walls were bare. If there had ever been any ornamentation or decoration in this part of the ancient Keep, it had long since turned to dust. The long hall that formed the backbone of the instruction, training, and research area ran perfectly straight and level for a mile or more. With the magic of the ring, Alexander could see the end nearing even though his sight was limited to the few dozen feet of light cast by the glow of the night-wisp dust.

Once they reached the last remaining steps of the hall, they found something they didn't expect. There was a line drawn straight across the hall from wall to wall, but that wasn't what stopped them all in their tracks. At the edge of their light, they could see the end of the hallway. An archway was sculpted into the wall with a protrusion of the same black stone but there was no passage beneath, only a stone wall where there should have been an entryway.

Standing in the middle of the hallway was a six-foot stone statue of a man in armor with both hands resting on the pommel of an oversized black stone sword. The statue was formed of the same black granite as the walls of the Keep, but it had a finely carved quality about it that made it look almost alive. The remnants of more than a dozen long-dead corpses were scattered around its feet.

Alexander knew instinctively that the line before him was a warning, that crossing it would awaken the sentinel. He could see the likely result of such an action scattered about the floor. Some of the skeletons were broken and dismembered. Others were intact, yet seemed to have crumpled to the floor, most likely after the length of a sword had been withdrawn from their bodies, leaving them where they fell in a carelessly discarded heap.

The Keep Master's tower lay beyond the stone sentinel. Alexander reached into the ring with his mind and looked for this place. The vast complexity of the Keep blurred past his mind's eye until he saw the place where he was standing. He saw nothing except the end of the passageway and a secure portal leading to the central tower. There wasn't a sentinel or a line on the floor or any indication of a guardian.

He stood at the threshold, looking at the sentinel. He'd traveled so far and endured so much to bring him to this place. The simple choice that lay before him was to cross the line or turn back. He knew even as the thought formed that he wouldn't turn back. The only course he could choose was forward. To turn back was to abandon reason, life, and the future. With the calm certainty of a decision made, he turned to Isabel and smiled.

"I love you," he said and then stepped over the line.

The line on the ground shimmered and the plane it described across the hallway solidified into a shield of invisible magical force enclosing Alexander with the sentinel in a battlefield every bit as inescapable as a gladiator's arena. He could hear his friends gasp and Anatoly curse when the sentinel came to life.

Its sword whirled up into its hand and its eyes began to glow behind its carved stone helmet, faintly at first, then more brightly until they resembled the fall of sunlight on fresh snow. The sentinel didn't advance but stood its ground, regarding Alexander with newly awakened awareness.

Alexander didn't waver or show any threat. He stood and waited. He could hear Lucky curse from beyond the shield at being denied entry. Alexander was alone, but then he knew he would be. This was a test. A final guardian set by Mage Cedric to ensure that only an acceptable champion would be able to proceed.

The sentinel spoke with a hollow-sounding voice devoid of inflection or emotion that seemed to come from a great distance away. "You face three tests."

Alexander held the brightly glowing eyes without faltering. "Proceed." He could feel the silence of his companions behind him.

"Touch the stone of Mage Cedric's ring to the stone of wall or floor."

Alexander lowered himself slowly to the floor without letting go of the sentinel's gaze and gently but firmly rested the ring against the stone of the floor. A moment passed before he felt a tingle of magic in the air. With his second sight, he saw a wave of color expand from the point that the ring was touching and race up the walls and down the hall as if awakening the entire Keep to his presence. He stood slowly, his gaze never wavering.

There was a long pause. "The ring is recognized. You have passed the first test." Still the sentinel did not move, its sword held high and ready.

"You must forfeit the life of one of your companions. Choose."

Chapter 55

A tingle of icy dread raced up Alexander's spine and was answered with a drip of perspiration trickling down his back. He stood stock-still in disbelief and horror, dumbfounded by the demand. How could Mage Cedric place such a monstrous burden on him? It was inconceivable. Almost as a subconscious act, he catalogued each of his companion's names in his mind and saw the inestimable value of each life.

His love. His sister. His protector. His teacher. His friend.

They were all precious to him. But more than that, each was precious in his or her own right. Each was a unique life of incalculable worth. How could he choose one of them to die? The demand penetrated into him like the cold penetrates after a plunge into icy water. He felt numb disbelief. He wanted to believe that he'd heard wrong or that he'd misunderstood. But he knew that he hadn't. Yet, how could he choose?

For a long moment he stared at the glowing eyes of the sword-wielding statue and struggled to make sense of the demand. He felt like every assumption and belief he held, his every conception of morality, was built on a bed of quicksand. His mind refused to work in the face of the decision hanging in the air like a sentence.

Mage Cedric had placed this test before him. Why? Alexander felt certain of only one thing. He must understand the reason before he uttered an answer. What could be the purpose of such a test? Was the long-dead wizard testing his resolve? His determination to do whatever it takes to succeed? And if he was, what then? How could he possibly choose? When he tried to consider the thought with any seriousness, he felt a wave of revulsion and repudiation well up from the depths of his being. He knew the answer with unspoken certainty even before he was able to put words to it in the quiet privacy of his own mind.

He could not choose.

He would not!

And yet, there he stood, looking into the face of such an impossible demand that he had trouble reconciling it with what he knew to be true. Mage Cedric had been committed to the Old Law. Alexander remembered the words cut into the stone of the Bloodvault.

You have a right to your life because you are alive. You have a right to your liberty because you have free will. You have a right to your property because it is the product of your labor. You forfeit these rights when you take them from another.

Cedric had placed those words there. He expected Alexander to show allegiance to the Old Reishi Law in order to enter the Bloodvault, but now he demanded that Alexander violate the most basic premise of that law.

And then he knew.

He heard his father's voice as if he were standing right beside him, speaking in the calm and reassuring tone of a man who is certain of his words.

"There are no contradictions, only false premises. If you believe you are facing a contradiction, you are not. You simply misunderstand some aspect of the situation. Correct your misunderstanding and the contradiction will vanish."

Alexander was faced with a contradiction and understood with building clarity that this *was* a test of his commitment, but not in the way he first thought. Cedric was testing his commitment to the Old Law, not his willingness to do whatever it takes to win. The realization settled his anxiety and washed the panic out of the dark corners of his mind.

He hadn't moved since the sentinel spoke and realized that his every muscle was knotted with tension. With a little smile and a deep breath he relaxed.

"No," he said clearly. "If you must take a life, then take mine. It's the only one I have any right to offer."

The sentinel didn't react for a long moment. Alexander held his breath.

"You have passed the second test."

Alexander felt a momentary swell of confidence, which quickly vanished the moment the sentinel said, "On guard," and then lunged at him with a perfectly executed attack.

Alexander spun to the side, narrowly avoiding the point of the stone blade. He drew his sword in that same moment and deflected a blow that would have been a fatal cut. He regained his footing and faced his enemy. He could see his companions' fear and helplessness behind the invisible magical wall but didn't have time to offer them even a flicker of assurance.

He was in a fight and he had a blade in his hand. Everything else faded away as the enemy attacked.

The sentinel came at him with the measured precision and the fluid grace of a master swordsman. Alexander dimly recognized the pattern of the attack and narrowly escaped without injury. He realized a moment too late that he knew a counter for that attack.

The next attack came more quickly than the last, and again it was familiar. He blocked and avoided but again failed to counterstrike. When the sentinel rounded on his position and began a series of movements intended to end with a blade buried in Alexander's midsection, he saw the pattern the moment it began and attempted the counter. He failed, but managed to avoid the kill strike if only by an inch or two.

The sentinel attacked with techniques that Alexander had learned from the skillbook. Each attack pattern had a counter and each counter had a foil. His mind raced, trying to discern the reason for the attack, but he couldn't devote sufficient attention to the problem because he needed every part of his mind to survive the relentless assault.

Alexander met the next attack with the kind of awareness that is completely present. His whole consciousness was focused on the form of the attack, on the pattern through space that it described. He could see it with dry, academic precision in his mind's eye even as he employed the counter with energy and force driven by fear and anger.

This time he was successful. His counterstrike slipped past the defenses of the enemy and landed solidly, blunting the tip of his sword on the stone hardness of the living statue. The sentinel paused for a moment at the strike and the glow of its eyes pulsed. The pause gave Alexander a moment to step back, set his stance, and prepare for the next attack.

What followed was a contest of the mind more than flesh and steel. Alexander lost himself in the dance of battle. He recognized each attack and responded with the counter. The only respite he was granted was a brief pause when he landed a successful blow against the sentinel. He fought with everything he had: mind, strength, steel, and spirit. He lost himself in the contest and became the instrument wielding the blade. The purpose of his existence in those moments was to give motion and direction to the lifeless steel of his sword. He'd felt lost in battle before. He'd felt a connection to his blade before, but never like this.

Alexander didn't know how long he fought. He could feel the exhaustion in his arms, trembling from the weight of his sword. He could feel rivulets of blood running down his skin from small cuts suffered when he'd been too slow. His body was coated with a sheen of sweat, and his muscles were sore and strained, but his mind possessed a clarity like nothing he'd ever experienced. He was one with his blade. Their purpose was one and the same. Cut.

The fight ended suddenly. The sentinel simply stopped advancing and returned to its place in the middle of the floor.

Alexander stood holding his sword at the ready, breathing deeply, dripping sweat, and waited, watching the steady glow of his inanimate opponent's eyes.

"You have passed the third test. Blackstone Keep is yours." There was no emotion in the voice of the lifeless guardian. Nothing to match the elation and relief Alexander felt as he slumped to his knees, allowing the tip of his blunted and dull sword to rest on the stone floor beside him.

A moment later, he was surrounded by his friends. The invisible shield had fallen and the doorway that was once a wall of black stone faded into empty space, opening the way to the tower beyond.

Isabel was on her knees, holding his head in her arms. She said nothing and didn't need to. Anatoly passed him quickly and stood facing the sentinel. Jack and Abigail stood beside him, while Lucky knelt in front of him to appraise his multiple minor wounds.

"That was quite a show, Alexander," Jack offered. "I don't think I took a breath for the last hour."

Abigail gently kicked him in the knee. When he looked up at his sister, she gave him her sternest look and said, "Be more careful." She couldn't help smiling just a little.

Lucky took Isabel's arm and unwrapped it from around Alexander. "My dear, let me take a look at his injuries." She let go reluctantly but made no move to leave his side.

Alexander was exhausted. He rolled off his knees, sat down heavily and dropped his sword on the floor. Isabel handed him a water skin while Lucky fished around in his bag, muttering something about organizational skills.

"You should listen to your sister, Alexander." Isabel tried to look reproving but all Alexander could see in her beautiful green eyes was relief.

He nodded, squeezing her hand, then winced when Lucky cleaned a gash on his arm with a splash of spirits.

He rested his body while Lucky tended to his wounds, but his mind didn't rest. He retraced the steps of the fight, looking for a purpose, and then realized with a shock that he'd performed every sword form he'd learned in the skillbook. The sentinel had pushed him to apply every technique he knew with perfection. He discovered somewhere during the furious battle that he was no longer thinking about what he was going to do. He stopped planning his next move and released himself to the purpose of the blade. He reacted from a place more basic than understanding and knowledge—from a place where the action that was required sprang forth spontaneously and unbidden.

It had been more than a test. It had been a graduation examination. The skillbook had prepared him for this fight. Without the knowledge he'd learned from that magical tome, he would have fallen in minutes, but this fight had integrated that knowledge into his body and soul. He was more now than he had been before. This fight had completed his training with a blade.

Once Alexander caught his breath and Lucky had cleaned his several wounds, they made their way past the sentinel. The stone guardian was unharmed by Alexander's attacks, and its eyes still retained their brilliant white glow, but it didn't move or react in any way.

The room that lay beyond the arch was austere. It was perfectly circular and easily a hundred feet across. There was an ornate desk of finely carved and polished black oak set some twenty feet inside the room facing the archway. The desk had a single chair pushed in behind it but its surface was empty of everything except a thin layer of dust. On one side of the room was a spiral staircase going both upward and downward. There were four other open archways leading out of the circular room and a few benches along the walls. Otherwise it was bare.

Alexander consulted the map of the Keep inside his mind to confirm his path before he went to the spiral staircase and headed down. It wound around and around in a corkscrew through the black stone, descending deeper and deeper into the mountain. There were a few landings with passageways leading off into the darkness. Alexander passed them by without hesitation. When he came to a landing without a door or a passage, he stopped.

He held his vial of magical light higher and looked closely at the wall. "I don't understand ... it's supposed to be right here," he said with a frown.

He felt along the wall for some kind of catch or lever, then stopped with a rush of foolishness and stepped back.

"What is it, Alexander?" Isabel asked, standing beside him.

"The passage is supposed to be right here. I'm wondering if I can open it with the ring or if it's some kind of mechanical hidden door."

He closed his eyes and focused his view of the Keep's map to this place and saw that there was indeed a secure passage. He focused his attention on the wall before them and noted a sensation similar to what he'd felt with the bridge. With a flick of his mind, the wall vanished, leaving a dark passageway beyond.

"Huh," Anatoly said.

Jack chuckled, "Eloquent as always, Master Grace."

The passage led thirty feet into the stone and opened to a domed room forty feet across. It was identical to the room where they'd found the first Bloodvault under the palace of Glen Morillian. In the center of the room was another pure-white marble cube seven feet on a side with a band of writing carved into the stone seven inches from the top edge and wrapping entirely around the structure. On the far side, there was an outline of a doorway and the imprint of a man's right hand in the center of the door.

Alexander squeezed one of the gashes on his arm to produce a few drops of blood and smeared it onto his hand. He looked around at his friends for just a moment with a look of expectancy and excitement. "I'll be right back," he said as he placed his bloody hand firmly on the handprint.

A moment later a tracing of light raced from the two points on the floor where the outline of the door met the ground to the apex of the arched doorway. A heartbeat later, his hand pushed through the stone. He followed it into the tiny room beyond. There were three shelves of white marble. The one on the right held a large and very old-looking book. The one on the left held a finely crafted jewelry box fashioned of gold and silver and encrusted with gemstones of every color and cut. These things he saw with his peripheral vision because his focus lay on the item resting on the center shelf. It was a sword cradled by an ornate display rack.

The scabbard was black as night and crafted from some material that Alexander had never seen before. The hilt was made from similar material. Without touching it, Alexander examined it closely. The thing that struck him with the greatest force was the symbol on its onyx-black pommel. Inlaid in gold was the exact symbol burned into the side of his neck: the glyph of the House of Reishi. His second sight told him that this was an item of exceeding magical enchantment. The aura produced by most enchanted items was faded and lifeless. This was vibrant and intense like the aura of a living being, though much less complex.

He lifted it reverently. It was light and cool to the touch. Carefully, slowly, he drew the blade from the scabbard. It was a good thirty inches long and almost an inch wide. The surface was blacker than black. Light fell into the darkness of the blade as if being consumed by it. He turned the blade slowly to look at the edge. When he viewed it edge-on, the blade vanished! It was so impossibly thin that he couldn't even see it except by looking at the flat side.

Thinblade indeed.

He brought it up and noted how good it felt in his hand. It was lighter than any steel blade he'd ever held, with most of the weight in the hilt. The tip moved with lightning quickness at the flick of his wrist. Still holding the Thinblade in his right hand, he drew his battle-blunted sword with his left and spun it up in front of him. He held out the fine steel blade and flicked it with the Thinblade.

Alexander wasn't even sure he felt any resistance. The Thinblade cut his old sword in half with clean precision. He laughed as half the length of his old sword clattered to the floor.

He sheathed the Thinblade, strapped the scabbard to his belt, then gathered up the book and jewelry box almost as an afterthought and pushed through the door of the Bloodvault, smiling broadly.

"We've succeeded."

He handed Lucky the book and jeweled box and drew the Thinblade for all to see. There was silence in the room. Everyone simply stared in awe at the ancient badge of an Island King. He handed Anatoly the hilt half of his old sword. The old man-at-arms examined it and whistled.

Alexander was beaten up and exhausted but he walked with a light step back to the Ranger camp outside in the paddock. He'd endured so much in the past months, but now he was satisfied that he had lived up to the burden he'd been given.

He took Isabel's hand when they stepped out of the tunnel and into the sunshine of the late winter day. For the first time since he discovered his ancient birthright, he didn't fear the future.

Here Ends Thinblade
Sovereign of the Seven Isles: Book One

www.SovereignOfTheSevenIsles.com

The Story Continues…

Sovereign Stone
Sovereign of the Seven Isles: Book Two